# A ROCKY CHRISTMAS

## LEIGH JONES

Published by Leigh Jones

First edition. December 2025

Discreet cover **ISBN: 979-8-9995923-1-6**

Illustrated cover: **ISBN: 979-8-9995923-2-3**

E-book: **ISBN: 979-8-9995923-0-9**

Discreet Cover Design by Katie Jaspersen @kjaspersendesigns

Illustrated Cover Design by Ali Shearer of @juniper.charm

Copy/Line Editing & Proofreading by Caitlin Lengerich @chronicledbycait

Interior formatting by Kay Morton @kmortonedits

*For those who have been asking Santa for the love child of a Hallmark Christmas movie and a smutty romance novel, this one's for you.*

*Curl up with your favorite seasonal drink, have some tissues at the ready, and dive in.*

# CONTENT WARNINGS

This book contains mature themes and language, and is not intended for those under the age of 18.

While this is a romance novel, there are some serious themes such as physical abuse, sexual assault, rape, death of a child (not on page), depictions of grief and loss, and suicidal thoughts, that may be triggering to some individuals. There are also graphic depictions of sex between consenting adults.

If any of these topics are a trigger for you, please refrain from reading, or proceed with caution.

# PLAYLIST

A Drop in the Ocean - Ron Pope
cowboy like me - Taylor Swift
Before You Go - Lewis Capaldi
I Don't Know If I Should Stay - Alexz Johnson
Dial Tones (Acoustic) - As It Is
My Little Girl - Tim McGraw
Be More Kind - Frank Turner
'tis the damn season - Taylor Swift
This House - Will Varley
All Your'n - Tyler Childers
Misty Morning (Live) - Lawrence
Something In The Way You Touch - Boystown
Your Guardian Angel - Red Jumpsuit Apparatus
Temporary Bliss - The Cab
Start Over - The New Low
Stargazing - Myles Smith
The Way I Wanna - Max McNown
THE END - Bilmuri
Carry You Home - Alex Warren

Full playlist available here on Spotify.

# 1

## SYDNEY



My blood boils as Mr. Alino feeds me yet another excuse as to why I don't have the signed proposal for his renovation project on my desk yet. It's been nearly a month of emails and calls promising to deliver it, and him continuously failing to do so.

I bite my tongue, doing the deep breathing exercises my therapist, Dr. Camden, suggested as the old man drones on.

By the time I'm blowing out breath number three, Tony has stopped talking, and I've calmed the raging bitch inside me enough to respond with a level head.

"I understand that you're short staffed, Mr. Alino, but we've been going back and forth on this for almost a month. If you want me to break ground on the project in January, I need the signed proposal by end of day."

"Well, it's just that I ran into Harold Gregory on the golf course last week, and we got to talking..."

*Harold fucking Gregory.*

That snake has been trying to steal my clients for years now. Every goddamn time I'm about to get someone to sign a deal for over five million dollars, he slithers out of the woodwork and tries to snatch them up.

"With all due respect, Mr. Alino, this is not the first time I've had Mr. Gregory try to poach a client of mine. I can tell you with absolute certainty that the man is all talk. He'll send you a proposal that's not nearly as well thought out or detailed as mine, claiming that it's more structurally sound and that he can have it done in half the time, but what he's not telling you is that it'll cost you three times as much."

Walking over to my desk, I click open the design I created for Mr. Alino's project. "If that's not enough to convince you to stay with Wilson & Wu, maybe the fact that he's notorious for using the cheapest possible materials—guaranteeing that something will go wrong within the first year of construction being completed—will."

I don't need to see his face to know Mr. Alino has gone slack-jawed and red-faced. "That can't be true. Harold assured me—"

"*Harold* was blowing smoke up your ass," I say, cutting him off. "Aside from shoddy construction and bad designs, he wipes his hands clean as soon as he sends the drawings over to the builders. With us, that doesn't happen. We see you through every phase. *All* construction—with the exception of outsourced, highly qualified restoration specialists—is done with the highest quality materials by an award-winning team that is in-house, here at Wilson & Wu. You're just not going to get that kind of service with Gregory and Associates."

His silence is so loud I almost laugh.

There's nothing more satisfying than knowing I've taken Harold Gregory down a couple pegs.

Maybe this time it'll teach the fucker to keep his grubby hands off my damn projects. Nearly twenty-five hundred construction projects happen every year within New York City alone, and this greedy asshole has to try and steal *mine*.

Every bit of what I told Mr. Alino is true. I have a list of clients a mile long who have called me personally to bail them out when Harold screwed them over.

A muffled conversation happens on the other end of the phone and I roll my eyes.

*Is he seriously considering not signing the proposal after all that?*

How anyone could even think to work with Harold Gregory after the scathing online reviews from his former clients is beyond me.

Tony clears his throat. "You'll have the signed proposals by the end of the day. I'm tracking down a courier as we speak."

"Great. I look forward to working with you."

"Thank you, Sydney," his wife-slash-assistant, Sandra, says before the call disconnects.

I tip my head back against my black, tufted leather executive chair, giving myself a second to breathe and revel in the fact that I successfully closed another deal.

Maybe Dr. Camden was right about that whole meditative breathing crap. I thought it was a load, but that conversation would have gone very differently six months ago.

It's not very often I get to appreciate the office I worked so hard to get, *and keep*. But at times like these, I do. The corner office on the twenty-first floor overlooks Central Park. It's an egregious waste of space, but someone in my position is expected to have the best of the best.

Having an office bigger than a decent portion of the apartments in New York is a sign of wealth and power. As much as I hate it, there's no way around it without losing the respect of not only my peers in the industry, but the people who work for me.

After another minute of calming my mind, I get back to work, firing off emails to prospective clients, scheduling calls that will fill up the rest of my afternoon and opening up my design program to get started on the new project for Havershum.

Dr. Camden's breathing exercises might be helpful in the heat of the moment on calls, and in board rooms, but when I'm in the zone working, I turn into a different person. No amount of deep breathing can save me then.

There's a knock at my door, followed by the telltale squeak of my assistant's shoes. Katie strides up to my desk with a worried look on her face. "Ms. Wilson?"

"I'm a little busy at the moment, Katie. What do you need?"

She timidly fiddles with the pen in her hand and I just barely hold back an eye roll. "I know your schedule is packed, but do you—"

"Katie," I sneer. "Get to the point."

Clearing her throat, she squares her shoulders. "Your father called. He said it was urgent."

Groaning, I dig the heels of my palms into my eye sockets. *I don't have time for this right now.* There's too much on my plate, and far too many plates for me to deal with the happenings of a podunk town in Colorado. "I'll call him later. If he calls again, tell him I'm tied up in meetings, and will get back to him later."

"But—"

"But nothing, Katie. I don't have time for my dad's so-called urgent matters right now. I'll call him tonight, when I leave."

She purses her lips, clearly unhappy with my decision, but nods and scurries away like a scared little mouse.

One day she'll thank me for being hard on her. As a woman in this business, there's no room for coddling.

*I learned that the hard way.*

Diving back into work after the interruption, I get lost in the Havershum design.

Time flies by so quickly I don't even realize I've skipped lunch until my business partner, Paul Wu—the *Wu* of *Wilson & Wu*—strides into my office. He's in one of his signature three-piece suits. This one a deep red, paired with a crisp white shirt, black tie, and a pair of perfectly polished black derby shoes. "Wanna grab dinner with me at Monkey Bar?"

My mouth waters at the memory of their gorgonzola aged

prime rib with creamy horseradish sauce, but I quickly shake it away. "Can't. Don't have time."

He rolls his eyes so hard I can almost make out the sound of his eyeballs hitting the back of his head. "What can I help with?"

"I don't need help, Paul. I need more hours in a day," I say, looking down at my cell phone that's buzzing with another incoming call from my dad. I'm trying really hard to not blow a gasket, but I really don't have the mental capacity to deal with any of this right now. "And more importantly, I need my father to stop calling me and my assistant."

"What does he want?" he asks as he unbuttons his suit jacket and drops into one of the plush red armchairs across from my desk.

"Probably to invite me back to Colorado for Christmas, which is not happening."

He pours himself a scotch from the decanter on the coffee table, swirling it around the glass before bringing it to his nose for a sniff. "You never did tell me why you hate it there so much."

"And I never will." My stomach clenches even thinking about telling him what I ran from. "The past is in the past."

"Are you at least going to call him back?"

"Of course I am. I'm not some heartless bitch. I just have too much to finish before I head home for the night. Him constantly calling isn't helping."

"What if it's important?"

With a scoff, I click through the design I'm working on. "Last time he said it was something *urgent* he was calling to tell me that one of the horses broke free from the fence. There's really not much that happens in that shithole of a town. It's probably nothing."

"You know if you answered it, it'd get him off your back."

Answering means talking, and talking is going to lead to an hour long conversation that I don't have time for right now. I want to be able to sit down with a glass of wine on my couch and actually enjoy the conversation, not rush him off the phone because I'm buried in work and can't ask for help to save my life.

The glare I shoot Paul's way is enough for him to back off. "Forget I said anything." He sips his scotch. "I know you said no to dinner, but what if I order some takeout and we bang out the rest of your work together?"

I groan, leveling him with a look.

"We're business partners, Syd. Let me help."

My stomach growls loudly and Paul smirks at me. "Fine. But you're paying."

---

Forty-five minutes later I shift my attention from the Havershum design to my email when I see the pop up of an incoming email from my father.

*Will the man ever fucking quit?*

Pulling up the email, I read through it and my heart stalls in my chest when I see the words *car accident* and *hospital* in reference to my mom.

A chill runs down my spine and my stomach knots uncomfortably. I didn't think I could be taken to my knees by a single email, but I was so very, *very* wrong.

*Fuck, I'm such an asshole.*

The one time there's an *actual* emergency I blow it off like my parents mean nothing to me, which is the furthest thing from the truth. They're all I have, apart from Paul.

I need to do a better job of showing them that.

"Paul!" I shout, quickly stuffing my phone, iPad, and planner into my bag. "Paul!" I yell again.

He comes running into the room wide-eyed. "What? What's going on?"

"I-I have to go."

"Where?"

"Colorado. My mom was in an accident."

He swallows thickly and brings his hands to my arms. "Go. I'll handle what I can, and when you get settled back home give me a call."

"Shit! You don't know about the—"

"New property in the Bronx? I'm cc'd on all the emails, and I'm sure Katie can catch me up on anything else regarding it. I can handle this, Syd. I promise." A sad smile tips his lips as he pulls me into a hug. "Go pack and give your dad a call. I'll have Katie book you on the first flight out."

My eyes quickly fill with tears as I nod against his chest. "Thank you."

I practically sprint down the hall and into the elevator, smashing the button for the ground floor and then the *Close Door* button.

I get to the street, wave down a cab and hop in, rattling off the address to my brownstone.

When I get to my place, a text with the flight information comes in from Katie. The flight doesn't leave until tomorrow morning, thanks to one hell of a snowstorm rolling through the Rockies.

I take a second to collect myself and shoo the worst case scenarios from my head before calling my dad.

"Sydney Mae?"

"Hi, Dad." Despite calming myself down, my words come out shaky.

"I take it you got my email?"

"I did. How's Mom?"

"Oh, she's doin' okay. She's got a fractured wrist, some minor cuts, and a pretty bad bump on her head, but the doctors say she'll be just fine."

I blow out a sigh of relief. "Thank god."

He sniffles. "I'm sorry if I scared you. You know how I get when it comes to your mother. Only come if you want to—we can make do on our own."

"I got a flight out first thing tomorrow morning. I'll at least come for a few days and fly back before Christmas."

"It's up to you, sweetheart. Your ma is ticked I even called you. She was grumblin' on about how you hightailed it outta here faster than a bull that heard we were havin' Rocky Mountain oysters for dinner, and how I shouldn't't've bothered you when I knew she was fine."

A laugh bubbles out of me and I wipe a tear off my cheek. I never thought I'd miss his dropped *g*'s and the wild contractions, but I do.

Truthfully, I miss both of them more and more the longer I'm away, but the thought of stepping foot back in that town has stopped me from visiting.

At the time, leaving was my only option, but I hate that I left them to deal with the ranch alone. It was selfish, even though I was saving myself.

"I'm coming," I say, sure of my decision. "I want to see for myself that she's okay."

"All right, if you say so. I'll pick you up from the airport."

I smile, thinking about how he'll talk my ear off the whole drive with all the stories he's going to have for me. "Sounds good, Pops."

"I love you, Sydney Mae."

"Love you too, Dad."

# 2

## CHASE

I *hate* hospitals. They bring back too many memories, especially this time of year. The beeping. The overly sterile smell. The fake smile on the face of every nurse, convincing you everything is gonna be okay when it's not.

Everything about them makes me want to hurl.

When Bill called to let me know that Susan had been in an accident, I froze. My stomach knotted in fear and my feet refused to move—memories of the last time I was at the hospital flooding my mind. I felt my palms get sweaty and my heart was pounding in my chest.

I wanted to be there for him, for Susan, but I couldn't get out of my damn head long enough to do anything about it.

After almost four years of working for them, and living in their home, they're practically family. Considering I haven't spoken to either of my parents in ten years, Bill and Susan are pretty much all I have in the family department. Not showing up when they needed me hurt, but I knew I wouldn't be doing either of them any good if I went there and broke down because the past was coming back to haunt me.

My knee bounces as I wait on the couch in the living room for them to get home. It's been hours since Bill's first call, and even though he called back to let me know that Susan didn't suffer any major injuries and would be released later tonight, it didn't ease my worry at all.

Just as I'm about to pull out my phone and text the guys to let them know I won't be making it to the bar tonight after all, the front door opens. Susan walks in with a cast on her right wrist and a bruise on her cheek, but otherwise, she looks good.

"What in the heck are you still doin' here, Chase? I thought Tuesday was your night out with your buddies?" Bill asks, shutting the front door behind him as Susan shrugs off the coat draped over her shoulders.

I stand, rounding the couch to give Susan a once-over with my own eyes. "It is, but I wanted to make sure Mrs. Wilson was really okay before I went out."

Ever-sassy Susan huffs and waves me off when I step up to her. "That's sweet of you, but I'm fine, really. Go spend some time with your friends. You deserve a break from us geezers."

"Are you sure?"

"Absolutely." Bill smiles and presses a soft kiss to his wife's cheek. "She's a tough cookie."

"Okay," I sigh. "I'll be back around eleven, and I'll do my best to not make too much noise comin' in."

Susan grabs my hand with an appreciative twinkle in her eye. "You're always as quiet as a mouse, dear."

"I try. If y'all need anythin', I'm just a call away." I look to Bill, knowing that Susan would sooner crawl her way back to the hospital before asking for help. "I mean it."

"Thank you, sweetie."

---

I park my truck in the back lot of the bar and head inside, waving a quick hello to Scarlet, who's behind the bar, before making my way over to the high-top table where Noah and Logan are seated. I take the empty stool against the wall and run my hand through my hair to shake off the dusting of snow gathered there.

"Hey, how's Mrs. Wilson?" Logan asks.

"She's got a fractured wrist and some bruises, but she's good. Mr. Wilson's truck though..." I wince, remembering the sight of the well-loved truck when the tow truck dropped it off in the driveway earlier. "I'm not sure it can be saved. Sucks too. It was his father's—means a lot to him."

Noah flashes me a sorrowful look. "He's always treated that thing like his baby."

"Have him bring it to Harper's garage. They can fix anything over there."

"Bill is always talking about how Harper owes him one from years ago. Maybe he'll give him a good deal."

Noah nods, tipping a beer to his lips for a quick sip. "I'm sure he will. There's not a single person in this town who doesn't love Bill and Susie."

As I'm about to open my mouth to agree, Riley comes over to the table. She's in a pair of skintight black leather pants and an oversized gray sweater that's falling off one shoulder, teasing the lacy edge of her black bra. Her hair is half up with long, tight curls cascading down her shoulders and back.

She looks good. She *always* looks good.

But I don't let my gaze linger for too long. I *can't*.

"Hey, Chase." She smiles, flashing a set of perfectly straight, pearly white teeth with the slightest gap between the front two. "Can I get you a beer?"

"Yeah, that'd be great. Thanks."

Riley nods, giving me a look that I know is meant to convince me to go home with her tonight. "Sure thing. Be right back."

She walks away, purposely swaying her hips, and like the idiot I am, I watch her.

"I still don't know why you don't just go for it with her."

My brows draw together as I pull my attention away from

Riley's backside. "Riley?" I shake my head. "I couldn't. I'm no good for her."

Noah huffs a laugh. "You make it seem like you're a horrible person, Chase. You're the nicest guy I know."

"I'm still working on myself. Bringing someone into my life right now would be a mistake."

"You're too hard on yourself."

"They're right, y'know," Scarlet says, laying a hand on my shoulder. "You don't give yourself enough credit."

I shake my head. "It's complicated. I... Can we just drop this?"

With a sigh, Scarlet grabs the empty beer bottles on the table. "You're gonna have to forgive yourself for what happened eventually. It's been five years."

"I know."

My teeth clench and for the second time today I'm inundated with memories.

*December 17th, 2014.* The day my heart stopped beating. The day I've been trying to make up for for the last five years. The day I will *never* forget for as long as I live.

I miss her every single day—it's impossible not to. But there's nothing I can do to bring her back. It's not fair, though. She didn't deserve to leave this world so soon.

*If I had my wish, it'd be me in that box six feet under, not her.*

There's a voice ringing in my ear, but I can't make out what it's saying. The memories, *the pain,* is so damn overwhelming I can barely think—can barely breathe. It feels like an elephant is sitting on my chest.

A palm slides onto my forearm and I startle, turning my head to see Riley's dainty, deep umber hand resting there. My eyes flit to hers and I feel the pressure starting to release. She's standing next to me with a concerned look on her face. I take a quick glance at the rest of the table and I know that, mentally, I just checked out worse than I have in a long time.

It's not the first time I got stuck in the past and had to be dragged back, but no matter how many times it's happened, it's never any less embarrassing. "Sorry."

"It's okay," she whispers, softly squeezing my arm. "Here's your beer."

Riley slides the bottle in front of me on the table and I try my best to give her a grateful smile. "Thanks."

She eyes me warily for a moment before dragging her gaze away. "Can I get you boys anything else?"

They shake their heads, but Riley makes no move to walk away. I can feel her eyes on me, burning into the side of my face, but I don't dare make eye contact with her. I'm pretty sure I'll break if I do.

I take a sip of beer, trying my best to ignore her until she and Scarlet walk away.

"Holler if you need anything!" Scarlet shouts over her shoulder.

Silence settles over the table and I hate it.

I hate the awkward aftermath when no one knows what to say or how to act. Sometimes I wonder if it would be better if I was just a shut-in. If I kept to myself and didn't burden anyone else with my grief.

But then I remember that *she* would be disappointed in me if I were. So I force myself to be around people. I swallow down the desire to be alone and wallow in my own self-pity.

"You good, Chase?" Noah asks, knocking me with his elbow.

My thumbnail absently picks at the label on my beer bottle as I nod. "I will be."

After I got out of my head long enough to actually participate in conversation, we had a good time. I always do when I'm with them.

By the time I'm ready to leave, I realize I'd had one too many beers to safely drive home, and opt to walk instead.

The snow is still falling, but the crisp air soothes something inside me. Just being outside seems to do that lately. And more often than I'd like to admit, I've found myself staring up at the stars and talking to the one person I wish was beside me.

Life isn't always kind, or forgiving.

We pay for our sins.

We make good on our promises.

But that's still not enough.

On December 17th, 2014, when the doctors told me she was gone, I was left with an angel-sized hole in my heart.

I promised myself, and her, that from that day on, I'd be a better man—the best version of myself that I could be.

I'd make up for the lost time we could have shared together. I'd give back to the people who needed it most. Because even after suffering a loss as great as I had, there were others out there who needed help more than I did. Some who aren't lucky enough to have a guardian angel up there looking out for them. But I *know* I do.

Because I sure as hell wouldn't still be alive walking this Earth, if I didn't.

"If you're listenin' up there," I say to the dark night sky, "know that you will *always* be a part of me. I love you with all my heart, sweet angel."

# 3

CHASE

By the time I get back to the house, my head is clear. The pain of that day still lingers, but it's been a part of my daily life for what seems like forever now. It's manageable most of the time, but god damn does it hurt when it slams down on me like it did tonight.

"What are you doin' home so early, son?" Bill asks from his favorite recliner as the light from the TV flickers across his face.

I'm surprised the old man is still awake. "It's almost eleven. Better question is, what are you doin' up so late?"

He chuckles, lowering the footrest. "Ah, you know me, an old western I used to watch with my pa was on."

"Shoulda known."

"Damn straight, you should've." Clicking off the TV, he moves to stand from the chair, long days of working in the fields since he was fifteen making his joints stiff. He stretches with a groan before clapping me on the shoulder. "Just ended though, so I think it's about time I turn in."

I dip my chin. "G'night, Mr. Wilson."

"Oh, I have a favor to ask," he says when he gets to the bottom of the stairs. "My baby girl is flyin' in tomorrow. I told her I'd pick her up from the airport, but my truck's a wreck. Do you think you'd be able to get her for me?"

That can't be right.

As long as I've been here, Bill and Susan's daughter hasn't visited once. From what Susan has told me, she never would. "Your daughter is comin' here?"

He nods, grinning. "Yep. First time back here in, gosh, must be six or seven years now. She never really liked it here, always been a city girl at heart, so I understand her not wantin' to come back."

"Well, I'd be happy to pick her up." I smile. "Her name's Sydney, right?"

Bill beams. "Yep. My Sydney Mae."

"All right. I'll be sure to bring her home to you, safe and sound."

It's not hard to pick Sydney out of the sea of people huddled around the luggage carousel. Not just because there are pictures of her in the living room and a few in the hallway upstairs, but because she sticks out like a sore thumb with her fancy clothes.

Those pictures don't even begin to do her justice.

I haven't found many women attractive over the years. Not because they aren't, but because I haven't allowed myself to look. With Sydney, though, it's impossible not to.

She's *gorgeous*.

Without a doubt, the most beautiful woman I've ever seen.

Even with the tiny scowl that's been etched on her face since the second she caught my eye twenty minutes ago.

Her hair is a rich brown that fades into a lighter shade the exact color of the chewy caramel candies Susan makes three times a year. The subtle waves look like they'd feel like silk between my fingers.

She has soft features, despite her grimace, angular brows,

perfectly sculpted cheeks, with just a hint of color on them, and a set of pouty lips painted a wine red.

And her body? *God, it's perfect.*

Long, slender legs that lead to a round ass. Hips that flare out just a touch before curving into a trim waist and a flat stomach. The tight cream-colored sweater she's wearing clings to her ample chest and I've never wanted to bury my face in someone's breasts as much as I do hers.

*I'm screwed.*

I couldn't take my eyes off her if I tried.

She hefts her suitcase off the luggage carousel, fighting with the handle to get it up before blowing out an exasperated breath. I see her grumbling to herself as she rolls the hard black case toward the exit, looking around for her father.

Taking a tentative step forward, I hold up my hand. "Sydney?"

"Do I know you?" she asks, her tone laced with annoyance.

She's even prettier up close. Dark brown eyes so deep and warm it's like looking into pools of molten chocolate.

Dammit, I need to stop looking at her. If I don't, I'm gonna get myself in trouble.

"My apologies," I say, nervously lowering my hand. "I'm Chase. Your dad asked me to pick you up since his truck has seen better days."

"How sweet of him to tell *me* that." She scoffs, rolling her eyes. "If I had known, I would have just gotten a cab." Opening her purse, she pulls out her wallet. "How much do I owe you?"

"Pardon?"

"For picking me up. I know all too well that my father isn't paying you, so how much?"

I shake my head, covering her hand with mine, signaling for her to put the wallet away. It's a mistake, though. The warmth of her skin under my palm is intoxicating. It sends a flare of heat through my hand and up my arm, settling right in the center of my chest. I bask in it for a second until I see the deepened crease between her brows and pull my hand back.

*What the hell was that?*

Is that the kind of thing they talk about in movies? When you touch someone for the first time and you literally *feel* a jolt of electricity?

Whatever it is, I know that it's a bad idea to touch her again. No matter how badly I want to.

"I did it as a favor to him. I can't take your money."

"Riiight. Well, can we get going? I'd like to get this trip over with as quickly as possible. The less time I spend here, the better."

My brows draw inward. How can she say that when she hasn't seen her parents in years? I was under the impression that she *wanted* to be here, not that she was being forced. "I don't mean to be crass, but if you don't want to be here, then why bother comin' in the first place?"

"That's really none of your business."

"I just meant—"

"It doesn't matter. Can we go?"

I press my lips together, rolling them to keep my mouth shut, and nod.

*This should be an interesting ride.*

Thirty minutes into the drive, it's nauseatingly silent. She hasn't so much as looked over at me or uttered a single peep.

To make it worse, the radio in my truck is busted and the one CD, that is very *inconveniently* stuck, is a mix the previous owner's girlfriend made that has one song on it repeated twelve times. "A Drop in the Ocean" by Ron Pope.

It's fine the first two times.

By the third, my eyes are stinging with tears.

By the fourth, I have to pull over.

I didn't think a song about a relationship on the brink of failure, where leaving is utterly terrifying and staying is agonizingly painful, would affect me, but it does. So there's no chance in hell I'm putting it on.

Sydney already hates me. I don't need her to see me cry, or ask why I have a CD with twelve tear-jerking tracks.

She huffs, shifting in the seat.

"You okay?" I ask, peeking over at her profile.

"Are you going to drive this slow the whole time?"

"I'm doin' the speed limit." I look at her again and she rolls her eyes. Placating her I step on the gas, pushing the truck to go a bit faster. "So, your dad tells me you live in New York. That must be—"

"A million times better than a shitty small town in the middle of nowhere, Colorado? Yeah. It is," she says, cutting me off.

Her attitude shouldn't be so attractive, but it is. "You really hate it here that much?"

"Yes. Now can we please just spend the rest of the drive in silence? I'm really not in the mood for small talk with a country bumpkin."

*Thirty five miles left to go…*

By the time we get to the house, I'm half-convinced Sydney has concocted a plan to murder me in my sleep. If the glares and throat clearing any time the speedometer dropped below seventy were any indicator, I'm well and truly screwed. I'm shocked she didn't tell me to pull over and drop her pretty self behind the wheel in my place.

Sydney blows out a breath before hopping out of the truck. I grab her luggage out of the bed and walk it up to the porch.

"Thanks for the ride."

"Of course." I dip my chin and give her a tight-lipped smile before heading for the door.

My fingers wrap around the knob and just as I'm about to turn it she says, "Wait, what are you doing?"

Smirking, I turn to face her. "Goin' inside to get changed so I can get to work."

"You *live* here? With my parents?"

I nod. "Have for about four years now."

Her eyes blow wide and those damn pouty lips pop open, forming a perfect little "O."

# 4

## SYDNEY

What the hell does he mean he's been living with my parents for four years? They haven't said a single thing about taking in a stray, but the look on his face tells me he's completely serious.

Is he just mooching off of them? Do they actually know anything about him? He could be a damn serial killer for all they know. Not that I think he is one, but that's not the point. With their stupidly big hearts, they wouldn't even think about something like that.

Being back here is stressful enough *without* having a houseguest to deal with. And to make it an even bigger *fuck you* from the universe, he's hot.

*Really fucking hot.*

I haven't given a man a second look in *years*. No one has even come close to sparking my interest, but I couldn't take my traitorous eyes off of Chase at the airport.

That sculpted jawline. Those gorgeous hazel pools that have the most immaculate combination of green, yellow, and brown. The fucking *freckles* dusting the bridge of his nose and apples of his cheeks.

*Fuck. My. Life.*

And that's just his face. I imagine the rest of him is just as perfect given the swells of his biceps visible through his thick blue sweater, and the meaty thighs in his dark jeans.

As soon as he spoke and that soothing deep timbre hit my ears, I knew I was fucked. Since when do I find someone's *voice* attractive?

Is that even a thing?

It was bad enough that I had to spend over an hour in the car with him, where my senses were assaulted by the heady mix of fresh air and whatever panty-dropping cologne he wears. I can't quite put my thumb on what it is, but *good lord* is it the most intoxicating scent to ever grace my nostrils.

To find out that he'll be at the house the whole time I'm here is just fan-fucking-tastic.

"Is that my baby?"

My head whips around to find my dad standing at the bottom of the porch. I smile. "Hi, Dad."

"You're not gonna make an old man come all the way over there to get a hug now, are ya?" he asks, wiggling his brows.

"Of course not." I can't help but giggle as I drop my purse on top of my luggage.

His arms wrap around me before I even hit the bottom step, and crushes me to his chest, my ribs threatening to crack. He's bonier than last time I saw him, but still has enough meat on him for me to not worry. The man has always been a glutton for Mom's cooking, so I know he'll never wither away.

His arms tighten and I feel the air leave my lungs.

"Pops, c-can't breathe."

Dad chuckles as he pulls back. "Sorry, Sydney Mae, it's just been so long. I missed the hell out of you."

Emotion swells in my chest. Six years is too long to go without getting a hug from my old man. "I've missed you too."

He smiles, pinching my cheek before draping his arm over my shoulder and leading me back up the steps to the front door. "I hope you were kind to Chase on the way here."

My cheeks heat knowing I was definitely *not* kind. "Sure was," I lie. "Right, Chase?"

"Yeah," he agrees, walking down the few steps to join us.

"I knew you two would get along." He claps his free hand on Chase's shoulder. "Chase has been workin' his tail off around here."

"That's great. I'm glad you have someone here to help." My eyes flick to Chase. He's staring at me with a softness in his eyes that makes me want to grovel at his feet for being such a bitch. I shouldn't have taken my hatred for this place out on him. My past is not his fault. I tear my eyes from him and clear my throat. "Where's Mom?"

"She's in bed restin', but I'm sure she wouldn't mind a visit from the likes of you."

"Okay." I pop a kiss on my dad's cheek and head for the door. "Thanks again for the ride, Chase."

He dips his chin, opening the door for me. "My pleasure."

I step inside and am thrown back in time. Everything is exactly as it was the last time I was here. From the vintage black and white Aztec-style rug on the floor leading to the makeshift mudroom at the bottom of the stairs, to the matching pillows on the bench seat. Even the walls are the same light sage color Mom and I painted them one weekend, back when I was thirteen.

Stepping through the doorway, I see the living room dons the same worn blue it always has, and the oversized grey couch looks as inviting as ever. I can only imagine that the rest of the house has stayed the same as well, with the exception of the kitchen I paid to have remodeled a couple years back.

I'm glad to know the converted old log cabin still has every ounce of charm it once did. It's just... cozy. Something I have yet to achieve at my place in New York.

Apparently I can make intricate and perfectly flowing designs for everyone else, but when it comes to my own home, I fail spectacularly.

The fourth step going up the stairs still whines under my

weight as it always did and I smile to myself. God, I've missed this house.

Pushing open my parents bedroom door I tiptoe inside, my nose instantly filling with my mom's signature scent of lavender and cedar. It's one of my favorite smells in the whole world, and it's entirely because of the woman it's tied to in my mind.

As I step closer to the bed I see the angry red lump on her forehead and a white plaster cast on her wrist.

"Mom," I whisper, gently nudging her shoulder.

Her hazel eyes slowly blink open and find mine. "Syd? Is that you? Oh, heavens tell me I'm not hallucinating."

"You're not hallucinating."

She perks up immediately, a smile tugging at her lips. "I'm so glad you're here."

"How are you feeling?"

"A little banged up, but I'll be just fine. Not sure I'll be able to make any more Christmas cookies with this thing though," she says, waving her cast at me.

"I'll help while I'm here, but for now, you should get some more rest. I have some work to catch up on."

"You work too much, Sydney Mae," she grumbles, settling back against the pillows.

I shake my head. "I'm fine, Mom. You don't need to worry."

"You're my little girl, I'll always worry." She reaches out her hand, softly touching my chin. "Especially with you living so far away."

Leaving her was easily the worst part of moving to New York. She was my rock through everything. It killed her to see me go, but I needed to.

"You know why I left, Mom."

"I do. And I'm proud of you for getting outta here when you did." She grabs my hand with her uninjured one. "I just want to see you settle down and be happy."

My eyes well with tears and I bite my cheek to stave them off. When I was younger I never imagined myself being alone. I always wanted to have a partner at my side. Someone I could lean on and trust. Someone I could raise children and grow old with. Someone to be the Bill to my Susan. I wanted a love like my parents from the minute I was old enough to understand what love was.

But after my last, and *only*, relationship, I convinced myself that wasn't in the cards for me. So, I buried myself in work and banished all thoughts of a future with someone. That doesn't mean a small part of me doesn't want it, though. I've just let the fear of history repeating itself control me for so long that I can't even picture it.

Maybe some day I'll be able to trust someone enough to let them in.

"I will," I say, blowing out a breath. "When I'm ready."

"That's all I can ask for."

---

Speaking with Paul eased *some* of my worries about being away. He seems to be holding the fort down pretty well, which is good, seeing as this town is still stuck in the damn Stone Age and has the shittiest Wi-Fi, so I won't be able to do much on my end.

Paul has never handled anything on his own, which is doing quite a number on my stress levels. He's the face that grumpy old men need to ease their mind because they don't trust a woman to handle a construction management and architectural firm. I do have to give him some credit, though. Over the years, he's earned a lot. I think seeing me screaming at contractors and zoning committees on a weekly basis has done him some good.

Actually getting him to work up the nerve to yell at someone is another feat entirely.

Which is exactly why, after talking to Paul, I call Katie.

"I need you to keep an eye on Paul for me. Any signs of pushback from anyone and you tell me about it immediately, understood?"

"I don't think that'll be a problem, Ms. Wilson."

"Good. I'll check in with you tomorrow."

"Okay. Have a nice night."

A strange, almost wet, slapping sound is in the background, and I swear I hear another voice whispering something before she hangs up, but I don't have the mental capacity to deal with it.

There's too much to worry about. Like making sure Paul doesn't run our company into the ground, and keeping my distance from Chase's stupidly-handsome freckled face and bulging biceps.

# 5

## CHASE

When I got back to the house after a long day of work, sweaty and covered in horse shit, the last thing I expected, or *wanted*, was an invitation to go into town for dinner with Bill, Susan, and Sydney.

I tried to turn it down, but I could see the excitement on Susan's face—I can never seem to say no to her.

So, I reluctantly agreed, and now, I'm crammed in a small booth with Sydney wedged in at my side, and Bill and Susan across from us.

No matter how far I scoot over in the booth, our thighs end up touching and my shoulder keeps bumping hers, earning me a scowl each time.

I can't lie, I *like* being this close to her.

There's something pulling me to her, but I haven't a single clue what it is. I just know that whatever it is, it's insistent.

It wants me to lean into her.

To get even closer than we already are.

But the glare on her face tells me otherwise.

We place our orders and the waitress comes back with our drinks. Sydney quickly downs a gulp of her red wine.

"I still can't believe you came all the way here, Sydney Mae,"

Susan says, shaking her head as she stirs a packet of sugar into her iced tea with a straw. "Your father really shouldn't have worried you like that."

"It's fine, Mom. Really." Sydney smiles, and *goddamn is she pretty when she smiles. Too pretty.* "I'm happy you're okay, and that I got to see that for myself."

"See?" Bill nudges Susan with his elbow. "She may be a big city girl now, but her heart will always be here, with us."

Susan rolls her eyes at her husband's antics and looks at me. "Chase, sweetie"—she raises her glass of tea—"thank you for joining us tonight."

"It's my pleasure," I reply, clinking my glass against hers. "Thank you for the invite. I haven't had a family meal in quite a while, so this is nice."

"Yeah. Lovely," Sydney says under her breath.

"Gosh, it's like my dreams are comin' true—my little girl and the son I always wanted in the same room."

Sydney stiffens next to me. "Gee, thanks, Dad."

Bill's brows dip together as the tension mounts, and Sydney stares back at her father like he's the villain in her story, when in reality, she's just hurt by his choice of words.

"Oh, Sydney, you know he didn't mean it like that."

She downs another gulp of wine, finishing off the glass. "It's fine. I'm just going to go to the ladies' room."

Sydney is out of the booth and walking toward the back of the restaurant before Bill can even finish saying, "Sydney Mae!"

A pit forms in my stomach. I can't help but feel like it's my fault. "I'll go talk to her."

Susan reaches across the table and grabs my hand to stop me. "It's best if you just leave her. She'll bite your head off if you try to talk to her when she's angry."

"Noted."

When Sydney came back to the table, things were even more awkward than before. She barely engaged in any of our conversations, and pushed the food around her plate rather than eat it.

It was impossible to miss the little black smudges of makeup under her eyes and the reddened tip of her nose—a sure sign she was crying in the bathroom.

I wanted to clear the air. To apologize for intruding on their family time because it was obvious that I'm the one that caused the tension, but I knew it wouldn't be well received. Not while we were with Bill and Susan.

It's nearly two in the morning now and I've been tossing and turning for hours. I can't stop thinking about her. About how I should have said more—should have *done* more than flash an apologetic smile in the millisecond she spared me a glance.

With a groan, I pull myself out of bed and throw on a pair of sweats to head down to the kitchen. I take the stairs from the attic to the second floor slowly, trying my best to make as little noise as possible, and do the same going down to the first floor.

The moment I turn the corner into the kitchen, I stop in my tracks.

Sydney is standing at the kitchen sink with her hands on the counter and her head dipped down. A white robe with soft pink flowers and pale green monstera leaves hangs from her shoulders to her bare thighs.

"Guess I'm not the only night owl," I say, making her jump.

"Holy shit, Chase! You scared the crap out of me!" she mutters, whipping around with a hand to her chest.

Her very nearly *bare* chest.

The robe is open, showing off a thin white tank top she's sporting with no bra and a pair of tiny sleep shorts that match the flowers on the robe.

*Holy shit is right.*

*She's...*

*Fuck.*

My eyes linger on her chest before dropping down to the rest of her.

She's exquisite. Every inch of her.

The rounded swells of her breasts and soft peaks of her nipples poking through the thin cotton.

The flat, toned stomach.

The drool-worthy way her damn legs look in those shorts.

And don't even get me started on the way my name sounded coming from her lips. I want to hear her moaning it between gasps for air as I work her over with my mouth and fingers—something I haven't even *thought* of doing to a woman in years.

"Look, I know it's a nice view, but I'd appreciate it if you didn't stare."

"Sorry." I feel my cheeks flush and I snap my eyes up to hers. Her face doesn't have a single stitch of makeup and I'm not sure I've ever seen someone so naturally beautiful.

*How is it possible that someone so gorgeous even exists?*

"What are you doing here?" she asks, crossing her arms and blocking the too-tempting view of her chest.

"Just came to get some water," I say, reaching for a glass in the cabinet next to her head. "You?"

Shrugging, she tucks a few stray strands of hair behind her ear. I don't miss the way her eyes linger on my shirtless chest and have to hold back a smirk.

"Can't sleep."

"Somethin' on your mind?"

She shakes her head. "You wouldn't understand."

"Try me." I fill the glass with water from the tap and take a quick sip.

She contemplates for so long, rolling her lips together as she traces the vein pattern of the white stone countertop with the tip of her index finger, that I think she's going to shut me out entirely.

"I know I let my dad down when I moved away." Her words are shaky, and she hasn't lifted her eyes to meet mine, so I keep quiet, letting her say more in her own time. "But I thought what I've accomplished for myself would've made him proud. I work my ass off doing something that I love because of *him*."

Those gorgeous dark eyes finally flick to me and I hate what I see in them. *Self-hatred. Shame. Regret.* All entirely misplaced.

"And all I get is a backhanded comment about how you're the *son* he's always wanted." She shakes her head to will away the tears welling up, but two slip free. "It's like me being *me* isn't good enough for him."

It takes everything in me to not reach across the small gap between us and wipe away her tears.

Guilt hits me right in the chest. If I hadn't been at that dinner, Bill likely wouldn't have made the comment that he did. They could have enjoyed the limited time they have together without me there, and avoided this whole thing.

But because of me, Sydney is upset and in a tough spot with her dad.

"He didn't mean it in a bad way, Sydney," I try to explain. "He's not saying he would have rathered a son, he was saying he's always wanted one. And if you think he's not proud of you, you're sorely mistakin'." I smile as memories flood my mind. "He talks about you constantly. Even slips up and calls me Sydney in the barn every once in a while."

"He does?"

"Yeah." I smile. "He'll talk anyone's ear off about you. You're his little girl. He'd—" I feel myself getting choked up and my words fail on my tongue. Taking a quick breath, I try again. "He'd be proud of you no matter what you did."

"Then why does he never tell *me* that?"

I shrug. "That I can't answer, but I promise, he's braggin' about you to any and everyone who'll listen."

She sniffles, hastily swiping away her tears. "Thanks."

A beat of silence passes and it's actually kinda nice. She's not biting my head off, or making rude comments, and she's looking at me with a softness in her eyes now.

It's like *this* is the real her.

A woman who's smart and successful as all hell, but just wants her father's approval. *His praise.*

I may not be even a fraction as successful, or smart, as she is, but I know what that feels like down to my core. Unlike her, my father will never give me his approval. "Y'know, you're not as scary at this time of night."

"You mean, I'm less of a cold-hearted bitch?"

"I wouldn't have used those words to describe you." I shake my head. "You're *guarded.* And probably for good reason."

Sydney chews her lip, studying my features. "You're the first person to not just assume I'm a bitch because I think I'm better than them."

"I like to see the good in people. Whether they deserve it or not, everyone has a reason for acting the way they do."

She snickers. "Well, I definitely don't deserve your kindness after the way I treated you earlier."

"Ah, it's nothin'," I say, waving her off with a smirk.

A smile tips the corners of her lips and it feels like I won the lottery. I want to see that smile on her face for the rest of the time she's here.

I have a funny feeling she doesn't smile often enough, and that's just a damn shame.

Even on the darkest of days, I've found a reason to smile. Sometimes that singular smile, brought on by a memory, or a picture, or even just feeling the sun shining on my face and realizing I'm still here, still *alive*, is the only thing to get me through the day.

"You seem like a good man, Chase. I'm happy my parents have someone like you looking out for them."

I can't help but return her smile. "It's the least I could do. They needed help and I needed a place to stay, so it was a win-win."

"Either way, I appreciate it. It takes a little bit of the pressure off me knowing they have someone they can count on."

"My pleasure."

I desperately don't want this conversation to end. I want more smiles. Maybe even a laugh or two. Anything that would make her want to stay here in this kitchen with me all night. "Your parents have told me a lot about you, but never mentioned why you left."

"I hated the small town, *everybody-knows-everybody* thing. I felt like I could never be myself—could never be free." The lie rolls off her tongue so easily it sounds practiced.

"I get that, but I meant the *real* reason."

Sydney drops her eyes to her bare feet. "That's a story for another time."

"You don't have to tell me anything, but I'm here if you want to."

She slides her tongue over her bottom lip before tucking it between her teeth as she shakes her head. "How do you keep doing that?"

"Doin' what?"

Her watery eyes flick up to mine. "Making me want to open Pandora's Box without giving it a second thought. I don't know *why* I want to tell you, I just have this nagging pit in my stomach that's telling me to." She rubs her eyes with a groan. "Did you slip truth serum into my wine or something?"

That makes me chuckle. "Can't say that I did."

"Anyone ever told you you're too nice for your own good?"

"Once or twice." I take a sip of water to hide my smile.

She snickers. "Sounds about right."

I don't want to get ahead of myself and say that we're friends now, but it definitely feels like something is shifting between us. That alone is enough for me.

# 6

## SYDNEY

The smell of coffee fills my nose as I roll over in bed.

*Heaven.*

My mom has always made the best coffee—better than any fancy coffee shop in the city or big chain. I wish like all hell I could figure out what she does to it because I've tried using the same brand of grounds and it never comes out like hers.

I would be so much more productive if I actually had *good* coffee to start my day.

Grabbing my phone off the nightstand, my eyes widen when I see the time reads six fifteen. I can't even remember the last time I slept past five.

It may not be late by a normal person's standards, but for me, sleeping until six *is* late. The only time I get to squeeze in a workout or a run is before I head into the office, so I've gotten used to 4:30 a.m. wake-ups.

Three hours of sleep is nothing to write home about, but I actually feel rested, which I haven't felt in years.

Not bothering with makeup, I put some dry shampoo in my hair and massage it into my scalp before spritzing some perfume on the inside of my wrists and neck. I throw on a pair of dark jeans, a slouchy gray sweater, and a pair of sneakers before heading downstairs.

"Morning, Sydney Mae," my mom says as she fills a mug with coffee.

"Morning. How are you feeling?"

"A little achy, but that's nothing new. Don't get old." She chuckles to herself.

Giggling, I breathe a sigh of relief that her injuries really aren't as bad as my dad made them seem with his insistent phone calls. "Good. I'm glad. Maybe we can finish up those cookies you were talking about later today."

"That sounds perfect. How'd you sleep?" she asks, placing a mug down on the counter in front of me and sliding over the small white ceramic sugar bowl.

I typically drink my coffee black, so I push it away. When you guzzle as much of the stuff as I do there's no time to fiddle with putting just the right amount of milk and sugar in. "Better than I have in a long time, actually."

She smirks. "That's what happens when you take a break from work for a little while."

"Actually, I think it was more because of something Ch—"

"Sydney, I-I'm surprised you're up so early," Chase interrupts as he slips by me on his way to the coffee pot.

"She's always been an early riser," Mom interjects. "Used to get up around four just to tend to the barn before school."

I smile, remembering my early mornings filled with fresh mountain air and the ever-present, but strangely comforting, stench of cow pies. "Some days I wish that was still my reason for waking up so early. The barn animals are better company— they don't talk back."

"You want to come help me with them this morning?" Chase asks, scooping two spoonfuls of sugar into his travel mug before twisting the lid into place.

Disappointment slams into me. I would love to spend my morning tending to the barn and getting my hands dirty. But after last night, I'm afraid of what will come out of my mouth around Chase. "Thanks, but I can't. I have some work I need to check up on."

"Well, if you change your mind, you know where to find us."

"Did you just refer to yourself and the barn animals as *us*?"

His cheeks flush pink. "I'm just gonna head out before I embarrass myself anymore."

A laugh bubbles out of me and I can't help but smile as I watch him walk away. My eyes drift down to sneak a peek at his ass in those jeans and now *my* cheeks flush.

*Goddamn, the man can fill out a pair of Wranglers.*

He has thick, muscular thighs leading to a sculpted ass any New York pilates instructor would be jealous of.

My fingers itch to grab hold of it to see just how firm it is.

Mom clears her throat, pulling my attention back to her. "You two seem to be getting along more than yesterday."

I take a sip of coffee, wincing at how hot it is. The taste settles on my tongue and I cringe. *Did mom lose her coffee god touch?* "The coffee is different."

"You're gonna ignore my comment, then?"

"Tell me why the coffee is different."

"I will"—she folds her arms over her chest—"when you tell me what changed between you and Chase."

I roll my eyes and slump into one of the chairs at the kitchen table. "We talked last night and I realized I may have misjudged him."

"He's a very sweet boy. Hiring him was the best decision your father ever made. Like you, he hasn't had the easiest life."

"What do you mean?" My brows draw together and a sudden sense of fear settles in my gut.

She shakes her head, rolling her lips together. "That's not for me to tell you."

"You didn't tell him about…" I can't bring myself to say his name, but she knows exactly who I'm talking about. "Did you?"

"Of course not, Syd."

Blowing out a breath of relief, a little bit of the weight that I always carry with me lifts from my chest. "Good." I take another sip of coffee and my nose scrunches.

"A spoonful of vanilla sugar should fix that," she says, tilting her chin toward my mug.

"But I always drink it black."

"Not in this house you don't." She grabs the sugar bowl from the counter and pushes it toward me. "Been sneakin' a spoonful in for you ever since you started drinkin' it."

My mouth drops open. "Are you kidding me?" I take the lid off the sugar bowl and see the fine white crystals flecked with dark brown. I drag my eyes back to her. "*That's* your secret to making it taste so good?"

"Yep. My momma made mine that way and I've never had it any other way."

"All this time I thought you had the perfect touch, turns out you've just been sneaking sugar into my coffee since I was, what, thirteen?"

"Sure have," she says as she spoons the sugar into my cup and gives it a stir. "Your father doesn't even know. Chase is the only one I've told."

I laugh until my stomach hurts.

They've been married for almost forty years, how has that man not figured it out yet?

When the giggles finally die down, I take a sip of my doctored coffee and warmth fills my chest. *This* is home.

This cup of coffee right here.

"It's no wonder no coffee has ever tasted as good. I tried for months when I got to New York and could never figure out what I was doing wrong. Turns out my mother is just a snake."

She shrugs, taking a sip out of her own mug. "You were always so worried about eating healthy because you wanted your father's figure and not mine. It's no secret that I could lose more than a few pounds, and I've been working on it, but I'll be damned if I give up putting a little sugar in my coffee."

"You look great, Mom. I hate myself for saying this, but as the daughter of a man who constantly makes dirty jokes and eyes you up like a Thanksgiving feast, Dad would be distraught if you didn't have *a little extra cushion for the pushin,* and lord knows the two of you are as freaky as ever."

"Couldn't keep his hands off me if I tried."

"Gross." My nose scrunches and I try to shake away the visual of the two of them. I walked in on one of their *rendezvous* when I was sixteen and have never been able to burn the image from my mind. "But that's my point exactly. If you want to lose weight for yourself, then do it, but if it's not affecting your health then fuck it. You're perfect the way you are."

"Oh, I know your father has no issue." She blushes and bites her lip, sending a shudder through me. "But my doctor said that if I did lose a bit it would be better for my joints."

"If you want, I could show you some easy pilates workouts you could do with a chair or on the couch while watching your soaps. Nothing too strenuous, and easily doable with your injuries, but it's great for mobility and strengthening your core."

Her eyes light up. "You'd do that?"

"Of course. Multitasking is my best friend. I'm all for a lazy girl workout routine. How do you think I make time for all the serial killer documentaries I watch?"

Mom chuckles and flashes me a bright smile. "I still don't know how you stomach those things, but I'd like that."

"Great. Let me check in with Paul and Katie, then maybe around ten we can go over some?"

"Sounds good to me. Thanks, Sydney Mae."

I stand, grabbing my mug and drop a kiss to her cheek. "You're welcome, Mom."

---

*I'm going to kill him.*

I can't even take five minutes to relax and enjoy a damn cup of coffee while having a conversation with my Mom without having everything turn to shit.

It's a miracle I've kept our company as successful as it is with him dropping a ball this big.

My fists clench as the line trills. He picks up on the fourth ring, way too late for my liking,. "Hey."

"What the hell did you do?!"

"Syd, what are you talking about?"

"The new property in the Bronx!" I shout, uncaring that my voice is as shrill as ever. "I got an email saying the material was never delivered. How could you drop the ball on this? You know how big this deal is, Paul."

He groans. "Let me call you back."

"Don't you dare hang up on me, Wu!"

The line disconnects and I nearly lose my shit. I feel my blood simmering to a boil and have half a mind to get on a plane this instant to get this situated.

Commercial locations in the Bronx are hard to come by. Our client, Klein Kovacs of Kovacs Inc.—a non-profit organization focusing on housing developments for marginalized and underserved communities—has been waiting for this land to become available for *years*.

He trusted Wilson & Wu to remodel an old warehouse in Brooklyn three years ago into a women's shelter. He offered us this job in the Bronx without shopping it around to other architecture firms because he knew we would get the job done on time and not fuck him over like our competition.

For Paul to drop the ball on this *day one* of breaking ground is enough to send me to an early grave. *No amount of deep breathing exercises will help me now.*

One day could be the difference in the zoning committee throwing a fit and revoking our permits.

They were hard enough to get as it is given that the housing development we're building is within a half mile of a school and the idiot lawmakers think that the development will only draw more crime and homelessness to the area. A load of absolute horseshit if you ask me, but we still managed to get the permits due to Klein's reputation.

I dial Katie and she picks up on the first ring. "I thought I told you to keep an eye on Paul! He was supposed to oversee the delivery in the Bronx."

"Ms. Wilson—"

"I swear, the only person I can count on to get shit done properly is myself! I knew I couldn't trust the two of you to make sure things went smoothly."

"Ms. Wilson—"

"Schedule me a conference call with—"

"Ms. Wilson, would you just shut up and listen?" Katie yells into the phone and I zip my mouth shut.

*Damn.*

*I didn't think she had it in her to stand up to me, let alone tell me to shut up. I'm impressed.*

"The delivery wasn't made because there was a delay with the trucking company. It has been rescheduled for tomorrow morning at seven. I already called the zoning committee so they're aware of the delay, and will ensure the permits are not going to be impacted."

I blow out a tiny breath of relief. "If that's the case, then why don't I have an email confirming it?" I ask, unable to settle my nerves.

"You do, Ms. Wilson. Maybe it just hasn't come through yet. You did say you don't have great reception or Wi-Fi there."

"I'm *very* well aware of that fact, Katie."

"You don't need to worry, everything is being handled. I'm taking care of it."

"Thank you."

"You're welcome. Now go enjoy the time you have with your parents. I'll call if there's anything I can't handle myself."

I roll my eyes, but can't hold back a chuckle. "You're really locked into boss bitch mode now, huh?"

"Sure am. Learned from the best. Talk soon."

She hangs up before I can get another word in.

Sighing, I click refresh on my inbox again and a few emails pop up.

One of them being the notification about the delay, and Katie's response. There's another one of her noting the name and direct line to the zoning committee person she spoke to regarding the delay with a timestamp and an attachment that I *know* is going to be an email she requested from the committee to have their acknowledgement and confirmation in writing.

I taught her well.

*Maybe I can enjoy my time here after all.*

———

After checking a couple of other emails and sending them over to Katie and Paul, I throw on a pair of leggings, quickly put on my signature wine-colored lipstick, and leave my room to head back downstairs for Mom's pilates lesson.

When I get to the end of the hallway, right before the stairs, I hear my mom talking to Chase. I take a step back and flatten myself against the wall.

"It's no trouble, Chase. Really."

"I should have known they'd come after me eventually."

*Who's after him? And for what?*

I know I shouldn't eavesdrop, but I can't help it, I need to know more about him.

"If you don't mind me asking, how much do you still owe?"

I hear him blow out a breath. "About $83,000 altogether, for the hospital bills and late fees."

*Hospital bills?* Is he sick? Is that why he's living here and scraping the barrel working for my dad?

My heart twists in my chest. *I shouldn't be listening to this.*

I should have walked away as soon as I realized they were having a private conversation.

But I'm desperate to know more about him.

So, however shitty it makes me, I stay.

"I'm so sorry, Chase. I wish there were something we could do to help."

"Thank you, Ma'am, but I'll figure it out. Y'all have already given me more than I deserve."

*They've given him more than he deserves?* What does that even mean? Did they give him money? Has he been taking advantage of their kindness this whole time? I don't want to believe he would, but I know almost nothing about him.

I do know that he's charming. All he'd have to do is flash them a smile and they'd be eating out of the palm of his hand.

"You know that we would never hold it against you if you wanted to get another job that pays better, right?"

"I-I couldn't do that."

"Sometimes it's okay to be selfish, sweetie. Especially when it's what's best for you."

"Bein' selfish is what got me into this mess."

*What the hell is your story, Chase?*

Hours later, after the broken-wrist-friendly pilates lesson with my mom, and a Chase-less dinner with no awkward mentions of last night's debacle, I hear a knock at my door.

"Syd?" I hear my dad ask. "I need to apologize to you about last night."

Ugh. Definitely not what I wanted to deal with.

"Come in, Pops."

He pushes into my room and gestures to the bed, asking permission to take a seat. I nod, knowing this conversation is going to happen no matter what.

"I'm sorry, Sydney Mae. I didn't mean to hurt your feelings at dinner."

"It's fine, Dad. Really," I say, trying to wave him off. My conversation with Chase helped quell my anger.

He grabs my hand. "We just miss havin' you around, and Chase has been such a big help to your mom and I. You'll always be my little girl, and I'm so dang proud of you, hon."

"Thanks, Dad. I miss you and mom too, but I can't just walk away from my life in New York to be here—it's too hard. There are too many bad memories."

"Your mother won't tell me what happened, but I know that if it were enough to have my beautifully strong baby girl runnin' for the hills, it can't be good. Maybe someday you'll be willin' to share that with me." He rests a hand on my shoulder and I get a good look at his misty eyes. "I'm not askin' you to move back or anythin'. Maybe just for you to come visit more. A couple times a year at most."

Chewing on my lip, I feel my eyes start to water. I don't think he knows how painful it is to be back here. I know they're getting older, and I've already missed so much time with them. I do miss them, but I don't know how often I can handle being here without fully breaking. "I'll try."

"I'd like that very much." He leans over, pulling me into a hug. "I love you, Sydney Mae."

"I love you too, Pops."

His arms give me a good squeeze before he releases me and stands from the bed. "Could you do me a favor and take it easy on Chase these next couple days? It's a rough time of year for him—Tuesday, especially."

The conversation I overheard earlier pricks at the back of my mind. Maybe the hospital bills aren't for him, but someone else.

Someone he lost.

I swallow down a lump of guilt lodged in my throat. "Okay."

# 7

## CHASE

Another sip of cheap vodka burns its way down my throat as I sit at a table in the bar by myself. I thought the taste would get better the more I drank, but now I'm well on my way to being drunker than I've been in years, and I can't say that it has.

*Drunker?*

No, that's not right. *More drunk.*

I'm *more drunk* than I've been in years. The C I got in English makes a whole lotta sense right now.

"*C's get degrees*," I mumble to myself as I tip the glass to my lips for another sip. "Except the only degree I have to my name is *World's Biggest Fuckup*, according to my parents."

I wince through another sip, toeing the line of drunk and trashed. Not my smartest decision, but after the day I've had, I deserve the leniency.

*Eighty-three thousand dollars.*

It's almost laughable how little money I have to my name. What I have in my bank account doesn't even come close to making a dent.

I knew it was only a matter of time before the debt collectors came after me. Of course it had to be *now* that they'd come.

When the five-year anniversary of the worst day of my life is just days away.

Swallowing down the last mouthful of vodka, I nearly gag.

*What the hell am I doing?*

"Chase, you okay?" Scarlet asks, sliding up to my table.

"Can I get a beer?"

Her brows furrow. "How about some water instead? Joe said you've been here since five."

I blow out a breath and run my fingers through my hair. "Yeah, I guess that's prolly a b-better idea."

She nods, and flashes me a sad smile. "Do you want me to call someone?"

"Like who? I got no one. Just me, myself, and I."

"That's not true, Chase. You have me. And Logan and Noah and Riley."

"Riley…"

Scarlet puts her hand on my forearm. "It's her night off, but I'm sure she wouldn't mind coming down here for you."

"No." I shake my head. "I'll make her sad."

"How about the boys then?"

I groan, digging the heels of my palms into my eye sockets. "They'll just take me to the Wilson's."

"Okay, well, what if you stay here and have some water and I can take you home when I close up?" she offers.

Refocusing my eyes, I swear I'm seeing things. There's no way she would be here, she's too good for this place. "Sydney?" I ask, convinced I'm going insane.

The blurry image of Sydney starts to focus when she takes another step closer.

She's in a pale pink sweater with a white collar peeking out from the neck and a slate grey buttoned skirt that hits mid thigh. Those damn long legs of hers are covered in a pair of sheer black stockings that lead to black booties. Definitely not clothing fit for a snowy night. *Or a dive bar.*

"Chase?"

"Sydney?" Scarlet says, making me feel less crazy.

"Scarlet?"

"Chase!" I say, popping to my feet. The room spins and I quickly grab the table and retake my seat on the high stool.

Sydney looks at Scarlet with a dip in her brows. "Is he drunk?"

"As a skunk," Scarlet confirms and I can't even be mad because it's the truth. "When did you get back to town?"

"Two days ago. I wanted to check on my mom after the accident."

"Gotcha." Someone calls out for Scarlet and she turns, holding up her finger to them before she brings her gaze back to Sydney. "Would you mind keeping an eye on him for a little bit? I could give you both a ride back to the house when I close up."

Sydney's eyes meet mine and I try to force a smile. "Uh, sure. Yeah."

"Thanks. I'll bring over some water for him and whatever you want to drink."

"I'm good with water," Sydney says as she slides into the stool against the wall catty-corner to me. Scarlet dips her chin in acknowledgement and heads back toward the bar. "Hey, Chase."

"Hi, Sydney Mae."

She cringes, her nose wrinkling. "Only my parents call me that."

"I think it's c-cute."

"At least one of us does." Scarlet drops off our waters before running off again, and Sydney takes a quick sip of hers. "I didn't take you for the kind of guy who'd be drinking alone on a Sunday night."

I shrug. "Shit happens."

"Do you want to talk about it?"

"You wouldn't understand."

She cocks a brow. "Using my own words against me, huh?"

"Maybe," I say, hiding a smirk behind my glass of water.

Sydney giggles, her cheeks flushing an adorable shade of pink.

When she tucks her plump bottom lip between her teeth it makes me want to pull it free and take it between my own. I've never wanted to kiss someone as badly as I want to kiss her. And I know that's not just the liquor talking. Even completely sober in the kitchen last night, I wanted to kiss her.

A nervous chuckle rattles my chest and I feel my cheeks heat. *Why the hell does she have to be so pretty and easy to talk to?*

My lips have a bad habit of spilling my secrets when I drink, but now is *not* the time to open up about the shit that haunts me. There isn't a single chance I'd be able to get through my story without breaking down after the day I've had, and knowing what's coming two days from now.

Sydney's eyes flash over my shoulder and her face drains of color. She goes still, apart from the rapid rise and fall of her chest. Her lips part and little shuddering pants blow past them.

My eyes lock with hers and I can see the panic in them.

The fear.

It shocks me sober almost instantly.

I look over my shoulder and see a guy about my age. He's in a leather jacket with the sleeves pushed up to his elbows. Thick black lines of tattoos are scratched on his exposed forearms and knuckles.

Generally speaking, he's a good-looking guy, with lightly tanned skin, cool blue eyes, and a strong jaw. The only noticeable flaw is the nasty scar cutting across the bridge of his nose.

I've seen him around a bunch of times, but Noah and Logan have warned me to keep my distance. They say he's bad news, and based on Sydney's reaction alone, I can tell they're right.

Turning back to her, I see she's now as white as a ghost.

"Are you okay?"

"C-can we get out of here?" she asks, barely above a whisper.

I nod and drop a twenty down on the table before hopping

down from my stool. Placing my hand on the small of her back, I lead her out the door, using my body to shield her from view.

The cold night air stings my face as we make our way through the parking lot and onto the well-worn path toward the main road that will bring us back to the Wilson's house.

She's silent the whole time, power-walking ahead of me.

There's an uneasy feeling in my gut that won't go away no matter how far we get from the bar. *I need to know what happened back there.*

"Sydney?"

She doesn't turn back and doesn't acknowledge me, she just keeps on walking.

I pick up the pace, jogging a couple steps to catch up to her. "Syd," I say softly, the nickname sliding off my tongue far too easily as my hand lightly wraps around her wrist.

"What?"

Spinning her to face me, I see the defeat. Her eyes are brimming with tears, and it's so damn tempting to pull her into my arms.

"Talk to me," I plead.

Sydney shakes her head, a tear falling free. "I can't."

"You can."

Taking a shaky breath she looks into my eyes, searching them with such hopelessness. I can see her hesitation. She doesn't know if she can trust me. "I-it's hard for me to talk about."

I nod, stroking the skin on the wrist I'm still holding with my thumb. "I know." I flash a half smile. "It's okay if you don't want to tell me, but I need to know that you're okay."

"Not even a little bit." She shudders and chews her lip. "That guy in there… Jack Dugan." She pauses, wincing at the thought of the truth coming out. "He's my ex."

"You dated that guy?"

Her eyes well with fresh tears as she nods. "I was young and stupid and it turned out to be the biggest mistake of my life." She wipes the tears from her cheeks angrily, like she hates giving him the power to affect her. "I wish I never met him, Chase. Things would be so much easier if I hadn't."

My stomach sours and a protective instinct I haven't felt in years flares inside me. "Did he hurt you?" I ask through clenched teeth.

Her silence is so loud I already know the answer.

Whether it was with his words, or his hands, he hurt her—there's not a single doubt in my mind. And I'll bet anything on him being the reason she left.

"Chase, I—" she starts, but a sob bursts from her.

Watching her break down is killing me.

It's like someone is driving a knife straight through my heart. I wish I could take the pain away, erase the memories that haunt her, because that's exactly what they're doing, *haunting* her.

She ran from here and didn't look back because of *him*.

She missed time with her parents because of *him*.

She buried herself in work to escape what *he* did to her.

I want to comfort her. Wrap my arms around her and pull her to my chest. Dry her tears with my thumbs and press my lips to her forehead. Let her know that no matter what, he will never hurt her again.

There's an insistent urge in my chest pounding against my ribcage and I realize it's my heart. The damn thing begging me to do something.

*Fuck it.*

My arms sling around her and I tug her into me, letting her bury her nose in my chest. She bawls, each rough intake of breath cracks my heart just a little bit further.

*God, I feel so useless.*

All I can offer her is the ounce of strength I have left in myself, but I'll gladly give it to her if it means her tears will dry.

Seeing a woman as beautiful and strong as she is cracking under the weight of her past sucks. She shouldn't have experienced that hurt to begin with. And she definitely shouldn't have to see the bastard that caused her pain.

I rub circles on her back, trying to soothe her. "Shhh, it's okay, Sydney Mae." Squeezing her tighter, I rest my cheek on the top of her head, inhaling the mellow citrus notes of her shampoo mixed with the soft, fruity florals of her perfume. "I've got you."

"I hate him," she says through a sob. "I hate him. I hate him. I hate him."

"I know."

"It hurts."

"Get it out, beautiful," I whisper. "Let it all out. He doesn't get to win. He doesn't get to control you."

Her chest rattles with a few more sobs before her tears start to slow, her breathing evening out. With a sniffle, she pulls back from my hold just enough to look up at me. "T-thank you."

I nod, not knowing what to say. All I know is that she feels too damn good in my arms. I don't want her to leave them, but I know my time is coming to an end.

There's a storm rolling in and the temperature is dropping. I need to get her home.

"I thought I was ready to talk about it, but I'm not. I don't know if I'll ever be," she admits.

"That's okay." I take her cheeks in my hands, using my thumbs to gently wipe away the makeup smeared below her eyes. "How about we get you back to the house?"

"Yeah."

---

The walk home was pretty quiet, neither of us knowing what to say, but she stayed close the whole time.

I sent her up to bed and told her I'd grab her a glass of water, knowing I needed a second to calm myself down.

Somewhere along the walk home, the desire to keep her safe and comfort her morphed into anger. I felt my fists clenching at my sides and my mind was whirling with ways to make things right.

By the time I make it to her room, she's already changed into a sage green, short-sleeved button-down sleep set and cleaned off the rest of her makeup. Her bottom half is tucked under the covers and she's resting her back against the headboard.

I set the glass of water down on her nightstand. "You need anythin' else?"

She rolls her lips together and her cheeks flush slightly. "Do you think you could stay with me? J-just until I fall asleep."

*Shit.*

There's nothing I want more than to slip in bed beside her and hold her close, but I know it's not a good idea. Despite *feeling* like I'm sober, I'm not. And I don't trust myself not to touch her. I've starved myself of any sort of physical connection for so long that I haven't a single clue what would happen if I gave in.

She may not have told me what happened with Jack, but I have a pretty good idea, and me pawing at her is only going to make things worse. Even if that *weren't* an issue, I'm too angry to sit still. Angry for her. Angry for Bill and Susan. Angry that Jack gets to walk around without a care in the world when she's been fighting just to keep her head above water.

"I don't think that's a good idea."

"Please?" she pleads, meeting my hazel eyes with her dark, chocolatey ones.

*Dammit. How am I supposed to say no to that face?*

"Okay," I say, resigned, taking a seat on the floor beside her bed.

"I meant—"

"I know, but this is what I can give you, Sydney Mae."

She flattens her lips in disapproval but nods anyway. Settling down into the pillows, she hangs her hand off the bed, wiggling her fingers until I slip my hand into hers. "Thank you, Chase."

*Don't thank me yet. You'll hate me again by morning.*

# 8

## CHASE

My head throbs something fierce as my alarm blares. I'm tempted to throw the damn thing at the wall but that would require too much moving.

Reaching out my arm, I smack the flat wooden surface of my nightstand a couple times before my palm meets the alarm clock, silencing the ear-splitting sound.

I blow out a breath into my pillow and nearly gag at the stench of alcohol. With a groan, I roll onto my back and crack open my eyes, wincing at the sandpaper-like feel of my eyeballs.

Why the hell did I drink so much last night?

*Guilt.*

*Worry.*

*Doubt.*

*Debt collector.*

*Eighty-three thousand dollars.*

*Five year anniversary.*

It was all too much. It felt like the weight of the whole world was on my shoulders. There was nothing I could do to stop that weight from crushing me into the ground, so why not at least ease the pain a bit?

But I don't feel any better today. If anything, I feel worse.

*God, I'm an idiot.*

Drinking has only ever gotten me into trouble, and last night was no exception. Drunk Chase doesn't exactly make the best decisions.

The mere thought of getting out of bed and tending to the barn makes my stomach roll, but I know I have to. Bill is counting on me.

My bare feet touch the cold hardwood, sending a shiver up my body. Cold mornings call for a shower before heading out into the freezing temps. I'm no stranger to freezing my ass off outside in the winter months, but being hungover *and* cold seems like it'd be a death sentence.

*It probably wouldn't hurt to wash the lingering odor of bad decisions and distillery off me, either.*

The hot water scalds my skin as I stand under the spray with my head dipped between my shoulders. My head is throbbing and every time I move, the room spins.

I swallow down the bile rising in my throat and get to work washing my hair before scrubbing my body clean.

By the time the water starts to cool, I'm clean and feel half-human again.

Stepping out of the shower, I bring my hand to the mirror and wipe away the steam, getting my first look at the shiner on my left eye. I knew it wasn't gonna be pretty, but I wasn't expecting it to look *this* bad. At least, not so soon.

Staring at myself in the mirror, the events of last night crash into me. Fuck, I shouldn't have gone back to the bar.

*Pushing open the door to the bar, I see Jack standing right where he was when we left, with a bottle of beer in his hand, chatting up a girl who's wearing far too little clothing for a Colorado winter.*

*She's biting her lip and batting her eyelashes, falling right into the trap he's laid for her. If she's smart she'll realize nothing good will come of letting him woo her, but something tells me Jack has a way of getting women to do whatever he wants.*

*Sydney didn't tell me much, but it was enough for me to make my own assumptions about him.*

*I make my way across the room and tap him on the shoulder.*

*He shrugs me off, his attention locked on the chesty blonde.*

*"Jack," I grumble, tapping him again.*

*"Little busy right now, buddy."*

*"It won't take long."*

*The blonde rolls her eyes. "Just talk to him so we can get out of here."*

*Jack turns around and levels me with a glare. "Do I know you?"*

*"No."*

*"Okay, then what is this about?"*

*"Does the name Sydney Wilson ring a bell?"*

*His brows dip for a second before he smirks. "Many." He licks his lips and I clench my jaw, choking down the urge to strangle him. "Haven't heard that name in years but,* **damn** *do I wish I still had my little pet."*

Little pet.

*One minute of talking to him and I know he's not the kind of man I'd ever picture Sydney with.*

*Sydney deserves to be treated like a damn queen. There's not a single chance in hell he actually respects women. I don't even want to think about what he put Sydney through.*

*I'm no saint, but in comparison to him, I sure seem like one.*

*It's no wonder Sydney ran as far and as fast as she could. I get her distaste for being here. I wouldn't want to visit either if I were her.*

*"Listen, buddy, I got better things to do then talk about my whore of an ex. What do you want?"*

I think the fuck not.

*"To give you this."*

*I don't think, I just swing my arm. My fist connects with his jaw, a satisfying crack ringing through the air. He stumbles backward a step before regaining his balance by grabbing the neck of my sweatshirt.*

*His fist is flying at me before I have a chance to dodge it. It slams into my eye and my vision blurs.*

*"What the fuck is your problem?" he asks, standing nose to nose with me.*

*Pain is radiating up my arm and my eye is throbbing, but I shake it off. "You're my problem. Pieces of shit like you who go around preying on women—using them and then tossing them aside. You're a pitiful excuse for a man."*

*Jack slides his tongue over the split on his lip as he huffs a laugh. I think he's going to say something, but he stays silent, a sneer on his face, as he throws another punch.*

*It lands in the exact same spot as last time and I fall to the ground with a hard thump, my skull rattling against the sticky floor.*

Fuck, that hurt.

*I roll onto my side, bringing my hands to cover my face. It's a feeling, a basic instinct. And apparently, completely warranted.*

*His foot connects with my ribs and the breath leaves my lungs on a cough.*

*"Tell Sydney she knows where my bed is if she wants to take a walk down memory lane." He kicks my ribs again and stars flood my vision.*

*Then, everything goes black.*

Regret floods me as I shake away the fuzzy memory of last night.

The outcome was clear to me the second I made the decision, but in my inebriated state of mind, nothing was going to stop me from picking a fight with Sydney's ex. Any time I tried to talk myself out of it, I remembered the fear and pain in her eyes.

I'd be lying if I said I could ever forget that look.

It wasn't my place to defend her, but I took it upon myself anyway—someone had to. But she can never know. I can't imagine the hell she'd raise if she found out.

I shake my head as I make my way back up the stairs to the attic to get dressed before heading down to the barn.

By the time the sun rises fully in the sky, casting some of the chill out of the air, I'm ready for the day to be over. Between the splitting headache, nausea, and general discomfort of being hungover, I'm basically a walking zombie.

The looming reminder of what tomorrow is isn't helping with any of it either.

*I wish it would end.*

Wish I could sleep through the next two days so I don't have to live, and relive, the pain of losing her again.

But who am I kidding? Sleeping through the anniversary of her death won't make the memory go away, I'd just be pissed at myself for not celebrating the life I had with her.

"Chase?" I hear from behind me as I run a brush over Storm's sleek chestnut coat.

My body stills.

*Sydney.*

"Now's not a good time," I say, keeping my back to her.

Snow crunches under her foot as she takes another step closer. "Are you okay?"

"No." The word comes out too harsh and I want to take it back as soon as it rushes past my lips.

"If this is about last night—"

"It's not," I lie. "Just go. Please."

"Okay." There's a moment of hesitation before she says, "I'm sorry."

My heart constricts in my chest. The last thing I wanted was to make her feel guilty for something that she has no control over. Even my going to confront Jack wasn't her fault, it was my own.

I want to turn around and tell her that, but I can't open that can of worms.

Not now.

Her footsteps slowly walk away from me and I breathe out a puff of air, watching as the cloud of condensation mixes with the air and slowly disappears.

I feel like a dick for snapping at her, but I'm at my breaking point. I don't know how much more I can take before fully breaking down, and that's the last thing I want her to witness.

About an hour later, as I'm putting Storm back in his paddock, there's another set of footsteps behind me.

"Hey, Chase," Riley's smoky voice calls as she walks into the barn.

"Hey. What are you doing here?" I ask with my back to her.

"Scarlet told me about last night," she says hesitantly, leaning against one of the closed stall doors. "With Jack."

*Of course Scarlet told her.*

"You shouldn't have come. I'm fine."

"We've all told you how dangerous Jack is—he's bad news, Chase. What were you thinking?" she asks, resting her hand on my forearm.

"I wasn't!" I snap, spinning around to face her, and immediately realize my mistake.

"Oh my god, your eye!"

Her dainty fingers reach out toward my face, but I turn away before they make contact. "Don't."

"Are you okay?"

I tongue my cheek and nod. "I'll be fine."

"Even with tomorrow being..."

"I know what tomorrow is, Riley. I don't need to be reminded of it."

She frowns, chewing her lip. "I'm sorry. I just thought I could help."

A sarcastic laugh bursts from my lips, cutting her off. "Help me? Newsflash, Riley, I don't want your help—hell, I don't want anyone's help!" My fingers dig through my hair, yanking at the strands. "I need her heart to still be beating! I need her to not be gone!"

"I know how hard it must be, but—"

"You don't have the slightest idea of how hard it is!" I shout, feeling every muscle in my body clenching, heart included.

*How could she know?*

She didn't have to watch the person she loves most in this world fade away day by day. She didn't experience the pain of the loss, or have to cope with the overwhelming and uncomfortable feeling of losing a part of herself.

No one, other than someone who has gone through it, will *ever* be able to understand how hard it is to even get out of bed in the morning.

"I—I didn't mean to upset you."

"Just leave before I say somethin' I can't take back."

Her eyes well with tears before she dips her chin. "I'm sorry, Chase. It's gonna be okay."

*She's wrong.*

*It will never be okay.*

# 9

## SYDNEY

After last night, I thought Chase and I were moving in the right direction, but his chilly attitude earlier made it clear that I was wrong.

*Was it because I asked him to stay?*

I know we don't know each other well, and it was probably a bit out of left field for me to ask, but in that moment, I just needed someone to settle the unease in my chest.

Even so, I don't think that a slightly awkward situation warrants his iciness. There has to have been something else.

Oh god, what if...

*What if I said something embarrassing in my sleep.*

Chase finding out the truth of my history with Jack is one thing—it seems inevitable at this point. I can tell that if I spend more time with him, the truth will come out. He's far too easy to talk to.

But him finding out that I've been practically drooling over him since the moment he stepped into my life? That would be enough to send me to an early grave.

And apparently enough for Chase to avoid me at all costs.

*Ugh. I can't think about it right now. If I do, I'm afraid I'll drive myself crazy.*

With a groan, I grab my phone and try to bury myself in work instead.

"You know, you don't have to check in every day," Paul says in an unamused tone when he answers the phone. "You should be enjoying your time with your parents."

I scoff. "I am, Paul. But this company is my baby."

"*Our* baby, Syd," he corrects and I feel like an asshole.

"Right. Ours."

"Look, I told you I could handle it. I know I haven't given you much reason to trust me in the past, but I have Katie, and she's basically the mini version of you."

That makes me smile. I knew she had it in her. "I don't know whether I should fire her or promote her."

"Well, she's running the show right now and doing a damn good job of it. You should have heard her screaming at the trucking company when they said they were going to miss the delivery."

"Guess I taught her well."

"You did."

"Are you sure everything is going okay?"

"Yes," he says through gritted teeth. "Now stop calling every hour on the hour. If there's something Katie or I can't handle ourselves, I will call you. I want you to forget about being a boss for a bit, okay?"

"Easier said than done, but I'll try."

"You're only there for another three days and then you get to come home and everything will go back to normal. Just try to enjoy your time there while you can."

"I will. Thanks again, Paul."

There's a soft knock at my door a couple minutes after hanging up with Paul.

For a split second, my brain force-feeds me hope that it's Chase. That he came to apologize for this morning and we can clear the air. That he felt something between us last night when he stayed with me.

But that'd be crazy, right?

I don't even know that *I* felt anything last night, other than the comfort of knowing he was there with me. So there's no way he feels any differently.

"Come in," I say, shutting my laptop.

The door creaks open and my mom pokes her head inside. "Do you have a minute, Sydney Mae?"

I nod, trying to swallow down the disappointment. *Should have known it wouldn't be him.*

She comes in and takes a seat on the edge of my bed, next to the vanity-turned-desk. "Sweetie, did you and Chase go out last night?"

"Uh, kind of? I went into town to clear my head and stopped at the bar to warm up a bit before heading home. He happened to be there and Scarlet asked if I could stay with him for a while because he was drunk."

Mom fiddles with the hem of her cardigan. "Is there something you'd like to tell me? Maybe something about a certain someone who shall not be named?"

I chew on my lip. "Did Chase tell you?"

"He didn't have to," she says with a slight shake of her head. "I heard you in your sleep last night, Syd. You were crying and pleading for it to stop. Damn near broke my heart to know being home brought back all those memories."

*Shit.*

*Maybe Chase did get the full truth about Jack last night after all.*

The dreams—more like nightmares—didn't stop when I went to New York, but they definitely haunted me less often.

At one point my mom slept in my bed every night so she could pull me into her arms when the worst of them hit. She'd squeeze me tight and run her fingers through my hair to calm me down.

I hate that just *seeing* Jack again brought the dreams back. "I-I didn't realize I was talking in my sleep. I saw him at the bar but Chase helped get me out before he could see me."

She places her warm palm on my cheek, softly stroking it with her thumb before dropping it to my shoulder. "Are you okay?"

"Yeah." I blow out a breath, trying my best to quell the tears threatening to spill over. "Just kinda makes me want to get on the next plane out of here and never look back."

"I'll understand if you want to, Sydney. I hate that you have to worry about running into him when you're here, checking in on me."

I shake my head. "I'll be okay. It's only a couple more days and if I stay in the house maybe it won't be so bad."

"Only if you're sure."

"I am."

My phone dings on the vanity, pulling my attention away. It's a confirmation email from Katie letting me know that the delivery happened without incident and they are officially getting started on the Bronx project.

"Okay, well, I'll let you get back to it," Mom says as she stands from the bed and presses her lips to the top of my head. "I love you, sweetie."

I smile. "Love you too, Mom."

***

I'm a mess.

Half of me is begging to go back to New York—to escape the hell of being here, surrounded by the memories threatening to drown me.

The other half is begging to stay—to fight the demons and conquer the fears that I left behind.

For the life of me, I can't figure out what to listen to: my heart or my head.

I know, mentally, I'd be much happier back in New York—at least until the guilt of leaving my parents again would start to eat away at me.

Emotionally, I'm not the same person who ran from here. If I stay, I know if I were to face those demons head-on I would kick their ass.

*Okay, maybe not kick their ass, per se, but I'd definitely give them a beating.*

I reach for the glass of wine I poured twenty minutes ago and finally take a small sip.

Mom's *Two Buck Chuck* is not nearly as bad as I thought it'd be. It's better than some of the house wines I've been served at galas and charity events.

"Hi," Chase says, startling me.

"Thought you were avoiding me?" I turn around, bringing the glass to my lips.

My gaze rakes up his body from his bare toes, to the dark grey sweats slung low on his hips, to the hard lines of his bare abs—*and those stupid lickable V-lines*—to the nasty bruise that's now his left eye.

"I was."

My tongue pokes the inside of my cheek as I look him over, having to pinch my thighs together to quell the growing need there. It should be illegal for a man to look so good. My gaze flicks back to his face in a desperate act of self-preservation. "Your eye looks pretty bad."

He nods. "It is."

"One of the cows kick you or something?" I ask, knowing there's only one reasonable explanation for how he would have gotten the shiner. There's no way he got into a fight, though. He *couldn't.* From the moment I met him, I could tell he was a lover, not a fighter. Him getting into a fight doesn't make sense.

Chase stays silent, a guilty look on his bruised face.

I chew on my lip as I place my glass of wine back onto the counter, and bring my eyes to his. There's something sorrowful in his good eye, and that's when it clicks.

An uncomfortable feeling of guilt covers me like a scratchy blanket. But there's also a warmth that spreads through my chest. "You went back there and got in a fight with Jack, didn't you?"

He takes a deep breath, giving me the subtlest of nods.

"Why the hell would you do something so monumentally stupid?" I ask, hating the shrill tone of my voice. "He's not worth it, Chase."

"He might not be, but *you* are."

I shake my head, brows drawing together. "You don't even know me."

Chase groans, muscles flexing as he crosses his arms over his broad chest. "I don't need to know you to know that he's a piece of shit. No one should know the pain I saw in your eyes last night, Sydney."

"I don't need your pity," I say weakly, as angry tears well in my eyes. I *hate* that I'm crying because of Jack again. I haven't let him have this much power over me since I left. "And I sure as hell don't need you fighting battles that I fought myself years ago!"

A sob rips through me as I try to take a steadying breath, leaving my tears no choice but to fall down my cheeks. I pinch my eyes closed in embarrassment.

*Why the hell am I still letting him affect me? He doesn't deserve a single one of my tears.*

I feel Chase's large, warm palm drop to my hip.

My eyes flash open to find him staring back at me, brows bent with concern. I should hate that he's touching me. Should hate that I'm not repulsed by the mere thought of being this close to him, but I'm not. I fear his touch is welcome.

It's grounding.

*Comforting.*

A little piece of softness in a world that's nothing but hard edges coming at you from every angle.

"I didn't mean for it to upset you." His other hand comes up to my face, softly wiping away my tears. "I was just tryin' to help."

I sniffle, leaning into his touch. "You're eleven years too late, Chase."

"I know. I'm sorry."

Licking my lips, I shake my head, hating that he put himself on Jack's radar for me. "How do your ribs feel?" I ask, running my hand over the ghost of bruises that used to live on my side for weeks at a time. "Mine hurt for weeks."

Chase's face twists in pain when I reach out and brush my fingers over the heated and reddened skin of his torso. "They'll be sore for a while."

I bring my watery eyes back to his. "Do you know what it feels like to be pushed face-first into a gravel road?" I don't wait for him to respond. "It's like ten-thousand tiny little knives digging into your cheeks and knees and palms. And it only gets worse when you fight to get up."

I feel a tear track down my cheek, but Chase quickly wipes it away.

*Jack doesn't deserve any more of my tears.*

"But when you're seventeen and scared out of your mind, being raped by your *boyfriend* for what feels like the hundredth time that week, the fear wins. You're powerless against it. Your body's natural reaction is to try to get away—to, at the very least, stop the pain, even though you know it's futile." I swallow thickly. "I fought against him every damn time. And every time, it hurt too much to keep going. I was too weak. Too broken and defeated because he *made* me that way. Even when he wasn't forcing himself on me, he had plenty of other ways to kill every last ounce of hope I had inside."

Chase's hands cup my cheeks and he leans his forehead against mine. "You never should have gone through that, Sydney. No one should." His head rocks side to side before pulling away. "How did you get away? How did you get out from under his thumb?"

"One night, fighting back wasn't pointless." A small smile curves my lips knowing that I got myself out. "He was too hopped up on whatever cocktail of drugs he was taking that night, on top of being piss drunk." My smile grows as I remember what happened that night. "It wasn't easy, but I managed to push him off of me and then basically ran like hell until I got home. I was on a plane the next morning. Not before leaving Jack a parting gift though."

Bringing my hand to Chase's face, I use my thumb to trace the path of the scar I left Jack with—from the middle of his left eyebrow, across the bridge of his nose, to the soft flesh under his right eye.

"That was you?" he asks with a grin. "How'd you do it?"

"There was a decent-sized hunk of concrete on the ground, and once I got out from under him, I rolled, grabbed it, and smashed it into his face."

"Badass."

I shrug, resting my hand on the counter next to my wine and popping my hip. "I like to think it reminds him of what a piece of shit he is every single day. It probably doesn't, but it makes me feel a bit better knowing I left a mark on him just like he did to me, so many times."

"I'm sorry, Sydney." Chase rests his hand next to mine on the marble. "Sorry for everything you went through, and that no one was there to help you back then."

I roll my lips together to hold back the impending tears. "I never wanted to leave my parents, I just didn't have any other choice. Jack wouldn't have let me go willingly. I knew if I got away once, it needed to be for good."

He nods, inching his hand closer until his fingers brush mine. "I wish I knew you back then so I could have done something."

"I'm afraid even if you tried, I probably wouldn't have listened."

"For what it's worth"—his fingers cover mine—"I won't let anyone hurt you while you're here. Especially not him." His thumb slowly strokes my knuckles and I feel a flutter of something in my stomach.

*Are those... butterflies?*

No.

No, that's not possible. I don't get butterflies.

And I definitely don't get butterflies from someone touching my knuckles.

Chase flashes me a crooked smile and the weird flutter happens again.

*Shit. Definitely butterflies.*

"T-thanks," I choke out as I pull my hand out from underneath his, immediately feeling awkward. "It's late, and it's been a pretty long day. I think I'm gonna head to bed."

He dips his chin in acknowledgement, but I can tell he's disappointed. "Sleep well."

"You too."

I dump the rest of my wine and fill the glass with water before heading toward the stairs. "Hey, Chase?"

"Yeah?"

"Thank you, for being stupid."

His lips curve up in a shy smile as he chuckles softly. "Anytime."

# 10



## DECEMBER 17, 2019

Every year, I think this day will get easier, and every year I realize just how wrong that line of thinking is.

Time is meant to heal wounds, to ease the pain of your loss. To bring clarity and acceptance. But to me, it seems more like time is just letting the wound fester. Becoming more raw and inflamed with each passing year.

The grief that slammed down on me before I even opened my eyes this morning was overwhelming. My brain reminded me what day it was with a barrage of memories, as if I could ever fucking forget.

Shouldn't I feel some sort of relief by now?

Shouldn't it feel less like my heart was ripped out of my chest just a minute ago?

It's been five years.

One thousand eight hundred and twenty-six days of her being gone, yet it still feels like it was yesterday that I held her in my arms.

God, where did the time go? How the hell did I survive *this* long without her?

*And why the fuck isn't it getting any easier?*

I talk to her every day. I feel her presence. I know in the very deepest pits of my heart that she's in a better place now.

She's not in pain. She's not suffering. She's living the life she should have lived, just apart from me. That should all be comforting. It should ease the ache I constantly feel—like a phantom limb.

But it doesn't.

Nothing makes losing her hurt any less.

After taking care of the barn to clear my head, I run back to the house and change into a clean pair of jeans, a thick sweater, and boots before heading out to the dock.

The ten-minute drive from the Wilson's house is lonelier than usual today. I pass the bare pine trees and snow-covered fields that are typically lush with green or wheat. The silence in the cab of the truck is deafening.

If there were ever a day to not listen to the jammed CD, today is definitely that day. I think "A Drop In The Ocean" would get me as soon as Ron Pope sings his first falsetto—no amount of choking it back would matter. My cheeks would undoubtedly be wet with tears.

I hop out of my truck and let my feet carry me up the small rocky hill that leads to the base of the mountain where a trail begins. Off to the left, there's a well-hidden path that hugs the side of the mountain before opening up to a field that butts up against the shore of the small lake.

Tucked at the water's edge, about three hundred yards from the clearing, is my favorite place in the whole world: the dock.

Unsurprisingly, also *her* favorite place.

It's become a bit of a tradition for me to come here on the anniversary of her death to spend the day with her. More often than not, I find myself here on the days I feel detached from her.

As I get closer to the dock, I see a figure standing at the railing overlooking the water. Of the thousands of times I've been here, I've never seen another soul.

Another few steps and the person standing there starts to come into focus.

Soft waves of caramel-brown hair fan over her shoulders to the middle of her back. The silhouette I've been dreaming about for the last three days is covered in a pair of dark wash blue jeans and a grey wool coat.

"Sydney?" I step onto the dock, catching her attention and making her turn around. "What are you doing here?"

"I should be asking you that." She grins. "I've been coming here since I was a kid."

I smile. "Weird. I've never seen anyone else here before."

"How'd you find it?" she asks, leaning her hip against the white vinyl railing.

"It was an accident, actually."

"Saw the lake from the top of that cliff, right?" Sydney asks, pointing up toward the camouflaged lookout on the mountain.

Not many people stop to take a look from that peak because it's only about halfway to the top, and most of the year it's covered by the thick brush of pines. But if you're someone who stops frequently to take water and rest breaks in the early months of fall, when the pines are shedding their needles, the lake is a picturesque sight.

"How'd you know?"

"My dad used to take me hiking up that trail every Sunday. One time, I got tired about halfway up and saw it by chance. I said, 'Daddy, we need to go down there! We need to find the lake with the pretty dock!'" She smiles, tucking her bare hands into the pockets of her jacket. *God, she's gorgeous.* "It took a couple hours to figure out how to get down here, but we eventually did. Since then, we've skipped the hike and came straight here. We spent hours just staring out at the water. To this day, it's still my favorite place."

"When was the last time y'all were here?"

"Mmm, probably about six years, or so, why?"

My heart squeezes in my chest. "It was you..."

"What?"

"Around six years ago, we were hiking and saw two people standing out here on the dock."

"We?"

I shake my head and chew on my lip. It's been years since I've told anyone. *Years since I've wanted to tell someone.* "Me and my daughter, Macie."

"Oh, I didn't know you had a daughter. How old is she?'

"She was born when I was seventeen. She would've been eleven, but she, uh—" I stop myself, taking a shaky breath. "She passed away five years ago today."

Sydney sucks in a quick breath. "Chase, I'm so sorry," she says, reaching out and placing a comforting hand on my forearm.

"It's okay," I lie.

Her hand falls from my arm and I instantly miss the contact. "If you don't mind me asking, what happened?"

"She was really sick for a while. She was diagnosed with Acute Lymphoblastic Leukemia when she was four. We did chemo and blood transfusions for a little over a year, but she got tired of being stuck in a hospital all the time. She just wanted to be a kid." *On that point, I never argued. How could I?* "The treatments were never a guarantee, and I wanted her to enjoy whatever time she had left. Whether it be five months or fifty years, she deserved to have a good life. So, we stopped treatments."

To this day I still beat myself up for stopping, even though I know that continuing would have just made both of us miserable. But there's still that small part of me that wonders if Macie would still be here with me today if I had pushed her to keep going.

"She was still sick, but she was happy, and that was all that mattered to me. I tried to give her the best life that I could. We spent almost all our time outside. Most of it on hikes, which typically ended with me carryin' her because she'd get tired real easily. That's how we found this place." I smile as I look out across the lake. "Much like you, she saw the lake with the pretty dock, only there was somethin' else that caught her eye."

"What?" Sydney asks so innocently I want to giggle.

"You and your dad. She turned to me and said, 'That's gonna be us one day, Daddy!' And just like you and your dad, we came down here and it became her favorite place. Whenever she was havin' a bad day, she'd ask me to bring her here because it made her feel better."

"I've always told my dad the dock has some kind of magic in it. Maybe I was right."

I snicker. "Macie thought so too."

"Great minds." A small dimple pits Sydney's lower right cheek.

"Definitely."

"So, I guess that means you came here a lot then?"

"We did," I confirm. "And five years ago today, we had just gotten back from almost a full day here. Macie went to the bathroom to wash up while I started dinner, I noticed she had been gone for a while, so I went to go check on her." My heart squeezes in my chest as I relive the memory of that day. "T-that's when I realized she must have fallen in the bathroom and hit her head." I pinch my eyes closed. "By the time I got her to the emergency room they said she had lost too much blood. I—" Bile rises in my throat cutting me off.

Shame, guilt, and regret all drop like bricks on my shoulders. *Idiot.*

My head has always done a fantastic job of telling me everything I did wrong when it came to Macie, and right now is no exception. It's something I'll have to live with for the rest of my life.

*I was supposed to protect her.*

"I should've checked on her sooner. I shouldn't've taken her on such a long trip that day. She was too weak. I should've forced her to stay on treatments for just a little longer. Should've gotten a second opinion, or—"

"No," Sydney blurts, silencing my ramble. She shakes her head, brushing away the tear streaking down her cheek before she reaches out to wipe at my own. Her small, cold hand stays on my cheek, thumb gently stroking back and forth. "You gave her the life she wanted, Chase."

"I-I didn't get to say goodbye." I chew on my lip, trying to hold back more tears, but it's useless. "Usually when you've got a sick kid, you get to say goodbye. You prepare for the inevitable. But it wasn't the cancer that took her from me, it was my own stupid mistake."

Sydney steps closer, the hand that was on my cheek dropping to cover my heart. The battered muscle thumps heavily in my chest. "It was an accident, Chase. It wasn't your fault."

"I should've been more careful with her."

"If you were more careful, you might not have found this place. And then she wouldn't have had those happy memories here with you."

"You're right, but—"

"No buts." Sydney's lips curve up in a small but brilliant smile. "Macie got to live her life to the fullest it would allow because of *you*. *You* did everything you could, everything *she* asked for. And because of that you still have this place to share with her. A place to come and be with her and remember all the times where it was pure magic for her. Don't belittle the happiness you were able to give her because of an accident that could have happened on anyone's watch."

A tear rolls down my cheek. I don't think anyone has ever found the words to comfort me like she just did. Most of the time I get pitying looks and a sorrowful smile.

But not Sydney. She reached into the depths of my soul and put a Band-Aid on a slow bleed that hasn't stopped in five years. "Thank you, Sydney."

"I'm sorry she's gone. And that I never got the chance to meet her. If she was anything like you, I know she would have grown up to be an amazing person."

That makes me smile. "Yeah, she would've."

Macie was the best kid there ever was, and I'm not just saying that because I'm biased. She was literally an angel. From the second she came into this world, until the moment she left, the world was a better place. There was absolutely nothing better than seeing that little smile on her face, or hearing her sweet giggles.

*Fuck, I miss her so goddamn much.*

Sydney's eyes drift shut as she takes another step closer and wraps her arms around me. They hang around my waist as she slowly rests her cheek against my chest.

I feel my heart stutter.

Never in a million years did I expect Sydney of all people to comfort me like she is now. The icy woman I met a few days ago is nowhere to be seen. She stays there for a few minutes, not saying a word, as my heart settles back into a normal rhythm.

"Do you want to stay here with me for a little while?"

She nods against my chest before pulling back and looking up into my eyes. "If you want me to."

"I'd like that. A-and I think Macie would like it too."

Sydney slides her tongue over her bottom lip before she tucks it between her teeth on a nod. "Then, yeah, I'll stay. For you, and for Macie."

I couldn't hide the smile that curves my lips if I tried. The fact that she wants to stay here for Macie... I don't even have words for how kind that is.

# 11

SYDNEY

*How the hell does Chase do it?*

He lost his daughter, an actual piece of himself, and he's not a mess or a raging asshole twenty-four-seven.

If it were me, I don't think I could live a single minute without letting the anger and bitterness seep out of me. Not to mention the overwhelming amount of sadness and grief that would leave me in a constant state of agony.

Chase still finds a reason to smile. He finds a reason to be positive and see the bright side of things after everything he's been through. I don't think I could ever be as strong as him.

He spends hours telling me stories about Macie. From the first gummy smiles and her first word being "Dada," to her singing along to his early 2000s emo and pop-punk bands in the car.

And possibly the cutest thing he told me, is how she would insist on bossing him around the kitchen on Sunday mornings. She'd tell him to make the strangest combinations of things, and he'd eat it all, no matter how disgusting, just to see the giant smile on her face.

He said the worst was pickle pancakes with a side of strawberry jelly eggs and ketchup toast.

"I can't help but notice you never mentioned anything about Macie's mom when you were telling me about her. Is there a story there?"

"There's really not much to tell." He shrugs. "Cara and I fooled around for a couple months, mainly at parties or when we were cuttin' class. She found out she was pregnant and then bailed a couple weeks after Macie was born."

"She left you alone with Macie?"

Licking his lips he takes a look out across the water and nods before looking back to me. There's a strange look on his face that I can't put my finger on. Resentment, maybe? "She told me she couldn't handle bein' a mom. Even tried convincin' me to give her up for adoption, but I didn't want to. I couldn't. She was my little girl—there's no way I could give her up. So, I raised her alone."

"Did you at least have your family to lean on for help?"

He huffs a laugh. "My uh… my parents haven't spoken to me since the day I told them I got a girl pregnant."

"Wow."

"Yeah. Luckily my Aunt Brenna took me and Macie in for a little while and helped out when she was able, but she got promoted at work and moved to Missouri after about a year."

My chest tightens. "So where did you go?"

Chase blows out a breath and I can see the shame on his face. "Depended on the season. I, uh… I had a job workin' at a gas station mini-mart that was about a mile away from a really shitty motel. I made friends with the kid at the front desk and he'd slip me the key for vacant rooms each night."

"In exchange for what? He couldn't have been doing it for free."

He winces, looking up to the sky. "Cover your ears, Macie," he says under his breath. "I'd steal packs of cigarettes, porn magazines, and condoms for him. Every once in a while, he'd ask for lottery tickets. I'm not proud of it, but when the temperatures dropped in the winter, livin' out of my car wasn't exactly an option."

I shake my head, blowing out a breath. "I'm not judging you, I'm just… fuck, Chase, I'm sorry."

"It is what it is." He shrugs. "I did what I needed to do to keep my daughter warm and fed."

"I don't understand how you're such a good man after everything you've been through."

"I was a different person before Macie."

"How do you mean?"

"I never cared about anyone but myself, treated people like shit, and constantly got in trouble at school and at home for bein' disrespectful, or not listenin'. But as soon as Macie came along…" He pauses to smile, like he appreciates the impact she had on him. "She changed who I was down to my core. She taught me love, patience, and kindness. She grounded me. Made me realize that the world *wasn't* out to get me. She gave me a purpose, apart from just bein' a piece-of-shit kid who didn't listen. When we got her diagnosis, I knew there wasn't much I could do for her. I could try to get her treatments and try to make her comfortable, but in the end I knew I couldn't help my daughter the way she needed. So, when she passed, I promised myself I'd be the best possible version of myself for her. Promised her I would show the world the kindness she showed me."

*God.* He's so… *good.* That's the only way I can think to describe him. I can tell that the love he has for his daughter will never change. She's clearly the most important person to him, even though she's no longer earthside. "She'd be really proud if she could see you now, Chase."

That earns me a smile. "I like to think she's lookin' down on me every day."

A chill rolls through me and Chase notices, touching my cold cheek with his warm thumb. "We should head back. Snow will be startin' soon."

"Five more minutes?" I ask, turning toward the lake and resting my hands on the railing. "I'm not ready to say goodbye to this place yet."

Chase's chest meets my back and he drapes his arms over my shoulders, sharing some of his warmth with me. "I'm not ready either."

Just like last night, his touch is welcome. It's kind of concerning how much I don't hate the way he touches me. My cheeks flush as his crisp masculine scent fills my nose. "Let's make it ten then." I melt into his touch. "For Macie."

"For Macie."

Ten minutes turned to an hour.

Neither of us wanted to leave the little bubble we created at the dock, despite the snow steadily falling.

We were both shivering by the time we made it back to his truck.

The beat-up old Ford's looks are deceiving. There's a weathered, rusted-out frame around the rear tires and the bed's gate is held shut with a bungee cord, but the interior looks fairly new.

Apart from the CD jammed in the disk player, and the heel hole dug into the floorboards by the gas pedal, I'd think this truck was only a handful of years old. The heat really cranks—thawed us both out pretty quick.

Our drive was relatively quiet, but I didn't mind it, I needed time to get my head back right.

I'm not usually one to admit when I'm wrong, but *fuck* was I wrong about Chase.

He's one of the most genuine people I've met in my entire life. A real breath of fresh air compared to all the fake, materialistic people I deal with on a daily basis back in New York. It's crazy that just three days ago, I thought he had nefarious intentions when it came to my parents. Now, I know that that couldn't be further from the truth. He would gladly run himself into the ground for them.

Kinda wild to think that one moment, one truth, can change your whole perception of someone.

I look across the cab of the truck as he shifts it into park and flashes me a lopsided smile.

We both push open our doors and hop out. He rounds the cab and shoves his hands into his jean pockets.

"Thanks for the ride back," I say, tucking my nose into the big, oversized maroon scarf around my neck as the wind whips by.

"My pleasure."

We walk side by side over to the porch steps, and just as I'm about to climb the first one, my dad's voice rings out behind me. "Sydney Mae, you got a minute?"

"Sure." I turn to Chase, giving him a sympathetic look. "Are you gonna be all right?"

He nods, giving me a tight smile. "I'll be fine." Squeezing my forearm gently, I try my best to seem unaffected and return the smile, but I can tell my cheeks are flushing. Thankfully, it's probably not noticeable after spending the afternoon out in the cold.

"Thanks for everything, Sydney."

"You're welcome." I swallow and blow out a breath as I head toward the large garage off to the left of the house. "What's up?"

Dad tosses a red towel covered in motor oil down onto the makeshift bench of two sawhorses and a piece of plywood. "Did you spend the day with Chase?"

"Unintentionally," I say as I nod. "I went to the dock to get some time in there while I was home and he showed up. He was as surprised as I was to see another soul there. I thought for sure you cracked and told him about it or something, but then he told me about Macie."

"You must be special to him. He doesn't usually open up about her so quickly."

Shaking my head I stuff my hands in my pockets. "I don't

know about that, Pops. I think it was more just me being in the right place at the right time."

"Ah, maybe you're right."

My spidey senses start to tingle as my dad scratches at the back of his neck while looking anywhere but at me.

"I hate to ask you this, but I'm in a bit of a jam." *Called it.* "With the truck bein' wrecked, and the mortgage due on top of your mom's hospital bills, I—"

"How much?" I ask, cutting him off.

"I'm not lookin' for a handout, Sydney Mae. I'll pay you back like last time, I just..." He brushes his hands down his face, showing more signs of stress than I've seen on him in a long time.

It drives a knife straight through my heart. I feel like a huge asshole. I have more money than I know what to do with and my parents are here struggling.

How did I let myself get so far out of touch? I used to be the kind of daughter that helped without a second thought. Before school, on weekends when I could have been hanging out with friends, after school when I should have been doing homework.

Never in a million years would I have left my parents to fend for themselves. I hate that I let them suffer for even a second because I had my head up my ass.

Reaching out, I grab his wrist and slowly pull it away from his face. "It's fine, Dad. I should've been helping this whole time. I don't want you to pay me back. "

His eyes fill when he looks at me. "The bank said if we can't pay what we owe by January first we're gonna lose the house and ranch."

"I'll give you whatever you need, Dad. I won't let you lose this place."

"Thank you, Sydney Mae." He pulls me into a hug, his arms wrapping tightly around me. "Same deal as last time, okay?"

I nod against his chest. "It's just between us, I promise. Mom will never know."

# 12

## SYDNEY



Ever since Chase told me about Macie two days ago, something has been off with him. He's made himself scarce during the day. The only times I've seen him have been late at night when we both can't sleep and migrate to the kitchen for water. Even those encounters aren't nearly as long, *or as personal*, as they were the first few nights I was here. I can't tell if it's because I know about his daughter now, or if there's something else that's bothering him.

Both of my parents have made a point to mention that this is a hard time of year for him, and after learning about Macie, I can understand why. But this seems different—*personal*. And I don't like it.

It might sound crazy, but our late night run-ins have become part of my nightly routine. I look forward to them. *Crave* them. And as much as I hate how vulnerable I am around him, I have to admit it's been nice to have someone to talk to.

And I don't hate the way he always seems to find a reason to touch me, either. Even just him tucking some rogue hairs behind my ear makes my heart rate pick up a bit.

I can't remember the last time I was actually looking forward to sharing parts of myself with someone for the sake of conversation, let alone a man. But Chase is here, ruining all of my prior perceptions.

Maybe tonight I'll ask what's bothering him. That wouldn't be weird, right? Even if it is, it's my last night here, and I probably won't see him again anyway.

With a pair of dark wash jeans, a thick beige sweater, and a borrowed pair of my mom's snow boots, I throw on my heavy wool coat, buttoning it up all the way to brave the cold.

Wind whips at my cheeks, causing me to wince and bury my nose further into the same red scarf I wore to the dock as I make my way to the garage. I'd love to turn around and head back into the house and cozy up next to the fire with a cup of tea, but I can't. The deadline to pay back my dad's debt is closing in, and I promised him I would take care of it before I went back home, and I'm already cutting it close, considering I leave tomorrow.

---

After a very slow drive down the snow-covered streets in my dad's rental car, I made it to the bank in one piece. It's borderline embarrassing how long it took me. I'm rusty enough behind the wheel as it is, add snow to the mix and I'm surprised I didn't end up in a ditch.

It only took me about ten minutes to settle everything my dad owes to keep the house and barn. I even went ahead and pre-paid for the next five years.

Guilt from the other day, when he told me how much they were struggling, stuck around like a bad cold. I couldn't in good conscience leave them to deal with the mortgage and taxes on their own when I have enough to rent out an entire building on the Upper East Side for *years*. Makes me feel like an even bigger asshole for not helping them from the minute I deposited my first big check.

My job has never been about the money for me. Sure, it's a great perk, but personally, it doesn't matter if I'm making ten thousand or ten million on a single job. So long as I can keep a roof over my head, and pay all of the people who work for Paul and I, I'm happy.

Paying off my dad's debt and pre-paying for the next little while is what the rich assholes I work with would call pocket change. I've never been arrogant enough to think that my wealth and success couldn't disappear in an instant.

The *only* reason I didn't fully pay it off is because I knew my dad would throw a shit fit. He's a prideful man, and sometimes he lets that get in the way of letting people help him. It's honestly a huge surprise that he hired Chase.

I didn't think the stubborn old man would ever willingly seek out help like that. Then again, knowing my father, it's likely that Chase only has a job because *he* needed the help, not my dad.

Smiling to myself, I push open the door to the bank and take a left, heading for the cafe a few storefronts down, on the other side of the street. I might as well take advantage of the good cell service to check in with Paul while I'm out, and I'm never one to say no to caffeine.

Opening the door to the cafe, I sigh in relief when the warm, coffee-scented air wraps around me. I order myself a chai latte and a cinnamon crumble muffin before snagging an empty seat in one of two oversized leather armchairs near the fireplace.

I pull out my phone, shooting off a quick text to Paul.

How are things going?

Really...

Can you just answer the question?

Everything is fine. Nothing is on fire and I have plenty of backup with Katie. Enjoy your last day with your parents and forget about work for a little while.

You know I can't.

Will you please chill the fuck out for like twelve seconds.

PLEASE.

I roll my eyes, but can't help the laugh that bubbles out of me. Before I can respond, my phone vibrates with an incoming call from him.

"Yes?"

"At least give me the satisfaction of knowing that I made you laugh with that one."

"My god, you're needy."

"You know I live for validation."

Shaking my head, I try, and fail, at holding back a smile. "Fine, yes, you made me laugh."

"Good."

"Is that really all you wanted?"

"Mhmm."

The call disconnects a second later and another laugh tumbles from my lips. When was the last time I felt this carefree? This light and airy?

*Sophomore year of high school, maybe?*

*Before Jack…*

That was the last time I recall being truly happy at least.

Is that what I am now? *Happy?*

I shake my head. No, definitely not *happy.* Content, maybe, but even that seems a little too generous a term.

The barista brings my order over to the table and I immediately dig into the warm muffin, my eyes rolling at the taste. God,

I can't remember the last time I indulged like this. Hell, I can't even remember the last time I went to a coffee shop myself, let alone stayed long enough to enjoy a drink and a treat. Because that's what a muffin is for me, a treat. My diet almost exclusively consists of salad, protein shakes, rice cakes with peanut butter, plain greek yogurt and black coffee.

My life back home doesn't afford me the luxury of kicking back and basking in the little moments like this, it's always go, go, go. I'm constantly doing something. The time I put into my clients and prospective clients is just as important as the time I spend making sure every aspect of a design is just right. I don't have time to dilly-dally in a coffee shop and drink a cup of tea or eat a muffin.

Bringing the paper cup of chai to my lips, I let the cardamom and clove fill my senses. I take a small sip, savoring the warmth of the spices as they settle on my tongue before I swallow it down.

*Fuck, that's good.*

My eyes drift closed and I soak up every last bit of comfort all of this is bringing me.

I should find time to relax like this more often when I get back to New York.

Ha. Who am I kidding? That's never going to happen.

"This seat taken?"

A chill runs down my spine at his familiar voice, and my stomach clenches.

*Fuck. This can't be happening right now.*

Slowly peeling my eyes open, I can feel my heart beating erratically in my chest.

My gaze settles on Jack, and I can't stop the panic rising in my chest. He wouldn't do anything to me in a public place like this, would he? I know he's an idiot, but there's a reason why he was able to get away with his abuse for so long. That doesn't make me feel any better though. He could snap at any moment.

Jack settles into the chair next to me and helps himself to a piece of my muffin before turning and reaching for my cup.

I'm frozen.

Shocked.

I can't bring myself to open my damn mouth to tell him off, or snatch my cup away before it's in his hand. He's controlling me without saying a single thing, and I hate that after all these years, I still cower in his presence. Still give him power.

He licks his lips and leans back in the chair, making himself comfortable. "Had a feeling you were back in town," he says before taking a sip from my cup.

I stay silent, unable to get any words to come out no matter how hard I try. It's like someone smacked a piece of duct tape over my mouth, or cut the tie between my brain and my tongue, leaving me mute.

Jack smirks, satisfied by my silence. "You know, I'm honored that after all this time I'm still on your mind." A shudder runs through me. "I gotta be in that pretty little head of yours if you told that bitch boy about me." He leans forward, resting his elbows on his knees. "Cute of him to try to stand up for you. Shame I had to mess up his pretty face."

My jaw clenches thinking about the shiner on Chase's face because of him. I never should have told him. All it did was cause trouble.

"I asked around about him—*Chase*. Apparently he works for your parents—lives there too. Maybe I should pay them a visit, make sure they know the kind of man they hired."

"No," I say through gritted teeth.

He cocks a brow at me. "What's the matter, *princess*?"

Every muscle in my body tenses at the pet name he gave me years ago. Memories of him using it as he forced himself on me and told me it would all be okay flood my mind. My hands start to shake and my stomach turns.

*I need to get out of here.* Need to get as far away from him as possible.

Pushing to my feet, I'm about to make a run for it when Jack grabs me by the arm.

"Where the fuck do you think you're going?" he asks with his teeth bared and his brows bent together in rage.

"Home."

He huffs a laugh, letting his tongue slip over his teeth. "I'm not done with you yet."

"Yes"—I rip my arm from his grasp—"you are." My body smartly reminds me of the hours spent at self-defense classes. "I'm not the weak little girl I used to be, Jack. And I'm sure as hell not your fucking toy. You so much as set a single foot on my parent's property and you'll be looking down the barrel of my dad's shotgun."

"You think your old man is a good enough shot to take me out?"

"No, but I know for a fact that *I* am." Slowly reaching into my jacket pocket, I pull out my phone and shakily dial 9-1-1, hovering my finger over the green *Call* button while showing him the screen. "I'll call, Jack. I'll call and I'll give them every piece of evidence I have against you. Every threatening text and voicemail. Pictures of every bruise you ever left on me. I have it all documented."

*Lies, but he doesn't need to know that.* I have some pictures, but not enough to send him away.

His brows pinch together in what looks surprisingly like concern. "If you had anything you would have turned it in years ago."

"The only thing I was concerned with back then was getting as far away from you as humanly possible. You took *everything* from me, Jack. My life, my hope, my friends, my parents. I've missed out on so much time with them because of *you*. I've been terrified to step foot back in this town because of *you*. And for what? Because you were an abusive, controlling asshole who used fear to control me? Well guess what, I'm not afraid of you anymore. You *can't* control me. You can't snap your fingers and make me fall to my knees for you. I'm. Not. Yours." Each word rolls off my tongue with more and more disgust. "Don't you dare think for one fucking second that I won't do everything in my power to put your ass in a cell where you belong."

He's the one stunned silent now, his mouth popped open, cheeks turning pink. The other cafe patrons are staring at us, but I couldn't care less. I would love it if everyone in this town knew what a manipulative, abusive, asshole he is.

I grab my jacket off the arm of the chair and slip it on as he stands there, dumbfounded. "Do me a favor and forget I ever existed," I say over my shoulder as I make my way to the door.

---

For the first time in what feels like years, I can actually breathe. I didn't realize how freeing telling Jack off would be, but *god* did it make a difference. The look on his face was priceless. I wish I'd taken a picture so I could remember the day that I finally stood up to the bastard who ruined my life, but the memory alone should suffice.

Shutting the car door behind me, I lock it and start for the house, but something is telling me to not go inside.

I look toward the barn and the wind whips across my cheeks, sending a chill down my spine. Shaking it off, I take a single step toward the house when I notice something shiny on the ground by my foot.

Bending down, I see a penny, face up, nestled in the snow.

Smiling to myself at the year engraved on the front, I pick it up, slip it into my pocket, and head for the barn.

Chase is in the middle of moving bales of hay from the bed of his pickup into the haymow on the left side of the barn. He looks dangerously hot in a pair of well-worn Wranglers. The sleeves of his red flannel shirt are rolled up to his elbows, showcasing his sinewed forearms. There's sweat dripping down his temples and his cheeks are flushed from the manual labor.

He tosses the bale onto the ground, the ties popping open and scattering the hay. I can't help but admire the way his lips part as he dips his head back and wipes the sweat off his forehead before turning to head back to the truck.

It's crazy to me that he's sweating when it's barely twenty degrees outside, but then I remember the icy mornings when I took care of the barn. I would have to change before school because my clothes would be soaked through.

He stops in his tracks when he spots me, flashing me that damn crooked smile of his. "Hey, what are you doin' in here?"

"I uh, I just got back from being in town and I found this on my way into the house." I reach into my pocket and pull out the penny, holding it out for him.

Chase takes off his gloves, tucking them into his back pocket before taking the penny from me. "A penny?"

I nod, barely able to contain my smile. "It was face up."

His brows draw up in the most adorable way. "Is that supposed to mean somethin'?"

"Some people say it's a sign of good luck. Others take it as a sign that you're on the right path. And then there's pennies from Heaven."

"Pennies from Heaven?"

"Mhmm. There are loads of people who believe that when you find a penny, especially face up, that it's a sign from a loved one that you've lost, letting you know that they're looking down on you."

Chase looks down at the penny in his palm and then back to me. "Who did you lose?"

"I didn't. But you did."

"Macie?"

Nodding, I take a step closer. "Look at the date."

"2008." His eyes flick to mine. "That's the year Macie was born."

"Somehow I don't think that's a coincidence, Chase."

He bites down on his lip. "But why now? And why would she send a penny to you?"

"Maybe she's just dropping in to let me know that she's watching—I don't know. I'm not really a spiritual person or anything like that, but a good friend of mine from college lost his mom when he was young and used to talk about how she would leave him pennies all the time, especially on hard days."

"Are you having a hard day?"

Shrugging, I chew on my lip for a moment, contemplating if I should even tell Chase. "I ran into Jack while I was in town."

He stiffens, his jaw clenching. I can tell he wants to say something, but doesn't open his mouth.

I shake my head, a small smirk tipping the corner of my mouth, almost not believing that it actually happened. "I told him off and feel really good about it, and myself, for the first time since I left."

Chase smiles back at me and gently squeezes my forearm. "You did?"

"Yeah. I mean, I might not ever be allowed back into The Brew Lounge, but it was worth it to finally get everything off my chest and let him know that I'm not afraid of him anymore."

Squeezing my hand, he lets his smile grow until it's crinkling the corners of his eyes. "I'm proud of you."

"Thanks."

His demeanor changes almost immediately, a guilty look clouding his bright hazel eyes. "I'm sorry I wasn't there. I promised I wouldn't let him hurt you while you were here and—"

"Chase, it's okay, really. You've done more than enough for me already by just listening."

"He didn't hurt you, did he?"

Telling him about how Jack grabbed my arm will only make him feel even more guilty, so I choose to keep it to myself. I'll have to remember to check for bruising and make sure it stays covered. "I'm okay."

He looks into my eyes, searching them for the lie. If he finds it, he doesn't call me out on it. "Good."

Silence settles between us for a few moments, but it's a welcome one. I don't know what it is about him, but I have this urge—this *need* to be around him. Even in the quiet moments where we're just near each other, I feel at ease. Like I can breathe without fear of having the air knocked out of my lungs.

I watch as he takes in every last inch of my face, studying it like he's going to be quizzed on it later. When his gaze lands on my lips, a wave of heat rolls through me, and I feel my cheeks flush.

The sound of a whistle I know all too well rings through the air, catching our attention. We each take a step in the opposite direction, putting a bit of distance between us.

A few seconds later, my dad walks into the barn and stops in his tracks when he sees me. His brows shoot to his barely-there hairline. "Sydney Mae, I wasn't expectin' to find you out here."

"I stopped in to talk to Chase when I got back from the bank."

"Oh." Dad shifts his gaze to Chase quickly before bringing them back to me with a worried look on his face. "Were you able to…"

"I took care of it," I say. "You don't need to worry about it for a while. I don't want you getting so close to losing this place again, okay?"

He rubs at the back of his neck and nods. "Sorry for makin' you have to dig me out again."

"It's okay, Dad. I'm happy to help. Really."

"Well, all right. Thank you, Sydney Mae," he says, kissing my hair before clapping a hand on Chase's shoulder. "Don't tell the missus."

He nods. "My lips are sealed, sir. I'm in no place to talk about someone else's financial situation."

Dad dips his chin in acknowledgement, a slight edge of embarrassment passing over his features. "Susan said Sydney's last supper will be ready in five minutes." He walks out, leaving Chase and I alone again.

Is it bad that I don't like the space between us? I'm wracking my brain for ways to get back to the way we were, but I'm coming up empty.

After another couple seconds he does it for me. He takes one large step and he's standing close enough to touch again.

"You're leavin' tomorrow?"

"My flight's at ten."

"Do you—" He clears his throat, awkwardly running his fingers through his hair. "Do you want me to drive you to the airport?"

"Are you gonna drive faster than a grandma this time?"

He juts his bottom lip out as he shrugs. "Probably not."

I giggle, my lips parting as a smile takes over my face. "Yeah, I'd like that."

Chase's cheeks tint pink as his eyes widen, clearly surprised by my answer. "Cool."

"Cool." That weird feeling from the other day returns. Only this time, there's no mistaking that they're butterflies.

He's quiet for a moment, absentmindedly running the pad of his thumb over the shiny copper-colored coin. "You really think it was Macie?" he asks, holding the penny up between us.

"I do."

"Thank you, Sydney."

"You're welcome." I dip my chin, and break eye contact with him, knowing that if I don't my eyes will inevitably start to water at the thought of all he's lost. "Are you ready to head in for dinner?"

Chase shakes his head. "You go ahead," he says with a sad tilt to his lips. "Enjoy the rest of the time you have with your parents."

"You're not coming?"

He shakes his head, looking down at the penny in his hand once more. When his eyes flick back up to mine, I can see the pain in them. "I don't think I'll be very good company tonight, and I don't want to bring y'all down. I'll grab the leftovers later." He waves me off.

"Chase—"

"I'm all right, I just… miss her. And I think I need some time alone for a bit."

I bring my hand to his arm. "Okay. I'll see you in the kitchen later?"

He smiles weakly. "Yeah."

<hr>

Morning comes and Chase never met me in the kitchen. He also doesn't need to drive me to the airport because my flight got canceled thanks to the blizzard-like conditions outside. Even worse, the next direct flight out of the tiny Colorado airport is after Christmas.

If it wasn't a four-hour drive to Denver, I'd go from there, but I can't inconvenience Chase like that. Not when I know he's so sad.

I click the *Call* button on Paul's contact and am met with his voicemail. *What else is new?* It's like he doesn't want to answer my calls so I can't tell him what to do. I mean, I can't exactly blame him for not wanting to be bossed around, but still.

I hang up without leaving a voicemail, and call Katie instead.

She answers on the first ring, slightly out of breath. "H-hi, Ms. Wilson."

"Hey, Katie. Can you let Paul know that I won't be home this afternoon after all? My flight got canceled, so I decided to stay until after Christmas."

"Oh, wow. Okay, yeah, I'll let him know."

"Thanks." I chew the inside of my cheek for a second, thinking over something that Chase said in the kitchen a couple nights ago. It was weird to talk business with him, but he made me realize what a shitty person I've been for working everyone to the bone. Everyone needs breaks every once in a while. "I've also decided that we're going to be taking a couple days off. Just until after the holidays when I get back. I'll send out an email when we hang up."

"What?" I can practically hear her eyes bulge out of her head. "Are you feeling okay?"

I blow out a breath and chuckle to myself. "Look, I know I'm not the greatest boss. I'm a bitch, and I'm mean, and I raise my voice more than I should, but you're doing a great job, Katie. I wouldn't have stepped a single foot on a plane if I didn't think you would be able to handle things while I was away. Taking a couple days off isn't going to be the end of the world. Our clients are more than likely spending time with their own families anyway, so I don't see why we shouldn't be able to do the same."

"W-wow. Thank you, Ms. Wilson."

"If it's not too late, why don't you catch a flight down to Florida and spend some time with your parents. Use the company card."

"Ms. Wilson, I—"

"Katie," I interrupt. "Just do it."

This time I can hear the smile on her face when she says, "Okay, I will. Thank you so much. Merry Christmas."

"Merry Christmas."

The call disconnects and I get to work typing up emails to send out company-wide, and to all of our active construction clients.

By the time I hit *Send* I have a huge grin on my face, and I can't help but want to thank Chase for being the one to put it there.

# 13



**DECEMBER 23, 2019**

I hear footsteps behind me as I pour myself my afternoon cup of coffee. Not only does it help with the midday slump, it helps to take the chill out of my bones on days like today, when it's bitterly cold, snowing, and there are vicious winds that feels like needles against your skin.

"Hey."

Turning around, I don't bother hiding my smile when I see Sydney standing there with her hip leaning against the counter and her arms crossed over her chest. Her oversized white sweater is hanging from one shoulder, showing off her dark red bra strap. And as for the skin-tight black leggings covering her legs, all I can say is *damn*.

Just like every night we've met up in the kitchen, her hair is piled atop her head in a neat, but messy bun, and her face is free of makeup.

She's gorgeous no matter what, but this look is my favorite. Maybe it's because this is how I got to know the *real* her. Or maybe it's because I've been picturing waking up to this version of her every morning. I quickly shake that thought out of my head. I can't think about her like that.

Clearing my throat, I smile. "Hey."

"Coffee this late in the afternoon? It's no wonder you're up so late every night," she teases.

"We both know it's emotional trauma keepin' me up, not caffeine."

She giggles and tucks her bottom lip between her teeth. "I wanted to thank you for what you said the other night about giving people breaks. You'll be happy to know that I sent out an email telling everyone that, effective immediately, they're off until the day after Christmas."

My eyebrows raise toward my hairline. "Wow. That's great, Sydney. Are you giving yourself time off too?"

"Yeah. I think I need it. I can't remember a time when I ever gave myself a few days to just relax and decompress. It's been like an hour, and I already feel so much better."

"Good. I'm glad." I take a sip of my coffee, letting the warmth seep into my bones. "I know you're probably not interested, but Scarlet is having a Christmas Eve Eve party tonight. You're more than welcome to join if you'd like to get out of the house."

Her eyes light up, but I can see the hesitancy on her face. "Really?"

"You deserve to have some fun while you're here, and what better way than reconnecting with your old friends?"

"Right…" She chews her lip. "Can I think about it?"

"Sure. I'm planning to leave around eight, so I'll check in with you around seven thirty?"

She smiles softly. "Sounds good."

We stand there in silence for a few moments, both of us with a hint of a smile on our lips. I don't think I'll ever get over how pretty she is. It's far too easy to get lost in the idea of her.

"I should—" I say at the same time she says, "Do you—"

I chuckle. "Go ahead."

Sydney shakes her head. "It's silly. Nevermind."

"Ask. Please."

"Do you ever wonder if things would have been different with Macie's mom around?"

Definitely wasn't expecting that question. "Not really. Even on the most basic level, Cara and I were never a good match. We were bad for each other. And I think had she been around while Macie was still here, our relationship would have become even more toxic. Sure, payin' the hospital bills and gettin' Macie to and from doctor's visits would have been a hell of a lot easier, but then I would have had another person to constantly worry about."

"What do you mean?"

"Cara was the definition of a wild child. She had been suspended a bunch of times for smokin', skippin' class, cursin' at teachers. I'm not sayin' I was a saint by any means, but she was the one who led me down the path I was on. My life was on a downward spiral before Macie even came into the picture. I think my parents were plannin' to send me off to the military when I turned eighteen because they thought I was throwin' away my future by hangin' around people like Cara. It would have been completely justified too. Back then I didn't have a single thought that was my own. Everythin' that went through my head was put in there by her."

Sydney's brows furrow in the most adorable way as she chews her lip. "So was Macie your scared-straight moment?"

I chuckle. "Absolutely. As soon as Cara said the words, *I'm pregnant*, it was like this switch flipped in my head. Without her even being a livin', breathin' part of the world, she changed who I was. I wasn't some punk who constantly got in trouble, I was a dad—h*er* dad, and I knew the moment she took her first breath, that I would always give her the best version of myself."

"I bet she loved the shit out of you, huh?"

A smile spreads across my face. "She did, yeah. And the feelin' was mutual."

"I know I've said it already, but I'm sorry, Chase," she says, dragging her fingers down my arm.

My heart stutters in my chest and I feel a buzz of pleasure shoot to my groin. *How can she make such a simple touch feel so damn good?* She's telling me she's sorry that Macie died, and I'm two seconds away from sporting a semi for the rest of the day.

What the hell is wrong with me?

I clear my throat and subtly take a step back. "T-thanks. I don't mean to cut this conversation short, but I should really get back to work."

"Right... Sorry."

"Don't worry about it." My feet reluctantly drag me away from her. When I reach the living room, I turn around and find her staring back at me. "For the record, I'm glad your flight got canceled."

Her cheeks flush and a tiny smirk tilts her lips. "Me too."

***

Trying to concentrate was near impossible after my conversation with Sydney. My favorite horse, Storm—a mellow chestnut-colored stallion with a perfect diamond-shaped white patch on his forehead—could tell my head wasn't in it. I swear at one point he even rolled his eyes at me.

It's funny how in tune with our emotions animals are. The minute I walked over to his stall his ears twitched like he was ready for me to spill my guts to him.

And despite thirty-five minutes of trying to hold it in, I couldn't stop myself from blabbing to him about the way her fingers felt on my skin, or the look that flashed in her eyes when I told her I was glad her flight was canceled. How something about her soul, no matter how hidden behind years of mistrust and unbreakable walls, is calling to me.

Everything in me wants to take them down brick by brick, making a space just big enough for myself to crawl inside.

It's been hours now, but I can still feel her touch lingering on my skin.

Can still feel the way she sparked something inside me that has been dormant for so long.

I step out of the shower, wrapping a fluffy white towel around my hips and use the side of my fist to clear the steam off the mirror. The bruising around my eye is mostly faded, apart from the gnarly greenish-yellow spot.

The pair of eyes staring back at me have much more light in them than they did the morning after I earned the shiner. I have a sneaking suspicion that that's thanks to Sydney.

After getting dressed in a pair of my least-ripped black jeans and an ugly Christmas sweater with a hideous cartoon Rudolph, I head down the stairs to Sydney's bedroom door. I take a deep breath and blow it out before raising a fist and tapping my knuckles against it, twice.

The seconds pass like hours as I wait, and when she finally opens the door, and I'm met with her makeup-free face and the slouchy white sweater from this morning, I try to hide my disappointment.

"You're not comin', are you?"

She chews her cheek as she shakes her head. "I'm sorry. I'll just stay and bake cookies with my mom or something, but you should go."

"When was the last time you let loose and had some fun?"

She shrugs. "I don't know, college, maybe?"

"That's it. You're comin' with me whether you like it or not. You can go back to bein' all work and no play when you get home, but tonight you're gonna let me take you to Scarlet's and you're gonna have a good time. Got it?"

"Chase—"

"Please?" I'm not above begging at this point. I really want her to be there tonight, if for nothing else than to spend more time with her before she goes back home. "I'd really like it if you came. At the very least, you give me the perfect excuse to leave early. I appreciate the invite every year, and I do try to show my face for a little while, but the holidays suck no matter how much I distract myself. So you'd be the perfect scapegoat. Plus, you deserve to get out for a bit."

I give her my best puppy dog eyes.

She huffs out a breath and her shoulders slouch. "Fine. Give me a few to get ready?"

"Take your time. I'll get my truck warmed up."

"Thanks."

It was damn hard to keep my tongue from lolling out of my mouth when Sydney took off her heavy wool coat when we got to Scarlet's. She's in a deep red velvet skirt, that hugs her curves and highlights her trim waist, and a tied white button-down shirt with the top button open leaving a spectacular view of her cleavage.

At this point, I'm convinced that she knows how attracted I am to her and is just doing it to test my limits.

When we walk into Scarlet's living room, Noah and Logan lose their shit. There's a flare of jealousy in my chest when they both pull her in for bear hugs, squeezing her tight, and telling her how much they've missed her. I knew she was close with Scarlet, but I didn't realize that *all* of them used to be such good friends. Even her and Riley.

"God, I really didn't think y'all would have stayed so close after all this time."

Riley scoffs and rolls her eyes. "Yeah, well not all of us decided to pick up and leave at the drop of a hat."

Sydney flinches next to me.

"Riley," Noah scolds, nudging her with his shoulder.

Riley rolls her eyes. "So we have to protect her feelings, but fuck all of ours, right?"

"Come on, Riles. It's in the past."

"Is it? Feels a hell of a lot like it always did with all of you taking her side."

Scarlet claps once, trying to diffuse the situation. "Anyone need another drink?"

"I'll take another hot toddy," Logan says, playfully massaging Riley's tense shoulders.

"Same here," Noah adds, finishing off his cup.

I shake my head. "I'll take a beer if you have one."

"'Course I have beer." Scarlet winks at me and then looks to Sydney. "Anything for you, Syd?"

Sydney shakes her head. "I'm okay for now, but I'll come help you." She turns around and flashes me a tight, fake smile before heading off to the kitchen with Scarlet.

"I didn't realize Syd was back in town." Logan takes a seat on the arm of the oversized beige couch. "Why didn't you mention anything?"

My mouth pops open in surprise. "I wanted to respect her privacy. Plus, she wasn't supposed to be here for this long."

"How long is she staying?" Noah asks.

I tuck my hands into my pockets. "Until the day after Christmas."

"Wonder if she'll say goodbye this time."

"Riley!" Noah scolds again.

Riley looks at Noah like he's a villain. "What? It's not like it's a lie."

"It wasn't just you she left, Riley. She left all of us."

"I was her best friend. The least she could have done was said goodbye!"

Anger flares just like the jealousy did. "I'm sure she had a good reason."

"That doesn't make it hurt any less."

Logan shakes his head. "Sure, the way she left sucked, but we had each other. She's here now. Why don't you go talk to her? Bury the hatchet or something."

"You're right." She blows out a breath and gives me a strange look that makes my gut clench before walking away.

*What the hell was that?*

"You don't think it was a bad idea to bring Sydney, right?"

"Nah. I'm glad she's here."

"Same," Logan agrees. "It's been a long time."

"I didn't realize you were all so close before she left."

Logan's blue eyes drift over to Noah who's giving him a strange look. "Until she started dating Jack and stopped coming around, we were all really close. Practically inseparable."

Scarlet fake gags as she walks back into the room holding our drinks. "Can we not talk about that jackass? It's bad enough I have to see him at the bar."

"Gladly."

She passes out our drinks, filling us in on how the other two girls are attempting to hash out their problems, and we settle into a casual conversation that has nothing to do with Sydney, or Jack, or anything that happened in their past.

But I can't help the thoughts racing through my head about the stories she'd told me regarding her relationship with Jack and how he destroyed every part of her little by little. Her head, her heart, her body…

*How did they not notice what he was doing to her?*

*How did* no one *notice?*

I shake my head and take a single sip of my beer before putting it on the coffee table and excusing myself to the bathroom.

Tossing some cold water in my face, I try to get out of my head. There's nothing I can do to change the past—*her* past. Dwelling on it and criticizing *her friends* for not knowing something so serious was going on with Sydney isn't going to help anyone. It'll just serve to piss me off and stress me out.

She got out.

She got away from him.

She made a life for herself in New York.

*She's safe.*

If I repeat that in my head enough times, maybe I'll believe it.

When I get back from the bathroom, I see Riley has rejoined the group and is taking long gulps of her drink with glassy eyes, but Sydney is still missing. Without a second thought, I step out onto the back porch and into the cold without my jacket, looking for her in the darkness.

I scan the backyard and don't see any footprints in the snow so I head back inside and search through the back half of Scarlet's house. I opened every door and she's nowhere to be found. She wouldn't have left, right? She would have told me that she wanted to leave so I could give her a ride.

Right?

Maybe I'm overestimating how much Sydney trusts me.

Pushing open the front door, my heart skips a beat when I see her standing on the porch with her face tilted up to the stars. Her eyes are glassy, just like Riley's, but there's a slight curve to her lips.

"Hey," I say, stepping out onto the small covered area of the porch. "I've been lookin' all over for you. I thought you left."

Her eyes don't leave the sky. "Just needed some air." I watch as she sucks in a deep breath and slowly blows it out. "Thank you, by the way."

"For what?"

"Tonight. I really needed it." She finally peels her gaze from the stars and settles her big brown eyes on me. "If there's one thing I regret the most about leaving, it's not saying goodbye to any of them. But I had a chance to get away from Jack and I couldn't give it up."

"I don't blame you. I would've done the same thing in your shoes."

She smiles at me. Not the brilliant one with teeth she's flashed me a couple times, this one is more reserved. "You know, I'm actually kinda sad that I'm leaving."

"You are?"

She nods. "Yeah. I guess I've always associated coming home with the bad parts, but there are good parts too. My parents. My friends." She licks her lips and her cheeks turn pink. "You."

"Me?"

"You've helped me a lot, Chase. I've only ever told my mom and my therapist about Jack because I was too afraid to face it, but I think keeping it suppressed for so long did more harm than good. Emotionally, I never recovered from what he did to me—I just closed myself off to everyone. Closed myself off to the possibility of ever letting anyone get close enough to hurt me like that again." Sydney takes a breath and I can tell she needs a second, so I stay silent, staring back at her. "And then you came along," she says as she scratches at the back of her neck. "With your little accent and your sad eyes that made me want to tell you every last thing about myself... I guess what I'm trying to say is that I'm glad I met you, Chase."

I feel heat skim my cheeks. "I'm glad I met you too. I don't really believe in fate, but it feels like I was meant to have you in my life. Almost like Macie sent you here so we could help each other heal. You are the girl from the lake with the pretty dock after all." She giggles and it soothes my soul. "She would talk about you for hours some days, making up stories of who you were and what you did for a living. It had to be one of the cutest things ever."

"I'm happy she found me, and brought me to you."

"Me too."

The small space between us practically disappears, the subtle scent of her peony and orchid perfume filling my nose. Something catches my eye and I look up.

"Sydney?"

"Yeah?"

"Mistletoe."

Her mouth pops open and something that looks a hell of a lot like panic crosses her face for a second. She draws her brows together as she looks up at the offending plant.

"It's just a silly tradition—we don't have to."

She shakes her head. "Isn't it bad luck to not kiss under the mistletoe?"

"Yeah, but—"

Sydney steps closer, bringing her hand to my chest. "I think it's safe to say that neither of us need any more bad luck."

"Are you sure?"

"Kiss me, Chase."

I swallow down the lump of nervousness in my throat and reach for her face. It's been over ten years since I've kissed someone, so I pray like hell that I didn't forget how. My thumbs stroke the pink apples of her cheeks as I stare into her eyes. The dark, rich brown is nearly black, but they're flecked with little pools of gold.

*Beautiful.* Just like her.

Leaning down, I take one last sip of air before I slowly press my lips to hers.

I thought feeling a spark when you kiss someone was a lie, but with her lips on mine, it feels like I'm being electrocuted.

My heart slams against my ribcage as I pull her closer. She fits perfectly against me. Her lips are warm, and so damn soft, that for a second I wonder if I'm dreaming. There's no way she should feel *this* good. That she should *taste* this good.

A soft whimper escapes her lips when my tongue slides over her bottom lip. I feel her quick intake of breath before she parts her lips, granting me entrance. Our tongues slide against each other in the most sensual way.

I've never felt this with anyone before.

Sydney fists my sweater, pulling me closer.

For the first time in five years, it feels like my heart is actually beating again. It's not broken or battered, it's *whole*, and practically pumping right out of my chest. I know she can feel it, but I can't find it in me to care. The only thing I can think about right now is how perfectly she completes me. How she makes me forget about everything else.

*How every part of me wants to beg her to stay so we can continue to heal together.*

I know that I can't, but fuck am I tempted.

She pulls away from the kiss, looking up at me with a dreamy look in her eyes. "We should go back inside," she says against my lips.

"Right."

"I wish we could stay out here forever."

"Me too."

Sydney is quiet for a moment, and then she tips her face up, letting her nose graze mine. "One more kiss wouldn't hurt, right?"

*Thank fuck.*

"I was hopin' you'd say that."

She smirks at me and nips at my bottom lip. "Then what are you waiting for?"

Flashing her a crooked smile, I lick my lips and dive back in.

I could kiss her forever—I *want* to kiss her forever.

The reminder that *forever* doesn't exist for us passes through my mind, but I shake it away. I'll figure out how to deal with the fact that we aren't forever later. Right now, I'm going to enjoy every last second of my lips on hers.

# 14

SYDNEY

*I kissed Chase.*

I *kissed* Chase.

I kissed *Chase.*

*Holy. Shit.*

It's been years since I've even wanted to look at a man, let alone kiss one. But as soon as Chase mentioned the mistletoe, a rush of excitement and need coursed through me. There was no way I was missing that chance.

The tension between us has been mounting since the day we met, and nothing could have prepared me for what it felt like when it finally snapped. I have never in my life felt so wanted. So cherished. And Chase did that with a single kiss.

His hand finds the small of my back as he leads me back inside the house. I immediately excuse myself to the bathroom, knowing that I need a second before I can show my face back in the room filled with my old friends.

I close the door behind me, taking a look at myself in the mirror.

My tingly lips are swollen, the wine-red lipstick painting them smudged around the edges making it pretty clear what I had just been up to. I snag a tissue and clean up my lipstick the best I can before taking a couple deep breaths and making my way back to where everyone is gathered in the living room.

Riley nearly knocks me over as she runs out of the room with tears in her eyes. Noah groans, chasing after her.

"What happened?"

"Ah, you know Riley." Logan fakes a smile, rubbing at the back of his neck. "Always crying over spilled champagne."

Confusion etches itself on my face. "What?"

Chase, whose cheeks are even redder than mine, clears his throat. "I'm pretty tired, you ready to get outta here?"

"Oh. Um, yeah. Sure." I look around the room and decide now is the perfect time to redo what I didn't get to in the past. "It was really good to see you, Logan," I say, pulling him in for a hug.

"You too, Syd. Don't be a stranger, eh?"

I smile, nodding as I move over to Scarlet. "Thank you for hosting. You have a beautiful home."

"My pleasure. I'm glad you could make it."

"Tell Noah and Riley I said goodbye?"

The two of them nod in agreement and when I turn back to Chase, his jaw is set in a hard line.

What the hell happened in the three minutes I was in the bathroom?

***

For ten straight minutes in the car, Chase was silent. I think the two-hour drive from the airport that first day was less awkward.

He pulls into the driveway and we walk up to the house together.

Shrugging out of our coats, he hangs them up on the hook by the front door and then lightly stomps the snow off his boots. "Sorry for cuttin' the night short."

"It's okay. I'm not mad." *Just really fucking confused.*

"I hope you had fun."

My stomach twists uncomfortably. Why is he being so weird now? "Yeah, I did. Thanks for inviting me."

"Of course… Well, I'm gonna head to bed. G'night."

I barely get out the word *Night* before he's halfway up the stairs.

*Ohhhkay then.*

Guess the kiss wasn't as great for him as it was for me?

Shaking my head, I let the embarrassment settle between my ribs as I head up the stairs.

An hour later, I'm in a pair of peach-colored silk sleep shorts and a matching bralette. This old house gets hot at night and I learned my lesson a long time ago that thick pajamas are a no-go. I'd wake up in a puddle of sweat.

With my face free of makeup and my hair twisted into a bun on the top of my head, I lie down in bed and stare up at the ceiling.

My lips burn and butterflies wreak havoc on my stomach. What the hell could have happened that made things between us so weird? One minute his tongue was down my throat, and the next he was ushering me out of the house like it was on fire.

I don't get it.

But I know that I long for another minute with him.

Another touch.

Another kiss.

Another moment where we can just *be* and forget about everything else around us.

*Fuck it.*

I throw the blankets off and take the few short steps to the bedroom door.

If I'm feeling this way, he has to be too, right?

Unless I've severely misjudged the kind of man he is, I can't be the only one affected.

Reaching for the doorknob, I let my eyes drift closed as I twist it and pull the door open.

I take in a steadying breath and slowly open my eyes.

My heart stutters in my chest when my gaze locks on a very handsome, *very shirtless,* Chase on the other side of the door. His hands are tucked into the pockets of his low-hanging sweats, almost like he's having the same internal battle as I am.

With his abs on full display I can't help but gape at him.

"Chase." His name comes out far too breathy.

Without a moment's hesitation he steps through the door and softly closes it behind him.

Grabbing my cheeks, he presses his lips to mine. Relief floods me almost instantly. The doubts and fears that filled my head just minutes ago fade into the background. I can't remember ever being kissed like this.

It feels like Chase would rather die than stop kissing me.

He scoops me up in one swift motion and walks us over to my bed, carefully laying us down. The muscles in his arms flex as he braces himself above me with his lips sealed over mine.

We melt into each other, both desperately addicted to the blissful escape from reality.

Our tongues tangle, our hands roam, our kisses grow more heated and passionate. I push my fingers through the short hair on his nape and wrap my legs around his waist, pulling him closer. I need to feel more of his weight on me.

More of *him* on me.

Shifting my hips, I grind myself against him and a groan pushes past his lips.

Chase tenses and tries desperately to pull his hips back so I can't feel the growing hardness in his sweats, but I tighten my legs around him, enjoying the feel of what I do to him.

A moan slips out of me when he smirks against my lips and lets his cock flex against my core.

We should really try to be more quiet considering my parents are asleep just down the hall, but I couldn't control the sounds coming out of me if I tried. After years of not having any physical contact, having Chase touch me is dizzying. He's driving me insane.

Breaking our kiss, Chase stares down at me for a second before tucking stray hairs behind my ear. "You're so damn beautiful, Sydney Mae."

I look into his eyes, nervous for what comes next. I haven't been with anyone since Jack. Not in this way, or any other. I've been too afraid that history would repeat itself, but Chase is different—I know he is. The thing that haunts him may be different from what haunts me, but he understands the constant pain I live with.

He understands my hesitations when it comes to putting myself out there again. But Chase makes me forget about my fears. He makes me forget all the shit that Jack put me through. He makes me feel safe—something I know I've never felt before.

So when his finger hooks under my bra strap and his eyes meet mine, my heart races faster than it ever has, but I give him a subtle nod.

Because Chase isn't Jack.

Far from it.

I feel my cheeks flush and my head falls back against the pillow as he kisses down my neck, slowly peeling my bra away the further down he goes. My nipples harden in anticipation as he bares my chest.

Letting out a stuttering breath, he looks up at me, those gorgeous hazel eyes sparkling in the dimly-lit room.

Chase's lips part and I watch in rapt fascination as he sweeps his tongue over my peaked nipple while his eyes are locked on mine. I arch into him on a moan as his hand cups my breast. He flicks the taught bud before closing his lips around it.

Snaking his hand between us as he shifts his weight, pulling his hips back. His hand slips between my legs, fingers grazing over my silk-covered core. I squirm in his grasp, wanting more.

*What the hell is happening to me?*

Never in my life have I let things move *this* quickly. I've kissed him twice before right now, but I can't for the life of me find a reason to stop what's happening here.

My fingers push through his hair as his mouth continues to work my nipple. He gives it a final suck before moving to the one he'd been neglecting.

Shifting to lay beside me, it's evident how hard he is. The front of his sweats are tented and the material jumps every few seconds, his cock begging to be set free.

Chase looks down as his fingers dip into the waistband of my shorts, tickling the sensitive skin there for a moment before flicking his gaze up to mine. "Is this okay?" he asks sheepishly, tracing circles gently along the skin just below the hem of my panties.

"Yes," I pant.

My eyes flutter shut when his fingers move farther south and tentatively brush my clit.

*Shit.*

That feels way too fucking good. He's barely touched me and it feels like I'm going to combust.

Is it him? Is he the reason that I'm so affected? Or is it because it's been almost ten years since someone touched me there.

And when he did, it was never this gently—this carefully.

Goosebumps litter my skin as he strums me expertly, like it hasn't been over a decade since he's touched a woman.

I open my eyes to see his gaze fixed on my face, searching for any signs of doubt or hesitation because that's just the kind of man Chase is. Grasping at his cheeks, I pull his lips to mine, needing him closer.

His deft fingers part my folds and they're met with my wetness, forcing a groan past Chase's lips. I let one of my hands travel down my body and grab hold of him over his sweats. The thick length of him throbs in my grasp at the same moment he sinks a single finger inside.

"*Chase.*" God, I sound so desperate. Needy.

He smirks and draws his finger out slowly before easing it back in again.

Two can play at that game.

I tighten my grip on him, doing my best to stroke him over his sweats. He hisses, letting out a soft "*Shit*" against my lips before regaining his composure.

Smiling to myself at the small victory, I pull my hand away and slide it inside his sweatpants. My fingers are immediately met with the warm silken skin of his cock.

*No boxers.*

Wrapping my fingers around him for real this time, I pump my hand as best I can within the confines of his sweatpants.

He pushes another thick finger inside and I feel the stretch. "Fuck," I curse, trying to keep my voice down, but it's impossible.

"You're so wet, Sydney Mae." His fingers pump faster and he lets the heel of his palm rub against my clit with each press. "Is this all for me, gorgeous?"

"Y-yes." I don't know that my pussy has *ever* been this wet. Not even when I've played with myself for hours at a time when I couldn't sleep. I know for a fact that, right now, I'm dripping for him. I can feel—and hear—the slickness as he fingers me. "All for you, Chase."

I whimper at the sudden loss of his fingers when he shifts on the bed so that he's kneeling between my legs. "What are you doing?"

"I wanna see all of you." He grasps at the top of my shorts.

I chew my lip, a sudden wave of nervousness passing over me.

Chase removes his hands from me, holding them up in surrender. "Can I?"

Taking a deep breath, I nod. If there's anyone I trust to see me in such a vulnerable state, it'd be Chase. I don't bother trying to figure out the logic or reasoning behind someone who is essentially a stranger to me having so much of my trust and faith, I just know that he does.

Carefully, as if I'll break if he moves too quickly, Chase strips me of my shorts and panties, placing them on the bed beside me.

He moves further between my legs and palms himself over his sweats as he lets his eyes rake down my naked body. "I don't think I've ever seen anythin' quite as exquisite as you, Sydney Mae."

I sit up and tug his pants down a little, tracing my fingers down one side of the delicious V that sits on his hip. Something I know he earned from hours upon hours worth of manual labor. "It's only fair I get to see you too."

A crooked smile tips the corners of his mouth and he brings his hand under my chin. "It's only fair."

We're still for a moment, neither of us daring to move—just living in the moment. Drowning our shared need for each other.

Chase dips his chin, flicking his tongue out to wet his lip before he gives me the slightest of nods.

Tugging his pants down, I watch as his cock springs free. He's bigger than I thought. Thicker too.

I lie back down and he starts to stroke himself as he watches me run my hands all over myself. My nipples stiffen under Chase's gaze and he groans at the sight, clearly enjoying the show.

One of his large hands comes to my waist and settles on my hip. My skin burns beneath his touch. It's like my skin is going to catch fire any moment now.

"Do you like the view?" I ask, bringing a hand to my chest to roll my nipple between my fingers. The sensation causes a jolt of pleasure to zip straight to my core.

"Like is an understatement, Sydney Mae." His knees part and he sinks down so he's more level with me. "I meant it when I said I hadn't seen anythin' quite as exquisite."

I watch as temptation fills his eyes and he grips the base of his cock holding it over my pussy, just high enough so he's not touching me. I can feel the heat of him there. He's so close. One move and he'd be inside…

"W-wait. I'm not… I don't—" I sigh. "I don't think I'm ready for… *that.*"

Chase shakes his head side to side and squeezes my hip. "I would never rush you." His eyes dance back and forth between mine, making sure I know down to my core. "And for what it's worth, I'm not either."

"So, what now?"

He smiles down at me and starts to lazily stroke himself again. "What happens now is I watch you play with yourself until you come apart for me. Does that sound okay?"

I moan, reveling in the fact that he's turned on just from seeing me pleasure myself, and let my finger start to circle my clit again. "And then what? Where are you gonna come?"

"Haven't decided yet." A downright sinful smirk curls his lips. "Maybe all over these perfect tits," he says, reaching up to grab a handful of my breast in one hand. His balls tap against my pussy with each rough stroke of his cock in his hand.

Heat rises in my cheeks, sending waves of pure ecstasy through me at the thought of him covering me with his cum. I flick my clit harder, seconds away from shattering for him.

"Would you like that, Sydney Mae? You want me to paint your pretty tits with my cum?"

"*Yes.*" I bite down on my lip, squeezing my eyes shut as pleasure races through me.

Hearing a deep groan and I know he must be close.

I open my eyes and they lock with his. We're both breathless, panting, barely keeping it together.

"I'm gonna come." His body stiffens, bottom lip tucked firmly between his teeth.

"Me too," I choke out as my fingers furiously rub at my clit.

My orgasm crashes into me at the feel of his warm, sticky

cum falling on my skin. My body is so overwhelmed with pleasure that my legs shake and my eyes roll back in my head.

"Holy shit." He lets his cock fall from his hand and looks down at the mess he made all over me.

My clit pulses, still recovering from the aftershocks of my orgasm. "I don't think I've ever come so hard."

Chase shakes his head, pulling his sweatpants back up. "Me either."

"I should probably go clean myself up," I say, running my finger through one of the pools of his cum on my stomach.

He chuckles, bringing his hand to my cheek and kissing my lips. "I'll take care of it."

My heart thumps wildly in my chest as his weight leaves the bed when he slips out of my room and into the dark hallway.

I stare down at myself, covered in him, and can't help but wonder what it would be like to be *filled* with him.

He pads back into the room and I quickly shake the thought from my head. I shouldn't be thinking like that anyway. When it comes to men, I run in the other direction, I don't give them a second glance or thought.

But Chase…

God, he makes it impossible to think about anything other than him. I want him in every way possible. Even the ways that scare me.

Hopping back on the bed, he brings a warm wet cloth to my chest and cleans me off. When he's finished, he tosses it onto the nightstand.

"Can you hold me for a little while?"

He brushes some hair from my face and cups my cheek. "I'd be happy to."

I curl into him, resting my head on his chest, and his fingers trace circles on my back.

"Thank you, Chase."

"For what?"

"For being you," I reply, placing my hand on his chest.

He squeezes me with the arm around my shoulders and kisses the top of my head. "My pleasure, Sydney Mae." Tilting my chin up with his free hand, he looks into my eyes. "Thank you for making my heart beat again."

I blush and bring my lips to his, getting lost in his kiss once more, and feeling happy for the first time in too long.

# 15

CHASE

Slowly cracking my eyes open as the soft, early morning light streams through the windows, they lock on Sydney. She's curled into my side with her cheek resting on my chest and her arm slung over my middle.

I haven't slept so soundly since before Macie was born. She rarely cried as a baby, but I was so anxious that something would happen to her in her sleep that I spent more time watching her sleep than I did sleeping myself.

Feeling Sydney's weight against me all through the night was something I've never experienced before. I never stuck around with Cara—I didn't care enough to.

But Sydney? Fuck, I would kill to fall asleep next to her every night. To wake up to her every morning too.

Never in a million years did I think I would find someone who settles my soul like she does. I'm amazed at how comfortable we are with each other when we're little more than strangers. I don't even truly understand how we got to the point we did last night. With anyone else, things wouldn't have gone so far.

Sex hasn't even been on my radar in the last ten years, and I know that, given her history with Jack, it hasn't been on Sydney's either.

Did things happen too quickly? Does she regret it?

I shake my head. *No.*

She had plenty of opportunities to stop things. Right?

My fingers absentmindedly toy with her silky soft skin as my mind races, running up and down her exposed spine for what feels like hours.

She stirs, sleepily nuzzling further into my chest before squinting her eyes open. Her cheeks flush lightly when her eyes meet mine. "You stayed." She seems surprised, but she shouldn't be. I couldn't've pulled myself away from her last night if I tried.

I nod. "I hope that's okay."

She smiles softly. "More than okay."

"Good." I chew my lip, wanting to clear the air about something. "Can we talk for a minute? I want to explain why we left the party so abruptly last night."

"Okay."

"Riley and I, we..." *Shit,* this already sounds bad. "Riley has a thing for me. And for a while it was mutual. She'd flirt and I wouldn't push her away when she'd get close to me. That probably makes me sound like a jerk, but the attention was nice after not havin' anyone close for so long." I see her brows furrow and a hint of worry creep onto her face. "Nothin' ever happened between us, but I think she felt betrayed when she overheard me say that we kissed. I always told her I wasn't good enough, or I had too much baggage to let myself be with anyone, so I'm sure there was a bit of animosity that I *picked* you. That you got a part of me that she never did. And after findin' out there was already a bit of bad blood between you because of how you left, I didn't know how to handle the situation. I don't want you to think that I was purposely shuttin' you out or that our kiss had anythin' to do with me actin' weird, I just—"

"Hey." She brings her hand to my cheek and smiles. "It's

okay. I know how Riley gets. It was a delicate situation and I don't blame you for wanting to get out of there when you did. Thank you for telling me."

There's some shuffling down the hall and then two pairs of footfalls on the creaky old stairs. "I guess we should probably head downstairs before your parents suspect anythin'. I don't know how much they'd appreciate it if they found out I spent the night with you."

"Five more minutes?"

I smile. "Five more minutes."

Sydney shifts, pushing herself up and pressing her lips to mine.

My worries of there being even a single shred of regret or concern about last night vanish when her tongue slides over my bottom lip, seeking entrance.

I reluctantly tear myself away from Sydney's lips thirty minutes later, knowing I need to get dressed and start the day before Bill has a chance to come looking for me.

In the four years I've been working for him, I haven't been late a single time, and this morning I'm cutting it dangerously close.

Stepping into my boots, I make my way downstairs and shrug on my heavy Carhartt coat and a beanie before heading for the barn. It may be Christmas Eve, but the animals we keep here still need to be fed. Their stalls still in need of mucking.

Two hours later, the realization that I haven't had coffee yet hits me. I think subconsciously, I didn't want to risk running into Susan because I can just tell that she has this innate ability to sniff out funny business.

And what happened between Sydney Mae and I was *definitely* funny business.

I take a breath and suck down my nerves, crossing my fingers that the kitchen is empty as I step through the front door.

After stomping the snow off my boots and hanging my coat up, I walk through the living room and into the kitchen, seeing both Susan and Sydney standing at the island chatting as they sip their coffees.

"Hey," I say, trying to maintain my composure as I make a beeline for the coffee pot.

I can feel their eyes staring at my back, but don't dare turn around.

"Chase, were your ears ringin'?"

Crap.

"What do you mean?" I ask, turning to find Susan with a wicked little grin on her face and Sydney looking like a deer in headlights.

"Well, I was just telling Sydney that Bill and I are leaving in a couple minutes to go to a Christmas party at the Bellingham house. I told her that she should come find you to keep her company."

Sydney groans. "Ma, I'm not five."

Susan rolls her eyes. "Don't remind me. But come on, Syd, it's Christmas Eve, you shouldn't be alone."

"I'm used to it," Sydney says, like it's the most normal thing in the world to be alone during the holidays. "I've been alone every year since I left.

"I don't mind," I cut in. "H-hangin' out with you, I mean."

Lifting her hands in a cheer, Susan beams at me and grabs my face with her good hand, planting a kiss on my cheek. "Thank you, Chase. Knock some Christmas spirit back into her for me, okay?"

I chuckle, but it quickly dies in my chest when I look at Sydney. Her arms are crossed over her chest and there's a hardness in her face that wasn't there this morning. "I'll do my best."

"Well, I gotta go get changed. You two kids have fun now, you hear?"

"Yes ma'am," I say at the same time Sydney grumbles something under her breath.

Susan leaves, humming a medley of Christmas carols as she makes her way upstairs.

Turning back to my coffee, I spoon in two scoops of vanilla sugar and stir for far longer than normal, trying to waste time until Bill and Susan leave.

I take a sip, basking in the warmth. "Do you need a refill?"

"No."

"So, your mom tells me you finally know about vanilla sugar."

"Yup."

Bill and Susan both make their way down the stairs. The pair are dressed in matching Christmas sweaters that Susan knit herself when Sydney was just a baby.

"Have fun you two!" Susan calls out, pulling the front door closed behind her.

I chuckle and turn back to Sydney, taking a step in her direction and reaching for her waist.

She shies away from my touch, giving me a strange look before tearing her gaze away and looking at the floor.

My brows furrow. "What's wrong?"

"Nothing."

"Sydney, talk to me."

She shakes her head, chewing on her lip, but refuses to make eye contact with me. "There's nothing to talk about."

"Okay, then why does it seem like you're pushin' me away now? Like you don't want to spend the day with me?"

"Because I am, Chase."

My chest constricts. *What the hell?*

"Why?"

"This was a mistake." She says the words with an air of indifference.

I huff a breath through my nose, not believing that for a second. "Didn't seem like such a mistake a couple hours ago when you kept beggin' for five more minutes and tellin' me how happy you were that I stayed the night."

"I-I shouldn't have said that. Can we just forget it ever happened?"

Crossing my arms over my chest, I match her pose. "No, I can't forget."

"Chase—"

"Why are you actin' like it meant nothin' to you? I know it did."

"Because I'm fucking scared, okay!" she admits with tears welling in her eyes.

"Of what?"

"You!" she shouts. "I'm scared of you, Chase."

My stomach rolls uncomfortably. *I think I'm gonna be sick.* I know things went far and fast, but she would have stopped me, right? She would have said she wasn't comfortable, right?

Fuck. Did I push her like Jack did? Did she feel like she *couldn't* say no?

God, I'm such a fucking asshole.

"Sydney, if I did somethin'—"

"No," she cuts me off. "It's not something you did, Chase. You were... you were everything. Sweet, kind, gentle. You made sure I was comfortable. It's how you make me feel that scares me."

"I don't follow."

"Last night was like a fairytale, but I can't do *this*. I can't let myself get more attached to you than I already am. It'll only make leaving hurt that much more."

I shake my head, running a hand down my face. "And what about me, huh? You think I'm not attached to you? Because I can tell you right now that I am." I take a step closer and this time she doesn't retreat. "You're the first person who has made me feel like I can breathe again since Macie died. Five years, Sydney Mae. Five damn years of this indescribable pain, and you changed that in one night." One more step and I'm right in front of her. I bring my hands to her face, stroking her cheeks with my thumbs. "No matter what, you leavin' is gonna suck, so why not enjoy the time we have?"

"I'm scared."

"I know, so am I. But I'm not askin' for forever, baby, just right now."

Her eyes frantically search mine before she nods slightly. "Okay."

Licking my lips, I slowly bring my face to hers. "What we do or don't do is entirely up to you. I'm happy with whatever you'll give me."

Sydney's dainty hand comes to my chest. "If you got to decide what to do for the next two days, what would it be?"

"Well, for starters, I'd kiss you again because I've wanted to do that since we got outta bed." She tips her chin up in invitation, but I deny her, needing to walk through our possible day. "Then I'd make you change into somethin' warm and take you for a ride on Storm. I can tell you've been dyin' to get back in the saddle, but it's been a while and you're worried." She rolls her eyes and giggles in a way that tells me I'm not wrong. "After our ride, we could come back here and order some takeout—spend the rest of the night watchin' movies, and if you're up for it, maybe we could have a repeat of last night."

"That sounds like a perfect way to spend the day."

"All of it?"

She smirks. "All of it."

"Can I kiss you now, Sydney Mae?"

She nibbles on the corner of her lip before nodding. "Please."

I don't waste another second before sealing my mouth over hers in a desperate kiss. If we only have two more days together, I'm determined to make it the best two days possible.

# 16



Cold wind whips against my cheeks, but I can't help the smile on my face as Ace, my old black horse with a pure white stripe running from his forehead to his snout, races through the snow-covered field alongside Storm and Chase.

I can sense his eyes on me—can practically feel the way his gaze is watching Ace's every move to make sure I keep my seat. He wanted me to join him on Storm, but I needed the freedom of riding by myself. And despite the years away from being on the back of a horse, it's something I could never forget.

My time in the city has made me forget how much I missed being on horseback. The feeling of the wind in my hair and on my cheeks. The familiar ache in my thighs. The connection to nature. It's the perfect combination you can't get anywhere else.

"You havin' fun?" Chase shouts as we slow to a trot.

"I don't ever want to get off."

He chuckles, clicking his tongue at Storm as he gently tugs on his reins, leading us toward the old horse stables on the edge of the property that my dad has always kept up for times just like these. "We should probably give these two a break, though. Snow's deeper than I thought."

In the winter months, back when I was younger, my dad

decided that instead of fixing up the snowmobile that had broken down, he was just going to maintain two stables. One for each edge of the property. It was a hell of a lot cheaper for him to keep up a smaller set of stalls on the north end than it would be to replace the snowmobile. And given how tight money has been for him, I'm not surprised that he still hasn't splurged for a new one.

"Okay." I give Ace's side a little nudge with my calf, signaling for him to follow Storm into the open stable doors.

Chase and I dismount, putting our horses in their own stalls and tossing out some fresh hay for them to snack on for a bit while they rest.

He grabs my hand and pulls me toward him. I go willingly, draping my arms over his shoulders as I melt into his chest. "Thank you."

"For what?" His palms slide into the back pockets of my jeans.

"Taking me for a ride. It's been too long."

"Happy to." Smirking, he dips his head and steals a kiss from my lips. "On the back of a horse, it's like you're a completely different person. I didn't think I'd ever see you smile so wide."

A giggle pushes past my lips, my fingers finding their way into his hair. It's so much silkier than I expected it to be. I've been dying to touch it again since last night. "I don't think I realized how much I missed it since I've been away."

"Maybe that should be added to your list of reasons to come home."

"That list is getting pretty long."

"Yeah? What's on it so far?"

"Well, there's my parents."

"Of course." He nods in agreement.

"It was really nice to get to hang out with Logan and Scarlet and everyone again, so they're definitely on there."

"Mhmm."

"Riding Ace."

"*Anyone* or anythin' else?"

I lick my lips before pursing them, then I look away. "I think that's it."

His hands squeeze my ass, sending a ripple of heat down my spine. "You sure?"

Shaking my head I tuck my bottom lip between my teeth as I let my gaze settle back on him. "No."

Pushing up on my toes, I tug him toward me.

With our faces barely an inch apart, his minty breath fans across my lips. "Who else is on the list, Sydney Mae?"

*God, it should be illegal for him to sound that hot.*

His normal voice is attractive—definitely on the sexier side, especially with his little accent—but this one? *Phew.*

This one is breathy and raspy, with just enough edge to leave you drooling. It oozes the kind of sex appeal that all those male narrators for naughty audiobooks have perfected over the years. Hearing it used on me from someone like Chase has me pinching my thighs together, trying to dull the ache growing between them.

"I think you know…"

The corner of his lips curve up in that perfect lopsided smile that I know I'll dream about for weeks once I get home. "Yeah, but I wanna hear you say it."

"*You.*" I don't bother hesitating, or covering up the unbearable need in my voice. There's no point.

He lets out a satisfied growl before erasing the remaining space between us. My back hits the wall at the back of the stable. Normally, that's when panic would set in—when I'd start to feel trapped—but Chase's lips feel like a little piece of heaven.

I didn't realize you could be kissed with so much passion. That a kiss so rough and claiming could be gentle at the same time. It's like Chase is pouring his soul into me and I never want it to end.

I'm enraptured by his very being.

His touch. His kiss The way he looks at me and holds me like I'm the most precious thing in his world.

*It's too much and not enough all at once.*

I want to drown in Chase Phillips.

Pushing off the wall, I untangle my arms from around his neck and spin us so his back is against the wall. Bringing my hands to his waist, I slowly work open his belt, then unbutton his jeans.

The weight of his cock forces the zipper open, and I smirk against his lips. *Guess that means he's feeling the same thing I am.*

Need.

Hunger.

Desire.

My palm presses against his stiff length and he breaks our kiss, but doesn't pull away. "Sydney," he warns, breathless.

"Yes?" I ask, hooking my thumbs into the wide elastic waistband of his dark blue boxer briefs.

"What're you doin' to me?"

"The same thing you're doing to me." My lips brush against his as I drag the tight material down. He sucks in a breath when I take him in my hand and give his length a stroke. "Making me want to be reckless."

A muffled curse rushes out as his head tips back against the wall.

I slowly sink to my knees, coming face to face with Chase's hard cock.

Pumping my fist once, a bead of precum leaks from the tip and I lean forward, letting my tongue lick it up.

"Fuck." The head of his cock flares as a pulse of want ripples through him. His fingers find my chin and he tips my face up to look at him. "You don't have to do this, Sydney Mae."

"I know." This time, I lick around his crown, then take him between my lips for a second. "It was never a choice before. Now, it is. I want to do this, Chase. Please don't stop me."

He runs the pad of his thumb across my wet bottom lip. "You're sure you want to?"

I smile, not bothering to respond before I take him into my mouth and tease the head with the tip of my tongue. Chase's uninhibited groan sends a wave of heat straight to my core.

It never crossed my mind that giving him a blowjob and pleasuring him would compound the desire for him that's already burning inside me.

Drunk with need, I take him to the back of my throat and let my tongue glide over the swollen veins on the underside of his shaft. My eyes flick up and I find his lips parted in pleasure. His cheeks are tinted pink, and there's an edge of lust in his eyes.

I swallow around him, letting my throat close around the tip. My eyes water, but I don't dare pull my gaze from Chase. He looks too perfect right now. *Too mine.*

With another slide of my tongue over the ridged veins, I pull back, coming off his length with a wet *pop*. "Does that answer your question?" I ask, bringing my hand to the base to stroke him as my lips part and I take him back inside.

His eyes roll and his grip on my hair tightens, using it to feed his cock into my mouth. "Yes," he hisses.

I smile around him, letting his words spur me on as I take him to my throat again. I really shouldn't like that sensation as much as I do. Maybe I wouldn't if it were anyone else, but Chase? Everything about the man is a turn on.

The softly commanding hand in my hair, guiding me. The sex-soaked tone of his voice. The taste of his desire for me. Even him in general, out of any sexual context, is hot enough to melt even the thickest ice.

It's infuriating how perfect he is.

"Fuck, Sydney Mae, your mouth feels too damn good."

My core aches, clit throbbing with need. Flicking open the button on my jeans, I shove my hand inside and am immediately met with my slick slit.

Before last night, I can't remember the last time I got even a little turned on, let alone got myself off. I have a nightstand drawer full of fifteen different kinds of vibrators and dildos, but never use them. Dr. Camden recommended I see a sex therapist, and part of my therapy was getting comfortable with myself and knowing my own pleasure before I attempted to give it to someone else.

Even after reclaiming that part of myself, it was never something I *needed*, just an added bonus on super stressful days, but now I *need* it.

My fingers slip over my clit, applying *just* the right amount of pressure and my eyes roll back.

"You playin' with yourself, baby?"

I hum in acknowledgement, letting my tongue do the talking as I keep up a steady rhythm.

Chase moans, tightening his grip on my hair. His lips part in awe as he watches me. "Rub that pretty clit faster for me," he commands.

*Who am I to deny this man a single thing? Especially when it feels so damn good.*

My fingers pick up their pace, brushing over my clit with precise flicks that I know will get the job done.

"That's it. Get yourself there. I want us to come together, okay?"

I nod, not sure what kind of wizardry he's performing, but it's working.

Within a minute, I'm panting around his length and everything in my body tenses before my orgasm sends a wave of euphoria passing over me.

"Shit," Chase curses. "You're gonna make me come. Tell me where you want it," he says with a frantic edge to his voice.

"My mouth," I say around him.

His pupils blow wide right before his eyes slam closed and the first jets of his warm cum hit my tongue. I swallow down every last drop, savoring the slightly salty taste of him, sighing contentedly before he pulls himself out of my mouth.

"Are you okay?" Chase asks, quickly tucking himself back into his boxers before dropping to a knee on the concrete floor beside me. He grabs my face in his palms, stroking the reddened apples of my cheeks.

I giggle, dragging my teeth over my bottom lip as he scours my face for any signs of regret. "I'm great, actually."

"You're sure I didn't hurt you or make you uncomfortable or anythin'?"

"Chase, I'm fine. I'd kiss you right now to prove it, but I just had your dick in my—"

He crushes his lips to mine in a searing kiss that melts away the last shreds of ice around my heart. When he pulls away, a slow smile spreads across his lips. "If you want to kiss me you damn well better do it, no matter what. You understand me?"

One last spark of pleasure pulses through me making my clit throb. "Yes."

"Good." He blows out a breath and shakes off the bossy facade, the sweet country boy settling back in. "Are you sure you're okay?"

"I'm sure. I am a bit cold though. Do you think we can head back to the house?"

He chuckles and presses his lips to mine again. "We can do whatever you want after that."

***

Two hours later, we're showered and cuddled up on the large grey sectional in our pajamas with Chinese take-out containers on our laps, and Macie's favorite Christmas movie, *How The Grinch Stole Christmas*, on the TV.

By the time the credits are rolling, the takeout is long forgotten and half of our clothes are missing. Thankfully my parents have always been dirty stay-outs on Christmas Eve, opting to party hop like the party animals they are. One year, they didn't come home until nearly midnight.

Chase's fingers hook into the waistband of my loose-fitting plaid pajama pants, dragging them down my legs. His lips meet the skin on my hip and I squirm. "You gonna let me return the favor?" he asks, looking up at me from between my legs as his mouth hovers over my aching pussy.

My lips part when he blows a breath right at my clit, sending goosebumps shooting across my skin. "Y-yes."

*Yes?* What the hell is wrong with me? No one has ever gone down on me before. Jack was disgusted by the idea, and I wasn't with anyone before or after him, so that doesn't leave much room for experimenting.

The thought alone makes me want to run as far away as possible.

But then Chase smirks, and keeps eye contact with me as his tongue slowly drags up my slit.

*Holyfuckingshit.*

My brain nearly short circuits when his tongue narrows in on my clit, flicking the stiff bundle with expert precision. He gives it a suck and my head shoots back against the couch cushion.

*Jesus, nothing has* ever *felt so good.*

The tip of his finger teases my entrance before easing inside as his tongue works its magic. He groans against me when he feels just how wet I am for him. I honestly don't think I've ever been so wet in my entire life.

Chase presses another finger inside and it's almost embarrassing how quickly he has me ready to explode. My nipples peak, and that familiar tingle in my lower belly intensifies.

"Chase," I pant, bringing my hand to his head, lacing my fingers in his hair just like he did to me. Pushing my hips forward, I use his hair to hold him closer to my pussy.

I feel him smirk before he doubles his efforts, pumping his fingers in and out at a fast pace as his tongue lashes against my clit.

Stars flood my vision as my orgasm crashes into me, sending me spiraling to a completely different universe as Chase continues to feast on me like I'm the most delicious thing he's ever tasted.

My grip on his hair loosens and he chuckles, finally breaking the connection between his mouth and my pussy.

He licks his lips clean and presses a single kiss to my clit before he pushes himself up so he's hovering over me. "Did I do okay?"

"I have nothing to compare it to, but you get an A++."

Chase chuckles and leans forward, kissing me slowly, a different taste lingering on his lips than I'm used to. My taste.

And I think I may want to taste myself on his tongue more often.

---

Waking up in Chase's arms for the second morning in a row was like a dream. A very dangerous dream, because I didn't want to wake up from it.

Even now, as we're sitting around the kitchen table with my parents eating dinner, I can't shake the nagging little voice in the back of my head telling me to stay. To see if this thing with Chase could actually work out, instead of wondering if it's so good right now because we know it has an expiration date.

"We got you a little somethin', sweetie," Mom says, handing Chase a wrapped box.

"Oh, you didn't have to do that. You've already given me enough."

Dad shakes his head, waving him off. "Ah, everyone deserves a little somethin' on Christmas."

Chase's lips spread into one of his gorgeous crooked smiles. "Thank you," he says as he slips his finger under the wrapping paper and tears it open. He lifts the lid off the plain white box, revealing a mass of tissue paper. Reaching inside he pulls out a new pair of camel-colored leather work gloves and a black beanie. His eyes flash up to my dad. "These are one of the most expensive brands on the market. I-I can't accept these."

"Sure you can," he insists. "Think of it as an investment in all the work you'll be able to do with them."

Chase still seems skeptical, so Mom chimes in. "It's really not nearly enough for all you do, honey. Please, take them."

He dips his chin, saying another quiet thank you.

"Your turn, Sydney Mae." Mom holds out my gift.

I grab the flat square box. "What is it?"

"Open it up and you'll find out." Dad shakes his head, turning to Chase. "She's been askin' that same question when openin' gifts for as long as I can remember."

Chuckling, I open up the lid, revealing what looks like a scrapbook. *Wilson & Wu Est. 2014* is etched onto the silver plate attached to the soft black leather. "Is this…?"

"It's all the pictures you've sent over the years, plus all the times you've been in the paper or on some fancy website. I know it's not much, but I wanted to make sure you knew how proud of you we are."

I sling my arms around my dad's neck, pulling him in for a tight hug. "Thank you, Pops. That means a lot."

"Do you mind if I take a look?" Chase asks, holding up the portfolio.

"Not at all."

He flips through the pages and pages of sketches, final drawings, renderings, photos of before and after each job site, and of me standing in the middle of construction zones with a hard hat on as if they're the most interesting thing in the world. He's taking in every detail, being nearly as diligent as I am when designing. "Wow. You did all this?"

My cheeks flush. "I designed them all, yeah. I have a team of builders that did the actual construction."

"This is amazin', Sydney Mae. I can tell why you're so in demand back in New York."

My cheeks flush. "Thank you."

The rest of the night passes by in a blur of laughter, smiles, and hidden touches.

---

Before I know it, Chase and I are at the airport.

His fingers lace through mine. "I'm gonna miss the hell out of you."

"I'm gonna miss you too. Thank you for everything, Chase."

"My pleasure, Sydney Mae."

I take a deep breath and nuzzle my cheek into his palm. "I should get to my gate."

He smiles shyly as he nods his head, removing his hand from my cheek without saying another word.

My feet drag me away from him reluctantly.

When I'm about twenty feet away I hear his voice from behind me say, "Wait! You forgot somethin'!"

I turn around to see Chase jogging toward me. "What?"

"This," he says right before he grabs my cheeks and dips his head, kissing me until my toes curl.

He's smiling as he pulls away.

"What was that for? I thought we agreed that last night was our goodbye?"

"Don't know. It just felt right. Like those cheesy scenes in romance movies where the guy runs through the airport to stop his girl from leavin'."

"Oh? Is that what I am? Your girl?"

"Maybe." He shrugs. "I definitely wouldn't hate it."

I giggle. "Dork."

"I know that frozen heart of yours melted, don't even try to lie."

"It did."

"Good." He steals one last slow kiss. "I'll let you go now. Have a safe flight."

# 17



**FEBRUARY 14, 2020**

My body aches as I climb off of Storm after a long day repairing the fence on the north end of the property. I have no idea how there's always something that needs to be repaired when we're meticulous about maintaining it, but here we are.

I lead Storm into his paddock, giving him a couple nose scratches. "Good work today, boy," I praise. "I hate to cut this short, but I gotta get my ass movin' so I can see my favorite lady. I'll give you an extra long brush tomorrow though, okay?"

Storm, being the well-adjusted adult that he is, winnies softly and turns around, not upset at all that I'm changing our nightly routine on him because I want to surprise Sydney Mae.

We might not be *official* or anything, but I've never really had anyone to celebrate Valentine's day with before, and the romantic in me is excited to experience it for the first time. I saved up for a month to be able to send her a bouquet of red roses. If I could afford it, her whole office would be filled with them. But since that's not in the cards, I spent an extra twelve dollars to add a small teddy bear holding a heart.

Racing back to the house after locking up the barn, I pass Bill and Susan on their way to their Valentine's Day tradition of spending the night at the Windrift Lodge about thirty miles away. They order room service and get massages, even splurging to upgrade to a newlywed suite every year. Apparently, they've been doing it for as long as they can remember. Back when Sydney was too young to stay by herself, the Bellingham's would watch her.

Lord knows the two of them earned every last ounce of pampering.

I hope someday I have a Valentine's Day tradition. Most people complain about how it's a Hallmark holiday, created by, and for, the commercial companies to have a reason to hike up prices and create specialized products. While I can't say I disagree, having another reason to show the one you're with that you care is never a bad thing.

I've never had someone to spend this day with, and even though I might not be physically with Sydney Mae, I'm gonna make damn sure she knows that she's mine.

Rushing through my shower, I brush my teeth and change into a pair of jeans and a red flannel, opting to keep it open to show off the crisp white tee underneath. I run my fingers through my damp hair and take a calming breath.

A pit of anxiety forms in my stomach. What if she's busy and doesn't have time to talk? What if she thinks it's dumb? What if she's one of those people who think Valentine's Day is just one big scam? What if she doesn't want to be my Valentine?

Fuck, I can't remember the last time I was this nervous.

I take a few deep breaths to calm myself down and settle onto the couch in the living room.

A quick look at the time tells me that it's almost eight in New York, and if my calculations are correct, Sydney should be wrapping up at the office right about now, given that it's Friday. I shoot her a text to make sure.

> Hi, beautiful. What are you up to?

Hi, handsome. Just packing up at the office. About to head home and stare at the flowers this really hot guy got me. You?

I feel my cheeks warm at the fact that she called me hot.

Glad you liked the flowers. I just got in from fixing the north fences. Your parents are at The Windrift Lodge tonight so I have the house all to myself.

God, I still can't believe it's Valentine's Day already.

Yeah, been meaning to ask you, by the way...

Will you be my Valentine?

My heart slams in my chest and there's a knot of anticipation in my stomach as I wait for her response. It comes through three minutes later.

It'd be my honor.

A dopey smile stretches across my face.

I'm definitely not smiling like a damn idiot right now.

Paul just asked if I'm feeling okay because he's never seen me smile so big or blush so hard.

Think I'm gonna need proof.

A picture comes through a minute later. She's in a navy blue blazer with a white V-neck blouse. There are hints of dark smudges under her eyes, probably from lack of sleep, but she's still as gorgeous as ever as she grins from ear to ear.

I wish like hell I could be with her right now. That I could pull her into my arms and kiss her all over.

Satisfied?

Never. I could stare at you all day.

Do you have time for a video call when you get home?

Of course. I'll call when I get settled.

Great. See you soon.

I breathe a sigh of relief and head to the kitchen to grab a glass of water and the small box of assorted chocolates Susan got for me along with a bag of my favorite jerky.

Forty minutes later my phone rings and I couldn't tamp down the excitement in my chest if I tried.

"Hi," I say, answering the call as I lean back against the couch cushions.

Her hair is wet and she's wrapped in a pale pink robe. "Hey. Sorry I took so long, I wanted to shower real quick."

"Don't be. I'm just glad I get to see your face."

She smiles softly. "Happy Valentine's Day, Chase."

"Happy Valentine's Day, Sydney Mae."

Giggling, she grabs a glass of wine, swirling the deep red liquid around the glass goblet. "So, I have some news," she says before taking a small sip of wine.

"Oh?"

"Paul and I were approached by one of our competitors, Juliano Riviera. He's retiring and wants Wilson & Wu to absorb Riviera Developments."

My eyebrows shoot to my hairline. "Wow. That's amazing, Sydney Mae."

"We still haven't decided if we're going to do it or not, since it'll be a huge undertaking, but Juliano isn't interested in selling to anyone else." I love listening to her talk about work. She's a total shark and really knows what she's talking about. It's so damn hot when I get to see the boss side of her pop out. "He's been a fan of our work since we started and as much as he's our competition, he's passed along clients to us that he doesn't have the capacity to take on himself. He said if we don't take the deal, he'll be forced to stay on until he finds another company he feels comfortable taking over for him."

"Seems like there isn't really a decision to be made."

She sighs. "Yeah. It's just going to be stressful taking on such a big book of business."

"If anyone can do it, you can, pretty girl."

A small smile curves her lips. "Thanks. It's a lot to think about, but I know that in the end, it'll definitely be worth it." She clears her throat. "But, let's not talk about work. It's Valentine's Day and I've never had a valentine before. What exactly does being someone's Valentine entail?"

"I'm not sure, actually. You're my first."

Sydney brings her wine to her lips and takes a sip, giving me a sultry look. "Does that mean we can make it up?"

"I don't see why not." I smile. "Did you have something in mind?"

Her cheeks flush as she nods, leaning forward to place her wine on the coffee table. The pink silk shifts, giving me one hell of a view of her full chest. "I can think of a thing or two," she says, her voice thick with lust as she traces the line of bare skin along her collarbone and down her chest.

*Fuck.*

Of all the scenarios that ran through my head, this was *not* one of them. This was supposed to be a sweet virtual date, and the look she's giving me is anything but *sweet.*

Before Sydney came along, my hand and I were pretty well acquainted, given the eleven years I was celibate, but since I've met her, we've become best friends. Maybe even a little *too* close, but I can't help it.

She's constantly on my mind. The risqué photos we've sent back and forth definitely don't help. The one of her in the bath with the rosy tips of her breasts peeking out from the bubbles is hands down my favorite. It's sexy as all fucking hell and I've used it to get myself off far too many times to count.

In the weeks she's been back in New York, we've gotten each other off a handful of times over the phone, but they've all been rushed. We haven't had the luxury of being able to just sit around and have fun with it, but now seems like the perfect opportunity to finally have that chance.

When she leans back against the cushions, the lapels of her robe fall open, just barely covering her breasts. I can see the faint markings of her peaked nipples poking through the thin fabric and I wish I were there to play with them. To pinch and lick and suck them until she's a panting mess for me.

I shift in my seat, adjusting myself at the thought.

"Whaddya say, cowboy?"

Smirking, I bring the phone closer so I can get a better view. "I say that robe needs to go."

"Yeah?"

"Yeah," I grit out, feeling my cock thump to life. "I wanna see every inch of you, Valentine."

Her fingers work to open the loose knot on her robe's belt, biting down on her lip. "Is that all you want to see?"

I shake my head roughly. God, she's going to be the death of me. "Wanna see you come all over your fingers for me too."

She lets out a breathy laugh. "That can be arranged." Her fingers drag down the edge of her robe, inching it over so her hard nipples are exposed.

When we first started the call, I thought for sure she was wearing something under her robe, but to find out she's bare under there has my cock throbbing. *Dammit I want to be there with her.* I should have just said fuck it and gotten myself tickets to go see her. "You're a naughty little thing, huh?"

"Just for you."

I smile and prop my phone up on the other end of the couch as I strip down until my chest is bare and my jeans are pushed down around my knees. I don't miss the way Sydney's eyes widen at the sight of my cock straining in my boxer briefs. "See somethin' you like, Sydney Mae?"

She nods, her hand snaking down her body and settling between her legs. "Can I see more?"

"Show me that pretty pussy first."

With her lip tucked between her teeth she brings her laptop onto the couch and spreads her thighs.

"Fuck," I curse, shoving my boxers down and wrapping my hand around my shaft at the sight of her soft pink lips.

"You're already so hard."

I give my cock another slow stroke. "Sure am. Fuckin' look at you, Sydney Mae. You're a goddamn sight."

Her cheeks flush as she squirms, shifting her hips forward a bit more.

"Is my girl wet?"

"Yes."

"Prove it," I practically growl, unable to control myself.

Her fingers dip between her legs and she circles her clit for a second before slipping them through her lips and opening herself up for me. Her pussy is glistening. I can practically see her dripping from here. "It's all for you, Chase."

"Yeah? What would you let me do to you if I were there?"

She lets out a little moan and her mouth pops open as she sinks a finger inside her tight pussy. "Anything. E-everything," she corrects.

My cock leaks pre-cum and I nearly combust at the confession. Neither of us were ready for *everything* a couple months ago, but now... Now it seems like so much has changed between us. It feels like I'll die if I don't get to have her soon. I'll never rush her into something she doesn't want, but fuck I want her so bad. "You want that, pretty girl? You want me to slide my cock inside and stretch that little pussy of yours?"

Her eyes roll as she nods and she brings her other hand to her clit, letting her fingers flick back and forth. "*God, yes.* I want all of you."

She adds a second finger and hisses at the stretch.

*Fuck, I want that to be me more than I should.*

I hiss as I tighten my grip on my shaft to mimic how tight I think she'd be.

When she pulls her fingers free and brings them to her lips to suck them into her mouth, I see the moment she realizes just how much power she has over me.

"How do you taste?" I ask, barely recognizing my voice.

She moans in response, making a show of running her tongue between the two digits. "Like yours. I wish you could taste me."

"Oh, you have no idea how badly I want to taste you again, Sydney Mae."

Bringing her hand back down, she slips two fingers back inside and slowly rubs her clit. "Have I told you how often I look at that picture you sent me two weeks ago? The one of you on the bed with just a cowboy hat covering your—"

"Cock?" I smirk at the reminder of the racy photo. "Yeah, baby. You told me you were gonna make it the background on your phone."

She giggles, nipples tightening. "I've been dreaming about coming home from work one day and finding you just like that on my bed."

"Yeah?"

"Mhmm."

"And what would you do if you did find me like that?"

Her lips part and she pants as her fingers pump in and out of her. "I'd crawl on the bed, take the hat off and swallow you whole."

"Fuck."

"Chase, I—" Her head tips back and her fingers pick up their pace as they race over her clit. "I'm gonna come."

I nod and match her pace with my fist. "Let go for me, sweetheart. Let me see you come all over those fingers as you dream of swallowing my cock."

Sydney comes on a loud cry, her whole body taking on a pink flush. My orgasm crashes into me a second later and I cover my chest with ropes of cum. She pants for breath as she pulls her fingers free, showing how wet they are to the camera before sucking them into her mouth once more.

"God, you're fucking perfect, Sydney Mae."

"I could say the same about you, cowboy."

I chuckle and blow out a breath, looking down at the mess she made of me. "Happy Valentine's Day, pretty girl."

"Happy Valentine's Day, handsome."

# 18

## SYDNEY

MAY 14, 2020

My head pounds as I stare blankly at my computer screen. The design for Havershum—that he *still* hasn't approved—stares back at me. It's been six months of going back and forth with this absolute pain in my ass and I've just about had it with his Mr. Big-Dick-He-Man-Woman-Hater's-Club attitude.

He thinks that just because I'm a woman I'm incompetent and have no business being in the position that I am.

*Fucking pig-headed men.*

"Syd?" Paul's voice pulls me out of my daze. I look up from the screen to see him standing on the other side of my desk with his arms crossed and a concerned look on his face. "When was the last time you slept?"

"What kind of question is that? I slept last night."

"I don't mean to sound like a prick, but you look like shit and those are the same clothes you had on yesterday."

I roll my eyes and lean back in my chair. "Fine, I didn't sleep, *per se*. I accidentally took a nap in the conference room while looking over blueprints, and just started working again when I woke up."

Before he can even open his mouth I can sense the lecture coming. "Syd—"

There's an unrelenting throb behind my eyes, shrinking my patience further than normal. "I'm really not in the mood for this right now. I'll have Katie go to my apartment and pick me up some new clothes."

"Or you can just go home and get some rest. This is the third time in two weeks you've *accidentally* slept in the conference room. I'm starting to get worried."

"There's nothing to worry about. I'm fine."

"You're not fucking fine, Sydney!" he shouts, sufficiently tipping my give-a-fuck meter off the charts.

"Get out." I feel the vein in my forehead start to bulge.

Paul's brows pinch together. "Sydney…"

"Get the fuck out!" I scream.

He scratches at the slight stubble on his chin and clicks his tongue as he walks out.

*Fuck. I really need to get back in to see Dr. Camden.*

It's been months, and clearly I haven't been using her deep breathing techniques nearly as much as I should be.

About a week after Valentine's Day, Paul and I decided to take Juliano Riviera up on his offer. We took on his entire book of business at an extremely affordable price since he was in a hurry to retire. He said he had made enough money over the last forty-five years and didn't need any more than necessary—his priority was making sure that all four hundred of his clients were in good hands. *Our* good hands specifically.

The only downside was a massive increase in all of our workloads. I definitely took the brunt of it, which has led to more sleepless nights than I'd like to admit. If I'm being honest, I don't even know the last time I slept in my bed. If I'm lucky, I make it as far as the couch.

Closing my eyes, I lean my head back against my office chair as I attempt the deep breathing even though at this point it's useless. It couldn't hurt to at least calm down a bit though.

Ten minutes into a mindful meditation playlist, the song is interrupted by an incoming call.

*Chase.*

God, it feels like forever since we've talked. With the acquisition piling onto my workload and the time difference, it's so much harder than I thought it'd be to keep in touch.

"Hello?"

"Hey. You busy?"

"Incredibly."

"Oh." He blows out a breath. "Okay. I'll give you a call a little later then."

"You sound upset."

"It's nothing. I'll be fine."

My chest tightens uncomfortably. *Fuck, I miss him.* I quickly unplug my laptop from its docking station and pop it into my bag. "Would you look at that, I'm done with work for the day. Let me just get home and then we can video chat, okay?"

"You don't have to. It's okay. Really."

"I want to. I'll call you in like thirty minutes."

I hang up before he can protest and tuck the rest of my things into my bag before heading toward the door.

Stopping at Katie's desk on my way out, I see her typing up an email to a client. "Katie, I have to go. I have the new proposal for Havershum ready to go. Can you just look it over quickly and send it to his assistant?"

"Sure. Do you want me to cancel the rest of your meetings for the day too?"

I nod. "Yes. And I know it's an absolute shitshow right now, but only call if it's an emergency."

"Got it."

"Thanks."

The anticipation makes the twenty-minute cab ride feel like an hour. By the time I push inside my brownstone, kick off my shoes, and quickly change into comfortable clothes, I could honestly go right to bed. Instead, I force myself to open my laptop and call Chase.

His solemn face fills the screen. "Hey."

"Hi. You're at the dock?" I ask, noting the unmistakable backdrop.

"Yeah."

"Is everything okay?"

Chase chews his lip for a minute before shaking his head. "Today would have been Macie's twelfth birthday."

*God dammit.*

With everything going on, the date completely slipped my mind. He even told me last time we spoke that her birthday was coming up. I was planning to make an impromptu trip so he wasn't alone, but then everything got so busy and I forgot to book a flight.

Fuck.

"Oh, Chase. I'm sorry I'm not there to celebrate her day with you."

"It's okay. I kinda just wanted to hear your voice. It's been a while since we last spoke."

"I know," I say on a sigh. "I promise, I'll call more."

I see the muscle in his jaw tick. "You said that last time."

"I'm sorry."

"When are you comin' to visit again?"

"I'm not sure. I'm hoping for Christmas."

He can't hold back his look of disappointment. "Baby, it's May. Christmas isn't for another seven months."

"It's not a good time right now, Chase—there's too much work to do. I can't just leave. Once things start to settle down I'll try to come."

He blows out an exasperated breath. "Okay."

I can hear in his voice that it's far from okay, but apart from dropping everything and going to see him, there's not much else I can do. There are quite literally not enough hours in my day to go see him right now, no matter how badly I want to.

My phone buzzes on the counter next to me, and I groan seeing Katie's name on the screen. "It's work."

Chase runs his hand down his face, clearly upset with the way this conversation is going. "Take it. It's probably important."

"I'm sorry, Chase. I wish things were different."

"Yeah, me too."

He disconnects the call before I can and I don't miss the look of resentment on his face. It kills me that I can't be there for him the way I want to be.

I've never felt like a bigger asshole in my whole life.

# 19



I knew Sydney going back to New York was gonna be hard, but I never expected it to be *this* hard. When she first left, we talked almost every day. Then every day slowly turned into once a week, then once every two, and now I'm lucky if we talk once a month.

The worst part is that I can't be mad at her for being busy with work because I know how important it is to her. I could never ask her to give that up for me, but dammit, I just want to be selfish sometimes. I don't want to come second to work every damn time.

With each day that passes, I can feel her slipping away from me. And the longer this goes on, the less hope I have that things are actually going to work out.

Our conversation has me in such a sour mood, I don't even want to be at the dock. I feel like being pissed and lonely is going to taint the magic of this place, and I don't want that for Macie. Especially not today.

I take one last look out across the water and then let my face lift toward the sky. "You are, and always will be, my greatest gift. Happy birthday, Macie Moo. Daddy loves you so much."

The ride back to the Wilson's takes me three times as long

since I have to keep pulling over to cry my eyes out thanks to the stupid CD jammed in my truck's player. On a normal day, I'd get the tears out and be able to move on with my life, but today the lyrics are hitting just a little too close to home.

It feels like Sydney and I are the ones he's singing about.

***

"Chase, sweetie, is everything okay with you?"

"Yeah," I sigh, scooping a spoonful of vanilla sugar into my morning coffee.

"You sure?" she presses, giving me a knowing look. "I can't help but notice you've been a bit down lately. I know it was Macie's birthday a couple weeks ago, but it seems like you were in a bit of a funk before that too."

I shake my head, trying my best to plaster on a smile as I bring my coffee to my lips. "It's nothin'."

"It's Sydney Mae, isn't it?"

Coffee nearly shoots out of my nose. "What?"

"Oh, honey, I know you two had somethin' goin' on when she was here. I saw you all cuddled up on Christmas Eve."

*Shit.*

"I swear, I didn't mean for anythin' to happen. We just got… caught up in the moment. I know I shouldn't have crossed that line, and I'll understand if you wanna kick me out. I just—"

"Chase, calm down," Susan says, reaching out to touch my arm. "I'm not mad."

My brows furrow. "You're not?"

"Of course not, sweetie. How could I be? I haven't seen Sydney let someone in in a very long time. Even if it was just for a couple nights, I know you're special to her. She wouldn't've let you stay with her if you weren't." She flashes me a smile. "Sydney is my little girl, and I love her to death, but she hasn't been the same since—"

"Jack."

"She told you?"

"I had my assumptions after we saw him at the bar. He's the reason I had that black eye. I couldn't handle knowin' he hurt her, even if it wasn't my place."

Susan smirks. "I'm glad you did. Lord knows I would've done it myself, but Sydney didn't want Bill to know, and it'd be a little hard to explain how I ended up in jail for deckin' that little prick in the face."

A chuckle rolls through me at the thought of Susan landing a sucker punch to Jack's nose. "What was she like back then?"

"Oh, gosh. She was the most radiant and carefree young woman. Always had the biggest smile on her face—I rarely ever saw her without one. But then she met Jack and I watched that smile slowly fade from her face until one day she was just a shell of the person she was." Susan shakes her head like she can't believe her own memory of the worst part of her daughter's life. "Between the pills and whatever else he was givin' her, I barely recognized her. My happy little girl was replaced with a sad, scared one, and it damn near broke my heart."

"I'm sure it did."

"But I saw some of her old self comin' back out when she was with you."

"I wish I could've been there for her back then."

She licks her lips as she picks up her mug. "I wish I could say it would have changed somethin', but I'm sure she would've pushed you away like she did everyone else. But she has you now, and that's the important part."

"Right..."

I blow out a breath trying to hold it together. Sydney doesn't really have me... not the way she should.

# 20

SYDNEY



My office door creaks open and Paul steps inside. Things between us have been weird since I screamed at him last month, but I feel like we're making strides to repair our partnership, *and friendship.*

"I'm heading out."

"Lucky you."

"You should take a break, Syd. You've been working on the redesign for three days now."

*I love when he tells me what I should do, as if I'm some sort of incompetent child.* "I know I should, but I have to finish it so I can send it over first thing in the morning."

"Anything I can do to help?"

"No."

Paul crosses his arms over his chest, giving me a disapproving look. "I thought we talked about how you were going to start letting me help more. Let me pull equal weight as your partner."

"We did, but this is—"

"Beyond my capabilities?" he finishes for me. "That's the

same bullshit excuse you use all the time, Sydney. I can't help you if you don't let me. You take on all these projects by yourself when you know full well that I can do half of them. But I guess once a stubborn control freak, always a stubborn control freak."

*Ouch.* He's not entirely wrong, but it still sucks to hear. "You're being a dick."

"Maybe, but I'm doing it for your own good. You can't keep doing this to yourself. You don't sleep. You barely eat. You practically live within the four walls of this office. You're like the walking fucking dead. Do you expect me to just sit back and watch you destroy yourself, because I hate to break it to you, but I can't. You're too damn important to me."

I bite the inside of my cheek to stop myself from tearing up. The stress of the job and knowing I'm letting Chase down is really starting to get to me. I don't know how much more I can take before I break. "I'll do better," I promise. "I'll ask for help and I'll start going home at a reasonable hour, but I can't tonight. Tonight I have to finish this redesign."

"Fine, but you're coming with me to get some fresh air first."

"Paul—"

"I'm asking for thirty minutes here, Syd."

He levels me with a look that I know from experience means he's not backing down. Rolling my eyes, I follow him out the door.

Central Park at almost 7 p.m. in June is surprisingly peaceful. The semi-fresh New York City air filling my lungs is magical. It's not even close to the crisp, clean smell of the air in Colorado, but it's already clearing my mind in ways I didn't think possible.

Sitting on a bench beside Paul, I take in a deep breath, basking in the feel of sunshine on my face.

"Can you be honest with me and tell me what's really going on with you?"

My teeth drag over my bottom lip. "I feel like nothing I do is ever enough anymore. I work non-stop, but have nothing to show for it. Most days I want to give up. Like if I quit tomorrow I'd be better off."

"How could you ever think that what you do isn't good enough?"

"The redesign for Havershum. This is the eighth time I've redone it and every single time he finds something wrong."

Paul knocks his knee against mine, making me look up at him. "Your original design was perfect," he says with such confidence I actually believe him. "He's a moron for not seeing that. Change it back to that one and tell him you're not changing anything else."

"I can't." I shake my head. "He has three other projects in the pipeline. If we lose his account, we'd be taking a pretty big hit."

"Who gives a shit. If you take him off your plate you open up space for ten other clients who are better than him. Havershum is the biggest asshole I've ever met. It has nothing to do with your designs and everything to do with the fact that you're a woman, and a fucking talented one at that. We should have terminated his contract months ago."

I run my fingers through my hair. "That doesn't make me feel any better. I feel like we've wasted so much time and energy on it that it would be stupid to drop him now."

"Then let me take over the account. I'll submit your original design with my name on it. He'll see that it's an original Paul Wu design and approve it without a second thought."

"You really think that'll work?"

"Pfft. Of course it will. On the off chance it doesn't, we tell him we can't work with him anymore. I'm not letting you run yourself into the ground for that asshole anymore."

I lean my temple against his shoulder, a rare showing of physical affection. "Thank you, Paul."

"You don't have to thank me, it's what I'm here for. We're partners for a reason, you just need to *let* me be your partner."

"I will."

"Good. Now let's go grab your stuff and I'll walk you home. I want you to take the day tomorrow."

A thought runs through my mind and I couldn't tamp down the spark of excitement if I wanted to. "Do you think you could hold down the fort for a little longer than just tomorrow?"

Paul smiles through a chuckle "Take all the time you need, Sydney. It's beyond well-deserved at this point."

My heart flutters to life and I desperately try to hold back my smile at the prospect of seeing Chase. "Thanks."

# 21



**JUNE 3, 2020**

Tossing the last bale of hay down in the hay shed, I wipe the sweat from my face with my forearm and pull on the T-shirt hanging from my back pocket. It's been one hell of a long day. The sun beat down on me all day long, and there was nowhere for me to hide out to escape the blistering heat.

I'm delirious with exhaustion. All I want is to go inside, take a cold shower, and pass out. Tomorrow will come sooner that way, but the bone-deep ache and the heaviness of my eyes is a sure sign that I need the rest.

Halfway to the house, I see a man who's become all-too familiar—*the debt collector*.

Before I can think better of it, I make a hard left, heading toward the main road that leads to town. I feel like an asshole for making the Wilsons deal with my issues, but I can't handle that conversation today. I'm barely holding myself up at this point. The heat and manual labor alone is enough to take me out. Add in the emotional toll of not hearing back from Sydney in days, I'm about ready to break.

My feet drag me down the well-worn path to the bar and I settle onto a stool, ordering a beer and basking in the crisp air conditioning cooling me to my core.

Bud, the daytime bartender, passes my beer across the bar.

I take a sip, basking in the coldness. There really is nothing better than an ice cold beer after a long day. Especially a hot one.

"Hey," Scarlet says, coming through the door from the back storage room. "What're you doing here so early?"

"Don't know," I lie. The crew knows most everything about me, but they don't know that I'm eighty thousand dollars in debt. If they did, I know they'd all chip in to help me pay it off, and I can't let them do that. It's my problem to deal with, and eventually I'll get it taken care of. Until then, no one else needs to know.

"Is everything all right?"

That's one hell of a loaded question. I snicker, taking a quick sip of beer. "Not really."

"Wanna talk about it?"

"Yes and no."

"I'm guessin' it's about Sydney?"

My eyes flick to hers and I'm met with her cocked brow. I blow out a breath and nod my head once. "Partially, yeah."

"What happened?"

Shrugging, I run the tip of my finger down the cold glass. "Things were good in the beginning, but it feels like she doesn't have time for me anymore. I get that she's got a life, and I don't expect her to drop everything just to answer my calls, but it's been *days* since I last heard from her. I miss her so much it physically hurts, and the worst part is not even knowin' if she misses me too." I groan, running my fingers through my hair and pulling on the strands. "I know it's crazy to be so attached to someone I spent three nights with almost six months ago, but..." I chew the inside of my cheek. "She changed my life, Scarlet. Made me feel like I was alive again after losin' Macie. I don't think I could let that go."

"I hate to say this, but, what if all you were meant to have were those Three nights? Three nights where you both let go of everything you're afraid of and moved on from the things haunting you."

I'm stunned silent, staring at the half-empty pint of beer and wondering if she's right. What if that's all we were ever meant to be? What if we were brought together to heal and nothing more? *Could that be true?*

"I'm not tryna be the bad guy, Chase, I just hate seeing you so hurt."

"N-no, you're right." I swallow down the lump in my throat —the one that's there because there's this voice in my head telling me she is. That she hit the nail right on the head. "Maybe we've been foolin' ourselves this whole time, holdin' out hope for somethin' that could never work anyway. Maybe thinkin' about sayin' goodbye hurts so much because I know it's the right thing to do."

Her lips twist in a sad smile. "You're a great guy, and you deserve to be happy."

"I know I do."

"I'm sorry I didn't give you the advice you were lookin' for, but sometimes, you gotta just rip the Band-Aid off."

I nod, taking another sip of beer. "I appreciate it. It's just a lot to think about. I don't know if I'm ready to say goodbye to her just yet, even if it does hurt like hell."

"Y'know, goodbye doesn't have to be forever... It could just be for now."

*Huh.* Goodbye *for now.* Maybe she's onto something.

"Thanks, Scarlet."

"You're welcome."

Pulling out my wallet I place a ten on the bar and tap it twice before dragging my ass off the stool and heading to the dock for a couple hours to decompress before going to the Wilson's house.

As soon as I get back, I head right to the shower, needing to wash the day's worth of dried sweat off me before I even think about getting in bed. I brace my palms against the tile wall, letting the water ease the tension in my shoulders until it runs cold.

Throwing on a pair of sweats and a plain white T-shirt, I head to the kitchen to grab a glass of water. Memories of my late night run-ins with Sydney bombard me, but I quickly shake them away. There's no use dwelling on the past. And right now that's exactly what she feels like—*the past.*

I want more than anything for her to be my future, but currently, I'm nothing more than an afterthought to her. I'm always the one reaching out. I'm the one constantly left feeling dejected, and I can't take it for much longer.

Climbing into bed, I settle against the pillows, staring up at the ceiling. How did I let her slip away? I refuse to believe that what we had was just a fleeting moment in time. We're more than that—*I know we are.* I can feel it down to my core. She's the only thing I've thought about for months, yet I don't even know where I stand with her.

My phone vibrates on the nightstand, sparking hope in my chest. I quickly reach over and grab it, only to find a notification from my weather app saying there was lightning detected in my area.

Sighing, I pull up my conversation with Sydney and look at the unread message I sent her two days ago. I scoff and chew on my lip. *My weather app messages me more than Sydney does.*

That's just sad.

I go to call her and then notice the time. It's just after six here, but knowing Sydney, she's still working despite it being after eight for her, so I decide to text her instead. Even if she doesn't get them for a couple hours, I need her to know how I'm feeling.

> I know you're probably still working, but I need to get this off my chest. I miss you. Your voice. Your smile. Your laugh. How you used to video call me to tell me about your day and then fall asleep. All of it, Sydney.

> I miss you so damn much, and that's why this is so hard to say…

Please don't say what I think you're about to say.

*Shit. She wasn't supposed to see these until later.*

Chase.

Chase, please answer.

*Fuck, what am I supposed to do?*

> I'm sorry.

Can we talk about this?

A call comes through, but I send it to voicemail knowing I'll crack the moment I hear her voice, and for my own sanity, I can't do that.

I can't lose you, Chase.

Please pick up.

Another call comes through, but I give it the same treatment and type out a message. I feel my heart crack in two, but I hit send anyway.

I don't want to lose you either, but this hurts too much.

Three little dots appear to let me know she's typing but then they disappear.

A minute.

Five.

Twenty.

She never responds.

I don't know if a response would have changed anything, but not getting one at all?

*I guess I know where I stand.*

# 22

## SYDNEY



"Katie, do you have a sec?" I say into the phone.

"Sure, I'll be right in."

A minute later she walks into my office, heels clicking against the white marble flooring. "What's up?"

"I have to leave early for a therapy session. I was hoping you could move around my schedule a bit? I know it's not your job anymore, but—"

Katie cuts me off with a giggle. "Just because I'm a junior designer now, doesn't mean you're not still my boss. I am still very much your assistant, just a hell of a lot less of a lackie."

"I know, but it feels weird asking you to do things like this now."

"Don't worry about it. So, do you need me to reschedule your meetings for tomorrow?"

I smirk. "Actually, why don't you take them?"

"Me? But I don't—I'm not…"

"You're a mini me. I trust you. It's two meetings with our easiest clients. They've already sent the proposals and approved them, they're just signing the contracts so we can get started on them next week. Now is as good of a time as any to show Paul and I you're ready to take on more."

She chews her lip for a second, an adorable little crease of worry forming between her brows.

"Katie, I wouldn't be asking you to cover the meetings if I didn't think you were fully capable."

"Okay." She blows out a breath. "Okay, I'll do it, but if I somehow eff everything up, I'm quitting."

"You won't be quitting."

Katie grumbles under her breath as she walks out.

She's come a long way from the meek little mouse she was a year ago.

When I got back from Colorado after Christmas I sat down with Paul and we had a long discussion about how Katie deserved a promotion. She kept this place running while I was gone. That alone was enough, but Paul came with his own list of reasons. We agreed we'd be idiots if we let someone like her slip away.

I pack up the rest of my things feeling like a weight has been lifted from my chest.

Stepping into Dr. Camden's office always makes my stomach knot up. It's incredibly uncomfortable and I would very much like to never step foot into her office again, but the bi-weekly appointments for the last three months have been the only thing keeping me sane.

"Hi, Sydney," she says with a smile as I step into her office.

"Hi, Eleanor," I reply, hanging my purse on the hook by the door before taking a seat in the most comfortable oversized armchair.

"How are you doing today?"

"Good, actually. Katie is taking some meetings for me so I could be here, and things seem to finally be settling down after the acquisition. I'm leaving the office at a reasonable hour most nights, and I've been delegating more work to Paul, letting him actually be my partner."

She jots something down in her notepad as she nods along. "It sounds like you're making some good strides on your work-life balance. Have you been keeping up with your journal?"

I shake my head even though I know what's coming.

"Remember the deal we made when I gave it to you?"

"Yeah," I sigh, picking at my cuticles.

Eleanor looks at me expectantly for a moment before dipping her chin and taking her glasses off her nose. She folds them, placing them, and her notebook on the coffee table between us. "Then you know what I'm going to ask you about."

My stomach clenches and I feel my heart start to pick up its pace.

*Dammit, it's been three months, why does it still hurt this much?*

"Yes."

"If you're not ready, it's okay, Sydney."

I feel my nose sting and I look up at the ceiling to keep the tears from welling in my eyes. "A deal is a deal, right?" I say, trying to put on a brave face.

"Yes, but I'm not going to push you. You'll tell me when you're ready."

Her words spur on the memory of our first night together. When our first kiss quickly turned into something so much more. I was so damn nervous that things would move too quickly, but he eased that worry.

*"W-wait. I'm not... I don't—" I sigh. "I don't think I'm ready for... that."*

*Chase shakes his head side to side and squeezes my hip. "I would never rush you." His eyes dance back and forth between mine, making sure I know down to my core. "And for what it's worth, I'm not either."*

"Sydney?" Eleanor softly calls.

My eyes flick over, but all I see is a blurry version of her. One blink and tears slip down my cheek, hot and fast. They sear my skin, burning as they collect under my chin, then fall onto my dusty blue blouse.

*How the hell could I have let him get away?*

"Chase broke things off." The words tumble past my lips and there isn't a single ounce of relief. "I don't even know if that's the right word for it. It's not like we were ever really together… Not fully, at least."

"Fully or not, you still cared deeply about him. Did he tell you his reasoning for ending things?"

I nod, poking my tongue into my cheek to keep the anger toward myself at bay. I'm the only one I can be mad at. I'm the one that lost him. "He said trying to make things work hurt too much."

"How did that make you feel?"

My lips roll together as my gut clenches. "Fucking awful."

"Why?"

"Because it was my fault," I admit. "I didn't make the time for him like I promised I would. It was a conscious decision to brush off his messages, and tell myself I would get to them later, then completely forget about them."

Eleanor grabs the tissue box and leans forward, holding them out to me. I hadn't realized I was still crying. I'm sure my mascara is halfway down my cheeks at this point, but I can't even bring myself to care. I fucked things up with the man I could easily picture spending forever with, and for fucking what?

"I'll go grab you some water," she says as she slowly stands from her chair and starts for the door.

"I love him." My words shock me, even though they're true and I've said them hundreds of times in my head.

*I love Chase Phillips.*

Dr. Camden stops short, turning back to me with wide eyes. "Have you told him that?"

I chew on my lip, remembering the day three months ago

that left me crying outside of my brownstone without a single shred of hope left inside.

*Pain.*

*Fear.*

*Guilt.*

*Heartbreak.*

*All things I've felt before, but never like this. Never all at once.*

*It feels like my heart was forcibly removed from my chest and smashed against the sidewalk as the rest of the city went about their day, walking by as if it were a completely normal sight to see a grown woman crying so hard she was gasping for oxygen.*

*The tears raced down my cheeks one after the other, my stomach sinking to my ass as his last message repeated itself in my head over and over.*

I don't want to lose you either, but this hurts too much.

*My fingers shakily type a reply that I'm too afraid to send.*

*Looking down at the message that reads,* I love you, *I erase it one letter at a time.*

*It doesn't matter now.*

*Nothing matters anymore.*

*I was too late…*

"No." I sniffle. "Chase has no idea."

Eleanor's face falls, her lips pinching together. "Why not?"

"It wouldn't have changed anything. If I had told him that day when he ended things it would have been a cheap shot. He doesn't deserve to hear that I love him for the first time like that."

"Have you thought about reaching out to him?"

"Every day."

"Have you?"

"No."

"What's stopping you?"

I shake my head, feeling my insides twist uncomfortably. I hate the thought, but I say it anyway. "Knowing that he might have moved on."

"Why would you assume he's moved on?"

"Just a feeling."

Eleanor grabs her notebook and glasses, slipping them back on her nose. She writes something down quickly. "Do you think you're getting that feeling because *you've* moved on?"

I shake my head, my ribs feeling unnaturally tight. My mouth opens and I'm about to tell her that I haven't—*that I couldn't if I tried*—but it wouldn't entirely be the truth. I'm *with* someone else, but things are *complicated* to say the least.

How could they not be when Vikram, my close friend from college, found me crying my eyes out on a New York City street? Vik carried me and the bags I had packed to take to Colorado with me inside the night that Chase shattered my heart, and he's been trying to piece it back together ever since. He's made himself a permanent fixture in my life and I really don't know what I'd do without him.

He's single-handedly responsible for me functioning enough to go to work every day. For three months now, he's been my rock, and I'd be lying if I said there wasn't a small part of me that has feelings for him.

Chewing on my lip, I feel my eyes well with tears again.

*Shit. I haven't cried this much at therapy since I told her about Jack.*

"It's okay if you're not ready to answer that."

I nod, hastily wiping the tears from my cheeks.

"Okay, well, we're coming up on our time, but I want to ask you to do something as a homework assignment for me this time."

"Okay?"

"I want you to write Chase a letter." I open my mouth to refuse, but she holds up her hand. "Before you say no, I'm not asking you to send it. I think it would be a good exercise to get your feelings out. There are still things you're keeping to yourself, and that's okay, but it's not healthy to hold onto the things that are hurting you. So, write it down in a letter. Get it all off your chest."

"And then what?"

"Burn it. Throw it in the trash. Put it through a shredder. It doesn't matter. What matters is that you get it out of your head and you set it free."

I lick my lips and nod. "Okay."

"Good." Eleanor smiles at me. "Remember, if you need anything at all, you can call the number I gave you at any time and I'll pick up, okay?"

"Thank you."

Silent sobs wrack through me the entire cab ride home. By the time I step through the door of my brownstone, my head is pounding and I'm sure that I've cried off all my makeup.

*Sometimes, I really fucking hate therapy…*

"Syd, that you?"

My heart flutters at the sound of his voice. "Yeah," I say back, hating the nasally sound to my voice. I kick off my heels and make my way into the kitchen, a mixture of Indian spices wafting through the air. "Mmm, please tell me that you're making those little fried potato and cheese balls in the yummy red sauce."

His deep chuckle rumbles in his chest. "Yes, I'm making you Malai Kofta, and some Garlic Naan."

"Oof. I swear, I'm gonna need to bring my pants to the tailor to have them let out if you keep cooking for me like this."

He scoffs as he wipes his hand on a dish towel before dropping a kiss to my hair. "You look beautiful. And I'll stop cooking when I'm confident that you can feed yourself."

"I can."

"Ordering takeout doesn't count."

I roll my eyes and tap his stomach with the back of my hand. "Then I guess you're stuck with me."

Vik smiles. "Gladly. How was therapy?" he asks.

"Do you need to ask me that given the state of my face? I

caught a glimpse of myself in the mirror by the front door and I'm honestly surprised you can even stand to look at me."

He sighs and wipes his thumbs under my eyes before tucking a lock of hair behind my ear. "Do you want to talk about it?"

"Not even a little."

"Okay, then go get in the bath and I'll bring you some wine. Dinner will be ready in about an hour."

My brows knit as I look up at him. "You're too good to me."

"You deserve it." He kisses my forehead and then grabs my shoulders and spins me around, gently nudging me toward the bathroom. "Go relax."

I make it halfway up the stairs before I turn around to find him staring at me with his arms crossed and a dreamy look on his face. "Thank you for everything, Vik. I really don't know what would have happened if you hadn't found me outside that night."

"You would have picked yourself up eventually."

"I don't know if I would have."

His lips curve into a shy smile and he shakes his head. "You don't realize how strong you are, do you? You didn't need me then, and you don't need me now. I'm here because I *want* to be, not because I think you can't do it on your own."

My lip wobbles. *God dammit, I thought I was done with crying today.*

"Thank you."

# 23

## CHASE



My phone alarm blares through the small room and I nearly fall out of the unfamiliar bed when I'm kneed in the gut.

"God, how can it be morning already?" Riley says as she grabs a pillow and shoves it over her face.

Chuckling, I reach across her to the nightstand and silence the alarm. My blurry eyes focus on the time and I sigh. *4:10 a.m.* I need to get moving, but the thought of getting out of bed after just falling into it a little over two hours ago is the purest form of torture.

Riley rolls over and cuddles into my side. I'm content at first, living in the hazy memory I have of waking up with Sydney curled into me, but then Riley kisses my neck and I fight back a flinch.

"Don't leave," she whispers, just before softly feathering her lips over mine.

My stomach knots as guilt settles between my ribs.

*God dammit.*

It's been three months since things with Sydney ended, and I still can't help but feel like I'm doing something wrong by being with Riley. I don't understand why either. Sydney and I were never *officially* together.

My relationship with Riley didn't start until over a month after Sydney and I called it quits. It wasn't like I actively sought out a relationship, it happened by chance one night.

The whole crew was at the bar, and slowly but surely, everyone else started heading home except us. I walked her back to her place because I didn't want her walking alone, and when we got there, she kissed me. It was nice to feel wanted again after fighting so hard for Sydney's attention, and thanks to the six beers in my system, I didn't push Riley away.

After that, we started talking and hanging out alone more, and it all kinda spurred from there. Things have been moving slower than a snail's pace.

I have nothing to feel bad about, but there's this nagging feeling in my gut, and my head, that I can't shake no matter what.

"I'm sorry, I have to get to work."

"Can't you just call out or something? I don't want you to go."

I shake my head, subtly trying to extricate myself from her hold. "I can't. Sorry." I pull on my jeans from last night and then search the floor for my shirt. "But I'll see you on Saturday for our date."

"Right." There's an edge of disappointment in her voice, probably due to the fact that I've rescheduled this date about as many times as possible, and it's likely she doubts we will actually make it to the date.

I tug my shirt over my head and lean down, pressing my lips to her forehead before heading toward the door of her studio apartment. "Saturday," I say, pointing at her.

"Okay."

"Bye, Riles."

"Bye."

There's another pang of guilt that rolls through me when I

pull the door closed behind me and use the key she gave me to lock it.

Sliding behind the wheel of my truck, I make my way to the Wilson's in silence, knowing all too well that if I were to even think about listening to the stupid CD jammed in the player I would break down.

I haven't so much as thought about letting the dreaded thing play in the last three months.

When I pull up to the house, none of the lights are on and I say a quick *thank you* to whatever higher power is letting me get inside without Bill or Susan noticing.

Toeing off my boots, I quickly make my way to the kitchen to turn on the coffee pot. Flicking on the soft light above the island, I feel my heart drop to my ass when I find Susan standing there with her arms crossed over her chest and a disapproving look on her face.

"M-Mrs. Wilson."

"Chase."

"G'mornin'."

She looks me up and down, her brows knitting when they catch on the clothes she saw me in at dinner yesterday. "You just comin' in, or are you headin' out?"

I clear my throat, and scratch at the back of my neck. "Bit of both, actually. I crashed at a friend's place."

"So, Riley's just your friend, then?"

My mouth pops open, but words fail me. Heat rushes to my cheeks. How the hell does she know I was with Riley? It's not like there's been an official announcement or evidence of it on social media that she could have seen.

"It's a small town, Chase. And people in small towns like to talk. Gale Harper told me she saw the two of you out and about a couple times." Susan cocks her eyebrow, silently asking me to explain.

I run my fingers through my hair as I blow out an exasperated breath. "We're seein' where things go..."

Susan nods with a slight tilt to her lips.

"Sydney Mae and I… We didn't work out." That truth hurts harder than admitting I was with Riley last night. I think my heart will ache for Sydney as long as I live.

"I know, she told me. And I can't say I blame you for cuttin' ties." She takes a step toward me and reaches out her hand to rest on my arm. "For what it's worth, I'm sorry things didn't work out between you two. It may have been a short time, but I could see how happy you made each other."

*This morning fucking sucks.*

I swallow the lump in my throat and try my damndest not to cry because she's right. We *did* make each other happy. At least I know she made *me* happy. I can't say for sure she felt the same.

"I'm sorry too."

Her lips pull to the left in a tight-lipped lopsided smile. "If you'd like to invite Riley over for dinner one night, that would be okay with me."

The thought of Riley occupying the space I once shared with Sydney doesn't sit right with me. These five hundred acres of land feel like *ours*. Having Riley here would taint that. And as much as I want to move on, I don't think my feelings about this place will ever change.

"Thanks, I'll think about it," I lie, knowing that I never will.

# 24
## SYDNEY



Paul unbuttons his suit jacket as he returns to his seat in the executive chair across from me at the large conference table after grabbing himself more coffee. We decided to sit in one of the conference rooms rather than in my office to go over the drawings the junior architects submitted to us for review.

Thankfully, we're in the home stretch, and so far, there have only been minor adjustments needed.

"Have you heard from your parents lately?" he asks, as he goes over the next drawing from the pile as I read over the proposal.

"Yeah. We've been talking at least once a week and I text my mom from time to time."

He nods. "How are they?"

"They're doing well. Seems like they had a really productive summer season and they're excited for the winter months to slow things down a bit."

"Are you planning to visit soon? Maybe spend Christmas there like you did last year?"

"No."

My answer catches him off guard, even though it shouldn't. "Why not?"

"You know why."

"Are you going to avoid seeing your parents forever?"

I shake my head as I chew on the inside of my cheek. "Until *he* moves out, yes."

"You're not even gonna try to talk to him?"

Leave it to Paul to make me feel like even more of an asshole. "For the sake of my sanity, I don't plan on seeing, or *talking*, to him ever again."

"Syd, you lov—"

"Don't," I cut him off. "Just let it go, Paul. Please."

He levels me with a pleading look and I can't help but feel a pang of guilt. I want more than anything to talk to Chase again. To see him. To know how he's doing. To be able to go see my parents whenever the hell I want, but I can't. I can't face the mess I left behind. The thought alone makes me want to curl in a ball and hide until I disappear.

"You're gonna have to face him eventually."

"I know."

There's a knock at the door before Katie pops her head in. "Ms. Wilson, someone is here to see you."

"Who is it?"

"They wouldn't say."

My stomach rolls. I'm not expecting anyone. There are hundreds of possibilities of who it could be, but my mind stupidly locks on one thanks to my conversation with Paul.

*Chase.*

There's no way it could be him, right? He wouldn't have flown out to see me after breaking things off. He didn't even fly out while we were still whatever the hell we were.

Unless he wants to talk through what happened in person.

God, I hate this.

"Do you want me to let them in or…?"

I blow out a shaky breath and stand from my chair, trying to swallow down the bile rising in my throat. "Yeah."

Katie walks out, softly closing the door behind her.

"Why do you look like you're going to throw up?" Paul asks, standing from his side of the table.

"What if it's him? W-what if it's Chase?"

He shakes his head and rounds the table, coming to stand in front of me. "Hey, I'll be right here the whole time, okay? If, on the off chance it is him, I'll kick him out if you want."

"Kick who out?" A familiar voice rings through the air. "I hope not me," Vikram says as he smiles in the doorway of the conference room.

"Vik!" I say, a little too excitedly as I rush over to him and wrap my arms around his waist. He lets out a breathy chuckle, letting his arms settle on my shoulders. "What are you doing here?"

Vikram drops a kiss to my hair. "Thought I could take you out to lunch."

He never ceases to amaze me with his thoughtfulness. "That's sweet." I pull back from our hug, and look up at him. "But Paul and I—"

"Were just finishing up," Paul cuts me off. "I'll handle the last two on my own."

"Are you sure?"

Paul nods. "Positive. Go enjoy lunch for once." Paul flashes me a quick smile and then moves toward Vikram to give him one of those guy hugs where you clap hands and then smack each other's back. "Good to see you, Vik."

"Likewise, we still have to get that drink."

"Maybe you can convince this one to come out with us. It'll be like a Columbia reunion."

Vik laughs, and winks at me before looking back to Paul. "I'll do my best."

With a nod, Paul walks out of the conference room, leaving Vik and I alone.

"Hi, gorgeous," Vikram says as he leans and sips a kiss from my lips.

I smile into the kiss, thankful that it was only Vikram. "Hi."

He pulls back, inspecting me. "What's going on in this beautiful head of yours?" he asks, tapping his index finger on my temple.

"I don't really want to talk about it right now. I would, however, like to know where this spontaneous side of you came from."

"My staff meeting ended early and I figured I would surprise you."

"I like it."

"You do? I thought you'd hate it."

Vik has a way of calming my racing mind, so him being here after the mental toll of thinking about Chase is incredibly welcome.

I shrug. "I mean, I don't like being interrupted at work, but lunch with you sounds fantastic right about now."

"Well, I have some bad news." He drags his nose against my neck and then kisses it, whispering, "I'm the only thing on the menu…"

"Oh, you are, hm?"

He nods.

I can't help but chuckle. We've barely gone past first base.

It shouldn't be that surprising that our relationship is starting to shift, but I still can't wrap my head around it. I've known him since freshman year of college, and there's always been a sort of comfort between us. There weren't many times I went to parties, but when I did, Vikram and I would always wind up finding each other. He was that little piece of safety I knew I could always count on.

Crossing that line of friendship has definitely been interesting. Vik's touch is welcomed, as are his kisses. I don't mean to push him away, or pump the brakes when things start to get heated, but my body is craving *Chase's* touch. When the realization that Vikram is not Chase sinks in, I'm far too in my head to let anything happen.

But I'm trying.

"I like the way you think, Anand."

Vik brushes his lips against mine again. "Is that all you like?"

"Definitely not," I say, kissing him again.

OCTOBER 15, 2020

My knee bounces up and down as I watch Riley talk to Scarlet and Amelia, Noah's girlfriend, from my seat on the couch in Scarlet's living room. Noah and Logan are next to me, their full attention on the TV as they watch the Braves play the Dodgers in the game four matchup for the National League Championship.

I bring my beer to my lips and take the last sip before resting the empty bottle on the arm of the couch. My thumbnail picks at the label as an awkward, uncomfortable sensation settles in my chest.

Every time we come to hang out at Scarlet's, I get the same feeling, and I know it's because of Sydney. It all started here, under the mistletoe on Scarlet's front porch. I can't even drive by without thinking about that moment when I first felt her lips on mine.

There's a part of me that has avoided coming here so I wouldn't be bombarded with the memories of Sydney, but it seems like a moot point when she's constantly on my mind anyway. I couldn't exactly tell Riley that's why I didn't want to come tonight though. She's been pushing me more and more lately, and I could almost guarantee that she would have some choice words for me if I told her I wasn't coming.

It's not that I don't want to hang out with my friends, because I do, but it fucking *kills* me that they constantly bring up Sydney Mae. Just ten minutes ago, Logan was telling a story about how Sydney never missed a single one of his baseball games their sophomore year and that happened to be his best season ever.

I didn't think I could get jealous of the friendship they had with her, but I did, and it put me in such a shit mood.

"Here you go," Riley says with a smile as she eases herself onto my lap and hands me another beer.

A sour taste settles on my tongue. "Thanks." I take a sip to avoid having to say anything else.

She splays her hand out over my chest, popping open the top few buttons on my flannel. When the tips of her fingers meet my skin, I feel heat rush to my cheeks.

I grab her hand, trying my best not to flinch away from her touch, I'm really not doing a very good job of that. "Don't," I say as gently as I can, grabbing her hand.

If there's one thing I've always hated, it's PDA. I don't like seeing it, and I definitely don't like being a spectacle to those around me, but I choke back the desire to pull away entirely and rest my hand on her hip.

Her brows furrow and those pouty lips part. "Was it something I did?"

My teeth grind. "No. I'm just feelin' off tonight, I guess."

"We can go back to my place if you want," she suggests, slinging her arm over my shoulder.

"It's fine." I half smile. "I think I just need some air."

"Do you want company?" she asks, sliding off my lap and onto the couch.

Chewing my lip, I contemplate my answer and shake my head. "I won't be long."

"Okay."

An hour later, I still haven't gone back inside. It was in the mid-fifties when we got here, but now it's down into the thirties and I'm really regretting not grabbing my coat before coming out. My fingers went numb twenty minutes ago, and I think the tip of my nose may actually fall off.

The image of Sydney with a red-tipped nose and rosy cheeks fills my mind, and I itch to reach into my pocket to take a look at the picture of her saved on my phone.

She sent it to me months ago from a jobsite she was on. The temps had plummeted into the teens and she was all bundled up in a thick wool coat and black beanie, but the wind had whipped at her cheeks for too long, marring her perfect skin.

It's one of my favorite pictures of her because it was just for me. I remember exactly what went through my head when her message came through too...

*Mine.*

The thought was promptly followed by an intense want to wrap her in my arms and drag her onto the couch until she was warmed up.

There's a creak of the door behind me and I let my eyes drift shut as I dip my chin to my chest. I don't need to turn around to know that it's Riley, the telltale scent of her jasmine and rose perfume fills my nose.

She comes up next to me and rests her forearms on the railing beside me. "I think we need to talk."

"About what?"

"Us."

My brows pinch and I try to ignore the slight relief that she's the one that's bringing it up first, playing it off like I don't know what she's talking about. "Is somethin' wrong?"

"You tell me."

"If you're askin' if I want this, I do." Not entirely a lie since I do enjoy spending time with her, but I'm not sure if we're a good fit romantically.

Riley scoffs, tonguing her cheek. "Are you sure about that, Chase? Because to me it seems like you're only half in it. You have been from the start."

"What does that mean?"

"Physically, you're here with me, but your mind is thousands of miles away." *One thousand eight hundred and fifty-six, but who's counting?* She crosses her arms over her chest, closing herself off. Her head shakes from side to side and I watch as her dark eyes fill with tears. "I thought that time would make it better. That you would get over her, but it's only made it worse. Every single day I wake up thinking that you'll choose me, but you never do." A tear races down her cheek. "I know I'm not the one you want, Chase, I'm just holding her place."

"Riley—"

She holds up her hand, silencing me. "I deserve to be with someone who wants *me*, and only me. Someone who pictures a future with *me*. Someone who's not in love with someone else. And right now, that person isn't you."

I blow out a breath, seeing it fill the air in front of me. "I'm sorry," I say, knowing that she's right. If tonight was any indication of my feelings, I shouldn't have even attempted to make this relationship work. It was hopeless from the start. Not a day goes by that I don't want Sydney back, and that isn't fair to Riley. I can't give her what she deserves.

"Don't be." She sniffles and a watery smile curves her lips for just a second. "It wasn't our time."

*That's the understatement of the year...*

The reason why things worked between Sydney and I while she was here—and the first few months she was gone—is because we both brought a shit ton of baggage to the relationship. We each had our own demons, but with Riley, I'm weighing her down. It's why I was so against anything happening between us to begin with, even before Sydney came into the picture.

I tried to convince myself that I was fine, that I could move on.

"Do you hate me?"

She chuckles, taking a single step closer and rests her warm palm on my cheek. "I could never hate you, Chase. I'm just not the one that's going to make you happy. And you deserve to be happy. Just like I do."

"Thank you, Riles."

"I hope you know that I'll still be here for you for whatever you need."

I flash her a tight smile. "I do."

"Good." She wraps her arms around my waist and pulls me into a hug. "For the record, I hope you get your girl."

"Me too."

My fingers fly over the keys as I respond to emails from the couch. I've started this new thing where I respond to urgent emails as they come in, but save the less pressing ones until later at night. There's something soothing about clearing out my email inbox right before going to bed.

"You coming to bed anytime soon?" a shirtless Vikram asks from across the kitchen.

I chuckle, and push the blue light glasses up the bridge of my nose. "In a couple minutes. I have three emails left."

"Okay. Don't forget to plug your laptop in before you do."

"Thanks."

Vik walks away, the chords of muscles in his back and legs flexing with each step. He keeps in really good shape. Better than I remember him being in college.

He's always been a good-looking man, but there's something about the confidence he walks around with now that is most attractive. He's got the head honcho, don't-fuck-with-me vibe down pat after four years of owning and operating one of the nicest and highest-rated hotels in the city, The Windmere.

His three-hundred-room hotel is the reason for our rekindled friendship. After college, Paul and I lost touch with him until a couple of years ago when he was shopping around for estimates and renderings for the hotel from various firms.

As soon as he found us, there was no doubt about who he was going to work with. The construction took about a year, and we spoke nearly every day during that time, but lost touch again when the hotel opened.

Vikram has always been someone I knew I could count on. Back in college, he would walk me to some of my classes. And now he's done enough for me that I owe him a lifetime's worth of favors.

Memories from that fateful night where I felt my heart shatter in about a million pieces swirl around my head. He was nothing short of kind back then, and it only seemed to have gotten more prominent.

The way he carried me inside and nudged me toward the bathroom, insisting I take a long hot bath. How he ordered takeout and then hunkered down with me on the couch as I stared into space for hours. His gentle tone when he asked about how, and why, he found me at such an astronomically low point in my life.

My story with Chase hit home with him. He had gone through something similar with his ex. Apparently she left him because he wasn't making enough of an effort with her, and he's been trying to do everything to prove to himself that it wasn't his fault the relationship failed. He's said multiple times that he understood the devastation that I felt that night, and that he wishes he had had someone to help pick him up off the ground.

When I told him I wasn't planning to go to Colorado anymore, but still wanted to take a few days off to get my head on straight, he suggested I stay in one of his luxury suites for a few days to take advantage of massages, facials, pedicures, and every spa treatment imaginable.

He took my phone and only agreed to let me have it if it were an emergency because Paul knew where to find me if needed. I think he could tell that I needed that separation, otherwise I would have dwelled on my last conversation with Chase, and been too anxious about getting a message from him to actually enjoy myself.

And he was right. Having that freedom of not being tied to my phone and getting pampered was easily the most relaxed I had ever been.

As a bonus, I got to spend time with Vik each night, rekindling our friendship at the Michelin star restaurant on the ground floor that's exclusive to guests.

From that point on, things between Vik and I happened pretty naturally. He would come over every night after work to make me dinner because he didn't trust me to feed myself. Most nights, he'd wind up staying over because we had either indulged in too much wine, or because he could tell that I needed to not be alone.

After about a month, we decided to give dating a shot, and the transition was pretty seamless. It was more about *knowing* I had someone I could count on than anything else. Of course there were the occasional flirty comments and pecks on the lips, but for the most part, things stayed pretty much the same from when we were friends.

Vik gave me the hope I needed to know that I could find happiness again after Chase. At first, I didn't think it was possible, but now, three months in, the pain of losing him isn't nearly as bad as it was in the beginning.

Don't get me wrong, I miss Chase every day, but I've come to terms with the fact that it was *my* fault things ended. I'm the only one who I can be mad at for letting Chase slip through the cracks.

I don't think I'll ever be able to forgive myself for losing him.

My laptop dings with an incoming email and I smile when I see my dad's name. He's been sending me weekly updates of the goings on back in Colorado, and it never fails to make me happy.

The subject reads: *The newest member of the Wilson family.* My smile grows, pitting my left cheek with a dimple. It's probably a new calf or foal, maybe even a goat. Whatever it is, I know it will be absolutely adorable.

Ignoring the rest of my emails, I click open the new one from my dad, reading his short message. *I'd like to formally introduce you to our newest family member, May. And before you ask, no, she's not named after you. Her name is May because this is the first calf we've had out of season in a long time. Usually all the new babies are here by May, but apparently Darla and Hank got a bit frisky on their own time. Hope to see you soon, Dad.*

I chuckle at the ridiculous names for my dad's other cows before clicking open the attachment with the picture of May.

My heart stalls in my chest. I feel it roll and squeeze, and I'd do anything to go back in time to three seconds ago before I looked at it.

It is in fact the new calf, probably one of the cutest ones I've seen. Brown and white with a soft pink nose and big brown eyes that make her look like a cartoon character. But it's not the calf that has my attention. It's the man holding her.

*Chase.*

He looks good. A bit more filled out and buff than I remember, but the extra muscle looks good on him. *Really good.* He's wearing a plain white T-shirt with a dark forest green flannel that perfectly compliments his deep hazel eyes.

Even with the bright smile on his face as he's holding the squirming calf, I can see the sadness in his eyes.

*I don't want to lose you either, but this hurts too much.*

I scoff, and close the email, trying like hell to hold back the tears, but no amount of staring up at the ceiling and willing them away will stop them from falling down my cheeks.

Chase was right.

The way things were going did hurt, but that hurt is *nothing* compared to the constant ache in my chest knowing I don't have him at all.

# 27

CHASE

Pulling on the reins, Storm slows as we near the barn. He's been my saving grace the last week after I twisted my ankle when May decided to dart in front of me while I was carrying two huge buckets of feed like the little psycho she is.

I've always loved when there are babies here, but fuck, does May wreak havoc. It's like she was put on this earth to test my patience and the strength of ligaments. The worst part? May is hands down one of the cutest calves I've ever seen. I can't do anything in the barn without her nipping at my jeans or knocking her head against my legs because she wants attention.

She's obsessed with me.

Not a single day has gone by since she came into this world that she hasn't done something to garner my attention. I swear, her squeaky little moo rings through the air any time I'm within earshot of the barn. It's like she has some kind of spidey sense and can tell when I'm nearby.

"Atta boy," I say as I dismount Storm and tie his reins to the hitching post before unsaddling him and making my way inside the barn. There's no need to actually tie him up, he's the most well behaved horse I've ridden in my time here, but with that devil May running around, I can never be too safe.

I toss Storm's saddle over the red pine saddle stand before grabbing the grooming box. As I turn around to head back out to where Storm is hitched, the little menace is standing there, blocking my entrance.

"Shit." I take a slow step toward her. "May…" Holding my hands up in surrender I make a slow approach.

She tilts her head at me and flicks her ears.

"Don't even think about it," I warn and I swear, I see her smirk before she charges at me, ramming her head against my thigh. "Ow! Jesus, May. Can we have *one* day without you bein' a threat to my well-bein'?"

May pulls back at that, looking up at me with those huge brown eyes. There's a singular moment of peace. She lets out her signature squeaky moo and then nips at my shirt sleeve.

"Okay, fine, I'll give you back scratches." My hand drops to the mass of brown and white hair and I start scratching.

Her moo turns soft, almost like a hum when something feels good.

"We gotta come to an agreement here, little lady. We can't keep doin' this. You're gonna get big soon."

She nudges her nose against my thigh when I stop scratching.

"Can't we make a truce? I give you back scratches every day and you stop tryin' to take me out. Does that sound good?"

*God, I'm really starting to lose it. I'm talking to a fucking cow and actually expecting it to answer me.*

May nips at my hand before nuzzling her cheek against my arm. She lets out a resigned moo and then flicks her tail before walking out of the barn toward the rest of her small herd.

*We'll see how long this truce actually lasts.*

Two hours later, I push open the door to The Brew Lounge and am immediately met with the sight of Noah and Amelia sucking face. I roll my eyes, turning to the left and see Logan running his fingers through his messy brown hair as his girlfriend, Selene, wipes the corners of her lips. Both of their cheeks are flushed, and it doesn't take a genius to figure out that they were just making out too.

"Y'all know this is a public place, right?" I tease as I take the empty armchair near the window.

"Shut up," Logan and Noah say at the same time.

"That color looks great on you, Noah. Where'd you get it?" Selene asks.

I look over at Noah and see his lips painted with the same deep red that Amelia is donning and can't help but smile.

Noah quickly wipes at this mouth with the sleeve of his black quarter zip.

"Where's Scarlet? I thought she was coming with you," Logan asks, pulling Selene onto the couch next to him.

"She decided to have a girls night with Riley and Lorena instead."

Gotta admit, being stood up by Scarlet so she could hang out with her girlfriend didn't bother me until I found out that Riley was gonna be there too.

I hate that it's been a little over a month, and Riley and I still keep avoiding each other. It's not fair that our friends have had to pick sides. I *knew* going into it that it would get messy if we didn't work out, which is another reason why I was so hesitant to start something between us.

"How are you dealing with all that by the way? You haven't said much about it."

I can't say I don't miss her, because I do. But she was right, it wasn't fair to her. I had one foot out the door because something was holding me back. Well, *someone*. *Sydney*. Even after all this time, part of me still regrets sending that message to her that night.

*I don't want to lose you either, but this hurts too much.*

The way things were going did hurt, but that hurt is *nothing* compared to the constant ache in my chest knowing I don't have her at all.

"Chase?"

"Hm?"

"You good? You spaced out there for a minute."

I blow out a breathy sigh. "Yeah. I, uh… I think I'm gonna head home."

Selene's brows pinch together. "You just got here."

"I know, but I'm not in the mood to be the fifth wheel tonight. I'd probably only make you all miserable anyway."

Noah and Logan share a concerned look, but know that there's nothing they can say to change my mind.

Walking toward the door there's a pang of guilt in my gut, but I try to ignore it. The only person I can blame for this situation is myself.

On my walk back to the Wilson's I stop and take a second to look up at the stars. The sky is filled with them tonight. There isn't a single cloud in the sky.

I smile to myself as a shooting star passes across the sky.

"Hi, Macie Moo." It's like she always knows when I need her. I feel bad relying so heavily on her to take the proverbial weight off my chest, but then I remember the times when she was fussy as a baby and just hearing my voice would soothe her to sleep. "I hope you don't mind me botherin' you all the time, but it feels like you're the only one I can talk to lately."

Chewing the inside of my cheek, I look out across the expanse of stars. "I need you to give me a sign. Somethin', anythin' to let me know that she's okay. That she isn't as miserable as I am. That she…" I shake my head, hating the thought, but say it anyway. "That she's happy, even if it means she's with someone else, because I don't think I could live with myself if I knew this is how she felt all the time. I need her to be doin' better than I am." Tears race down my cheeks and there's no point in trying to stop them. "Please, Macie. I need to know that she's okay."

# 28

## SYDNEY

I've had a lot of bad days at work. From being yelled at by clients, to constantly having to prove myself in this industry, but this one was by far the worst.

Never in my life have I felt like such a complete and utter failure.

As if losing a bid to Harold Gregory wasn't bad enough, the asshole called to gloat afterward like the douche canoe he is.

I have *never* felt so goddamn small.

Telling me I have no place in this business is one thing. Accusing me of using the fact that I'm a woman to win deals is beyond insulting, not only to my character but to the entirety of the business I've created over the years.

*None*, and I truly mean none, of my clients have ever agreed to a deal because of how low-cut my shirts or how tight my pants are. But it hurts to know that my peers, my fellow competition, apart from Harold, are probably thinking the same thing —that I'm seducing my way into deals.

It's humiliating.

I've always known that to some degree that's what people thought, but to hear it out loud, with such conviction, was like taking a knife straight to the chest.

Apparently crying on the cab ride home from work is becoming a new normal for me, and I fucking hate it.

Pushing open the door to my brownstone, I smell a familiar aroma pouring from the kitchen.

*Braised short ribs.*

It's the perfect comfort meal on a day like today. I can't wait for the deep, rich taste to settle on my tongue, and the mashed potatoes to stick to my bones.

"How do you always know when I need a hug in the form of food?"

Vik chuckles, turning around with a glass of red wine in his hand and drops a kiss to my forehead. "Paul told me about your conversation with Harold this morning."

"Of course he did."

"You know there isn't an ounce of truth to anything he said, right?"

I nod. "Yeah, but it still hurts that *anyone* could think that. Even him."

"I know." He grabs my chin and tilts my face up. "Why don't you go relax on the couch while I finish up dinner. There's a new episode of that serial killer docuseries you've been binging."

"You know, the more episodes I watch, the more adept I'll be at murdering you for leaving dirty dishes in the sink."

Vik shakes his head, lips curved into a devastating smile. "No murdering happening tonight. I promise to leave the kitchen spotless."

I giggle, feeling some weight lifting off of my chest. "Thank you, Vik."

---

An hour and a half later, my belly is full and my glass of wine has been emptied twice. Vik had to go check on something at The Windmere, and I agreed to do the dishes. He truly deserves an award for being so patient with me.

After nearly five months of dating, the most action he's seen is kissing and cuddling. I don't know why I still freeze up any time he asks if I want to take things further.

That's not entirely true. I know exactly why I freeze up and it's a six-foot-two ranch hand with a panty-dropping smile and the most gorgeous hazel eyes, but we don't talk about him.

Or think about him.

No, we definitely *don't* think about him.

With the kitchen back to rights and my docuseries over, I head into my room to change into pajamas when I notice the neat stacks of clean laundry on my bed. Vik the saint must have reheated and folded the load I left in the dryer a week ago.

Smiling to myself, I grab the first stack of leggings and tuck them into their drawer before reaching for the pile of perfectly folded socks. I shove them into the drawer and pick up the over-sized T-shirts from the bed.

My pajamas used to consist of lace and silk, things that made me feel sexy, but now I prefer a man's shirt that acts as a nightgown.

There's one shirt in the stack that has received *a lot* more love than the others. The white cotton tee is so thin it's practically see-through. It's impossible given the amount of times it's been washed, but I *swear*, I can still smell his scent lingering.

I pull open the drawer, ready to cram the too-tall stack of shirts into the drawer when I notice the corner of a piece of paper peeking out from beneath the neglected silk and lace in the drawer.

My heart rate immediately kicks up knowing that it's not just a piece of paper. It was buried at the bottom of the drawer for a reason. I couldn't bring myself to throw it away, but the thought of coming face to face with it every day made me want to hurl.

I set the pile of shirts on top of the dresser and pluck the paper out from the drawer. The well-loved note feels so goddamn heavy in my hands.

Chase must have slipped it into my suitcase before I left. I found it when I was unpacking and couldn't help but swoon at the thought of him sneaking away to write it and then putting it into the zippered pocket where he knew it'd be safe.

Reading it back now is even harder than it was the day I shoved it in the bottom of my drawer after he ended things.

> You're heading back to New York today and I wish I could ask you to stay. With me. For me. I know I can't, but man, am I tempted. You've changed my life, Sydney Mae. I hope you know how much that means to me. You will always have a place in my heart. Please, don't be a stranger.
>
> -Chase

Tears race down my cheeks as the proverbial knife twists in my gut.

*God, it fucking hurts.*

I grab at my chest, clutching at my aching, battered heart as I fall to my knees. Silent sobs wrack through me with every passing second. The searing pain of losing him is just as fresh as it was five months ago. It's as if no time at all has passed, and the gaping hole he left has just been ripped back open after I barely stitched it together.

"Shit!" Vik says right before I watch his blurry form race across the room and drop in front of me. He plucks the note from my hand and carefully places it on the dresser before pulling me to his chest. "It's okay, Syd."

"W-why does it have to h-hurt so m-much?" I choke out through watery sobs.

Vik rubs gentle circles on my back. "Because you love him."

I shake my head, taking my first steady breath. "He broke my heart, Vik."

"I know he did." He gives me a sad smile as he wipes away my tears. "I don't think I'll ever forget the sight of you crumpled up on the ground crying your eyes out. But I've always known that your love for him runs deeper than you let yourself believe."

"That's not true."

"It is. And that's okay. All I've wanted to do since that night is help. Whether it be helping you move on, or just being a placeholder, I only care about you being okay."

Sniffling, I rest my cheek on his chest. "How can you be okay with that?"

I feel his chest rumble with a slight laugh. "I know what it's like to have the love of your life walk away from you. I wish I had someone to help me back then. So, if I can make things even a little bit easier for you, that's what I want to do. More than anything, you deserve to be happy, Sydney."

"I hate him."

"There's a difference between hating him and hating what he did, and you wouldn't be crying in my arms right now if you didn't still love him."

Chewing my cheek, I try to stave off more tears, but they well up in my eyes anyway. He's right. I don't hate Chase. Not even a little bit. And it's not fair to put all the blame on him when I know I'm just as responsible for my own heartbreak. "I don't know what I'd do without you."

"You won't ever have to find out." He presses a kiss to my temple. "Friends, more than friends, however you want me in your life, it doesn't matter, I'll be there."

"I know it'll never be enough, but thank you, Vikram."

He smiles at me and I see just a hint of sadness in his eyes. "You're welcome, Sydney."

# 29

CHASE

After the walk home from The Brew Lounge, I grab myself a glass of water before heading up the stairs. I'm about to round the corner to head to the attic stairs when a scent that's been haunting my dreams fills my nose.

There's a spark of hope in my chest. Could she be here?

I tiptoe down the hallway and push open the slightly ajar door to Sydney's bedroom before popping my head inside. The room is exactly how she left it nearly ten months ago. The bed is perfectly made, the borrowed pair of Susan's old boots she'd tucked next to the nightstand of her bed right in front of the radiator to dry out the wet toes, but there's no sign of her.

No suitcase.

No coat haphazardly thrown over the chair of her vanity.

No Sydney Mae.

Just the lingering scent of her perfume, and the misplaced hope that one day we might be able to fix things between us.

My eyes scan the tops of her dressers, noting the picture frames filled with photos of when she was younger. There aren't a ton, but the unmistakable faces of Logan, Noah, Riley, and Scarlet are scattered in them. She's smiling from ear to ear and making goofy faces, but she's still just as gorgeous.

Blowing out a sigh, I take a seat on the edge of her bed and hang my head. My fingers run through my overgrown hair, tugging on the strands.

"Chase, sweetie, what are you doin' in here?" Susan's soft voice asks as she steps through the doorway. She's wearing glasses and her hair is in rollers with a matching purple flannel sleep set and a pair of slippers.

*Shit, I probably woke her up.*

"S-sorry. I just… I wanted to—" My brows pinch and I shake my head, not wanting to lie, so I cut myself off.

She half smiles as she takes a seat beside me, resting a reassuring hand on my forearm. "I come in here when I miss her too."

I feel my eyes start to water. Why the hell is this so hard? There's no reason why I should still be *this* miserable without her. My knee bounces up and down as I look up at the ceiling to prevent the tears from falling. "It smells like her."

"Oh, honey, I'm sorry." Susan squeezes my arm. "She left behind a bottle of her perfume and I spray it every once and a while so it feels like she's here."

"I thought maybe she… Nevermind."

"She'll come back, Chase. You just have to give her time."

My tongue slides over my bottom lip before I tuck it between my teeth. "I know."

Susan puts her hands on her knees before pushing off the bed. She places her hand on my cheek. "You're free to stay in here whenever you like, I know the attic room is a bit small."

"Really?"

"Of course. I should have offered sooner."

"Thanks, Mrs. Wilson."

She smiles, lightly pinching my cheek. "You're welcome. Sleep well, Chase."

"You too."

An hour later, I slip under the covers of Sydney's bed after grabbing a few essentials from my room and spending far too long contemplating whether or not it was a good idea.

Even if it isn't, it's just one night.

One night of sleeping in her bed and then I'll go back to my room.

---

*So much for one night…*

I've spent every night of the last month in Sydney's bed.

Every single night, the smell of her perfume fills my senses and soothes the ache in my heart. It eases my mind of the fact that she's no longer a part of my life. Because as long as I'm in this room, it doesn't feel like I lost her. It doesn't feel like I made the biggest mistake of my life by letting her go.

I turn my head and look over at the clock on Sydney's nightstand, noting the time of eleven-forty five.

"I know I've asked you for signs before, but I could really use one right now, Macie Moo."

Staring up at the dark ceiling I lie there, waiting for a sign. Something, anything to let me know that I'm not crazy.

My phone vibrates on the bed next to me and I blow out a breath. "Is this the sign?" I ask Macie as if she'll be able to answer me.

Picking up the phone I see an unknown number and pause for a moment before sliding my thumb across the screen and holding it up to my ear. "Hello?" I wait for a response, but none comes. "Hello? Is anybody there?"

There's a soft sniffling sound on the other end and I feel my heart squeeze.

"Sydney?"

Silence settles on the line again and I hate the spark of hope that blooms in my chest.

"Sydney, if that's you, I'm sorry. I didn't mean what I said." I pause for a second, trying to settle my nerves so my damn voice will stop shaking. "I didn't mean what I said… I don't care if it hurts, baby, I need—"

The call disconnects and my heart sinks.

I huff out a breath. "It probably wasn't even her," I whisper to myself.

And if it was, she clearly doesn't care. If she did, she would have said something the night I ended things. But she didn't. I should know better than to get my hopes up.

DECEMBER 14, 2020

Walking through the doors of The Windmere, I'm greeted with bright smiles, but the last thing I want to do today is smile. It feels wrong.

Stepping up to the front desk, Amaya, Vik's most trusted employee, waves. "Hi, Ms. Wilson, are you here for Mr. Anand?"

I dip my chin. "Yes. Is he available? If not, I can wait."

Amaya clicks around her screen, eyes scanning what I can only assume is Vikram's calendar. "He's just finishing up a walk-through with our new facilities manager, but should be free within the next five minutes. Why don't you go wait in his office."

"Great. Thanks, Amaya."

She flashes a shy smile as I breeze past her toward the long hallway that leads to Vik's office.

I absolutely adore this building, and it's not just because *Wilson & Wu* did the work. The place is perfectly styled and elegant, but it's not one of those super fancy hotels that you feel like you can't actually exist in. It's luxury with a cozy home feel.

Vik has worked so hard getting this place in tip-top shape

and I'm so damn proud that I had a hand in at least a little part of it. He deserves every bit of success that has come from it.

By the time I make it to his office door, I hear my name called from behind me.

"What are you doing here? Did something happen? Are you okay?" He races to ask as he grabs my cheeks and looks me over from head to toe.

I chuckle, pulling his hands away from my face. "I'm fine, Vik."

"I thought we didn't lie to each other?" he asks, cocking a brow.

"We don't. Technically, it isn't a lie. Physically, I'm fine. Mentally and emotionally, I'm a fucking train wreck."

"What's going on?"

Blowing out a breath, I lean my back against his door. "Paul kicked me out of the office and told me I couldn't come back for at least a week."

"What? Why?" The panic in his eyes is evident.

"I was scheduling meetings this morning and had a breakdown when I realized that it was a year ago today that I first met Chase, and in the heat of the moment I booked a flight to Colorado."

The realization slammed down on me and flooded my mind with the memory of meeting him for the first time.

*My eyes scan the terminal around the luggage carousel, but my dad is nowhere in sight.*

*Typical.*

*"Sydney?" a rugged voice calls out from my left.*

*I turn and have to clench my jaw to keep it from hanging open.*

*He's easily the most attractive man I've seen in years. From his cheeks dusted with freckles, to the easy, crooked smile on his lips and those deep, sad eyes, I'm powerless. I feel a flutter in my stomach just looking at him, but I know better than to trust an attractive man. I did once, and I don't think I'll ever give someone that power again.*

*"Do I know you?" I ask, trying to ignore my attraction to him.*

*"My apologies," he says with an edge of nervousness in his voice. "I'm Chase. Your dad asked me to come pick you up since his truck has seen better days."*

Fuck. My. Life.

*He has an accent too?*

*"How sweet of him to tell* me *that." I scoff and roll my eyes. Anything to take my eyes off the handsome stranger for a second. "If I had known, I would have gotten a cab." I reach into my bag and pull out my wallet. "How much do I owe you?"*

*"Pardon?"*

*"For picking me up. I know all too well that my father isn't paying you, so how much?"*

*He shakes his head, pushing my wallet away. I feel a spark when his hand touches mine and I immediately pull my hand away. "I did it as a favor to him. I can't take your money."*

*"Right… Well, can we get going? I'd like to get this trip over with as quickly as possible. The less time I spend here, the better."*

*His brows pinch together. "I don't mean to be crass, but if you don't want to be here, then why bother comin' in the first place?"*

*Guilt weighs heavy on my chest, but for my own sanity, I can't apologize for wanting this trip to be over before it ever really begins. He doesn't need to know that though. "That's really none of your business."*

*"I just meant—"*

*"It doesn't matter," I cut him off. God damnit I need to get out of here. I need to be away from him. "Can we go?"*

*He rolls his lips together and nods.*

*I'm not sure why I thought being in a confined space with the hot stranger would be better, because the smell of his cologne invades my senses, and of-fucking-course it's intoxicating.*

"So, you're going to Colorado then?" Vik asks, his eyebrows raising to his hairline.

I shake my head. "I haven't decided yet." He gives me a look and I know what he's going to say before he even opens his mouth. "You think I should go."

Vik shakes his head, tucking a lock of hair behind my ear. "What I think doesn't matter. You have to do what feels right for you."

"Right."

"When is the flight?"

"Wednesday."

"So you still have time."

I nod, but can't shake the uneasy feeling in my gut.

---

A day later, I'm starting to worry that I'll never be able to make a decision. I'm running out of time, and I know if I talk to my parents, they'll convince me to come home. More than anything, I want to see them, I'm just not sure if I'm ready to see Chase again.

Would he even *want* to see me after everything?

Does he ever think about me?

Does he miss me as much as I miss him?

There's really only one way to get answers to those questions, and that's going back. I just don't know if my heart could take it if the answer to any of them is *no*.

# 31

## CHASE



"Do y'all have questions about anythin'?" I ask Noah and Logan as we walk toward the exit of the barn after giving them the low-down on what they might need to help with while I'm gone.

"Nope," Logan says at the same time Noah shakes his head.

"I'll only be gone for a couple days, and I think Bill should be able to handle everythin' on his own, but I really appreciate you guys offerin' to help out."

"Of course."

"Are you gonna tell us where you're going?" Noah asks.

I shake my head. Telling them would lead to them telling me I'm crazy. They'd try to talk me out of it when I've already talked myself *into* it. By no means does that mean I want to go, but I'm a man of my word. So whether I like it or not, I'll be leaving this afternoon and heading toward the one place I vowed I'd never set foot in again.

*Rock Springs, Wyoming.*

Home.

Or where I *used* to call home.

"Maybe when I get back."

"Is everything okay?"

*That's a loaded question if there ever was one.* I can't exactly tell them that I got a call from my ex last night asking for me to come home so we could talk. After spending five minutes trying to tell her that I have nothing to say to her, she turned it around and said she had some stuff she needed to tell me.

It feels like that's a load of crap, but at this point I've already committed. "It will be."

---

Later that morning, as I'm packing my bag, I find a polaroid Sydney and I took on Christmas morning. Our lips are swollen and there's a dreamy look in both our eyes.

The memory settles my mind. I would do anything to go back to that morning, or *any* of the mornings I spent with her.

I shoved the picture in the bottom of my drawer, needing it out of my sight after I broke things off, but I couldn't bring myself to throw it away. I wanted the reminder of the good times we had together, but couldn't stomach the thought of seeing how happy we were every day.

Taking one last look, I tuck the picture back into my drawer. I know I need to put the past behind me. She hurt me just as much as I hurt her and dwelling on what we *could* have changed isn't going to do either of us any good.

I zip up my duffle and sling it over my shoulder as I head down the stairs.

Susan is already standing at the landing with a brown paper bag in her hand and a forlorn look on her face.

"I made you a turkey sandwich for the drive. And I threw in a little baggie of vanilla sugar so at least I know you'll be havin' good coffee. There's also this." She reaches onto the bench we all usually use to put our shoes on and hands me a canvas bag. "I put some snacks in here for you. I even had Bill get that jerky you like from the market."

Chuckling, I take the bags from her hand and then wrap my arms around her shoulders, pulling her in for a hug. "Thank you, Mrs. Wilson."

She swats at my chest as she steps back from our hug. "No need to thank me, Chase. Do you have everythin' you need?"

"Yeah." I nod and run my sweaty palms over my jeans. "All packed and ready to go. You promise y'all will be okay without me for a couple days?"

She rolls her eyes, pinching my cheek. "For the millionth time, yes. We'll be just fine. If we need anythin' we'll give Logan or Noah a call."

"Okay."

"Are you sure you want to do this, sweetie?"

I can't help the small huff that leaves me. "Not even a little bit." How could I willingly *want* to go back home after all the shit I've been through? It's not like anyone there has missed me in the years I've been gone. I don't get cards or text messages wishing me a happy birthday. I'm consistently let down by everyone I left behind, yet for some reason I feel like I owe it to myself to go.

"So why are you?"

"I've put it off for long enough."

Susan shakes her head and I see the beginnings of tears forming in her eyes. "Well, you just remember that *this* is your home now, all right? No matter what, you have a place here, Chase."

"Thank you," I say, feeling myself get choked up. "And thank you for keepin' this between us."

"Don't make me regret it."

"I won't."

"Drive safe now, y'hear? And call when you get there so I know you made it okay."

I smile at that and give her another quick hug. Susan is more of a mom to me than my own mother. "I will. Thanks again."

The drive back to Rock Springs wasn't as bad as I thought it'd be. I had plenty of time to think and because I was thinking ahead, I downloaded a bunch of music on my phone and brought a speaker with me so I wouldn't have to listen to the stupid song that's made me cry one too many times lately.

When I left Rock Springs, Macie was just a baby. We had to stop for me to change her diaper or feed her what felt like every hour, making the drive feel like it took forever. This time, the five-and-a-half-hour drive feels like it happened too quickly.

I wasn't ready to step foot back in the town where everyone let me down. My parents, Cara, the people I thought were friends who very quickly dumped me when they found out I was going to be a dad.

Sometimes I wish I had grown up in Slate Ridge with Logan and Noah and the others. My life probably would have turned out much differently.

Maybe I could have saved Sydney from Jack. Maybe she never would have started seeing him in the first place.

*Maybe Macie could have been ours…*

I quickly shake that thought from my head.

Slamming the truck door behind me, I make my way toward the only motel in town. The bell dings as I push open the rickety door.

Behind the front desk is an old man who looks like he's been here since I was born. Grey hair, overgrown beard, and a shirt that clearly doubles as a napkin. "W'canah doya fer?"

"Pardon?"

The man clears his throat, sitting up straighter. "What can I do ya for?"

"Oh. One room please. Two nights."

"Any guests joining? That'll be an extra charge."

"No, sir."

He tips his head and reaches behind him to the wall of keys, grabbing the one with the number eleven on it and hands it over. "Eighty-seven dollars. Pay when you leave. Your room is outside and to the left."

"Thank you."

Walking into my room, I'm greeted with an aggressive floral-patterned bed spread and dark green carpet. The walls look like they were white at one point, but now have a yellow hue to them, likely caused by the lingering smell of cigarette smoke.

"It's only two nights," I remind myself before dropping my duffle and the bag from Susan on the small table under the window.

Tempting fate, I take a seat on the edge of the bed and am pleasantly surprised at how soft the mattress is.

I pull out my phone and quickly dial Mrs. Wilson.

"Chase, sweetie, is that you?"

"Yes, ma'am. I just wanted to let you know that I made it to Rock Springs."

"Oh, thank goodness. I was starting to get worried."

It's not even been twelve hours and I already miss her.

*Damn Wilson women…*

"Did you remember to eat your sandwich?"

Chuckling, I shift the phone to my other ear. "Yes. It was delicious, thank you."

"Good. We missed you at dinner tonight."

"I missed you too."

There's some shuffling on the other end of the phone before she says, "You get what you need done up there and then you come back home to us, y'hear?"

"I promise."

I know if I could see her she'd have a sheen of tears in her eyes. "All right."

"Have a nice night, Mrs. Wilson."

"You too, Chase."

The call ends and I immediately miss the connection. The

Wilson's have changed my life for the better. I really couldn't imagine it without them now.

My stomach rumbles and I take it as a sign to go out in search of food.

It's been a long time since I've had a burger from my favorite burger place, The Rail Yard, and my hungry stomach likes that idea.

On the drive over, I pass the block I grew up on. For a moment, I think about stopping by, just to see if my parents are home, but quickly change my mind. I haven't spoken to them in eleven years. They haven't made a single effort to try and repair our relationship, so why should I bother?

I pull into the parking lot and hop out, the smell of greasy burgers and perfectly seasoned fries wafting through the air.

My mouth waters.

There's really not much I miss about this place, but damn do I miss these burgers.

I reach for the spatula-shaped door handle and pull it open, immediately being greeted with the heavenly scents that molded my childhood.

Heading toward the back of the restaurant where there's a bar, I weave through the tables, passing happy couples and families indulging in the goodness The Rail Yard has to offer.

A woman with a stroller comes toward me so I take a step to the right, wedging myself between two tables. She waves a silent *thank you* as she passes me.

When the walkway is cleared, a couple comes into view and my heart drops through my ass.

What kind of sick hell is this?

Balling my fists, I shove them in my pockets and turn around, making a beeline for the door, but there's a traffic jam of people leaving their tables at the same time.

"Chase?" I hear called from behind me.

*Damnit.*

With nowhere else to go, I slowly turn around, and stare back at the woman who brought me into this world. "Mom."

My father comes up behind her, resting a hand on her shoulder. "What are you doing here?" he practically spits.

I click my tongue, trying desperately to fight back the very choice words I have for the man that was single-handedly responsible for me being disowned and kicked out of the house. "Don't worry, I won't be in town long enough to tarnish your reputation any further."

His brows furrow and I see my mom wince at the edge in my voice. "You will not speak to me that way."

"Okay, I won't speak to you at all then," I say with a shrug as I turn to walk out the door.

He catches my elbow. "Don't walk away from me."

"Isn't that what you wanted me to do eleven years ago?" I pull out of his hold. "Walk away and pretend like I never existed so I wouldn't ruin your sparkly reputation?" I huff a sarcastic laugh and tongue my cheek. "I see not much has changed after watchin' your only son walk out of your life."

"Chase, please, can we—" Mom starts but I level her with a glare. "We're sorry, honey."

I nod, feeling myself get choked up. "If you truly meant that, you would've been there for me when Macie passed." An angry tear races down my cheek, but I ignore it. "You would have called, or come to the funeral, but you didn't. It's been six years and I haven't heard a single word from either one of you about how you're sorry that my daughter is gone. That she left this earth and left a hole in my heart that I will *never* be able to fill. You kicked me out of your life and haven't had a single ounce of remorse about it since. And you want to know why? It's because you don't *fucking* care. You don't care about me, you never cared about my daughter, and it probably would have been better for you if I never existed. So, why don't you just go on pretendin' I don't? It would make all of this a hell of a lot easier."

"Watch your tone, young man," Dad scolds.

Scoffing, I clench my teeth and my fists, wanting so badly to deck my asshole of a father right in the mouth. He's been like this my whole life. It's why I acted out as a teenager. Why I tried so damn hard to be everything that he's not.

He cared more about how people would view *him* for having a son that fucked up and got a girl pregnant before graduating high school than he did that he was going to be a grandfather.

Not once did he ask how I felt about the situation. He never checked in to see if I was doing okay knowing that my life was about to change in more ways than I could ever imagine. He didn't care that while he was kicking me out of my home and taking away any sort of safety and comfort I had, that I was scared shitless.

I didn't know the first thing about being a father. Didn't know how often babies needed to be fed or changed, or how long it would take their umbilical cord to fall off.

All I knew is that I wanted to be the exact opposite of the man standing in front of me right now.

"As far as I'm concerned, you stopped bein' my father the day you kicked me out. So I'll talk to you however I damn well please."

Mom covers her mouth with a shaky hand as twin tears roll down her cheeks. I know that seeing me filled with so much disdain for them is killing her, but she made her choice. She chose to stay with my father and live under his repressive thumb. If she truly wanted a relationship with me she would have fought for one. She could have easily kept in touch when he was out of the house, but she didn't, and for that I don't think I'll ever be able to forgive her.

"Whoever taught you that this attitude is acceptable clearly needs a lesson on respect."

My teeth grind. "Wasn't it you that taught me respect is to be earned, not given freely? If anyone here needs to learn a thing or two about respect, it's you, *sir*." I practically spit my last words.

His face reddens, the look of pure hatred and disgust I've

always been privy to taking over his features. He takes a step closer, coming nose to nose with me, a viscous look in his eye. "Get out of my damn sight."

"Gladly," I say through my teeth. My eyes flick to my mom, and for a split second, I think about saving her from him, but then I remember the years worth of pain and suffering that I went through entirely alone. "Have a nice life."

Turning my back on them, I make my way to the door. Behind me I can hear my mother's sobs and my dad cursing up a storm, but I ignore it, just like they ignored me for the last eleven years.

I don't wish ill on anyone, and for my mom's sake I truly hope she wakes up one day soon and realizes what a manipulative piece of shit my father is, but I hope to never lay eyes on either of them again.

They have no impact on my life. I've gone through enough of it without them in it, so it's no loss to continue.

I walk back into my motel room hungry and emotionally drained. I'm tempted to give up completely and go to bed at 7 p.m. when my eye catches on the canvas bag Susan gave me. My eyes immediately start to water.

The Wilson's have shown me more love and support in the five years I've known them than my parents have my entire life. They took me in as a complete stranger and let me live in their home without question. Never once did they make me feel like an outsider, or that I didn't belong. The first time I stepped through their door I immediately felt like I was home. Like I was safe.

I'll be indebted to them forever, but honestly, I don't mind. At least around them I know that there are two people who care about me regardless of my past.

At the end of the day, isn't that what everyone wants? To feel cared for? Like they have a place? To know if they were to leave and never come back, that they'd be missed?

Wiping my tears away with the back of my hand, I grab the

jerky with a watery smile. It's my *real* favorite jerky, not the cheap one I always *say* is my favorite because I don't want them wasting their money on me.

I make a mental note to save up and buy Susan that decadent chocolate cake she loves so much from the small bakery two towns over.

*If I have nothing else in life, at least I know I'll have them.*

# 32

SYDNEY

After a full day of freaking out, and a panicked call to Dr. Camden, it was clear that I needed to go to Colorado for the sake of my sanity. Trying to avoid the situation any longer was going to make me go crazy. At some point, I would need to talk to Chase again anyway. Not going would only be delaying the inevitable.

That doesn't mean I'm not scared shitless though. The entire car ride to the airport, Vikram had to convince me that going wasn't a huge mistake.

He held my hand as he walked me to the door and then spun me to face him, tucking a lock of hair behind my ear. "If you need me, just call and I'll be on the next flight out, okay?"

"Thank you." I smile up at him. "I'll let you know when I land."

Vikram nods, returning my smile. "I've been thinking… and I want to take a break while you're gone."

My heart clenches. A break? He can't mean that. "W-what?"

"Until you come back with all the answers to the questions spinning around your head"—he taps my temple with his index finger—"and the closure that you need to move on from this once and for all, we're on a break."

I shake my head, feeling my eyes well with tears. "Why are you doing this?"

"You need to follow your heart, Sydney, and I know you won't if we're still together." Vikram cups my face, softly stroking the apple of my cheek with his thumb. "I don't want you to miss out on the opportunity to be with Chase again just because you're tied to me."

"Vik—"

"I may have lost my chance at happiness with the love of my life, but *you* haven't. You still have time to change your future with him," he explains. "And now, there's nothing standing in the way of you taking that chance."

My mouth opens to reply, but nothing comes out.

I knew Vik was selfless, but I didn't think he was *this* selfless.

"More than anything, I want you to be happy, Sydney. Whether that's with me, or with him, it doesn't matter."

"Thank you, Vikram."

The corner of his lips curve up. "You're welcome."

"I love you."

"I love you too." He presses a kiss to my forehead, letting his lips linger there for a moment. "I'm looking forward to you coming home and telling me you're no longer mine."

I giggle and push at his chest. "Shut up."

"I'll see you soon, okay? Have a safe flight."

I nod and roll my carry-on behind me toward security.

This time, I won't take a single second I have to spend in Colorado for granted.

An hour of being stalled on the runway due to a small lightning storm passing through means I have effectively run through every single one of my encounters with Chase from this time last year.

Meeting him at the airport and being a cold, unfeeling bitch.

The moment in the kitchen after dinner with my parents where the first of my carefully constructed walls started to crumble.

When I felt his hands on my waist for the first time after he swooped in and saved me from an encounter with Jack.

And the second when he pulled me into his chest as I cried.

Hearing how he fought for me without question, and then telling him about my past.

The day at the dock when he first opened up to me about Macie and the things that haunt him.

Our first kiss.

Our first night together.

Waking up wrapped in his arms.

Sneaking away on Christmas day to make out in the barn.

Saying goodbye and feeling my heart tear in two.

I remember every moment we spent together like it happened yesterday.

Every word. Every stolen glance. Every touch. Every kiss.

And if I were given the chance to go back and relive it all, I would without a second thought.

But would he?

I grab the key from under the mat and unlock the door, pushing inside and out of the cold.

"Mom? Dad?" I call out, toeing off my boots.

"Sydney Mae? Is that you?" Dad calls out from the other room.

I giggle to myself. "Do you have any other children I don't know about?"

My mom turns the corner, her face immediately lighting up.

Her arms wrap around me. "Oh, we tried like hell to give you a sibling. Just wasn't in the cards for us."

"Still try twice a day though," Dad notes, winking at me over Mom's shoulder.

"Gross." Cringing, I pull away from Mom's warm hug. "I don't need to know about your sex life. I'm still scarred from that one time when I was sixteen."

They both chuckle and then get goo-goo eyes, clearly remembering their tryst. I don't think I'll ever be able to get the vision of my parents doing it out of my head.

It's burned there permanently.

"What on earth are you doin' here, Sydney Mae?"

"I missed you. Thought I'd come spend some time here like I did last year." The lie rolls off my tongue too easily. As much as I *am* here for them, Chase is the reason I came.

It's weird not seeing him in the kitchen or on the sofa in the living room. He's typically a fixture of my parent's nightly routine.

"Well we sure are happy to see you, kiddo." Dad drapes his arms over my shoulder and pulls me in close enough to drop a kiss to my hair. "Why don't you go wash up from the plane and we'll get some supper heated up for you."

"We?"

He rolls his eyes. "Your mother. I'll get the coffee goin' though." Mom cocks an eyebrow. "All right, fine, she's gonna do all of it, but I'll be watchin' her. It's one of my favorite things to do."

I laugh, smiling at my mom. "Thanks, Mom."

"Oh, it's nothin'. Go get cleaned up."

---

My room feels different than it did last time. I'm not sure if it's because of what happened inside these walls when I was here last, or if it's that in my mind, he'd still be in here waiting for me.

Sitting down on the edge of my bed, I pull out my phone and call Vik.

"Hey, sorry I forgot to call when I landed. I just got to the house—trying to find a car service was nearly impossible because of the time."

"No worries. I tracked your flight the whole time and then stalked your location. Were your parents excited to see you?"

I smile. "They were. It's good to be home."

"Have you seen Chase yet?"

Chewing my lip, I shake my head even though Vik can't see me. "Not yet. He must still be in the barn. I thought about going down there, but I think I should let fate decide when I see him instead."

"Who are you, and what have you done to Sydney?"

"Shut up."

"I love you, not-girlfriend."

"Love you too, not-boyfriend."

I smile to myself when the call disconnects. For as often as Vik talks about how he wants me to be happy, I don't think he realizes that I already am. Without him I'm not sure I'd smile any day, let alone all of them.

After changing into a pair of black leggings and an oversized red crewneck, I head downstairs, finding my parents on the couch and a covered bowl sitting in front of my favorite chair.

It warms my heart that they'd remember something like that.

I dig in, enjoying the rich, elk stew that takes the chill right out of my bones as my parents pepper me with questions about how things have been going since we last spoke. I happily report that my entire backlog of clients that came over from the acquisition have now all been officially welcomed and their plans all approved and set into motion for the coming months.

Being able to tell them I've actually been taking time off work and sticking to a bi-weekly therapy schedule definitely helped ease some of their worries of running myself into the ground.

"Well, I sure am glad you're doin' better than you were this time last year. And I'm happier than a pig in shit that you're actually here," Dad says, resting his palm on my knee. "This old man has got to get some shut-eye though." He stands and kisses my forehead before turning and planting an excessively long kiss to my mom's lips. "It's so nice to have my two favorite girls here. Sleep tight, Sydney Mae."

"Night, Pops."

Pulling the blanket up around me, I let my eyes roam to the door once more. He still hasn't come home. Surely if he moved out, my parents would have told me, right?

What other explanation could there be for him not being home yet? It's nearly nine; he should have come inside hours ago.

"All right, spill."

"Spill what?"

"You've been starin' at the door all night long waitin' for a certain someone to come in."

"What? No I haven't."

She cocks her brow at me like she did to Dad earlier. "Don't bullshit me, Sydney Mae. Practically every time the wind blew outside, your eyes went straight to the door."

*Shit.* I didn't realize it had been that obvious.

"You didn't come home to see your father and I, did you?"

"Of course I did. Why would you think—"

She cuts me off by holding up her hand. "You told me y'all had a fling and that it didn't end well, so don't bother lyin' about that, missy. If you're here to make things right with him, you don't need to pretend like you're not *here* for him."

"Fine. I came back to clear the air. There's a lot we need to talk about, and I figured the best way to do it would be in person. But he hasn't come home yet and I'm starting to worry he moved out and you didn't tell me."

"He didn't move out."

"Then where is he?"

My mom takes her glasses off her face and folds them,

placing the tortoise shell frames on the coffee table. "He's out of town for a few days."

*Out of town?*

My heart sinks. He's not here. I came all this way to talk and he's not here. I feel the tears well in my eyes and do my best to keep them at bay.

Clearing my throat, I grab my empty bowl and stand from the armchair. "I, um… I'm gonna head up to bed. Thanks for dinner," I say, before heading into the kitchen.

I load the bowl into the dishwasher and make my way toward the stairs. About halfway up, my mom calls my name.

"You should know that he's been stayin' in your room for the last couple weeks."

Stopping dead in my tracks I turn around to look at her. "What do you mean?"

"I caught him in there one night and told him it'd be all right if he wanted to stay. He just misses you so much, sweetie."

My eyes water and this time I'm not strong enough to hold back the tears. A twin pair race down my cheeks as I nod at my mom. "I miss him too."

Before she can see me fully break down, I retreat up the stairs.

When I'm locked in my room, I let my tears fall freely.

I understand now why it felt different before. It's because he's been staying here. His things are scattered all over the room.

A flannel hung over the chair of my vanity.

A pair of boots tucked away by the closet.

A picture frame I don't recognize on the nightstand next to my bed.

My heart thumps in my chest as I walk over to it and pick it up, looking down at the picture behind the glass.

The breath is knocked from my lungs when I realize who it is.

"Macie," I whisper, bringing a hand to my mouth. He'd shown me a few photos of her last year, and I remember this one being one of them. I can tell it's one of his favorites. He even has a copy printed and stuck in his phone case.

Looking at her again now, it's no wonder she stole his heart. She's got him wrapped around her little finger. How anyone could take one look at her and not immediately fall in love is beyond me.

She's practically Chase's twin, just smaller and with the cutest little dimples. The pastel teal headscarf she's wearing perfectly compliments the olive complexion she got from Chase. I think she may just be the cutest kid I've ever seen.

I know I haven't seen him in a while, but Chase looks so different. His whole face is filled with love and pride and pure happiness.

I want to see him smile like that again.

Not because he looks damn sexy smiling, but because he deserves to *be* that happy again. He deserves to find that sense of joy he felt the day they took this picture.

Placing the frame back down on the nightstand I lick my lips, tasting the remnants of my salty tears.

*I wish she were still here.*

I wish Chase hadn't lost her.

Even if that means that I never got the chance to fall in love with him, I don't care.

I would give *anything* to bring her back for him.

Because, above all else, Chase deserves everything good this world has to offer, and I want to be there for the day that his smile shines as brightly as it does in this picture again.

I promised myself that I wouldn't get my hopes up when I came back here, but now that I'm lying in my bed and I'm surrounded by his intoxicating scent, I can't help it.

He misses me.

Chase Alexander Phillips misses *me*.

Knowing that is one of the best feelings in the world, because it means I still have a chance.

And this time, I'm not letting him slip away.

# 33

CHASE

Walking into the diner and finding Cara waiting at one of the tables, I know I fucked up. I should have taken yesterday and the beyond shitty encounter with my parents as a sign to just get my things and hightail it back to Slate Ridge. Nothing good could possibly come from me being here.

Especially not where Cara is concerned. She hasn't changed much since I last saw her. Same messy, dark auburn hair that teases the tops of her shoulders, and she's wearing the same signature matte garnet-red lipstick.

Macie was basically my twin, but seeing Cara, I can see the subtle things that the two of them shared. Like the soft slope of her Grecian nose and the dimple pitting her cheek.

She spots me and lifts her hand in a wave.

*Too late to back out now.*

I slide into the seat across from her and her face brightens.

"Thanks for coming," she says with a smile, but it only serves to piss me off.

After last night, I don't have it in me to pretend like I want to be here. My patience is shot, and my ability to cover that up is nonexistent.

"What's this about, Cara? Last time we spoke you pretended

you didn't know who I was, so pardon my confusion that now you suddenly do."

Her mouth pops open. "I-I wanted to apologize. I shouldn't have left you and our baby."

"Macie," I grit out. The least she could do is call my daughter by her name.

"Right. Macie." She blows out a shaky breath, nervously stirring the coffee in her cup. "I was wrong to leave you all alone to raise her. The last time we spoke, I wasn't myself. It was a really bad time in my life, and if I'm being honest, I don't even remember it. But I need you to know that I regret it all, Chase."

I hold back the desire to shake my head. "Why now?"

"I'm in a rehab program and started seeing a therapist. They encouraged me to reach out to you to clear the air and make amends."

"Well, I'm glad you're in a better place, but I can't forgive you for leaving. I was the same scared seventeen-year-old that you were, Cara, but I didn't run. Macie deserved better than that."

She nods, chewing her lip for a moment. "How is she?"

The question is like a knife to the gut. It's bad enough that she's gone. Now I have to break the news to her? For a split second, I think about lying, about telling her that Macie is thriving and living her best life, but I know that I can't. It probably makes me an asshole for not telling her sooner, but I don't regret it.

"She's gone, Cara." There's a knot in my chest that feels like it'll never loosen. "She passed away six years ago."

Her hand comes to her mouth. "What?"

"She was sick. It's why I called you that day. For her sake, I was goin' to give you a chance to be there for her and get to know her before she passed, but as soon as I started talkin', you made it clear that you wanted nothin' to do with her life, or mine. So when she passed, I didn't think you'd care."

Shaking her head, I watch as her face contorts with anger. "You should have told me. She was my daughter!"

"No!" I shout, standing from my chair. "She was *my* daughter," I say through clenched teeth as I stare daggers down at her. "*I'm* the one that raised her. *I'm* the one that took her to all the different doctors and hospitals. *I'm* the one that held her hand through each round of chemo. *I'm* the one that had to say goodbye to the best goddamn thing that's ever happened to me —*alone*. I did it all by my fuckin' self, Cara. So, no, you didn't deserve to know shit about *my* daughter!"

"Chase, I'm sor—"

"Save it," I cut her off and drop back into my chair, crossing my arms over my chest. "I don't need to hear how sorry you are. If you truly wanted to have a part of her life, you wouldn't have waited so long to come to me. Maybe if you had, you would've gotten a chance to meet the most amazin' little girl."

"She changed you so much," she says, looking at me like I'm a stranger. "You're nothing like the Chase I remember."

I huff a laugh. "I was a teenage boy that didn't have the slightest clue what I was doin'. Can't exactly say I miss the old me."

"Do you think she would've changed me too? If I hadn't left?"

"Knowin' her, absolutely. But I think she was better off not knowin' you."

Cara winces and I realize that that may have been a bit harsh, but it's what I believe. It would have killed me to see Macie be anything like her.

"I wish I hadn't been so selfish back then," she says and I stay silent, not knowing how to politely agree. "I know you said you didn't want my apologies, but I really am sorry I wasn't there for you and Macie."

"Thank you."

Clearing her throat, she takes a sip of her coffee. "So, how long are you staying?"

"I'm headin' out in the mornin'." I don't bother telling her that tomorrow would be the six-year anniversary of Macie being gone. She doesn't deserve to know anything more about my little girl.

"Are you staying in town?"

"The motel down the road. It's all I could afford."

Her eyebrows pinch. "What do you mean?"

"I have a lot of debt from hospital bills and chemo treatments."

"Oh." She chews her lip. "I don't have much, but I could help."

I shake my head. "I don't want your money, Cara. Like I said, she was my daughter."

"Chase…"

"I'll be okay. It's not the first time I've stayed in a motel, and I'm sure it won't be the last."

One shitty diner cheeseburger and an awkwardly one-sided conversation later, I'm walking Cara down the dark alley to her trailer. I wish I had it in me to be an asshole and leave her to walk alone, but my conscience wouldn't allow it.

By the time we get to her place, it's five, and the sun has fully set in the sky.

"Do you want to come in for a drink?"

"I thought you said you were sober?"

She shrugs. "Drinking was never my issue. But you're right, I don't drink anymore. Some of my friends do though, so I have a couple beers in the fridge for them."

I know I shouldn't, but after the last two days, I could use a drink. Especially knowing that by the time I get home tomorrow, I won't get much time to spend at the dock with Macie. I was hoping to be able to leave tonight, but I know it's not a good idea to drive these roads at night on the little to no sleep I got last night thanks to my mind racing.

Had Cara not changed our plans, I'd be halfway home by now, but something came up and she needed to reschedule.

"Sure. But just one."

She nods and pushes open the door, leading me inside. It's a decent size for a trailer, and the interior is nicely done. If I hadn't seen the outside, I wouldn't know it was a trailer since it looks so much like a traditional home.

The walls are painted a soft grey and the large couch is a robin's egg blue. There's a tufted grey chair in the corner under a lamp that I settle into while Cara grabs me a beer.

"Do you think you'll ever stop hating me?" Cara asks as she extends her arm and I take the beer.

"I don't hate you." I twist off the top and take a quick sip. "You have Macie to thank for that. She made me a better person. And as much as I don't like to admit it, I wouldn't've had her if it weren't for you."

"Oh…"

Shrugging, I lean back in the chair. "Sorry if that wasn't the answer you were lookin' for, but it's the truth."

"No, it's nice to know you don't hate me. Even if it's only because of a technicality."

---

Two hours later, one beer turned into four and my judgement went out the window. "I should go."

"Or you could stay."

*Stay?* How in the world is *this* how my night is ending?

Cara gets up from her chair and comes to stand in front of me. She rests her hands on my shoulders and steps between my spread thighs. "Stay with me. It's not like we haven't done it before."

"Cara…"

"I want you, Chase." Her voice has a different edge to it now. It's thick with desire and I feel my gut churn. "Say you want me too."

"I—"

As if she belongs there, she drops herself onto my lap and brings a hand to my hair. Her small fingers run through it, earning a groan. "C'mon, Phillips. Don't you wanna know what it'd be like to be with me again after all this time?"

Cara leans forward, grinding her hips against me as she presses her lips to the corner of my mouth.

For a split second, I want to let her do whatever she wants. I want to fall and fall until I don't recognize myself anymore because there's nothing left to live for.

I lost Macie. I lost Sydney. Nothing better is ever going to come along for me.

But then I remember who this is, and just how far I'd be falling.

"No."

"No?"

She doesn't extricate herself from my lap soon enough so I pick her up and plop her back down on her couch. I need my bubble again—she just invaded the shit out of it. "I didn't stutter."

"You're turning *me* down?"

"I am. You haven't changed at all. You don't care about me, you never did. You're just tryin' to use me for a good time like you did back then."

"You used me too, Chase," she spits. "Don't act like you were such a damn saint!"

"I never said I was. But at least I can say I'm happy with the person I turned out to be. I'm not goin' around throwin' myself at the first person that's nice to me."

Cara scoffs a laugh, rolling her eyes. "You really think you're gonna find someone better than me?"

"I already have, and she's everythin' you're not."

"Bullshit. She probably just feels sorry for you, Chase. How could she even think about loving you? Think about it, you've got nothin' to your name and a dead kid that you won't stop cryin' about."

My heart squeezes so tightly it feels like it might stop working altogether. "Fuck you." The words slip off my tongue and I don't have a single ounce of remorse about them.

She bites her lip and stands. "You already did. Multiple times. That's how the dea—"

"You're a heartless bitch, Cara. How the fuck do you live with yourself?"

"Pretty easily, actually."

Shaking my head, I run a hand down my face. Why the fuck did I do this to myself?

"I hope you find someone that changes your life for the better because knowing Macie came from someone filled with so much hate and ugliness makes me sick." I make my way to the door and only when I pull it open do I turn back around. "Have a nice life, Cara. And just in case it wasn't already crystal fuckin' clear, don't contact me ever again."

Slamming the door to her trailer behind me, I hop in my truck and race toward the motel. I can feel the bile rising up my throat. I knew coming to see her was a mistake. I should've known nothing good would come of it. And the worst part is knowing *that's* how she feels about Macie. I couldn't care less what she thinks about me, but to call her what she did and talk about her like that killed me.

I'm not sure what I ever saw in her. And to think I almost gave in again.

For a second, I wanted to. I was so close to throwing away all the progress I've made since Macie was brought into this world, but thankfully, I didn't. I would have hated myself even more than I already do.

The moment I step through the motel room doors, a wave of

nausea hits me. I race to the bathroom and make it just in time to empty the contents of my stomach into the toilet.

I *definitely shouldn't've driven.*

I rinse my mouth out with water, still tasting the bitter acid on my tongue, and I take a seat on the edge of the bed.

A replay of the last two days flickers through my mind and I know for a fact that I never should have come here. It only served to make things worse. Because now I've started to believe the shit Cara said.

Maybe she was right.

Sydney could *never* love me. She's successful and smart and has her life together. I'm over here drowning in debt and living in her parent's attic.

*Fucking pathetic.*

Tears fill my eyes and I try to choke them back, but it's useless. They spill down my cheeks, hot and heavy. How could she ever love me?

*How could anyone?*

# 34

## SYDNEY



Waking up surrounded by Chase's scent is a cruel joke. My eyes fly open and I half expect him to be lying there next to me, but he isn't. I wanted, more than anything, for him to have come home in the middle of the night and slid between the sheets beside me, but apparently that could only happen in my dreams.

Pulling myself out of bed, I quickly change into a pair of dark-wash jeans and a grey-and-white striped sweater before heading to the bathroom to brush my teeth and fix my hair.

By the time I make it downstairs, it's nearly seven. I grab a cup of coffee, making sure to use a spoonful of Mom's vanilla sugar, and head out to the barn.

As I approach the doors, I see my dad, who's locked in a game of tug-of-war over a navy blue scarf with the small brown-and-white calf I recognize from his email. "Need some help, Pops?" I ask, trying to hold back a full-on belly laugh at the sight.

"Ah, crap. I was hopin' no one would see me like this." He tugs on the scarf, but it doesn't budge from between her teeth. "Dang it, May, I thought you only tortured Chase?"

Torture Chase? Now that's a story I gotta hear.

I swear she moos back a retort and this time I can't hold in my laughter. It comes out as a snort and I quickly bring my hand up to cover my mouth.

"This is the best thing I've ever seen."

"Oh, hush, Sydney Mae. I'd like to see you try."

I raise my brow at the challenge. "All right, old man. Watch and learn."

He drops his end of the scarf and May swings it around happily.

Taking a couple steps closer, I hold my hand up at the tiny terror as I click my tongue. "Hey, girl," I say just above a whisper as I extend my arm, letting her sniff me. "May, right?"

She snorts, tilts her head to the side, and eyes me skeptically.

"I'm Sydney Mae. My dad sent me a picture of you when you were just born and I gotta say, I think you've only gotten cuter."

Her eyes twinkle and she flicks her ears.

I turn my palm over and run my fingers through her soft brown-and-white fur. "Such a pretty girl you are, May." I scratch behind her ear and she lets out a soft moo. "That feel good?"

She moos again, louder this time, and I smile at her.

"Are they not feeding you enough around here that you need to eat scarves?"

This time she doesn't reply, just tilts her head again like a confused puppy.

"How about I give you a treat and you give me the scarf, huh?"

I reach for the shelf behind me, grabbing a small apple.

"Hm, does that sound like a deal?" I ask, holding the apple in front of her. She gives it a sniff and I can see the excitement in her eyes. I might be going crazy, but I think she actually nods before dropping the scarf and patiently waiting for me to feed her the apple.

Once I hold it out for her, she happily chomps on it and walks away, swishing her tail back and forth.

Grabbing the scarf off the floor, I hand it to my dad with a victorious smile on my face.

"You always had a weird ability to get animals to do what you want."

"What can I say? It's a gift."

He chuckles, tossing the now cow-slobber-covered scarf over the edge of the fence to bring home for a wash. "Yeah, yeah. Now, what are you doin' out here?"

"I figured since Chase was gone, I'd lend a hand."

Dad shakes his head, resting a hand on my shoulder. "I don't think so. You go inside and spend some time with your mother. I can handle the barn. And I'm not takin' no for an answer, young lady."

I roll my eyes. "Fine. But if she steals your scarf again, don't come cryin' to me."

It hits me when I see the calendar hanging in the kitchen that today is the six-year anniversary of Macie's passing, and that Chase isn't here to spend it with her.

Something about that doesn't sit well with me. She shouldn't be alone today.

Without a second thought, I grab a thermos from the cupboard and fill it with coffee and a couple spoonfuls of vanilla sugar to keep myself warm, and head for the door. I slip on a pair of boots and the heavy winter coat I left on the hook last night when I got in and am about to leave when my mom comes down the stairs.

"Where are you headed all bundled up like that?"

"The dock," I say as I see a knit hat on the bench and snag it. "Can I borrow this?" I ask, holding up the hat.

"Yes." She crosses her arms over her chest. "Why are you going to the dock?"

Licking my lips, I contemplate lying for a minute but decide against it. She already knows that Chase is the reason I'm here, so there's no point. "It's the anniversary of Macie's passing, and Chase isn't here to spend it with her."

"That's awfully sweet of you."

"It's the least I could do after all he's done for me." She flashes me a watery smile. "I should get going. I don't want her to think no one is coming."

"Wait, Sydney Mae." Reaching behind her, she grabs the keys for the new car I bought them as an anniversary present three months ago and hands them to me. "Take the car. The weather is supposed to get bad later and I don't want you walking."

I smile and take the keys. "Thanks."

---

Six hours later, I'm chilled to the bone, but my heart is fuller than it's been in years.

"I hope you don't mind me being here with you for so long," I say, looking up at the slowly darkening sky. "I admit I may have had an ulterior motive for coming here today. I wasn't lying when I said I didn't want you to be alone because your dad was out of town, but it's just that I know he would never miss coming to see you today. Even if it meant he wasn't here until the sun went down."

I chew my lip, feeling guilty for using Macie.

"I know I have no right to ask, but if you could send him a sign or something to let him know that I need to talk to him, I would really appreciate it."

A harsh gust of wind sends a chill down my spine. Hopefully that wasn't her being pissed at me for completely overstepping and then asking her to do me a solid. *Shit.* Am I really that asshole?

The poor girl is probably wishing I had left hours ago. I blabbed to her the entire time. She knows more about me than Dr. Camden does.

A car door slams in the distance and a weird feeling settles in my stomach.

*Please don't let that be a serial killer or something.*

I clear my throat and stuff my hands in my pockets as it starts to snow. "Well, I guess that's a sign, huh? Are you telling me to give up and go home?"

Dammit, I wish she could answer me.

*If I feel this way, I can only imagine how Chase feels.*

"I should get going. It was really nice talking to you today, Macie. I hope you feel the same. I'll come back to visit again before I head back to New York."

I turn around and my chest tightens uncomfortably. "Chase."

His lips part, and he looks at me like he thought I was just a figment of his imagination. "I didn't know you were home."

"I got in last night."

"And you came here?" He rubs at the back of his neck.

"I know what today is, a-and my mom said you were out of town, so I came to keep Macie company since you weren't here."

"You came so she wasn't alone?" There's a confusing combination of hatred and appreciation on his face.

I nod. "I'm sorry if I overstepped, I just—"

Before I can finish, he closes the gap between us, grabs my cheeks and kisses me.

My heart pounds in my chest as the world around us fades away.

All I can think about, all I can care about, is his lips on mine. It feels like heaven. Like coming home. Like everything I've been dreaming about for months on end. The breath I had been holding for five months finally escapes me on a cry.

I thought I'd lost my chance at being with him. I was fully prepared to live my life with only half a heart, but he's kissing me.

Chase is *kissing* me.

And every part of me that has been broken since that day starts to stitch itself back together. In this moment, with his mouth on mine, everything feels right in the world. Now that I have him back, I never want to let him go again.

"Thank you," he whispers against my lips before pulling back. "Thank you for being here with her when I couldn't be."

With wide eyes, I bring my fingers to my tingling lips, too stunned to speak, and nod.

Chase's demeanor changes before my eyes. His shoulders straighten and the softness that had settled on his face after our kiss fades away. I watch as his jaw clenches and he takes a step back, letting his hands fall from my cheeks.

Just by the look on his face, I can tell that he's about to break my heart all over again.

And I hate that I'm right, because before long, one of the happiest moments of my life, quickly turns into one of the worst.

In a handful of words, Chase tore apart everything we had built and I couldn't do anything other than stand there and watch it crumble.

---

I somehow manage to make it safely back to the house, despite the blur of tears clouding my vision. Slipping inside, I climb the stairs and race to my room, thankfully undetected by my parents.

My back collides with my bedroom door and I slide down the wall with a hand over my mouth as a heartbreakingly silent sob rips through me.

*Why is the pain so much worse the second time around? I never could have imagined what it'd be like to lose him twice.*

My heart feels like it was put through a blender and then battered and fried in too-hot oil—burning it so it'll never beat properly again.

Everything hurts.

I shouldn't have come back here.

Pulling my phone out of my jacket pocket, my shaky fingers dial Vikram.

He answers on the second ring.

"I need you."

# 35



Silence settles over the dock as Sydney's words replay in my head.

With tears in her eyes and a visible hole in her heart, she stared back at me like I was a stranger. *"I don't know what I did, but whatever it is, I'm sorry."*

I wish I could've told her that *she's* not the problem.

*I'm* the one who's not good enough.

*I'm* the one who can't give her the life she deserves.

*I'm* the one who doesn't have the slightest idea of how to be better for her.

So I had to let her go. I needed to free her from being shackled to someone so utterly useless and disappointing. If Sydney didn't hate me before, I'm sure she does now. Deep down I know it was the right thing to do, but *fuck* does it hurt like hell—more than it did the first time around. Maybe that's because now I know just how miserable life is without her.

Or maybe it's because I couldn't help myself from getting a taste of her again. I regret giving her the false hope I did, but I needed to know what it felt like to kiss her again. If I never get to do it again, at least I have this to remember her by.

What happened after was a disaster, but that kiss was damn

near perfect. And thank god it was, because I don't plan to kiss anyone else in this lifetime, or any other.

The cold wind whips against my cheeks and I shiver, being brought back to reality.

"I'm sorry you had to hear all that, Macie Moo. And I'm sorry for not bein' here with you today. I hope you can find it in that big heart of yours to forgive me." I sigh, tilting my head up to the starry night sky. "You're my little girl, and that's the one thing no one can ever take away from me." My eyes water and I quickly shake my head to banish them, but it's useless. After the few days I've had, nothing could stop the tears from brimming in my eyes. "Daddy loves you so damn much, baby girl. Don't you ever forget that."

I watch as Logan covers his couch with a sheet and drapes a blanket over the top before putting a pillow on the arm. "Thanks again for letting me stay."

"Anytime. Everything okay at the Wilson's?"

"Yeah, I just... I needed to get out of the house—needed some distance."

His brows pull together and his baby blue eyes look me over. "Did something happen?"

"Sydney Mae is here, and I think it'll be best for all of us if I stay away until she goes back to New York."

"What about work? Are you just gonna leave it all to Bill?"

I shake my head, pinching the bridge of my nose. "No, I can't. I'll still go, but I'll have to keep to myself and avoid going to the house for anything."

"Are you sure that's what you want?"

A sarcastic laugh bubbles out of me. *Not even close.*

I want to be near her. To take back everything I said earlier and talk to her for hours—get to know her even more than I already do. But I know that I can't.

That I *shouldn't*.

"No, it's not what I want, but it's what's best for her."

"According to who?" he challenges, with his arms crossed over his chest.

"Me."

Logan shakes his head and I watch as he pokes the inside of his cheek with the tip of his tongue. "You're lying to yourself if you think *not* being with her is what's best for her."

"You don't understand."

"Then explain it to me." He sits down on the arm of the couch without the pillow. "Please."

I blow out a breath and lean against the large table under the window across from the couch. "I can't."

"Because you know it's a load of horse shit!" I've never heard Logan raise his voice before. If I'm being honest, I didn't think he had it in him. "I've known her since I was in kindergarten, and if there's one person on this entire planet who deserves a girl like her, it's you."

"You're wrong. I'm not good enough."

"The only person who thinks you're not good enough is you, Chase. Sydney wouldn't've wasted her time on you if she didn't think you were worth it."

Licking my lips, I tuck the bottom one between my teeth to quell the urge to cry. *I'm tired of fucking crying.*

When I don't respond, Logan stands and walks over to me, putting his hand on my shoulder. "You're welcome to stay for as long as you want, but I won't stop reminding you what an idiot you are."

# 36

## SYDNEY

Vik's strong arms wrap around me as I'm curled into a ball on my bedroom floor. I don't even know what time it is, just that he used the key I told him was under the mat and snuck inside.

"Please don't cry, Syd. It's going to be okay. I promise."

"You didn't hear him, Vik. He—" I get choked up by another sob as I try to tell him.

"Shh." He soothes a hand over my back. "Take a couple deep breaths for me."

I do as he tells me, stuttering through the first few before finally getting my breathing back to normal.

"Okay, now, tell me what happened, but take it slow."

"I went to the dock to spend the day with Macie since Chase was still out of town. I stayed there most of the day and was just about to leave when I turned around and saw him standing there. We talked for a minute and then he rushed up and kissed me out of nowhere." I feel my chest tighten. "It was amazing. Everything about it was perfect, and then it just wasn't…"

*"I-I shouldn't have kissed you. I'm an idiot. I'm sorry," he rushes to say as he takes another step away from me. "I was caught up in the moment and couldn't help myself."*

*"You're not an idiot. I want—" I start, but he cuts me off.*

*"I'll stay with one of the guys until you go back to New York."*

*I reach out and touch his arm. "What? No." My head shakes side to side. "I want to talk about this—about us..."*

*"There can't be an us, Sydney. You deserve someone world's better than me. Someone who has their life together and can support you instead of bein' a burden. Someone who can take you to fancy restaurants and buy you nice things. And as much as I want to be that person, I can't. It's just not in the cards life dealt me.*

*"I don't give a shit about any of that. I don't want anyone else, Chase, I want you."*

*He licks his lips as he shakes his head. "You don't want me, you just feel sorry for me, and I don't need your pity."*

*It feels like he's using my heart like a punching bag. "You think I pity you? Chase, I envy how strong you are."*

*"I'm not strong, just good at pretendin'."*

*Angry tears well in my eyes. "You're wrong."*

*"You should go." His voice is cold and the look in his eyes is one I haven't seen before.*

*"Chase..."*

*"Go!"*

I shudder at the memory.

"It was like he was a different person after that kiss," I explain. "Something about him was just so jaded and negative. It was a side of him I'd never seen before. All he kept talking about was how he wasn't good enough, and that I deserved someone better. But I don't want someone better. I want him. I need him. He's perfectly imperfect and that's exactly why I love him."

Vik squeezes my hand. "Give him a couple days. You said it yourself—it's a hard day for him. His head probably isn't in the right place right now."

"You didn't see the look in his eyes, Vik. When he told me to leave it was like he never wanted to see me again."

"Just give him time, Sydney."

"I feel like I'm running out of it."

"You're not. It's gonna be fine."

I sniffle and rest my cheek on his shoulder. "Thank you for coming. I don't think I could do this without you."

"I'm not going anywhere. I'll be here whether things work out with Chase or not. I told you you're not losing me, and I meant that." He kisses the top of my head and I blow out a sigh. "Why don't you try to get some sleep? We can talk more in the morning."

"Okay."

Vik stands first and extends a hand for me to pull myself up. "Thank god you said yes. My ass was starting to go numb from sitting on the floor."

I chuckle and tap him on the stomach with the back of my hand. "Shut up."

"My work here is officially done. I got you to smile."

This time a genuine smile crosses my face. "Thank you for everything, Vikram."

After rolling out of bed and slipping into our clothes for the day —me in a pair of medium-wash jeans and an oversized tan sweater, and Vik a pair of dark-wash jeans and a dark-blue button down—we walk into the kitchen side by side.

My mom stops what she's doing to look Vikram over before flicking her gaze back to me. "And who might this handsome fella be?"

"This is Vikram. He flew in last night."

"Pleasure to meet you, Vikram." She reaches her hand out and Vik shakes it. "I've heard so much about you. It's nice to finally put a face to the name."

"You as well, Mrs. Wilson. You have a lovely home."

My mom smiles, a little spark of pride twinkling in her eye. "Well, it ain't a mansion, but we love it here."

"I've offered to do some renovations over the years, but the only thing they let me fix up was the kitchen," I say, crossing my arms over my chest.

"That's because the one time her father decided to cook he not only burnt dinner, but half the kitchen as well."

Vikram snickers as he looks over at me. "Apple doesn't fall far from the tree, huh?"

"Shut up." I glare at him.

"What'd she burn?"

"I couldn't even tell you what it was supposed to be," Vik says with a grin as he tries to hold back a laugh.

"I was trying to make you Indian food! Technically it was all your fault." I poke him in the chest. "You were having a bad week and I wanted to cheer you up, and nothing does that quite like vada pav."

"Oh, hush. Don't blame him for your shortcomings in the kitchen."

Vik crosses his arms and smirks, clearly smug that my mom took his side. "Yeah, what she said."

I groan. "You two are never allowed to be in the same room again."

"You know you love us," he says, kissing my cheek.

"Yeah, yeah. Whatever you say, traitor."

Mom clears her throat and I feel my cheeks flush slightly. "Sydney Mae, do you mind if I have a word?"

"Sure." I turn to Vik. "I'll be right back."

"Take your time. I have a couple calls to make anyway."

She ushers me through the kitchen and to the den on the far side of the house, sitting down on the small sofa under the window. "What's goin' on, Sydney? You locked yourself in your room when you got back last night, and now your boyfriend is here. Did somethin' happen?"

I chew my lip. "I saw Chase."

"Wasn't the whole point of you comin' here to see him?"

"Yes, but he wasn't himself." I shake my head. "He made it seem like he wanted nothing to do with me."

"And Vikram flew all the way out here to help you with Chase?"

Nodding, I take the seat next to her. "Vik knows everything. And technically we're not together right now."

"Are you sure he knows that? That boy seems awfully smitten."

"It was his idea. He wanted to take a break and told me to follow my heart with Chase."

"Just make sure you don't hurt him. He seems like a very nice man."

"I know he is, and I won't."

"Good. He might be okay with letting you go back to Chase, but I can tell he loves you."

My lips flatten. "And I love him, but it's a different kind of love, Ma."

There's a beat of silence between us, but Mom makes no move to leave. So I take the opportunity to ask, "Do you know who Chase went to see?"

"I do, but I told him I wouldn't say anythin'."

He's got secrets with my mom now?

Then again, I guess he always kinda did. *He knew about the vanilla sugar before I did.*

"Mom, please."

"I'm sorry, honey, but I can't. Just know that nothin' about the last couple days could've been easy on him. If he's acting off, it's likely because of his trip."

"W-what do you mean by that?"

She rests a hand on my knee, giving it a light squeeze. "You're a smart girl, Sydney Mae, you'll figure it out." She pushes up to stand and takes a step toward the door before turning back around. "You should get back to Vikram. And I'm sure whatever happened with Chase will blow over, you just have to give him a little time."

*Why the hell does everyone keep saying that?*

"Yeah, time... Heard that before."

"He's got a lot goin' on right now, sweetheart. Be patient with him."

"Right," I say dejectedly before my mom leaves me alone with my thoughts.

Where could he have gone?

I try my best to ignore the nagging in my gut that's saying to go find him outside, and head back to the kitchen.

"Why the long face?" Vik asks over the lip of his coffee mug as he takes a sip.

"I guess I didn't expect it to be this hard. I knew it wasn't going to be easy, but this limbo fucking sucks. It feels like coming here has just made things worse."

He places his mug down and leans a hip against the counter. "It might feel that way, but I promise, it's going to get better. Coming here will be worth it, you just have to keep your head up, okay?"

I nod and take a step toward him, resting my head on his chest.

"So, what did your mom say about me?"

"She likes you."

"What's not to like?"

Chuckling, I wrap my arms around his waist and tip my head back. "Almost nothing."

"Almost?" He gasps in mock offense. "What's my tragic flaw?"

"Two words. Dirty. Dishes."

He rolls his eyes. "Oh, come on! I've gotten so much better!"

I smile up at him. "You have. Was it all the serial killer documentaries I watched that made you change your ways?"

"That *may* have been a factor, yes."

We share a laugh.

"You're cute." My phone buzzes in my back pocket and I pull it out, seeing Katie's name on the screen. I told her to only call if there were any emergencies, so this must be important. "It's Katie, I should take this."

"Go ahead. I'm gonna make a fresh pot of coffee and then roam around for a bit."

My ears perk up at that. "Give me twenty and I'll join you?"

"Sounds good."

# 37

CHASE

Bill and I stand side by side as we wash off our hands in the barn's slop sink. We spent the day elbow deep in the tractor, even though neither of us know the first thing about how to fix one.

"Can I ask you somethin'?"

"Shoot."

"How'd you know Mrs. Wilson was the one?"

He turns to me with a giddy look on his face. "It was just a gut feelin'. Can't really describe it. Like how when I see her she takes my breath away and makes me feel like I can breathe all at the same time."

"When did you realize you loved her?"

"First time I saw her smile." His lips spread in a big dopey grin and he shakes his head. "She always had this mean scowl on her face, the kind that can make a grown man cry, and the first time that I saw her smile I knew I'd do anything to only see a smile on her face for the rest of my life. Now that I think about it, Sydney Mae has that same scowl."

My chest tightens. "Yeah, she does."

"What's with the sudden interest in love? There a special someone you haven't told me about?"

I nervously scratch at the back of my neck. "J-just curious."

"Well, I ain't Mr. Romance or nothin', but if you ever need advice, I'm here."

"Thanks."

He dries his hands off on the clean white towel hung beside the sink. "I gotta run into town for a couple things, you mind goin' up to the house and tellin' Susan?"

*Shit.* I can't go to the house. I know she's gonna be there and I can't do that today.

"I could go to town for you," I suggest, hoping like all hell he says yes.

"Nonsense." He waves me off. "You don't need to be runnin' my errands. Plus, I gotta stop by a buddy's house on the way home to help him with a mare."

"Oh. Okay."

"Thanks, son." Bill claps me on the shoulder. "Tell Sydney Mae to come down and help ya while she's here while you're at it."

*Double shit.* Going to the house is bad enough. Seeking out Sydney to deliver a message from her dad is absolutely not happening.

"I don't need any help. And even if I did, she's on vacation. It wouldn't be fair to make her work on vacation."

"All right, suit yourself." He starts walking away and throws a hand above his head and waves. "Thanks again, Chase."

I blow out a slow breath and let my eyes drift closed.

*Please don't be at the house, Sydney Mae.*

The thought of seeing her makes my stomach churn. Everything about it makes me want to run a million miles in the other direction.

I know she hates me. I know she'll never want to talk to me again after what I did.

And the worst part is that my feelings for her haven't changed one bit. I love her with every ounce of my soul. Sydney Mae is the only one for me. Knowing I fucked that up is going to go down in the history books as my greatest mistake of all time.

---

Taking a deep breath, I push open the door, stepping inside the house, and I'm immediately met with the sound of someone talking on the phone. I don't recognize the voice at all.

"I know it's the holidays, but you practically do my job for me on a daily basis. I'll be back in a couple days, a week at most."

Stepping into the kitchen, I make eye contact with the owner of the voice.

It's a man about my height with wheatish-colored skin and dark brown eyes. His nearly black hair that's trimmed short on the sides and longer on the top is neatly styled. He's dressed in a pair of jeans and a blue button-down, the scent of expensive cologne lingering in the air.

"Look, I gotta go," he says into the phone. "I'm just a call away if you need anything, Sam. Talk soon."

He hangs up the call, stuffing his phone back in his pocket. "Sorry about that."

"N-no, I'm sorry. I was just, uh, looking for Mrs. Wilson. She here?"

"You must be Chase. Sydney has told me a lot about you."

My brows furrow and an unsettling feeling churns in my gut. "You're a friend of Sydney Mae?"

"Yeah." He smiles a bright white smile with perfectly straight teeth and extends his hand out to me. "Vikram Anand, nice to meet you."

I shake his hand and nod. "You too. Uh, if you don't mind me askin', what're you doin' here?"

"Syd needed my help with something."

What could she possibly need help with?

"So you flew all the way out here?"

He nods, crossing his arms over his chest. "I'd do anything for her."

My heart feels like it just shit itself. I can see in his eyes how much he cares about her. "You must really love her." The words taste sour on my tongue. Thinking about someone else loving her the way I do makes me sick.

"I do."

A wave of emotion crashes down on me and it feels like I'll combust at any moment. I need to get the hell out of here. I can't be here. Can't look at the man that Sydney is so obviously dating.

I clench my jaw so tightly I think my teeth will crack. "Make sure you treat her right. She deserves happiness, and someone like you can give it to her."

"Only one problem."

"What?"

"She could never be *truly* happy with me."

I shake my head, confused by what he's saying. "I don't know what you mean."

"Vik!" Sydney screeches as her footsteps pound toward the kitchen. "Holyfuckingshit, Vikram! You'll never guess what—" She stops dead in her tracks when she sees me standing in front of her. "Chase," she says breathlessly.

"Sydney Mae…"

"H-hi."

An awkward silence takes over the room until Vikram clears his throat. "Uh, what were you so excited about?"

Her eyes leave mine and find Vikram. A slow smile spreads across her lips. She reaches into her pocket and pulls out her phone, tapping it a couple times before handing it over him.

"No fucking way." His eyes flash to hers, a look of wonder and pride shining in them. He drops the phone on the counter and wraps his arms around her, lifting her in the air. "You fucking did it! You got on the thirty-under-thirty list!"

Sydney giggles, her cheeks turning pink. "I made it on thirty-under-thirty!"

I've never felt more like an outsider than I do right now. Seeing her so happy and wrapped up in someone else's arms is like a knife to the heart. But for the life of me, I can't look away.

"I'm so damn proud of you, Syd," he says before placing her back on her feet and dropping a kiss to her hair.

It hurts enough that I need to look away for a minute to regain my composure. Knowing she has a boyfriend and seeing her with him are two different things. I don't care to know or see anything having to do with her relationship.

And that's when it hits me.

I kissed her last night.

I kissed her without knowing if she was mine to kiss or not.

God dammit, I'm such an idiot.

Vikram pulls away from their hug and grabs her shoulder. "You two have a lot to talk about." She nods subtly. "I'll give you two some privacy."

"Thank you, Vik."

"Of course."

"Wait," I say, catching him by the elbow. Something about this isn't adding up. "If you love her, why are you just wakin' away?"

The corner of his mouth tips up in a smirk. "She was never really mine in the first place."

He pulls out of my loose grip and makes his way through the house, leaving Sydney and I alone.

Turning back to her, I look her over, noting her sheepish posture and the way she's nervously chewing her lip. "You have a boyfriend."

"It's complicated." When I don't say anything she elaborates. "We're not together right now. We're... on a break."

"What does that even mean?"

"He wanted me to follow my heart, so I did." She blows out a shaky breath and finally looks me in the eye. "It led me here. I came for you, Chase."

I lick my lips, tucking the bottom one between my teeth and look away from her. "You're wastin' your time. I told you yesterday, I'm not worth it."

She shakes her head and takes a step toward me. "Can you just hear what I have to say? If you still feel the same after, then I won't bother you anymore."

"Fine."

Sydney takes a step closer to me. "I asked Vik to come here because I couldn't process what happened yesterday alone. I needed him to help me make sense of it." Her eyes turn glassy. "When you told me to leave it felt like my heart was breaking all over again."

My heart thuds in my chest and my eyes flick to hers. "Again?"

"*I don't want to lose you either, but this hurts too much.*" She repeats my text message back to me like it haunts her. Tears well in her eyes and are seconds away from spilling over. "That pain you saved yourself from by saying goodbye?" Her head shakes and the first tear falls. "That was hell for me, Chase. It took me *months* to be even a little okay. I couldn't eat, couldn't sleep, couldn't even make it through more than a couple hours without crying. I hated myself for not treating you like you were the most important person in my life, because you were. You *still* are. And hearing you say that you're not good enough, or not deserving enough, is bullshit. Whoever got that in your head is an asshole. I don't want someone who can give me material things, dammit, I want you!"

Guilt slams into my chest. "Why can't you just forget about me? You'll be better off."

"Because I love you!" she shouts and everything around us stops.

It's like the entire world fades away until it's just the two of us floating around beside each other. She loves me? I couldn't have heard her right. There's no way she could love me. I don't even come close to deserving her. "What?"

"I love you, Chase." She wipes at her tears and takes the final step to close the distance between us. Her hand comes to my chest and I instantly feel warmth spread through me. Feel every ounce of the love she has for me. "I wanted to tell you so many times."

"Sydney—" I try to cut her off, but she keeps going.

"I even typed it out the night you said goodbye, but I didn't think it would matter. I was too late."

Too late? How could she think it was too late? Couldn't she tell how much I loved her? I may not have said it out of fear of scaring her away, but I did.

With every broken and bruised piece of my heart, I loved her.

I never fucking stopped.

"You had already given up on me—on us, and I—"

I grab her cheeks and press my lips to hers, feeling a huge weight lift off my shoulders. It might take me some time to truly believe that I deserve her, but I'm not going to let what my ex said stop me from being with her. Not anymore.

Sydney is *mine*. From the moment I met her, she was *mine*. And I'm a goddamn idiot for letting her slip even an inch away from me.

"I never gave up on you," I whisper into the kiss. "Not for a single fucking second, Sydney Mae."

My tongue slips over the crease of her lips and she lets me in, her tongue tangling with mine. She tastes so goddamn sweet. Now that I have her, I never want to stop kissing her, but I have something I need to tell her. Something she deserves to hear.

Pulling away from our kiss, I look down at her, seeing those brilliant dark brown eyes staring back up at me with so much love and adoration. "I love you, Sydney Mae."

"You do?"

"Of course I fuckin' do, baby." I tuck a lock of hair behind her ear and stroke the pinkened apple of her cheek with my thumb. "It's impossible not to fall in love with you."

Her smile is blinding before she seals her lips over mine again.

Yesterday's kiss was good, but this one is *everything*.

It's the best kiss I've ever had because I know that this time, I won't let her go. No matter what, Sydney and I are in it for the long haul. I don't care if that means I only get to see her once a year, I need her in my life, no matter what that looks like.

# 38



My fingers toy with the buttons of Chase's partially-buttoned green flannel, letting my heart settle back into a normal rhythm as I stare up at him.

His cheeks are flushed, and his lips swollen, a look of pure joy clear on his face.

*He loves me.*

After all this time, and all the uncertainty yesterday at the dock, I finally know what he really feels for me.

I never imagined being the one to say I love you first, but if it's what snapped him out of his pity party and earned me a spot at his side for the rest of forever, I'll take it.

The way he was talking still isn't sitting right with me though. "Chase, what was all that stuff you said about not being worthy?"

His jaw clenches. "I let my ex get in my head. I never should've listened to her, but I was in such a shitty place that it was impossible not to believe every word she said."

My heart sinks. "You went to see your ex?"

"Yeah." He shakes his head in disbelief. "Saw my parents too."

"What? Chase, are you okay?"

Nodding he cups my cheeks and presses a kiss to my forehead. "I'm fine, I promise. It was a coincidence I saw them. And I can honestly say that I don't think I'll ever see them again."

"That bad?"

"I probably should've taken it as a sign to turn my ass around and come back home, but I guess I wanted to punish myself."

"Why did you go in the first place?"

He sighs, resting his hands on my hips. "Cara, my ex, wanted to give me some half-assed apology for leavin' me alone to take care of Macie. It was one of the worst days of my life." He takes a deep breath, blowing it out with a sigh. "When Macie first got sick I had called to let her know, and to see if she wanted to know Macie in any capacity, but she blew me off. She didn't care that our daughter was sick, or that she wasn't long for this world." There's a moment of hesitation. A moment where his brows pinch and I could see a hint of regret. "When Macie passed, I... I never told her. I honestly didn't think she would care. So, I had to break the news to her. Things went downhill pretty fast after I walked her home."

"Are you okay?"

"She yelled and screamed at me and said some really awful things. We got into a fight that I never want to relive. It's hard not to think she's right, at least about some of it."

My heart aches for him. "I don't know what she said, but I can tell you that she's wrong, Chase." I bring my hand up his chest, letting my palm rest over his heart. "I wouldn't have been begging you for a second chance if I didn't think you were worth it."

I can see him trying to make sense of the words, but not fully believing them. There's something that's still holding him back. "Will you feel the same in a year or two when what's standing in front of you is all I'll ever be able to give you?"

"I will never change my mind about you, Chase. *You* are all I need."

He pauses, jaw ticking as he looks down at me. "What about seein' each other? Is it goin' to be any different than the last time?"

"I don't know exactly yet, but I promise we can figure it out together. I'll fly back here every damn weekend if I have to."

Resting his forehead against mine he brings his hands back to my cheeks. "Are you sure about this, Sydney Mae? Sure about *me*?"

I can't help but smile, giggling softly. "I have never been more sure of anything in my life."

"You'll never be able to get rid of me. I'm not letting you off so easily this time."

"Good. I want you in my life forever, Chase Alexander."

"Did you just use my middle name?"

"Not so fun now, is it?"

He pushes his hips forward, pinning me to the counter behind me. There's an obvious bulge in the front of his jeans. "Hate to break it to you, but I liked it," he says with a smirk.

I haven't gotten nearly enough opportunities to fully explore all of Chase in that way, and *man* do I want to.

Therapy has been doing wonders. I was never afraid of men, I was afraid of *one* man. And now that I've seen that man cower before my eyes, he's not so scary.

Between self-defense classes every Saturday morning, and therapy every other week, I'm a completely different person than the one Chase met last year.

I'm stronger now. Him breaking me is what I needed to heal those last pieces of myself that had been left broken since Jack.

And now that I have him, I'm starting to feel whole again.

Chase stops himself from going too far, pulling his hips back, but in the same moment he leans forward, feathering his lips over mine in a near kiss. "We still have a lot to talk about," he says as his lips brush against mine.

"We do."

"But I don't feel much like talkin' right now."

"Why's that?" I ask, flicking my tongue out to wet my lips and inadvertently licking his too.

A groan rolls out of him. "Because I don't think I can wait any longer to kiss you again." He nuzzles my nose with his own. "I've been dreamin' about it for months."

"Then stop dreaming and do, cowboy."

This time, he doesn't hold back. His lips meet mine in a searing kiss.

It's the kind that makes your toes curl and your stomach do somersaults. His tongue seeks entrance and I happily part my lips for him, letting it slide against mine.

My hands roam his chest and stomach, noticing the much firmer muscles there now. He must have been working out for the last couple months. He was fit and muscular before, but now I can feel the deep definition between each one of his abs.

I can't wait to *really* get my hands on him.

# 39



When we tucked ourselves under the covers last night, I didn't want to close my eyes, just in case it was a dream. I fought sleep for so long, choosing to stare at Sydney Mae instead, but it finally dragged me under after about two hours.

Thankfully, when I woke up this morning, she was still tucked into my side with her head resting on my chest. It's the best damn feeling in the world to have her this close and know she's mine.

There isn't a single doubt about it anymore. Sydney *is* mine. Always will be.

I make a mental note to thank Vikram for taking care of her while I was too busy feeling sorry for myself to do it. I'm still not sure how he's so understanding. I know if I were him, there's no way I would let a girl like Sydney go back to someone like me. I would've kept her for myself.

And he very easily could, but even after only one conversation, I know he won't. He's a damn good man, and I'm incredibly grateful that he's not only prioritizing Sydney's happiness, but accepting that, in her eyes, *he* doesn't hold a candle to *me*.

Sparing a glance at the clock on the nightstand, I know I have to get up before I'm late, but for the life of me, I can't pull myself away from her. I would much rather spend the day cuddled up with her instead.

Taking one last long look at my beautiful girl with her long, dark lashes and a subtle smile on her lips, I slip out of bed, easing her onto a pillow.

After changing into my Wranglers, I search the floor of the bedroom for my shirt from yesterday, only to realize it's draped on Sydney's small frame. A satisfied smirk tips my lips. I'm definitely a fan of her in my clothes.

Leaning down, I press a featherlight kiss to her forehead.

Sydney stirs, slowly cracking open her eyes and reaching for me. "Morning, handsome."

"Good morning, gorgeous. How'd you sleep?"

"Better than I have in a long time."

I smile, squeezing her hand. "Me too. I know it's early, but do you have any plans for the day?"

She giggles and reaches for my belt buckle. There's a sultry look on her face that I remember from that day in the barn before she left. "Considering the only plan I had for coming home was winning you back and making things right, I can't say that I do."

"Well, I gotta take care of a couple things this mornin', but I want to take you out." I clear my throat, suddenly feeling awkward. "I-I know it's not much, but do you think I could take you out to the diner for lunch?"

She blushes, biting down on her lip as she nods. "I'd love that."

"Good. Then it's a date." I press a sweet kiss to her lips, momentarily getting caught up in the kiss before heading out the door and up to the attic to grab a clean shirt.

---

After about an hour of going through my morning routine at the barn, Bill drops by to see if I'm ready to give fixing the tractor another try.

"I asked Herman Harper if he knew anything about it and he said something about a hydraulic filter, so he gave me an extra his son had him order a while back. He says it's an easy fix, and if *that* doesn't work it's probably the gas filter."

"Is that also an easy fix?" I ask, pushing May's head away as she nips at the towel hanging from my belt loop.

Bill gives me a face while rocking the top of his head side to side. "Well, it would be if he had an extra gas filter on hand. Since it's an older tractor, it's hard to track down the parts these days. He said if it doesn't work, it may be best to just splurge on a new tractor."

"That wouldn't be a horrible idea. It was a rougher ride than usual this season. Might be better for peace of mind, knowin' it won't break down on us again."

His hands find his hips as he nods. "Yeah. But let's hope for the best, huh?"

"Of course." I chuckle, giving May another gentle shove. "Should we head out then?"

"There's actually somethin' I wanted to talk to you about first."

"What is it?"

Bill crosses his arms, looking more stern than I've ever seen him. "I want to know your intentions with my daughter."

I choke on my spit, coughing and taking a huge breath before looking back at him. "Pardon?"

"I know you two have somethin' goin' on, and Sydney Mae doesn't let just anyone into her heart, so you must be special to her. I just wanna know what your intentions are. Is it just a bit of fun while she's in town, or is it more than that?"

Shaking my head, I run my fingers through my hair and then sweep a hand over my mouth. How the hell am I supposed to answer that? I can't lie to him. The man can read me like a book. But if I tell him the truth, Sydney Mae is gonna kill me. I'm also not entirely sure *he* won't kill me.

I don't have much of a choice though. So, I guess it's an *ask for forgiveness, not permission* kinda situation right now.

Clearing my throat, I square my shoulders and look him right in the eye. "I'm in love with her, sir." I take a breath. "I have been since I met her this time last year. If you want to fire me or kick me out, I'll understand, but if you're gonna ask me to give her up, I can't do that—I won't. I just got her back. I'm not lettin' her go again."

"Woah, Chase, calm down," he says, holding his hands up in surrender. "I'm not mad, son. I'm happy for you. I just wanted to make sure you weren't in it for… well, you know."

"O-of course not. You oughtta know by now that's not the kinda man I am."

He nods, a sympathetic look on his face. "I do, but Sydney Mae is my little girl. I'm weary of any man in her life."

"I might not be able to give her the world, but I can sure as hell give her my heart. Hell, she's already had it for a year." I feel my chest tighten, knowing that there's only one other person who takes up as much room in my heart and mind as Sydney does. "She's everythin' to me, sir."

"That's all a father could ask for—someone he knows is gonna love his baby right."

There's a beat of silence between us and I can't help but feel a bit of weight come off my chest. "You're really okay with this?"

Bill chuckles and grabs my shoulder. "Would it change anythin' if I wasn't?"

"I don't think anythin' could stop me from lovin' her," I say, shaking my head.

"Good." He smiles and squeezes my shoulder. "Now get outta here and make the most of the time you have with her while she's in town. My baby is a busy woman, so you gotta take what you can get."

I chuckle as a slow grin tips my lips before I rush for the house, needing to have my girl in my arms. "Thank you, Mr. Wilson."

# 40



The cold air nips at my cheeks as I follow Vikram outside. He's in a pair of dark jeans and a thick cream sweater with a maroon button down underneath. His carry-on stands beside him with a backpack perched on top.

I wrap my arms around his middle. "Thank you for everything, Vik." I pull back from the hug and take a step away. "Are you sure you don't want to stay a few more days? I'd really like it if you got to know Chase."

"And I will, in time. But right now, I think it's more important that the two of you get some time alone."

"Okay." Chewing on my lip for a moment, I look up at him. "You'll still be at my place when I get home, right?"

He gives me a half smile and shakes his head. "I'll come over any time you need and we'll keep up our weekly dinners, but I think it'd be best if I moved back into my own apartment.

My bottom lips juts out in a pout. I'm gaining Chase, but losing Vik, and that realization twists my gut. I feel my eyes start to water but Vik grabs my chin. "Don't give me that face. It's for the best, okay? I love you, but I definitely don't need to hear you and Chase having phone sex for the foreseeable future. But I promise, anytime you need me, I'll be there. No matter the time."

I nod, giggling and quickly blinking away my tears. I hadn't thought about that, only that he wouldn't be a permanent fixture in my home. "I'm gonna miss you."

"I'll miss you too, Syd."

Vik looks at his watch and then blows out a breath. "I should get going." He wraps his arms around my shoulders, pulling me in for one last hug and drops a kiss to my hair. "Text me when you're on your way home and I'll come pick you up from the airport."

"Thank you. Have a safe flight."

A pair of boots clomp up the porch steps and Chase's broad frame comes into view. There's a flutter in my chest at the sight of him. *And maybe in another place too.*

"Safe flight? You're leavin' already?"

"Yeah. My flight isn't for a couple hours, but given the winding roads and incoming storm it'd be better to get there early just to be safe."

I see Chase's face fall. "I was hopin' to get to know each other a bit better. And thank you properly for lookin' out for Sydney in New York."

A smile takes over Vik's face. "There'll be plenty of time to get to know each other in the future. Like I told Sydney, I'm going to be in her life for as long as she wants me, so I'm sure we'll be seeing each other. As for the other thing, don't mention it."

I step toward Chase and fit myself under his arm.

Vikram holds out a hand and Chase takes it. "Take good care of her."

"I will."

"I know," Vik says with a smirk. He walks down the porch steps and tosses his suitcase into the back of the rental car before rounding the side to the front door.

He raises a hand over his head, waving goodbye before slipping behind the wheel and taking off down the street.

There's a pinch of sadness in my chest, but I know it's for the best that Vik is leaving and moving out of my place. He's right, Chase and I do need alone time together. We haven't exactly had that luxury since we met last year. And I'm sure when I get back to New York we'll have to get *creative* when it comes to spending time with each other.

I may be getting a *bit* ahead of myself on that front though. Nothing happened last night, and while I think we both *wanted* something to happen, we were more concerned with just *being* together.

As the taillights disappear down the road, Chase rests his chin on my head. "He's great, Sydney Mae. How could you pick me over him?"

"Vik is amazing, but he's not you. He's not the cowboy I fell in love with."

There's a dreamy look in his eyes when he hears the *L* word. He pulls me from under his arm and looks down at me. "Is that what did it for you? Me bein' a cowboy? Because I got some bad news for you, baby, I ain't a cowboy."

I bite my lip and press up on my toes, planting a soft kiss on his lips. I'll never get tired of being able to kiss him whenever I want, though we should probably try to keep it on the down low. If my dad found out, he would freak.

"And why don't you consider yourself a cowboy, hm?"

He steals another kiss from my lips that sends butterflies racing around my stomach. "No hat. No cattle to herd."

I look to my left, seeing the old hat my dad used to wear all the time that now lives on the well-loved rocking chair and pick it up, plopping it on Chase's head. "Problem solved. And I seem to remember you wearing a cowboy hat just fine, only on a different head."

He blushes as he runs his finger over the brim, tipping it

slightly before winking at me. "This really does it for you?" he asks.

*Dear god.*

"Maybe." My cheeks heat.

Chase drags me toward him with a hand on the small of my back and kisses me so passionately I feel my toes curl and a dizzying need pools in my belly.

"Let me go change and then we can head to lunch."

The last thing on my mind right now is food, but I nod anyway.

---

Chase and I had an amazing time on our date. We talked for hours about nothing and everything. It was great to reconnect in a way we hadn't yet had the chance to. There was a lot of ground to cover after six months of not speaking.

Including the fact that he dated Riley for a little while.

I couldn't ignore, or hide, the flare of jealousy when he told me. Something about the situation soured my stomach, but then I realized him being with Riley wasn't really that different from my relationship with Vikram. We both found comfort in other people when all we *really* wanted was each other.

I won't lie though, it was hard to accept the fact that in some way, the basis of their relationship started before I even knew him. Feelings make things complicated, and from what he's told me, there's still a bit of awkward tension between them.

It really put things into perspective for me. Had I been more open about my feelings from the start, maybe we would have been together this whole time. Then again, maybe the time we spent apart is what we needed—to hit rock bottom before we could slowly climb back up and into each other's arms.

There isn't a single doubt in my mind that Chase is the man I want to spend the rest of my life with.

By the time we get back to the house, the sun is already starting to set. With my hand in his, he leads me to the barn.

We sneak inside undetected and I'm flooded with flashbacks of last year when we went riding and then fooled around. The scene now is quite familiar. My back is pressed up against the wall, and Chase is pressed against me. The only difference is, this time, we're much more desperate for each other.

Not just emotionally, but *physically*.

I'm strung so tight I feel like a rubber band ready to snap at any moment. And by the feel of his hard length pressed against my thigh, he feels the same way.

Chase tilts his head to the other side as he devours my lips. The man is starved and it's making for one hell of a kiss.

It's passionate and fiery and unlike any kiss we've shared before. His soft lips move in perfect sync with mine. Every swipe of his tongue across my lips sends a wave of excitement through my body.

My fingers hastily undo the buttons on his solid black flannel before pushing it off his shoulders and letting my fingers dance across his skin.

Without breaking our kiss, he hooks his hands under my ass and lifts me up, carrying me over to one of the empty horse stalls that's primarily used as makeshift hay storage in the winter months.

Carefully laying me down on the fresh hay, he situates himself between my legs. "So damn gorgeous," he whispers, almost like he's saying it to himself, as he brushes a lock of hair behind my ear.

Blushing, I bring my hand to his cheek, guiding his lips back to mine. He must like the slight move of control because I feel his cock flex against my core.

I moan into the kiss and feel him smile against me right before he rolls us over so I'm straddling his hips. His hands fall to my waist and he stares up at me in amazement as I slowly unbutton my blouse. I shrug it off and toss it to the ground, then plant my hands on his chest, grinding myself on his obviously hard length.

I swivel my hips and it earns me a deep groan as Chase's hands make their way up my nearly bare back.

His fingers are cool against my heated skin, leaving a trail of goosebumps in their wake. "May I?" he asks, slipping his fingers beneath the band of my bra.

There's a moment of hesitation that flutters in my stomach, and I tuck my bottom lip between my teeth. I'm a fairly confident person. I know I take good care of my body, and have turned heads before, but there's a sense of insecurity when you're naked.

For some reason, right now, I can't shake it.

Our first time fooling around last Christmas Eve, my head was entirely clouded with want and need and desire. There was hesitancy, sure, but that vanished the moment I looked into Chase's eyes.

So, I look into them again, and the unspoken promise that he'll take care of me, that was present the last time, is still there now.

I give him a shy nod and he flicks open the clasp. The tightness of my bra releases, and my nipples harden at the mere thought of him seeing me.

With his eyes on mine, he slowly drags the bra down my arms and tosses it aside. He lets out a low groan and I feel his cock twitch again before he slowly cups my breasts, rolling his calloused thumbs over my peaked nipples. I'm powerless to hold back a moan, all sense of innocence and hesitancy flying out the window at the feel of him touching me.

Reaching down, I pop the button on his jeans before slowly dragging down the zipper.

Chase's palms roam up my thighs and over my ass to the small of my back, gently pulling me into him so my bare chest is in his face. He closes his mouth around my breast, circling the stiff point with his tongue.

He finally stops teasing me and sucks my nipple into his mouth, I can't stop the moan that falls from my lips. And when he nibbles down on it, letting his teeth graze my sensitive flesh, his name rolls off my tongue.

Wave after wave of heat passes through me, settling right at my core.

"God, Chase, that feels so good."

If feeling his smirk wasn't enough, he thrusts his hips up too, just to let me know he likes hearing my praise.

My fingers dive into his hair, desperate to keep him right where he is. I could stay like this forever. Having his mouth on me and feeling how much he's enjoying himself is enough to make my heart swell.

He pulls back, his mouth making a glorious-sounding *pop* as my nipple is released before grabbing my hips and softly laying me down on the hay.

Planting my feet on the ground, I lift my hips and shimmy out of my jeans as Chase does the same. He's hard and leaking, straining against the fabric of his grey boxer briefs.

"Didn't think you'd be one to stare," Chase says as he drops back to his knees.

I spread my legs and watch in awe as he comes between them, dragging his fingertips up my legs. The subtle grazing of his skin on mine sends a zip of excitement up my spine.

Chase palms himself over his boxers with one hand as he brushes his thumb up and down my covered slit. "Can I taste you here, Sydney Mae?"

Heat rushes to my cheeks. "Yes, please."

Reaching down, he grips the top of my panties and slowly pulls them down my legs, tossing them in the direction of the other clothes we've shed.

I squirm as I watch his head drop between my legs, his

mouth leaving a trail of wet kisses all along my inner thigh, building the anticipation the closer he gets.

With his eyes locked on mine, he places a soft kiss to my clit before swiping his tongue through my folds. My head falls back against the hay as pleasure rips up my spine.

Chase circles my clit with his tongue, just like he did my nipple, and I can't help the desperate sound that slips past my lips.

"Fuck," I purr, lacing my fingers in his hair and grabbing a handful, tugging his face closer to my pussy.

It feels *so* much better than I thought it would, and now I never want him to stop.

He smiles against me. "That feel good, baby?" he asks before diving back in and sucking my clit gently. One of his hands travels up my body, tweaking my nipple between his fingers and I feel the pressure building low in my belly.

I can't remember the last time I had an orgasm that wasn't achieved by a battery-operated friend while soaking in the bathtub, but the tingling is unmistakable. It zips down my spine and my lips part. Chase was always *very* talented at getting me there, even from nearly two thousand miles away.

Just when I think I can't get any closer, Chase switches it up, flicking his tongue over my clit like a madman and my eyes flutter closed.

"I'm gonna c—"

Before I can even get the words out, my orgasm crashes into me. I'm pummeled with wave after wave of pleasure, goose bumps fanning out across my skin, pebbling my nipples, and sending a shiver down my spine.

Chase slides his tongue against my core, lapping at my wetness and getting one last lick before removing his face from between my thighs. "God, you taste like heaven," he whispers, looking down at me.

I lie there, breathless, as he kneels between my spread thighs and pulls down his boxers, his gloriously hard cock on display.

My eyes widen in anticipation, and maybe a little anxiety for what comes next, but then Chase leans down, his face just inches from mine, with his hand braced next to my head. I grab his length, pumping it slowly in my fist. A bead of precum drips from the tip.

He sucks a breath through his teeth and I can see the relief on his face. Scooting closer, I bring the head of his cock closer to my core.

"M-maybe we should slow down," he says, pulling his hips back slightly. "We're movin' pretty fast, and I don't—" He sucks in a deep breath and I let my hand fall from his length. "I haven't had sex since before Macie was born."

My brows furrow. There's no way that can be true. "You and Riley never...?" Knowing the way Riley *used* to be, it's hard to believe that she would be okay with nothing happening between them.

"We fooled around a bit, but never sex." He licks his lips and softly shakes his head from side to side. "I-I couldn't. There was only one person I could picture myself being with after so long, and it wasn't Riley."

That's one hell of a statement. But one I completely understand because I feel the exact same way. Vikram and I may have barely rounded first base, but my hesitation was because of Chase. I knew I wouldn't be able to forgive myself for letting anyone other than him have me in such an intimate way.

"I couldn't either," I admit. "I haven't been with anyone since Jack."

Sadness and a hint of anger fills his eyes as he recalls what I told him last year. "Sydney Mae..."

I've spent twelve years waiting for the right person after Jack, and I can finally say that I found that in Chase. He's kind and thoughtful. Caring and gentle. The complete opposite of Jack in so many ways that it's laughable.

Chase Alexander Phillips is the closest thing to perfection that I'll ever know. After twelve years of being scared that history would repeat itself, I *know* I have no reason to be. I'm finally ready.

"I want you, Chase. Only you." I chew on the inside of my cheek as I reach out and take his hard length in my hand again.

He blows out a harsh breath and I think for a second that he's going to say he's not there yet, but his hand comes to my face, brushing his thumb over my lips. "I want this, Sydney. I want you. I'm ready as long as you are."

"Then make me yours, Chase Phillips," I whisper, lifting my hips and rubbing the head of his cock against my too-sensitive clit.

"With pleasure." He brings his lips, that are coated in me, to mine and I squirm beneath him.

The head of his cock nudges my entrances as his mouth devours mine and a shameless moan slips out at the contact. He's warm and hard and I can't wait to feel him stretch me.

"Shit." He hastily pulls back. "I don't have a condom."

Heat rushes to my cheeks. "I-I'm on the pill. But if you want to wait, we can."

With his eyes locked firmly on me, he shakes his head. "I don't want to wait any longer to have you, but are *you* sure?"

"Yes." I hook my legs around his waist and pull him closer, the head of his cock nudging me again. "I trust you, Chase."

He reaches down, grabbing hold of his length, and drags the bare head through my lips, letting my wetness coat him. Slowly, he eases himself inside, the flared head a tight fit. My eyes snap shut at the sweet pain of him stretching me.

Chase's hand finds my waist, holding me in place as he presses in further. My brows pinch as I bite down on my lip to stop from wincing.

"You're so wet for me, Sydney Mae." He ticks his hips forward, sinking in another inch. "So wet, but so damn tight. Relax for me, baby."

I open my eyes and find his locked on where our bodies connect as he watches his length gradually disappear between my legs. His mouth pops open, forming a small *"O"* as he moves deeper.

He's a damn snug fit and I cry at just how well he stretches me.

"Am I hurtin' you?" he asks, bringing his eyes to mine, halting his movement.

"I'm okay." My voice shakes. "You're just a lot bigger than he was, and I'm not used to the feeling yet."

I see a little smirk of pride tilt the corner of his lips as he brings his hand to where we're connected, letting his thumb stroke my clit.

"Is this makin' it any better?"

The sensation immediately relaxes me and I nod, dropping my gaze to get a glimpse of him filling me. He starts to move his hips back, pulling out almost entirely before sinking in fully, my pussy getting wetter with each stroke of his cock.

Moans tumble out of me as the slight pain turns to pure pleasure. "D-don't stop," I mutter, my body overwhelmed by what he's doing to me.

His thrusts are smooth, getting gradually harder each time and combined with the way he's strumming my clit, I can feel that familiar pressure low in my belly. My nipples tighten and I know it won't be long before I'm hit with another mind-numbing orgasm.

I clench around his length, feeling each of his deep thrusts more intensely.

"Fuck, Sydney," he curses through his teeth, "you're gonna make me come if you don't stop that."

"I'm too close. Can't. Feels too good."

He smirks and crashes his lips to mine, hammering into me as I shatter around him. Moans and gasps pour from my mouth, and my pussy flutters wildly around him as he desperately clings to control.

"Chase," I whisper, breathless from the insurmountable pleasure of my second orgasm.

Quickly pulling out, Chase hurriedly strokes his cock, chasing his own orgasm.

I see the moment when it washes over him. His lips part and his eyes glaze over as he sprays me with his cum, coating my stomach and pussy.

My chest heaves as I try to catch my breath, and I feel him rub my cum-covered clit. Looking down, I watch as he paints his cum up and down my slit with the head of his cock, slipping it through my folds before slowly sinking back inside me.

"F-fuck." He's breathless and shaking, the aftershocks of his orgasm still rolling through him causing his cock to twitch and flex inside me.

Once our breathing returns to normal and the fog of lust clears, Chase pulls out again and lies down beside me in the hay.

"Sorry," he says meekly.

"For what?" I roll onto my side to look at him.

He wraps his arm around my shoulder and meets my gaze. "The mess… I don't know why I did that."

I giggle and bring a hand to his chest, drawing circles on his skin with the tips of my fingers. "Don't be sorry. I liked it."

His eyes widen. "Really?" he asks, brushing his thumb across my cheek.

I smile. "Chase Phillips, I recently learned that, when it comes to you, I'm always sure."

A sexy, sure smile curves his lips right before he presses them to mine. "I love you, Sydney Mae."

*God, I'll never get tired of hearing that.*

"And I love you."

# 41

## CHASE

We lie there for a few moments, naked and carefree, completely blissed out. The hay isn't comfortable by any means, but having her so close to me more than makes up for it.

It's taken my mind a little while to catch up to the fact that I just had sex for the first time in over twelve years. If you asked me last week if I thought I'd ever get the opportunity to be with Sydney again I would have laughed in your face. Nothing about the way we ended, or the last six months, gave me any hope that we would make it to this point.

Truthfully, I still don't believe it. I'm waiting for the moment I wake up from this dream, because that's what this has to be—a dream. Only in my dreams do I get to have her like this.

A car door slams in the distance and we share a look. "I guess we should probably clean you up, huh?"

She giggles, her cheeks still tinted pink from our rendezvous. "Yeah, I guess so."

I reluctantly disentangle myself and hop up, quickly pulling on my jeans before heading to the small slop sink on the other end of the barn. Snagging a clean towel from the pile, I run it under warm water before jogging back to Sydney.

"Do you want to, or can I?" I ask, holding the damp towel out as I kneel beside her again.

She nervously chews her lips, her cheeks turning a shade darker. "You can."

Nodding, I bring the towel between her legs and carefully clean her. When I pull the rag away, panic sets in when I see that it's tinged pink. "I thought you said I didn't hurt you? You're bleeding, Sydney Mae."

"I'm okay," she says, gently strumming my cheek with her thumb. "It's probably because it's been so long, but I'm fine, I promise."

I blow out a breath and try to shake the worry. "Okay."

She smiles dreamily at me and it takes every ounce of strength I have to not claim her again. But I know that wouldn't be a smart idea. She may say she's okay, but I don't miss the slight wince when she moves to stand. I watch as she dresses herself and it shouldn't be such a turn on to see her skin disappear behind layers of clothing, but I'm nearly ready to go again.

Gentle hooves sound behind me and I know that sound all too well.

*Shit.*

My eyes snap to Sydney who is half-dressed, sporting only her pants and a lacy bra. I look down, noting I'm in a similar state of undress.

Before I can get a word of warning out, May barrels into the makeshift hay shed like a bat out of hell and looks up at me innocently. Sydney giggles as she watches the little menace stalk toward us.

"May," I say firmly. "Walk away now and I'll give you a treat."

Being the demon she is, May practically laughs in my face and struts over to Sydney. She inspects my girl, sniffing her like a family pet does to new guests and then nudges her head against Sydney's leg.

"Hey, girl." Sydney chuckles and rubs the calf's blocky head.

"You know, I didn't tell you before, but we're obsessed with the same man."

May's ears twitch and she looks from Sydney to me and back again.

She smiles. "Yeah, him. He's pretty great, huh?"

A long, soft moo sounds, almost like May agrees, and she nips at my jeans. "You're lucky you're so damn cute."

Sydney giggles and reaches for her shirt, but the moment it's off the ground May snatches it and makes a beeline for the exit.

*Dammit.*

"May!" I shout after her, hoping it'll make her turn around, but it's no use. Sydney's shirt is long gone.

"What in the hell does she have in her mouth now?" Bill's voice sounds through the barn.

My eyes immediately snap to Sydney, who's as white as a ghost. She searches the floor for something to cover herself with.

"Chase, I thought I told you to—" Bill rounds the corner, coming face to face with me. And my bare chest. And his shirt-less daughter as she hastily shrugs my flannel onto her shoulders. "Oh." His eyes bounce back and forth between the two of us. "Oh my."

*Shit.*

"Mr. Wilson, I..." How the fuck am I going to explain my way out of this one? "We were just—"

He holds his hand up to stop me. "Nothin' to be ashamed of, kids. Susie and I had our fair share of rolls in the hay. If I remember correctly, that's where Sydney Mae was conceived."

"Dad!" Sydney groans, burying her face in her hands.

"Right. Enjoy!" Bill smacks himself in the forehead. "Err…"

Sydney groans, running her hands through her hair. "Dad, just go!"

He nods and turns his back to us as he hightails it out of the barn. "Goin'!"

As soon as Bill is out of earshot, I turn toward Sydney. "Sydney Mae, I'm sorry. I never should have let us get—"

"Chase, it's okay."

"It's not." I shake my head, chewing on my lip. "I had a talk with him this mornin' about my intentions with you and he just walked in on us."

Her brows draw together. "You talked to him about us?" There's an edge of hurt in her voice that's like a knife to the gut.

"I didn't mean to. He confronted me about us and I couldn't lie."

"What did you tell him?"

"That I'm in love with you," I say, resting my hands on her hips. "And that I'm not the kind of guy who's only in it for one thing."

Sydney licks her lips. "You aren't."

"I know, but what he walked in on says otherwise."

Her arms drape over my shoulders and she runs her fingers through the hair at the nape of my neck. "Did his reaction make it seem like he was angry, or doubted any part of what you told him?"

I shake my head. "Not really."

"So, then apart from it being incredibly awkward, what's the issue?"

"I don't know."

"There isn't one," she says matter-of-factly. "And if there is, then it's something we'll deal with together, okay?"

Blowing out a breath, I rest my forehead against hers. "Okay."

---

After being caught by Bill in the barn, Sydney and I keep our *extracurricular activities* to her bedroom, or any other room with a locking door. We weren't worried about being caught again, per se, it was more like we didn't want a fan club there cheering us on.

If there was any question about whether or not Bill was okay with me and Sydney Mae, the next day at dinner it was clear that both he and Susan were *big* fans. They were both grinning from ear to ear.

Apparently Bill had been hoping for us to get together since last year. He's thrilled that he's one step closer to having me as an *official* part of the family. When I mentioned he may have been getting ahead of himself, he waved me off with a hushed, "Never say never." And Sydney Mae gave me a look that said maybe it wasn't such a crazy idea.

I couldn't help the big dumb smile that took over my face after that.

Things between us feel so much different this time around. I don't know if it's because we know what it's like to lose each other now, or if we're just different people than we were last time, but whatever it is gives me so much hope that we'll make it.

*Maybe too much.*

Losing her once was bad. I can't imagine doing it again.

"What's that face for?" Sydney asks, as she puts her earring in.

I take a seat on the edge of her bed and lock eyes with her in the vanity mirror. "Are you sure you wanna go to Scarlet's? Riley will be there, and I don't—"

"Is there anything you haven't told me about your relationship with her?"

"No."

"Then I don't see why we shouldn't go." She puts her other earring in and then turns around to face me. "If you don't want to, that's a different story." Climbing onto the bed, she straddles my thighs, settling onto my lap. "But if you're worried that I'll be uncomfortable"—she shakes her head, breathing heavily as she leans in—"don't be."

I groan, grabbing her waist. "Fuck, baby. You keep wigglin' around like that and we're not gonna leave your room at all tonight."

Sydney giggles and pecks my lips before pulling back. "Sorry."

"You're really okay with goin'?"

"Positive."

"I guess we should head out then."

She licks her lips and wiggles her ass on me. "I think we might need to take care of something first, hm?"

Heat rushes to my cheeks and I nod as I tip us back and quickly pin her to the bed. "Needy girl."

"Mhmm."

# 42



I told Chase that I was fine coming, and that his relationship with Riley didn't bother me, but I wasn't being entirely truthful.

The Riley situation is hard for me to get past. Not because of what he did, or how far things between them went, but because there were feelings involved that I *know* were there prior to their relationship starting. Something about that just feels *icky* to me. Like she was turned down and waited for the perfect opportunity to pounce.

Part of me wants to believe she didn't do it intentionally. That she wouldn't do something like that to Chase. But given our history, I wouldn't put it past her to do it to hurt *me*. She's not a malicious person, and I know she wouldn't deliberately hurt me emotionally, but she would absolutely find a way to shove a big fat middle finger in my face. Her being with Chase was that middle finger.

I've tried my best to bite my tongue over the last two hours, but if she makes one more snarky comment or rolls her eyes at something I say, I'm going to lose it. Don't get me wrong, I want to be here. I want Christmas Eve Eve at Scarlet's to be part of my tradition too, but I don't want to deal with the animosity that I can feel pouring off of Riley.

But for everyone's sake, I've ignored it and pretended like I don't notice the glare she shoots my way every time I talk.

"Bad news. The batch of hot toddy's I had next to the sink somehow disappeared," Scarlet says, holding up two empty clear mugs in each hand. "We have champagne, which Riley has almost finished, and plenty of beer, it's just not cold since I needed the room in the fridge for the cake."

"We could throw 'em in the snow outside for a little while," Chase suggests

Scarlet's lips pop open. "That's actually not a bad idea. And we could go down to the rink to waste some time while they're chilling."

It feels like I swallowed a brick and it's just laying uncomfortably in my stomach. If there's one place in this town I have no intentions of returning to, it's the rink. There are far too many memories there, and none of them are the good kind.

I feel the tell-tale burning in my nose right before the tears come, but I choke them back.

"Oh I am *so* down for that!" Logan practically jumps out of his chair. "Whatcha say, babe?" he asks the quiet blonde whose name I can't remember.

"That does sound pretty fun."

"I'm beyond awful at skating, and will absolutely fall on my ass a million times, but I'm down." Noah looks toward his girlfriend, Amelia, holding out his hand for her. "You wanna go?"

She giggles, and takes it, standing from her seat on the couch. "You do realize I was a figure skater for twelve years, right? Of course I want to go."

*Leave it to this group to be overly enthusiastic about ice skating.*

"Chase? Sydney?" Scarlet asks, turning to us.

How am I supposed to casually drop that there's no way I can come within a hundred feet of that place ever again?

"I've never been ice skatin' before, but I'll give it a shot." Chase squeezes my hand. "You want to?"

I shake my head. "I'll stay back and tidy up. You guys have fun though."

"What? Is everythin' okay?"

"I-I'm not really coordinated enough."

Riley scoffs and I don't miss the challenge in her eyes. "We used to go all the time, you're practically a pro."

"It's been years, and I just don't really want to. Let it go, please?"

Her eyes roll so far back in her head I think I might actually see her brain, before she stomps toward the back entrance, mumbling something under her breath.

"You guys go ahead. Sydney and I will stay here."

The group turns and walks out through the door that leads to the backyard.

"Chase, just go with them. I'll be fine by myself for a little while."

He shakes his head and grabs my cheeks. "I'm not going without you. Talk to me, baby. Please."

Emotion swells in my chest anytime he calls me *baby*, but especially right now, when it feels like my heart is in my throat.

Chase constantly argues that I deserve better than him, but he's wrong. It's me who doesn't deserve him. He's too good for me. Too sweet and kind. Too caring. Too close to perfect.

I lick my lips, trying desperately to hold back tears. "I used to go there with Jack, and none of my memories are good ones.

He smiles softly, an edge of sadness to it as he looks me dead in the eye. "Then how about we make some new memories?"

"Chase—"

"Look, I know I can never erase what he did to you, or take away the pain he put you through, but I can try to make your memories of home happy ones. And if that means makin' a damn fool of myself by fallin' on my ass ice skatin', then I'll do it. But I can only try if you give me a chance to." He bends his knees so he's eye to eye with me. "Please let me try, Sydney Mae. Let me make home a happy place for you again. A *safe* place."

My eyes water and I let a single tear fall as I nod my head. *Goddamn him.* "Okay," I whisper, clutching his hideous reindeer sweater in my hand.

He presses a soft kiss to the corner of my mouth, and then pulls back. "Thank you."

———

Walking the gravel road to the rink from Scarlet's house with Chase's hand in mine definitely helped ease some of the anxiety. Jack used to take me here most nights to meet his dealer. I hated every second of it.

But the rink is damn near unrecognizable from the last time I was here. Back then it was cold, and dark. Eerily silent. It was the place that most of my nightmares stemmed from. But now, it's filled with laughter and smiles and millions of twinkling lights dangling from above. It's the kind of place you'd see in those cheesy Hallmark Christmas movies set in a small town. It's beautiful, and that's not something I *ever* thought I would call it.

Plus, the cold doesn't seem so bad when you're hand in hand with the one you love.

We lace up our borrowed skates from the giant box of thrifted ones at Scarlet's and make our way to the ice. Logan, Amelia, and Scarlet are floating across the frozen surface with practiced ease. Noah, on the other hand, is fighting to stay upright, and just barely achieving that goal.

Scarlet's girlfriend, Lorena, and Logan's girlfriend, whose name I now know is Selene, are standing just outside the rink, recording the whole thing.

"You ready?" I ask Chase as we step onto the ice and he wobbles on his skates.

"As I'll ever be." He blows out a confident breath and then pushes off with his right foot.

The momentum carries him a couple feet away before his

legs kick out from under him and he goes crashing to the ice. I wince before effortlessly skating over to him. "Are you okay?"

Chase groans but sits up, hanging his forearms on his knees. "Never better, baby." A blatant lie he delivers with a smirk. "Can you help me up?"

I nod and grab his hand, balancing myself as I slowly pull him up to standing. This time he gets his bearings first before pushing off, and the crew cheers him on. He looks like a baby giraffe just learning to walk and I think it might be the cutest thing I've ever seen.

He sticks close to the wooden railing on the boundary of the rink, giving me a thumbs up as he makes his way around the edge at a snail's pace.

With a smile, I skate off, gliding across the ice, and feeling the cold air nip at my cheeks as I breeze past a wobbly Chase.

He whistles at me and I smile, tipping my head back as I continue to look up at the fairy lights, in awe of how much something as simple as lights can change a space.

I pick up speed, skating around the rink with my arms out wide, feeling *free* for the first time in as long as I can remember. Spinning around, I lift my hands above my head, twirling in a tight circle before skating backwards past Logan and Scarlet.

Once upon a time, Logan and I had a choreographed routine we thought was good enough to get us into the Olympics. Wildly optimistic, and not even a little true, but we were dumb fourteen-year-olds, and compared to the rest of our friends, we looked like professionals on the ice.

With a smile, I spin around again, skating like hell across the wide open expanse. I chuckle to myself, not knowing the last time I felt *this* good, when out of the corner of my eye, I see Chase's tall frame fall backward in slow motion.

"Chase!" I shout as I skid around, quickly changing directions.

He groans, lying on the ice, looking up at the sky, when I come to a stop beside him and drop to my knees.

"Are you okay? That one looked like a pretty hard fall."

"I've got a bit of a bruised ego, but other than that I'm fine." He reaches up and tucks a lock of hair behind my ear. "I really thought I was getting the hang of it, but I guess not. Why didn't you tell me you were such a good skater?"

I shake my head. "If I'm being completely honest, I didn't think I still would be."

"You sure you're not skatin' around the Rockefeller Center Ice rink every year?"

Giggling, I shake my head. "Definitely not."

"Could've fooled me."

He smiles at me and I feel a rush of heat settle between my legs.

*Why the hell is he so damn attractive?*

*And how on earth did I get so lucky?*

I lean down and feather my lips over his for a quick kiss, but his hand comes to the back of my head, holding me in place. "I can't wait to get you home," he whispers against my lips before his tongue butts up to mine.

There are hoots and hollers from the other side of the rink where everyone is clapping and cheering us on. For a moment, I forgot we weren't alone.

My cheeks heat as I pull back from the kiss, even though it's the last thing I want to do. "Let me help you up."

"Gimmie another minute, the ice feels good on my ass."

A cackle bursts out of me and I quickly smack a hand over my face to stop myself. "Sorry."

He chuckles like a champ and still makes no move to get up. "Ice skatin' is clearly not my forte, but I do like seein' you smile so much."

"If it makes you feel any better, you look *really* cute trying."

"Oh?" He smirks and I can see the air of mischief in his eye. "Is that right?"

"Mhmm."

Chase pushes up on his elbow and cups my cheek, leaning in for another kiss.

"Guys!" Scarlet calls. "We're all freezing so we're heading back to the house, you coming?"

"Uh, I think we're gonna head home unless you need any help cleanin' up?"

Logan shakes his head, waving Chase off as he slings one arm over Selene's shoulder and the other over Riley's. "We got it. You two lovebirds have fun!"

Riley scoffs and rolls her eyes, trying to wiggle out of Logan's hold. I can tell that she's the real reason they're all leaving. It wasn't my intention, but I can tell that my being with Chase is affecting her, and the PDA isn't helping.

"Nice to see you again, Syd!" Noah says, holding a hand in the air.

"You too. Merry Christmas!"

They all start to walk away but there's a nagging in my gut. "Riley!" I shout. She turns around with a pout on her face. I climb to my feet. "Can we talk for a sec?"

She chews her lip for a moment before nodding, and then I skate over to her.

"I owe you an apology," I say, keeping my voice down. This conversation is between Riley and I—no one else needs to hear it. "More than one, really."

"Okay." There's an edge of annoyance in her voice, and her crossed arms scream closed off, but I don't let that stop me.

"It was never my intention to hurt you. When I first left, it was purely for the sake of self-preservation. And I know I could have reached out to you once I got out, but I was so ashamed that I let things get that bad. I already regretted leaving my parents to fend for themselves, I couldn't face the reality that I left all my friends behind too." I take a breath and look over my shoulder to where Chase is standing with his hands stuffed in his jeans pockets. "As for Chase..."

Riley shakes her head, waving me off. "Don't apologize for loving him, Sydney. That man has only ever loved two people in his life—Macie and you. I never stood a chance."

"Still, you shouldn't have to be subjected to our relationship."

"It's fine, really." She flashes a half smile before looking to Chase herself. "If I only had a week and a half with him, we sure as hell wouldn't be at a Christmas Eve Eve party with our friends."

Warmth floods my cheeks. "His self-control is unparalleled. I currently feel like I'm going to combust."

Riley laughs, showing off a genuine smile this time. "You know I'm happy for you, right? Albeit a little jealous, but happy for you."

"Thanks." I reach out and grab her hand. "Are we good?"

"Yeah, Syd, we're good."

"Oh, thank god." A breath of relief leaves me and I pull her in for a hug.

"Just… don't be a stranger when you leave this time, yeah?"

I nod and give her one last squeeze before pulling back. "I can do that."

"Good." She smiles. "Well, it's freezing, so I'm gonna head out. Have fun with Chase, and Merry Christmas."

"Merry Christmas."

Riley walks away, leaving me alone in the middle of the rink. Turning around, I see Chase with his arms out like a *T* as he slowly shuffles over. Putting him out of his misery, I skate over and grab his hand. "Let's go home."

"If you're ready to. Or we can stay a little while longer so you can skate."

Shaking my head, I lead us toward the gap in the wooden railing and Chase blows out a breath when we're finally back on solid ground.

After a quick walk back to Scarlet's to grab his truck, we head out, taking the winding road toward my parents' house. Except, when we reach the fork and are supposed to go left to turn into the driveway, Chase makes a right.

"Where are we going?"

With one hand on the steering wheel and a smirk on his lips, he turns to face me. "You'll see."

Pulling to a stop about a mile away from the Wilson house, I put the truck in park and hop out, leaving a confused Sydney inside the cab. I smile to myself as I walk to the passenger side and open the door, offering her my hand. "You comin'?"

Her ass stays planted in her seat and she makes no move to grab my hand. She looks around at the thickly-wooded area around us and eyes me skeptically. "Is this the part where your true colors show and I find out that my suspicions of you being a serial killer from last year come true?"

I cross my arms over my chest and cock a brow at her. "You thought I was a serial killer?"

"For a brief period of time, yes."

Chuckling, I reach inside the cab and unbuckle her seatbelt. "No, I'm not a serial killer. I want to show you somethin'."

She rolls her eyes, but takes my hand. "That's what they all say."

Hopping down, she shuts the door behind her and watches as I reach into the bed and pull out a clear plastic tub with blankets inside. Removing the lid, I pull out two blankets, stuffing them in the crack of my elbow before putting the lid back on. "Ready?"

"Sure."

There's a slight shake to her voice letting me know she might actually be worried. I take her hand, lacing my fingers through hers, and start to lead the way down the short footpath, the moon hung high in the sky, lighting the way. "I promise, I'm not a serial killer, or an axe murderer, or anythin' like that. If I were, I probably wouldn't murder you on your parents' property. I just have somethin' I want to show you."

"Okay…"

I hold back a tree branch and signal Sydney to step through. She does without hesitation and then I see the moment realization sinks in.

A smile spreads across her face as she looks at the small round wood-paneled hot tub on a raised platform nestled between a bare spot in the trees, and the small bunkhouse a few hundred yards away. "I can't believe this thing is still here, we've had it since I was a kid." She turns to me. "Does it work?"

"Sure does." I walk ahead of her and lift the cover off. Steam billows up into the darkened night sky, and I place the cover off to the side. I had left it running earlier to keep it warm, just in case we found a reason to come. "I found it a couple months back and asked your dad if I could use it. He told me if I could figure out how to get it runnin' again and clean it up then I could use it all I wanted."

She nods and walks toward the hot tub. "So, what are we doing here?" she asks, dipping her hand into the water.

I smirk and shrug off my jacket before gripping the bottom hem of my sweater and pulling it over my head. Goosebumps pop up all over my skin when Sydney's eyes trail from my bare chest, all the way down to the waist of my jeans. "We're goin' in. My body is already hurtin' from fallin' on the ice so many times, and it'll help warm you up."

My fingers pop open the button on my jeans and I slide them down my thighs, leaving me in just a pair of dark blue boxer briefs. Sydney tucks her lip between her teeth as her gaze rakes over my nearly naked frame.

After climbing the four steps to the left, I sink down into the staking water. "God, that feels good," I practically moan as warmth surrounds me and starts to soothe my aching muscles. "You gonna stand out there and freeze your butt off, or come join me?"

"I don't have a swimsuit. Didn't exactly think it would be necessary considering it's the middle of winter in Colorado."

I cock a brow and rest my elbows on the edge. "I'm in my boxers. And I'm fairly certain that you've got a bra on under there," I say, tipping my chin toward her skintight leather pants and fuzzy sweater. "Close enough to a bikini top if you ask me."

She sighs. "I guess you're right."

"I know I am." Shooting her a wink, I settle back into the seat, letting the jets pound against my back as I watch my girl undress.

With a small sigh, she kicks off her boots, then she pulls off her jacket. Her sweater is next, leaving a deep red lacy bra. My mouth waters. She's so goddamn perfect. Her tight black pants go next, a matching red thong appearing.

Scurrying up the steps, she quickly sinks beneath the water to escape the cold, but keeps her distance from me. I see her bask in the warmth for a second before she looks across the steamy water at me.

"Nice, ain't it?"

"It's not bad. I'm still a bit cold though."

"Because you're too far." I stretch my arms out, just barely able to touch her silky soft skin. "Come over here and I'll help warm you up."

With a shy smile she closes the distance between us. "Now what?"

I smirk and grab her waist, pulling her through the water so she's straddling me. My dick stirs to life at the weight of her on top of me and I realize how big of a mistake this was.

"How's this?"

Her arms drape over my shoulders. "Better. Warmer now that I'm closer to you."

"Good." I kiss along the column of her neck and she wiggles in my lap. Dammit, that shouldn't feel so good. "I gotta admit, I don't have the purest of intentions right now, Sydney Mae."

"No?"

My fingers dig into her waist and I pull her tighter against my hard cock. "Not a chance in hell, baby."

She brings her lips to mine, kissing me slowly as she rocks her hips back and forth. "Is this what you had in mind?"

I smirk and nip at her bottom lip. "Not quite." My hand skates up her bare back and I unhook her bra before slowly peeling the straps off each shoulder. Sydney gasps at the cold, her nipples tightening to stiff points before my eyes.

Licking my lips, I lean in, flicking my tongue over the taut peak before sucking it into my mouth as I tease the other one with my thumb.

"Fuck," she hisses, tipping her head back with a moan.

She's practically purring.

My cock flexes against her at the sound. I don't think I've ever been so turned on in my life. I'm not sure if it's because we're outside—and even though we're on her parents' property, anyone could technically walk by and see what an utter fucking mess I am for this woman—or if it's just because of her.

Nearly twelve years without sex and now I'm a damn fiend for it. For *her*.

Since our first time, it's been nearly impossible to go more than a couple hours without wanting to be inside her again. It's never been like this with anyone else. I've never had this insistent need to claim someone.

But if I could have Sydney Mae a million times a day, I would in a heartbeat.

Her fingers brush through my hair, and she pulls my head

away from her chest, her nipple popping free of my mouth. "Why'd you do that? Sounded like you were enjoying yourself?"

"I was, but I don't think I can wait any longer." With a rough grind of her ass on me, she leans in, feathering her lips over mine. "I need you, Chase," she whispers, voice thick with need.

"Oh?" I tease, ticking my hips up into her. "And just how do you need me, baby?" I ask, slipping my hand between us.

My fingers press against her lace-covered pussy and her lips part at the sensation. "Need you inside me," she says breathily. There's a desperation in her voice that hasn't been there before. Like she might actually die if I'm not inside her in the next two seconds, and fuck if that isn't one of the hottest things ever.

"Lift up."

She does as I ask, whining at the loss of contact and I can't help but smirk at my needy girl. Gripping her panties in each hand, I tear them off her, watching in satisfaction as the jets carry the shredded lace to the other side of the hot tub.

Quickly pushing my boxers down my legs, I wrap a hand around my length, giving it a stroke. "Can you take me like this, baby?"

Sydney nods with her lip between her teeth and slowly sinks down.

I guide my cock to her entrance, teasing her pussy with the head before putting us both out of our misery, and pushing inside. We let out a collective moan as she eases onto my length, inch by inch.

Her hands come to my shoulders, nails digging in as she drops the rest of the way down, taking all of me in her tight pussy. "Fuck."

"That's it, baby." My hands fall to her waist, guiding her movements as she rides me. Each flick of her hips is like a little taste of heaven. "God, fuck, you feel so good. Just like that."

She pants, her warm breath fanning across my neck as her walls tighten around me. "Chase…"

I buck up into her, but it's not enough. I need more. She feels amazing like this, but it's not enough. The water is stopping me from fucking her the way I want—and the way I know she needs.

"M-more. I need m-more," she moans.

With a satisfied groan I pull out, lifting her off of me and spinning her around so she's folded over the edge, with her knees on the arm rest, lifting her ass out of the water for me.

A slow, loud moan tumbles from her, and I realize there's a jet right against her pussy. I chuckle as I grab the curve of her waist and sink back inside.

I feel her stretch around me, and it's insane how much tighter she feels like this. I'm already holding on for dear life. I bring a hand up, grabbing onto her tit and pinching the nipple between my fingers.

"Does that feel good, baby?" I ask, keeping up my slow, steady thrusts.

"God, yes," she whimpers, pressing her hips back. "Harder."

Bringing my hand back to her waist, I dig my fingers into her hips and slam forward, feeling myself bottom out inside her. We moan in unison as her pussy tightens around me.

"Fuck, Chase. Don't stop," she begs as she brings a hand between her legs.

I swat it out of the way, replacing it with my own. "Let me. I wanna make you come," I say, letting my fingers find her stiff clit.

Between my fingers and the work the jet did before, she's strung tighter than I've seen her. Panting and moaning, she turns her head, keeping her eyes locked on mine as I hammer into her with renewed fervor. There's words on her lips but they refuse to come out.

"That's it, baby. Let go for me."

Sydney's eyes roll back and her pussy clamps down on my cock like a vise as an orgasm races through her. "Fuck!"

*Ah, shit.* Her pussy flutters around me and I lose my rhythm, the once controlled thrusts now frantic as I chase my own orgasm.

My hips smack against her ass three more times before I explode, painting her insides with my cum. Then I rock in and out of her slowly as I ease us both down.

After a few gentle thrusts, I pull out, watching in awe as my cum drips out of her pussy. The sight alone is enough to have me ready to go again, and I have to hold back the urge to catch it with my fingers and stuff it back inside.

I ignore how dangerous that thought is.

Wrapping my arms around her, I pull her to my chest and drop back into the water to escape the chill in the air.

She nuzzles her face in my neck letting out a dreamy sigh. "You were right."

"About what?"

"It's freezing out here, but I've never been so warm."

I chuckle and tilt her face toward me, placing a soft kiss on her lips. "Told you I'd warm you up."

She blushes and chews her lip. "On second thought, I'm still pretty cold."

My cock thumps to life and I flash Sydney a look that tells her she's in for a long night.

# 44

## SYDNEY

Sticking with tradition, my parents left for the Bellingham house around ten in the morning on Christmas Eve and didn't come home until almost midnight, giving Chase and I the *entire* house to ourselves. We definitely took advantage of that for as long as we could, reliving Christmas Eve from last year all the way down to the takeout and cuddles.

If I could relive one day over and over again it would easily be that one. It was the best day I've had in a long time, and it was entirely because of Chase.

Knowing I have to leave in a couple days, and being unsure about when I'll be able to get away again is torture. Now that he's *really* mine, I don't want to be away from him for a second, let alone months at a time.

I look to my right and find his sleepy face half-buried in a pillow. I smile to myself and take a mental snapshot, wanting to savor him like this for as long as I'm able to.

"What's got you so smiley so early?" he asks without opening his eyes.

"You."

He hums and stretches, hunching his back and squeezing the

pillow under his head before letting his eyes slowly flutter open. "Oh?"

"Merry Christmas, Chase."

With a smile, he turns onto his side and pulls me flush against him. "Merry Christmas, Sydney Mae. I can already tell this is gonna be the best one in a long time."

I nod and press up until my lips meet his for a sweet, slow kiss. "Do you want help out in the barn this morning?"

Chase groans and rests his forehead against mine. "Yes, but no. I'll take care of it. You stay warm and spend some time with your mom."

Our old Christmas morning tradition pops up in my head and I can't stop the giggle that comes out of me.

"What?"

"Oh, you'll see."

He smiles and presses a kiss to my forehead before getting out of bed. His bare ass is a damn glorious sight as he walks to the dresser and pulls out his clothes for the day. "I can feel you starin' at my cheeks, Sydney Mae."

I shrug and roll out of bed, tying my discarded blue silk robe from last night around my waist. "Don't have such a nice ass then, cowboy."

A chuckle rolls out of him and he makes a show of pulling on his boxer briefs and snapping the band around his waist with a wink. "I kinda like that nickname now," he says, stepping into his jeans.

"Noted."

There are a few moments of silence as Chase finishes getting dressed and I make the bed, but they're welcome. Comfortable.

"Sydney Mae?"

"Yeah?" I turn around and find him nervously squeezing the back of his neck.

"I know it's not much, but I got you somethin'," he says, handing over a red and white striped gift bag with green tissue paper sticking out.

"You didn't have to get me anything, Chase."

"I know, but I wanted to. Go on, open it."

Pulling out the tissue paper and setting it aside, I reach my hand in and find a beat-up old notebook. My brows furrow. "What is this?"

"My journal."

I shake my head, not understanding. "Why are you giving this to me?"

"I started journaling when I was in a really bad place. Between missin' Macie and havin' this overwhelmin' sense of bein'... *stuck*, I was a mess. It was like nothin' good was ever gonna to happen to me because whoever makes the decisions up there surely doesn't care about me." He takes a breath, hanging his head. "But then I met you, and everythin' changed for me." His gaze settles back on mine, along with his hands on my hips. "You made me feel alive again, Sydney Mae. You lit a fire in me that I didn't know existed after Macie, and I don't think I'll ever be able to thank you for how much you've helped me. So I guess this is a start. I wanted you to see how big of an impact you made on my life. From the *moment* I met you, you changed my world in the best possible way."

Tears well in my eyes and I chew the inside of my cheek to keep them at bay. "I don't know what to say."

"Say that, when you read it, you won't judge me for hating myself." He licks his lips. "And that you won't judge my anger and resentment when I lost you."

My hand comes to his cheek. "Chase, I would never."

"I know, but I figured it wouldn't hurt to say somethin' considerin' there are some pretty heavy words in there."

I nod and give him a quick kiss. "I promise I won't judge a single word."

His lips curve in a weak smile. "Thank you." My hands absentmindedly open and close the journal. "You wanna read that right now, don't you?"

"I do, but I actually have something for you too."

He catches my hand when I go to reach for the nightstand. "Wait." Tucking a lock of hair behind my ear, his thumb strokes over the apple of my cheek. "Give it to me when I'm done out in the barn so I won't have to leave you right after."

"Okay."

"I love you," he says, brushing my lips with his own.

I smile. "And I love you."

Our lips touch and I feel my heart swell. *God, how did I get so lucky?*

---

After an hour of Christmas morning dance party time with my mom, and a guest appearance from my dad, I snuck upstairs and opened Chase's journal. He was right—there are a lot of hateful entries. And a hell of a lot of entries that would worry me had I not seen for myself that he was okay.

> September 12th, 2019
> I didn't think there could be so many consecutive days where I despise myself, but here I am. Day 11 of wishing that I could be poofed out of existence. There's nothing good left in this world anyway... it was taken away.

I can tell that he's in a better place now, whether that be because of me or if it's just time that's helping him heal his wounds. But he's happy, and not *afraid* to be happy.

There was one entry from before I met him that made me smile.

> October 26th, 2019

I had a good day today. One, singular good day, after nearly two months straight of feeling like crap. Logan and Noah asked me to go snowboarding with them since they had an extra lift pass. I haven't been since I was in high school, but apparently I still got it. The day ended too quickly for my liking though. I could have stayed on that mountain forever, breathing in the fresh air and feeling Macie's presence stronger than ever before.

The entry from the day I met him though… That one really made my heart clench.

December 14th, 2019

I just got home from picking Sydney up from the airport and she's gorgeous. Sydney Mae Wilson is hands down the most beautiful woman I have ever laid eyes on. I know the chilly exterior is meant to scare me off, to be a warning to tread carefully, but there's some-thing in me begging to be bold enough to break through the fortress she has built up around her. I want to know everything there is to know about her. I want to tell her that, because of her, I feel like I have something to live for for the first time in years. Even if that is dueling with a New York spitfire like herself.

It's scary as hell, but I can't shake the feeling that she's the kind of woman that would change my life for the better. More terrifying than anything though, I want to kiss her. I need to kiss her.

How does one recover from reading something like that? Is it even possible? I can't believe he felt so strongly after a single interaction with me, especially knowing how much of a bitch I was.

The next entry makes me blush.

December 15th, 2019
It's been less than twelve hours and I've already seen too damn much of her for my own good. I didn't need to know how good she looks when she's relaxed and about to slide between the sheets. And I definitely didn't need to know that her eyes wandered too.

The more entries I read, the more I can see that he invited light into his life again after living so long in darkness, and it's truly magical to read about. I flip through a few more pages, getting emotional at the one from the morning of Christmas Eve last year.

December 24th, 2019
I think I've known since I first laid eyes on her, but after last night, it's clear. I love her.

But then there's a span when that light and that joy starts to fade from his words.

> April 8th, 2020
> I'm losing her. No surprise there. Never in a million years would someone like her choose someone like me. What was I thinking?

And another where it completely vanishes, breaking my heart in the process.

> June 3rd, 2020
> For weeks I felt her slipping away. Felt her closing herself off to me again. And today, instead of desperately hanging on to something that isn't working, I let go. Fuck, does it hurt. I've felt this searing pain once before in my life, and to know losing Sydney hurts as much as Macie leaving me alone in this world, is... What the fuck is even the point anymore? I wish it would all just fucking end.

My gut clenches at the entries where he and Riley are starting to feel each other out. I hate that she got hurt in the process, but his thoughts during their relationship settle something inside me. It's not that he didn't want to be with her. It's that he wanted to be with me more.

> August 2nd, 2020

I kissed Riley and I don't know how I feel about it.

September 28th, 2020
I almost called Riley Sydney today.
Fuck, why can't I stop thinking about her?

October 15th, 2020
I feel like such an asshole, but I can't even describe the weight that fell from my shoulders when Riley broke things off. I should be sad, or at least a little upset, but it's more like relief knowing I don't have to go on pretending that every minute without Sydney Mae hasn't been gut-wrenching torture. No amount of time without her will ever change my feelings. SMW is the love of my life. And I hope I get to tell her that one day.

I can't bring myself to read about his meeting with Cara or his parents. I know the only thing that will come out of it is me hating them even more than I already do.

Skipping ahead a page, I see December 17th. My chest squeezes.

December 17th, 2020
Today always sucks, but this year, it sucks even more. Sydney came to stay with Macie while I was out of town. My heart damn near

dropped out of my ass when she said that. As much as I tried to hold back, I couldn't stop myself from kissing her. After months of not seeing or hearing from her, I needed to. But then everything Cara said started bouncing around in my head. She doesn't care about you. She just pities you. It's not real. She could never love you. That shook me right out of the moment because Sydney Mae deserves so much more than me. She deserves the world, and I can't give it to her. Maybe someday...

Tears drip down my cheeks and I snap the journal closed, tossing it on the bed. I hate that he believed even a single word out of her mouth. Chase is the one that deserves the world, not me. He deserves so much more than this life has given him.

There's a soft knock on the door before it's pushed open and Chase asks, "Can I come in?"

Sniffling, I do my best to wipe away my tears and give a shaky *yes*.

He closes the door behind him and comes to sit next to me on the bed, leaving barely any space between us. "You okay, pretty girl?"

I roll my lips and nod, leaning my head on his shoulder. "I am now that you're here."

"I'm sorry my present made you cry."

"It's okay. I think I needed that glimpse behind the curtain."

"Do you keep one?"

I shake my head. "Despite my therapist's best efforts, no."

"It's not for everyone. Someone in a grief group I went to a couple times actually suggested it. He had also lost a child and said that having the journal was his responsibility now that they were gone. Instead of taking care of them, he used it to take care of himself. It may seem silly, but havin' somethin' to occupy at least part of your mind for a little while really helps."

"Thank you for sharing this with me, Chase. It means more than you know."

He presses a kiss to my hair. "You're welcome."

Sitting up, I reach into the nightstand and pull out a red envelope with his name written in cursive on the front. I hesitate for a split second before handing it over.

Chase carefully peels open the envelope, smiling at the white card with a cartoon reindeer on the front. Opening the card, he finds a check tucked inside. He flips it over, reads the amount, and quickly puts it back in the card and closes it, trying to hand it back to me. "I can't accept this, Sydney Mae."

"You can."

"It's not your debt to pay, it's mine. Eighty-five thousand dollars is a lot of money."

"I know it is," I say softly as I grab his hand. "But it's not just yours anymore, Chase. We're in this together, and I want to help."

He shakes his head. "I don't want to be a burden on you, and that's exactly what I'm doin'."

"You're not, I promise."

"It's eighty-five thousand dollars. You're makin' it seem like that's pocket change."

I grab his hand, lacing our fingers together. "I never said it was, but I want to do this for you, Chase. Please let me."

He thinks it over, looking down at the check that would change his life. A single piece of paper that can lift such a heavy weight from his shoulders. I didn't give it to him to flaunt my wealth. I gave it to him so he doesn't have to constantly worry about it anymore.

For six years, his life has been constantly haunted by this debt looming over his head. A constant reminder that, no matter how hard he tried, Macie is gone. I couldn't imagine living like that.

Chase blows out a breath. "You're sure you can afford this?"

"Positive."

"Okay, but only on one condition."

"What's that?"

He grabs my waist and pulls me closer. "One day, when I get down on one knee, you'll say yes."

I smile, barely holding back a giggle. "I would have said yes either way. You're mine, Chase Phillips, now and forever."

"And you're mine."

# 45

## SYDNEY



After spending nearly three weeks in Colorado, walking away is almost impossible.

Between helping out in the barn, baking with Mom, and spending lots and *lots* of quality time with Chase, we rang in the New Year together. For the first time, I was actually *hopeful* for what this next year would hold, not just dreading the next three hundred and sixty-five days. For me, and for Chase.

We've both changed so much since we met last year, and I know that this coming one will only serve to change us even more, but in the best way.

"I'm not ready to say goodbye to you again," Chase pouts, resting his hands on my hips.

"It's not goodbye." I shake my head. "It's *see you soon.*"

He chews his lip, not believing me. "Are you sure about that?"

I nod, hating that he doesn't already know that this is nothing like the last time I left. "Things will be different this time." My hand comes to his chest, fingers toying with the buttons on his heavy blue flannel. "I'm not running from my feelings for you anymore. And I refuse to let work get in the way of our relationship again. You come first, Chase. Now and always, okay?"

"Sydney, I don't expect you to drop everythin' for me. I just want to know that you're thinkin' of me."

"I'll make sure I tell you every day just how much I miss you."

The most adorable smile curves his lips. I'll never get over seeing him smile. It's perfect. There should only ever be a smile on his face for the rest of his life—he's spent too long being sad for my liking. "I look forward to it."

An announcement comes over the intercom, reminding me of why we're standing in an airport. "Guess I should probably get going, huh?"

"Have a safe flight, beautiful."

Licking my lips, I press up on my toes and kiss him one last time. "I'll call you when I land and every free moment I have until I get to see you again."

He groans and steals another kiss. "I love you so damn much, Sydney Mae."

"And I love you, Chase Alexander."

I can feel how much different things are this time, and that makes it so much harder to walk away. But the time I spent with Vikram taught me that work doesn't always need to come first.

Spending time with the people I love does. And Chase is at the top of that list. Hell, apart from my parents, Chase *is* the list.

I've been so laser-focused on making sure I didn't have time to let the past catch up to me that I forgot to actually *have* a life. So this time, I won't be dumb enough to let him go.

---

"Well, well, well, it's about time you come back to work," Paul teases from my chair when I walk into my office for the first time in three weeks.

"Very funny." I whack his arm with the back of my hand. "What are you doing at my desk?"

"I missed you, and sitting in your chair made me feel close to you."

I drop my bag onto the chair across from him and cross my arms. "Aww. Bullshit."

He chuckles. "I like it better in here." Tipping back in the chair he tucks his hands behind his head with his elbows out wide. "Nicer view."

"I'm sure closer proximity to a certain someone doesn't hurt either."

"Katie?" His eyes light up just the slightest bit. "Yeah, but only because she's a mini version of you and yells at people for me."

Rolling my eyes, I sit on the arm of the chair. "Come on, Paul, I'm not an idiot."

"I have no idea what you're talking about," he says, still playing dumb.

I give him one last chance to tell me the truth, and when he doesn't utter a single peep, I pull out my phone and tap the screen a couple times before a security cam video fills the screen. I cringe, but hit play and the sounds of two people going at it ring out through the room. It's from mid-July, and I'd like to say it's the only one, but it's not.

Turning the screen to Paul he quickly leans forward and runs his fingers through his hair. "Shit."

"*Shit* is right." Pausing the video I stuff it back into my bag.

"Please don't fire her," he begs.

I scoff. "I haven't yet, and I've known for this long, so why would I do it now? This place would fall apart without her, we both know that. It has made me rethink my partnership with you though."

"Sydney…"

"How the hell could you be so stupid?" I ask, trying to keep my voice low enough that Katie doesn't hear. "Fucking anyone you work with is messy, but you, *a co-owner of this company,* having sex with a subordinate?" My mouth opens and closes, words failing me for a moment as I shake my head in disbelief. "You're setting us up for one hell of a lawsuit, Paul."

He licks his lips as he shakes his head. "It's not like that, Syd. We're not just… *fucking.* We've been together for over a year and HR has known about us since our first date."

"Good." I blow out a breath. That's a fucking relief. "At least you're smart enough to cover your ass even while you're thinking with your dick."

"I just told you, it's not like that."

"And her promotion? Did your relationship with her have any impact on you pushing for her to get it?"

Shaking his head, he runs a hand down his face. "Promoting her was your idea, Sydney. I just agreed to it. Regardless of my relationship with her, that girl works her ass off."

"I know she does, just wanted to make sure you knew it too."

He huffs a breath through his nose and turns around, looking out across the busy street to the snow-covered tree tops in central park. "Katie is… She's a lot of things—brilliant, beautiful, hilarious. I could go on for days about all she is, but if there's one thing I know for a fact, she's honest and fair. She didn't talk to me for like a week after we promoted her because she thought I was the one that was responsible for it. But she earned that promotion long before we gave it to her."

"I know," I say, coming to stand beside him. "It's why I didn't fire her when I found out about you two."

"Syd, I'm sorry. I can end things if you're not okay with it," he suggests, his eyes sad. "Or I can sell you my shares of the company and step down. We both know you do the heavy lifting anyway."

My chest squeezes. As much as I hate that he put us in such a vulnerable situation, I also know that you can't help your true feelings. "Do you love her?"

"With my whole heart," he says without hesitation.

"Then don't you dare break hers," I warn.

"I won't."

"I'm not kidding, Paul. I will kick your ass all the way back to bumfuck nowhere, Pennsylvania if you so much as make that girl shed a single tear."

Paul holds his hands up in surrender. "Promise. I think I'm more afraid of fucking things up than anything else."

"As you should be. That girl is a fucking catch."

He smiles. "Yeah, she is." A moment of silence passes between us. "You're taking this much better than I thought you would. I thought you'd freak out on me."

I level him with a glare. "Oh, I absolutely did freak out about it, but luckily for you, Vikram got the brunt of my meltdown. He convinced me not to beat your ass for being so stupid."

He clicks the side of his watch. "Siri, remind me to schedule a thank you dinner with Vikram Anand."

There's a robotic chime and then, *"Setting reminder to make dinner plans with Big Dick Vik."*

A cackle bursts out of me. "Holy shit. Did you do that?"

"Of fucking course I didn't! That asshole must have done it when we went for drinks back in November."

"God, that was amazing," I say through another laugh.

Paul rolls his eyes as his fingers furiously fly over his phone screen. "I'm gonna kill him."

I giggle. "On a more serious note, though, I need you to be more careful about what you do while in the office. I can't have you screwing all over this place."

Paul tucks his hands into the pockets of his navy blue suit pants. "Don't worry, Katie put the kibosh on PDA and in-office trysts almost immediately after Gerry the janitor walked in on us."

"Smart woman." I rest a hand on his arm. "As pissed as I am

that you put us in a shitty position, and kept it from me for so long, I'm really happy for you, Paul."

A shy smile tips his lips. "Same goes for you. I don't think I've ever seen you so happy and laid back before."

"Love is pretty great that way, huh?"

He smiles and slings an arm over my shoulder. "Yeah, it is."

# 46

## CHASE



"Holy shit!" Noah elbows Logan. "Am I seeing things, or is that Chase?"

Logan's lips split into a wide grin and he holds his hand out for me. "Where the hell have you been, man?" he asks, clapping my hand and pulling me in for one of those bro half-hugs.

"Sorry, I've been busy," I say, awkwardly squeezing the back of my neck. "Y'all don't mind if I stay, right?"

"Nah, of course not. We just ordered a fresh bucket, so have at it," Noah says, giving my outstretched hand a shake.

"Thanks." I take a seat on the high stool and shrug off my jacket, putting it on the pile the boys have already started on one of the empty stools before grabbing a beer and twisting off the top. "How have y'all been?"

Noah shrugs. "Good. Not much has changed for me really."

"Same here. Just work and trying to keep Selene happy. What about you?"

"I've just been workin' some odd jobs around town to make some extra cash."

"For what? I thought you paid off those medical bills?"

"I did. Well, Sydney Mae did," I correct. "But, I've been trying to save up some money so that I could pay her back one day. As of the current moment, she'll be paid back two lifetimes from now, on a Saturday, when I'm ninety-seven."

Noah's eyebrows raise. "Wasn't it like eighty grand? She must be making a killing out there in New York."

There's a swell of pride in my chest and I couldn't stop the smile that crossed my face if I tried. I won't go into detail about her financial situation, because it's not my place, but *holy fuck* is my girl doing well for herself. It nearly gave me a heart attack when she added me to her bank accounts and gave me access to every single penny in her name. Talk about feeling insignificant.

Jesus, I didn't know dollar amounts like that could exist in someone's personal bank account. I thought for sure that was just a rich-people-in-movies thing. It's safe to say that that was our first real fight.

I told her that I had no business having access to an account with so much money. She pushed back and told me, "What's mine is ours." Which is a load of shit. I've had a card for almost a month now and haven't even had the balls to activate it yet.

The last thing I need is to have all of her accounts drained because I was frivolous and bought a stupid T-shirt with May's face on it from some sketchy website. She told me I was being unreasonable, and that she wants me to not have to worry about money anymore, and to use it at my discretion. I told her that I would only use it for emergencies and that earned me an eye roll, but our fight otherwise flittered out when she cocked a brow, lifted up her shirt and flashed me her boobs on our video call. I was too stunned to speak, let alone continue arguing about her being rich.

Clearing my throat, I bring myself back to reality. "Yeah, she is. She just sent me her plans for this building in Manhattan and my god, she's brilliant."

I quickly pull out my phone and tap the screen until the photos of the mock-ups she sent earlier today fill the screen. Like a proud dad, I turn the phone toward the guys and look on with an unwavering smile when their faces fill with awe at what my girl did.

"Damn. She designed this all herself?" Logan asks.

"Yup. Her company will do pretty much every phase of the project too. She's got a real good thing goin' out there."

They smile back at me and nod, taking sips of their beers. "That's awesome, Chase. I take it that means the long distance thing is working for y'all?"

"I mean, it sucks to be away from her, but things are good right now. Really good. We're talkin' a lot more than last time, and in general I think we're both happy."

Our relationship has grown so much in just a couple months. We have a routine that works for both of us now, which is working out much better than winging it like we did last time. Would I like to see her more? Absolutely. But there's that old saying about distance making the heart grow fonder, and in this case, I do actually think that's true.

The more time that passes between when I get to hold Sydney Mae in my arms, the more I want her. I would give just about anything to be able to drop everything and catch a flight to New York to go see her.

"So, which one of you is gonna cave and move first?"

I shake my head and shrug. "She loves it in New York. She's got her company, and we might be talkin' more than ever, but they're busy enough to fill every wakin' minute of her day with work. If it weren't for Vikram and I forcin' her to go home at a certain time every night, she'd never stop. But I can't leave the Wilson's to fend for themselves, and I'm not a city guy."

"So this is what the rest of your life will look like?" Noah asks, brows drawn up. "Video calls and seeing each other a couple times a year?"

My chest squeezes and I drown the uncomfortable feeling with a swig of beer before nervously picking at the label with my thumb. "There's no one else I want to be with."

There's a beat of silence, before Logan breaks it. "But?" he asks, and my heart feels like it shrivels up in my chest.

What a loaded question for one single word. Three letters and it has the power to change your entire life. "But I don't think I could do this forever." The words burn my tongue as I say them, and I know the only reason they do is because it's true. I *don't* think I could do this forever. I have her attention this time, but I still don't have *her*. And she's the thing I want the most. *The thing I need the most.* "I miss her too damn much. I want her with me all the time."

The boys stare back at me with worried looks on their faces. "Have the two of you talked about it at all?"

My teeth clench and I bring my beer to my lips, taking a sip before answering. "It's come up a few times, but we both pretty much agreed if it ain't broke, don't fix it." Not exactly the approach I wanted to take, but if it means keeping her... "For now, what we have is great. I'm not gonna bring it up and risk losin' her because I wanna kiss her every night before bed."

"Makes sense. Just..." Logan sighs. "Just don't forget about yourself, okay? Make sure your opinion on things matters too. She might have the fancy job and the money and the New York prestige, but that doesn't mean she can strong-arm you into giving up what you have here."

I nod. "Yeah."

"Good. We're only saying this because we care about you, man."

"I know, and I appreciate it."

Noah stands from his stool. "I gotta hit the bathroom."

Logan waits a moment for Noah to be out of earshot before he speaks again. "We haven't really talked much since you spent those few nights on my couch. I just want to make sure you're good with everything—that shit you told me about your parents and your ex?" He shakes his head. "I don't know how you do it, man. I'd be a mess."

There's not really much to say to that so I just shrug.

"Have you heard from them at all?"

"Nope. I don't really expect to, either. If I never hear from Cara again it'll be too soon. And as far as I'm concerned, my *family* is the Wilsons. Bill and Susan took me in when I needed a place to stay. They've treated me like family since the moment I met them. I already know that if things between Sydney Mae and I don't work out, they would still look out for me."

Logan swallows thickly. "Good. You're better off without them anyway."

"Damn straight." My phone vibrates in my pocket and I smile before I even see Sydney's name on the screen. "I gotta take this," I say, taking a quick sip of beer before sliding my thumb across the screen and then bringing it to my ear. "Hey, hold on a sec."

The moment I step through the door, I switch it over to video and hold the phone up in front of me.

"Hi, handsome." Her sweet smile instantly warms my heart.

"Hi, gorgeous."

"Sorry to interrupt while you're out with the guys. I just wanted to say goodnight while I still could."

"I don't mind the interruption one bit. I missed your voice anyway." Taking a quick look at the corner of the screen I smile to myself when I see the time on the clock reads eight forty-five, meaning it's ten forty-five for her. "Early night for you, huh?"

She giggles, and more of her makeup-free face and the messy bun piled on top of her head come into frame. "Yeah, I have an early session with Dr. Camden tomorrow before a day from hell, and I know I'll be dead on my feet if I don't go to bed soon."

"Hey, that sounds like progress to me, baby."

"Yeah, I think so." I can see the sleepiness and a hint of dread on her face. "God, I wish things weren't so crazy right now so I could come see you."

I plaster on a smile. "It'll be okay. Just a couple more weeks, right?"

She nods. "Yeah, I think so. We should start upping our video calls to four times a week because I miss your face more than anything."

"I do too."

Sydney's jaw cracks in a yawn and I watch as she nuzzles into her pillow. *Fuck, I wish I were there with her. That pillow would be my chest and she'd sling her leg over my waist to make sure I couldn't go anywhere.* "Well, I won't keep you. Go have fun with the boys. Tell them hi for me, okay?"

"I will. I love you, gorgeous. Sleep well."

"I love you too."

Our call disconnects and there's a weight in my chest that wasn't there before. It's kinda fucked up how I always miss her even more after just talking to her.

When I get back to the table, Noah is chatting up a buddy of his from work and Logan is just cracking open a fresh beer.

"You know, I was thinking, If you ever wanna go to New York, I can help out at the Wilson's while you're gone."

Hope sparks to life in my chest but I quickly tamp it down. "You'd do that?"

"Of course, Chase. You work your ass off and never do anything for yourself. Not only do you deserve the time off, but you deserve to see your girl too." Noah rejoins the table at that moment and Logan slings an arm around his shoulders. "Plus, I'm sure Noah would be willing to help out too."

"If it means you getting to see Syd, then just say the word and I'll be there with my galoshes and overalls."

"Thanks, guys. That means a lot." I let a small smile curve my lips. "I might just take you up on that."

**MARCH 29, 2021**

My knee bounces up and down as I watch the minutes tick by. Our newest client has a knack for yapping and today is the worst possible day for yappers. I have places to be and a boyfriend to see.

I've been holding onto this surprise for weeks now. And I fear that Chase thinks I'm mad at him or something because of how short I've been the last few days. I just didn't want to ruin the surprise, especially since it's been three months since we've seen each other.

Michele Badini, the yapper, finally shuts her trap and I wrap the meeting up in record time, telling her that we will touch base sometime next week to go over the more intricate details of the plan. She must sense the edge of annoyance in my voice because she politely apologizes for the meeting going over and then hangs up the call.

Just as I'm about to open my mouth to shout out for Katie, she walks through the door. Her heels click against the marble and I smile at the little touch of me that's rubbed off on her. No more squeaky flats for her.

"Hey, I was just about to call you."

"Well, I hope it can wait because there's someone here to see you."

My brows pinch together. "I thought my schedule was free for the day? I have a flight to catch in three hours and I should have left for the airport twenty minutes ago because of the traffic, but the call with Badini went long."

"I know, and I'm sorry, but he's insisting on seeing you."

I blow out a breath and run my fingers through my hair. Of course I decided to go for a more casual look today with a pair of painted-on jeans, and a white blouse with a navy blue blazer. Groaning, I push out of my chair and tuck my blouse in. "All right, you can send him in, but could you tell Paul that I'll need him to come in and take over in five?"

"Sure." She smirks as she spins on her heel and clicks away.

Reaching into my desk, I grab the small handheld mirror and take a quick look at myself, making sure my hair isn't a disaster and I haven't nervously sweat off all my makeup. Whoever it is better make it snappy. I am long overdue for some Chase kisses, and I'll be damned if I miss my flight.

"Happy birthday, baby," an all-too familiar deep voice says from the other side of my office.

My eyes snap toward the door and my knees nearly give out when I see Chase's broad shoulders filling the doorframe. "Chase!" I shout before sprinting toward him. I crash into his chest, flinging my arms around him. "What the hell are you doing here?"

He chuckles and wraps me up in his strong arms. "I missed you too much and you hadn't mentioned anything about when you were comin' back next, so I decided to come to you. Figured it'd be a good birthday surprise."

"I was just about to leave for the airport to get on my flight. *I* wanted it to be a surprise."

"Guess I beat you to it."

I smile, bringing my hand to his chest. "Yes, you did."

He licks his lips and lets his gaze scan the office he's seen hundreds of times in our video calls. "It's okay that I'm here, right?"

"More than okay."

"Can I kiss you now, Sydney Mae?"

My cheeks flush and I tuck my lip between my teeth, nodding shyly. "*Please.*"

His hands cup my face as he leans down, a dopey smile gracing his lips right before he kisses me. And, *fuck*, does he kiss me. I melt into him like butter in a hot pan. My toes curl when his tongue slides against my lower lip and I'm barely able to hold back a moan.

I can't get enough of him.

And if he keeps kissing me like this, I'm gonna have to take a page out of Paul and Katie's book and let him fuck me against the floor to ceiling windows for the whole city to see.

Okay, maybe not *that* page, but an office romp, for sure. After this long without him, I honestly don't know if I'll be able to wait until we get back to my place. It's either going to be a quick shag at the office, or we're going to have a very scarred cab driver.

Whatever, I'll ask him to turn the music up and then throw him an extra three hundred bucks to get the interior professionally cleaned and call it a day.

My need for Chase far outweighs the need to be rational and clear-headed, or even a little bit ladylike. I'm living in a cloud of lust and longing. I can feel the need pooling between my thighs.

God, I've missed him so much.

Talking on the phone and over video call is a nice way to see him, but having him here physically is a dream. He's a dream. And he's all mine.

"Hey, you have that—Oh…"

I quickly pull away from the kiss. "Paul!"

"Shit!" he grumbles, quickly turning around. "Sorry."

Chase and I share a laugh. At least he didn't tell us to *enjoy*, like my dad did.

"It's okay. We probably got a little carried away anyway."

"I would say yes, but you've been apart for months, I get it."

Chase clears his throat and holds his hand out to Paul. "Hey, I'm Chase. Sydney has told me a lot about you."

"Likewise," Paul says, giving Chase's hand a firm shake. "Syd, I'm guessing you don't need me to take over this meeting after all?"

I giggle and feel my cheeks heat. "I think I can handle this one myself. Thanks though."

He dips his chin in a nod. "Enjoy your time off," he says as he strides toward the exit. "It was nice meeting you, Chase. Maybe we can all go out to dinner while you're here so we can actually get to know each other."

"I'd like that," Chase replies, bringing his hand to the curve of my waist.

"Cool." He smiles. "Happy birthday again, Syd."

"Thanks, Paul."

Paul, being the smart, amazing partner that he is, pulls the door closed behind him.

I spin around and bite down on my swollen bottom lip. "I still can't believe you're here."

Chase presses a kiss to my forehead, and then the tip of my nose. "Better believe it. I'll be here all week."

"Really?"

He nods, letting his laced fingers hang on the small of my back. "Mhmm. I figured If I was comin' all the way here, I might as well make it a worthwhile trip."

"And what were you planning on doing had I not already taken a week off to come see you?"

"Uh… I hadn't thought about that, actually." His eyes scan the office. "Probably sit in that chair over there and give you puppy dog eyes until you got off work." He gives me said puppy dog eyes and I immediately want to pinch his cheeks and then ride him in the chair.

*Jesus,* three months is apparently way too long without sex after being with Chase.

"I can assure you right now that I wouldn't have gotten a single shred of work done and would've caved within five minutes of you sitting there."

Chase smirks and licks his lips as his hands squeeze my waist. "That right?"

I bring my arms up and drape them on his shoulders, playing with the overgrown hair at the back of his head. "You're a hell of a lot more charming than you think you are."

"Thank you."

"Do you want a tour?"

"As long as I get to hold your hand, we can do whatever you want."

An easy smile curves my lips as I lace my fingers through his and lead the way to the elevator.

I knew coming to New York would be a shock, but I wasn't expecting it to be *this* overwhelming. Sydney fits right in. She's completely unfazed by all that's going on around her.

But between the cars, the honking coming from every direction, and the people racing by like everyone is late for something, I feel like my head is spinning. There's too much happening. Too many noises and competing smells. My nose is confused and my mind is in a constant state of alert to make sure I keep Sydney safe.

I've been here for five hours and so far the only thing that has calmed my anxiety was walking through Central Park, and the hole-in-the-wall cafe Sydney loves, where we got coffee that tasted almost as good as Susan's, and some truly delicious sandwiches.

By the time we got back to her brownstone, I heaved a sigh of relief to finally be away from the hustle and bustle and be able to just breathe for a second. I excused myself to the bathroom, and splashed some water on my face. I hope I'm not making it too obvious that I'm not a huge fan of the city, but I can't really tell. My mind was too preoccupied with worrying about being hit by a car, trampled by thousands of people, or jumped by any of the number of sketchy people we walked by on our way here.

When I come back out to the living room, Sydney gives me a quick kiss before heading to her bedroom to change out of her work clothes. Walking over to the window, I tuck my hands in my pockets and look outside, wondering how anyone could ever enjoy living in a place like this.

The sky is dark, but the amount of light pollution clouds the stars. Back home, Macie is always with me—I feel her in my bones, and in my heart—but here, surrounded by the people and the noise and the lightning speed pace, I can't *feel* her like I normally do when I look at the stars.

I've gotten used to missing her over the years. I've accepted that I'll never hear her giggles or see her smile. That I'll never get to hold her in my arms and kiss her dimpled cheek. But being this far from home, I ache to feel close to her again.

"Hey," Sydney says, wrapping her arms around my waist and resting her cheek on my back. "What's wrong?"

I sigh and turn in her grasp. "Just takin' it all in."

"You hate it here, don't you?"

"Hate is a strong word… It's more… strong dislike." I shrug. "I dunno. I guess it might take some gettin' used to. It's a big change from small town, Colorado."

She nods. "You're not wrong. I think that was the main appeal at the time. It was the complete opposite of everything I grew up with. After what happened with Jack I just… I needed to get away. To have a space that was entirely my own and wasn't tainted by him. A place that was bright and loud and filled with people so I wasn't alone. A place busy enough where I could blend in with the crowd and disappear."

"Do you ever miss it?"

"Colorado?"

I shake my head. "Not just Colorado, but the quiet. The openness. Fresh air. Bein' able to actually see the stars."

A resigned look passes across her face and her eyes have a slight gloss to them. "Daily."

"But?"

She licks her lips and steps away, looking out at the city I despise. "But this has been my life for ten years. The honking. The crowded streets. The smell that's both nauseating, and kinda comforting, at the same time. The bright lights. I don't know, I guess part of me loves it here, and the other part wants to run from it. To say fuck it and move back to Colorado and build a new business there. It's not like architecture is something that's only in New York."

"What's stoppin' you?"

"Fear of failure," she admits, getting visibly choked up when the words settle between us. "Staying in New York is safe—I know I'll always have work. There's new buildings going up, coming down, and being restored every single day. I guess it's just scary knowing that none of that is a guarantee in Colorado. I mean, in a very broad sense, it is, but I *know* it works here. I have a very successful business and I feel like it'd be a mistake to walk away from it."

"Makes sense."

A crease forms between her brows as she looks up at me with watery eyes. "You're not mad, are you?"

"Of course not." I cup her cheek, letting my thumb stroke over the apple. "I just want you all day every day, not just for a few at a time."

"I want that more than anything, Chase," she says, bringing her hand to my chest.

My gaze drifts back to the window, and all I see are lights. There's not a single star visible in the sky and my stomach knots. "I can't feel her as strongly here," I whisper. "I know it's silly because she's still with me—in here." I tap my chest right over my heart. "But I can't *feel* her around me like I do when I'm home."

"It's not silly," she says, and takes a step closer. "She's a part of you, Chase. I could never ask you to give up being close to her."

"Yeah." A half smile graces my lips for a second at how well she knows me before it disappears. Does hating it here mean the end of us? As much as she can't ask me to give up Colorado to be close to Macie, I can't ask her to give up her dreams and the business she's poured her whole self into for me. But I don't know how much of being here I can take. "It's probably no surprise, but I don't think I'm a city guy, Sydney Mae."

She chuckles sweetly, her cheeks tinting a soft pink. "That's okay. It's not for everyone." With a sigh, she laces our fingers together. "Some days I don't think I'm a city girl, either."

"Maybe someday things'll be different, right?" I ask with way too much hope in my voice.

I know it's not fair to make her be the one that uproots her life, but this place isn't for me. It was clear the moment I stepped off the plane.

"Right," she says with a sadness in her voice I haven't heard since she told me about her past.

Regret slams into me. I shouldn't have brought any of this up. Especially not on her birthday. I clear my throat. "Until then, we gotta make the most of the time we have together."

"Yeah, we do." She smiles. "Did you have anything in mind?"

Smirking, I lick my lips. "Well, for starters, you still haven't opened your birthday present."

"Oh? What is it?"

Leaning down, I bring my mouth to hers, just barely letting our lips brush. "I'm the present, Sydney Mae."

Her eyes flare with heat and her warm breath fans across my lips in a soft pant. She reaches for my belt and starts to slowly undo the buckle.

"W-what are you doin'?"

"My birthday." She sinks to her knees. "My rules."

Sydney's fingers work the buckle the rest of the way open before getting to work on the zipper.

In the blink of an eye, my jeans and boxer briefs are at my ankles and my hard cock is bobbing in her face. Her eyes widen at just how hard I am already, but what she doesn't know is that it's impossible to not be when she's on her knees for me.

The sight alone is enough to make *my* knees weak.

"Fuck," I curse under my breath when she leans forward and licks away the pearl of precum from the head.

Sydney smirks up at me, wrapping her hand around my shaft and pumping it along my length, earning a groan. "Did I ever tell you how much I like that you only curse when we're together like this?" she asks, before taking the head in her mouth for a quick suck.

My eyes roll back in my head at the feel of her tongue circling the tip. "No, you haven't."

She takes me to the back of her throat before pulling me out again, a line of spit connecting my cock to her lips. "Well, I do." Her eyes glaze over as she twists her hand and gives the head a hard suck. "It's like you can't help yourself. Like what I do to you drives you insane."

"You have no idea how fuckin' true that is, baby." I bring my hand to her hair, gathering it in my hand to guide her movements the way I know she likes.

"I like that I'm the only one who gets to hear your dirty mouth." She licks her lips before diving back onto my length.

"Only you, gorgeous," I say, holding her head in place and she does that wicked thing with her tongue along the underside of my cock. I nearly bust when she forces more of me into her mouth and swallows, her throat squeezing the shit out of me. "Jesus fuck, Sydney." Pulling her head back by her hair, she looks up at me with a sated smile and glossy eyes. "You're gonna make me come if you keep doing that."

A giggle bubbles out of her and she nods. "I want it." Her hand strokes my length at the perfect pace with just the right amount of pressure, and I can't help but hiss at how good it feels. Tingles shoot down my spine and I can feel my orgasm building as she keeps her eyes locked on me as she fists my length. "Want you to paint my throat, Chase," she rushes out before wrapping her lips around me again. She moans and reaches her free hand between her legs.

"Fuck, baby, are you touchin' yourself?"

She nods with her mouth full of me and my head tips back, not wanting this to end just yet, but her mouth feels like fucking heaven around me. Combine that with her hand working me in perfect sync—I don't stand a chance.

There's only one thing that I know feels better wrapped around my cock and it's her pussy. But the birthday girl wants my cum in her throat, so that's what she'll get. I'll fill her pretty cunt later.

I tighten my grip on her hair. "Are you gonna be a good girl and let me use your throat, Sydney Mae?"

She mumbles around me, nodding enthusiastically as her eyes roll back. Her hand falls from my length because she knows what's coming.

"That's my girl," I say with a swell of pride before I start to thrust my hips forward.

Moans pour from my lips and as much as I want to take my time fucking her throat, I know I'm way too close to coming already. She caught me off guard. I was planning on stripping her down and worshipping every inch of her body. Kissing that spot below her ear. Licking the column of her throat. Sucking the tight peaks of her nipples, and teasing them with gentle grazes of my teeth. Stroking my fingers over her clit until she was begging me to let her come, and then spreading her open and devouring her pussy like it was my last meal.

That's what I had in mind. That's the present I had planned for her.

But she had another idea, and there isn't a single chance in hell I could ever say no to her when she's on her knees for me.

My cock rams against her throat repeatedly, causing the most erotic, wet moan to come from her each time. Her eyes are watery and her cheeks are flushed, the hand between her legs hastily shoved into her pants and I can see just how quickly her fingers are racing over her clit.

"You there for me, baby? Gonna come as soon as you taste me?"

She nods weakly, her throat relaxing even more.

I smirk and fist her hair just a little tighter, thrusting into her mouth another three times before the most relieving orgasm races through me. My cum paints her throat just like she wanted, and a deep moan tumbles from me.

Sydney's eyes widen right before her brows pinch and then she falls apart, her own orgasm peaking.

"Fuck, you come so pretty, Sydney Mae." Easing my hips back, she swallows me down, licking up every last drop from my length. "Happy birthday, baby."

With rosy cheeks and puffy lips she smiles at me. "Best birthday present ever."

# 49

## CHASE



Susan wraps her arms around Sydney's shoulders, burying her nose in my girl's hair. "Oh, sweetie, I'm so glad you're here!" Susan gushes with a huge smile on her face.

"Me too, Mom," Sydney says, with an equally big smile.

We didn't tell her parents that she was coming home for my birthday because we weren't sure she was going to make it. She and Paul signed a huge deal last week and they're set to break ground tomorrow. I could tell she wanted to be there for it, but she's a much different person now than she was when we met. It doesn't take much to convince her to take a break now. And she said that the only thing better than being there, at the start of a new project, is being in my arms. I couldn't really argue with that considering I've been missing her something fierce since I last saw her in New York for her birthday.

Susan lets her go and Sydney grabs the counter for support, closing her eyes as she takes a deep breath.

"You don't look so good, honey," Bill says, resting a hand on her shoulder. "You're lookin' a little green."

Sydney plasters on a smile and waves him off. "It's nothing.

Just a rough flight. There was a ton of turbulence and my stomach was in knots the whole time."

"Exactly why I don't trust those things. I've gone fifty-seven years without gettin' on one and I ain't startin' now."

I chuckle, shaking my head at Susan. "I can't say I blame you. The trip to New York for Sydney Mae's birthday was my first time and I really contemplated hitchhikin' back home. That big of a thing shouldn't be able to stay in the air like that."

"You're both so dramatic," Sydney teases before clutching her stomach.

Her forehead is sweaty and the once green hue to her skin is now a pasty white. I brush the hair off her forehead and press my chin to it just like I used to do to Macie when she was little and running a fever. "You're burnin' up, baby. Why don't you go lie down for a bit?"

She pouts, but when she goes to retort her stomach must turn again.

"Come on. I'll tuck you in and then bring up some ginger ale and crackers."

Sydney licks her lips and nods shyly. "You really do love me."

I smile and press a kiss to her hair. "Ain't a single damn doubt about that, my love."

After tucking her in and delivering the crackers like promised, I make a quick run to the store to grab her some Pedialyte while she rests. She hasn't gotten sick yet, but I can tell it's coming, and she's gonna need to replenish her electrolytes to make sure she doesn't get dehydrated.

By the time I get back from the store she's out cold.

I sneak back out of the room, softly closing the door behind me and find Susan standing in the hallway with her arms crossed over her chest. "You're good with her," she says. "And good *for* her. She's lucky to have you."

"Thank you, ma'am."

"Smart thinkin' with the Pedialyte. She got sick while you were gone."

I nod. "The doctor really drilled the benefits of it into my head when Macie was sick during chemo. Bein' dehydrated was the last thing she needed when she was constantly bein' poked with needles."

"I bet she was thankful for that. I'm sure that little girl never said it, but I know for certain that she was grateful every day that you were her daddy."

The comment warms my heart. It's not often that I get to remember that I was a damn good dad to her. Most of the time I punish myself for not being able to give her a better life. If I had been richer, or had more people that I could rely on to help with her, maybe the outcome would have been different.

But thanks to Sydney, I'm trying to be better about that. Just because money could have bought her fancy treatments and more renowned doctors, doesn't mean anything. A client of hers, who is richer than she is, lost a child a few months ago, and they had access to the best the world could offer.

What really matters is that I was the best dad that I could be to her. That I gave her the best life I could with what I had. That I cherished every goddamn second I had with her.

"Thank you, Mrs. Wilson."

She dips her chin and squeezes my arm. "My daughter is one lucky lady. Thank you for loving her as much as you do."

"She makes it pretty damn easy."

---

Later that night, when I slip between the sheets after spending the day popping in and out checking on Sydney, she's finally starting to feel better. The color is back in her cheeks and her fever seems to have broken.

She rolls over and cuddles into my side. "Thank you for taking care of me today." Her fingers draw circles on my bare chest. "And I'm sorry your birthday isn't starting off as planned."

"Don't apologize, baby. I've got you here with me and that's all I care about. I could think of a lot worse ways to spend my birthday. Plus, I get you all day tomorrow too."

Sydney's eyes fill with tears. "I'm sorry I can't stay longer."

I tip her chin up, making her look at me. "Stop being sorry for things you have no control over. You're busy, and I get that. I'm happy I get any time with you and I don't want to waste what little time we do have bein' angry that I don't get you for longer. We have the rest of our lives together, Sydney Mae."

"How did I get lucky enough to deserve a man like you?"

"I'm the lucky one, baby." I lean in and press my lips to hers. "You changed my life."

She hooks her hand around my neck and pulls me down for another kiss. Her tongue slides against mine and I groan at the way her hips grind into me. "It's officially midnight," she whispers. "Happy birthday, Chase Alexander Phillips. I hope this is the best one yet."

I nuzzle my nose against hers and nip at her lips. "I think it will be. I've got you this time."

"What's your birthday wish?"

"I can't tell you, otherwise it won't come true."

"Just think it then."

Closing my eyes, I rest my head back against the plush pillows and recite my wish in my head.

*I wish to be with you for the rest of my life. I wish that one day I'll be able to give you a ring and a house—a life that you can be proud of here, where I spend every night and every day showing you just how much I love you.*

"Did you make your wish?"

"Yeah."

"I hope it comes true."

"Me too."

Before she has a moment to protest, I roll her onto her back and kick off the blanket, dragging down the flimsy sleep shorts I helped her change into after she choked down some crackers earlier.

"What are you doing?" she asks with an edge of panic in her voice.

"Claiming my birthday present."

Her brows furrow. "What are you talking about?"

I brush my thumb over her panty-covered core and she lets out a little moan.

"You sucked the life out of my dick on your birthday." I hook my finger inside the lace and pull it to the side. "It's only fair I get to eat your pussy until I've had my fill on mine."

Her cheeks flush a violent shade of red, but she puts up no further protests.

When she comes on my tongue for the second time, I can't help but agree with the words she uttered on her birthday.

"Best birthday present ever."

# 50

SYDNEY



Vikram comes back to the couch with a glass of water and sets it down on the coffee table. He eyes me warily as I cocoon myself further into the blanket. "You doing okay?" he asks, taking the seat next to me.

"A little better than yesterday." I sniffle. "Thanks for staying with me last night. I didn't know who else to call."

"I told you I'd be here whenever you needed me, and I meant every word."

I roll my eyes. "Yeah, but that was before you got with Bee. I doubt I'm her biggest fan at the moment."

"She knows about our friendship, Syd. She's also well aware of the fact that you're obsessed with a cowboy who doesn't pronounce his g's. I also know that if I get home and she gives me a look, all I'll have to do is make her vada pav and eat her out and all will be forgiven."

Giggling, I swat him with the back of my hand. "Shut up."

"It's the truth. The woman is a sucker for my tongue."

I shake my head. "You're crazy, but I'm really glad you found your person."

"Me too," he says with a bright smile. I don't think I've ever seen him look as genuinely happy as he has the last four months after Bee quite literally stormed into his life and never left.

A moment of silence passes between us and a guilty feeling settles in my stomach, along with an ache of longing in my chest. "What am I supposed to do, Vik?"

"Be honest with him. It's all you can do."

I chew my lip. "What if he hates me and never wants to talk to me again?" My eyes fill with tears. "I can't lose him again. I barely survived the first time."

His arms wrap around me and he pulls me to his chest. "That's not going to happen. You're not gonna lose him. You'll explain everything and it'll be okay, Sydney. I promise."

My lip quivers as I fight back the tears, willing them to not fall down my cheeks. "I hope you're right."

Vik presses a kiss to the top of my head, rocking me back and forth against his chest. "I know I am."

Eleven days later, I step out of a cab and make my way up the front porch of my parents' house with a small suitcase dragging behind me.

"I would say I'm surprised to see you, but Vikram gave me a heads-up that you'd be comin'," my mom says from the rocking chair on the front porch.

"You talked to Vik?"

She nods, writing out a word in a crossword puzzle before putting her pen down and taking her reading glasses off her nose. "I was worried something happened. Chase hasn't been himself lately."

"So you called Vikram instead of me?"

"Well, I'd like to think I know my daughter, and her stubborn ass probably wouldn't tell me anything, so I figured I had better luck with him."

I sigh, but can't argue with her because she's right. I wouldn't have told her anything. Not before I have a chance to talk to Chase in person. "I'll explain everything later, I promise. I just need to talk to Chase first. Do you know where he is?"

"I think he's helpin' your daddy out with the tractor in the field. Damn thing keeps stallin'."

"Again? Why doesn't dad just buy a new one already? Clearly that one isn't cutting it anymore."

My mom cocks a brow. "I'd love to hear you say that to your father."

"Well, I guess it's a good thing his birthday is coming up," I say before pushing my suitcase inside the house.

"Whatever it is you're so worried about, I'm sure it'll be okay. That boy loves you more than everything he has."

My chest squeezes. "I know. And I love him just as much."

---

I spot Chase standing alone under a tree getting some shade, and feel my heart skip in my chest.

My footsteps must startle him because he lifts his gaze from the piece of metal in his hands to find me. "Sydney Mae? What are you doin' here?" he asks, quickly closing the space between us.

"W-we need to talk."

A crease forms between his brows and I see him grind his teeth. "I've been tryin' to talk to you, but you've been actin' weird since you were here for my birthday."

"I know, and I'm sorry."

"If I did somethin' wrong, I didn't mean it. I thought things with us were good, but I guess I was wrong."

I shake my head and bite the inside of my cheek to stop my eyes from watering. "We're okay. I just... There's something I need to tell you, and I've been too afraid to do it."

He takes a step back and slides his tongue over his lip. I

can see the worry in his hazel eyes and I hate that I can't just spit it out already. "You're scarin' me, Sydney Mae. Are you okay?"

"I…" I take a breath and reach for his hand, needing to feel closer to him if this is the last time I'll be able to. "I love you so much, Chase. More than I've ever loved anyone in my entire life —fuck, more than I love myself. This last month I've been distancing myself because I've been too scared that you'd hate me for what I have to tell you, and then I'd lose you all over again. And I can't lose you again. I need you."

Chase squares his shoulders and looks away. "Did you cheat on me?"

"No!" I cup his cheek, turning his eyes back to me. "God no. I could never—I would *never*. You're the only person I want to be with."

"Then you gotta help me out here, Sydney Mae. What are you so afraid to tell me?"

I swallow the lump in my throat and nod. "When I got home after your birthday, I was still feeling a bit off a couple days later. I went to the doctor and they ran some tests, and that's when they told me I…"

"Told you what? Please, baby, tell me that you're okay."

"I'm pregnant, Chase."

He stumbles back a step, his lips parting. "Pregnant? You're… We're havin' a baby?"

My eyes fill with tears and I nod, feeling them streak down my cheeks. "In about five months. Turns out the turbulence wasn't the issue and I was actually just experiencing the first bout of morning sickness."

"Why were you so afraid to tell me?"

"I didn't know if you were ready, or if you even wanted to have more kids. We never talked about it. And after what you went through with Macie being sick, I wasn't… I didn't want you to worry about something like that happening again. O-or for you to feel like Macie wouldn't mean as much to you when this baby comes because that's not even a little true. Macie will always be your little girl. No one could ever replace her."

There's a long beat of silence and I can't help but hold my breath. The look on Chase's face isn't giving me much and that scares the shit out of me.

Could I do this alone? Raise a kid without his help? I don't know the first thing about babies. But I also know that I'd never be able to give this baby up. I've only known about it for two weeks, but it's already a part of me.

Panic starts to set in when Chase is still silent a full minute later.

"Say something. Please."

Chase blows out a breath and then takes one large step, closing the distance between us. He cups my cheeks and crashes his lips to mine. I sob into the kiss, clutching at his shirt and never wanting to let go.

When he pulls back he has a smile on his face. He rests his forehead against mine. "I'm not gonna lie and say that I'm not terrified of goin' through all of that again, but I've got you by my side, and that's all that matters to me. Whatever happens, we'll face it together."

"Thank fucking god," I blurt, wrapping my arms around his neck. "I was really hoping I wouldn't have to do this alone. Plus, I can't wait to see you as a dad."

"And I can't wait to see you as a mom." He places his hand on my small, rounded belly. "And to meet this little one that's part you and part me."

"She's gonna love you so much. Just like I do."

His eyes go wide. "S-she?"

"Or he. The doctor asked if I wanted to know, but I couldn't find out without you."

"I don't want to know."

I smile. "Then we won't know."

"Does this mean I should pack my bags so we can head back to New York?"

Shaking my head, I run my fingers through the hair at the nape of his neck. "I think I'd like to call Slate Ridge home again. If that's okay with you?"

A huge grin curves his lips. "You mean it?"

"Yeah, Chase. This is home. *You* are home."

He kisses me fervently, pulling me closer with each passing second, and I can't wait to spend the rest of my life kissing this man.

"I love you so damn much, Sydney Mae," he whispers against my lips.

"I love you more."

"Forever?"

I nod. "Forever."

# EPILOGUE

## CHASE

### TEN YEARS LATER — DECEMBER 17, 2031

Sometimes when you think there's nothing good left in the world, life throws you a bone. I went from having nothing and no one, to having everything I ever could have dreamed of and more. And that's entirely thanks to Sydney Mae.

She's easily the one of the best things that has ever happened to me. Along with our three perfect kids, and of course, my little angel, Macie Moo.

I'll never understand how I got this lucky, but you won't hear me complaining.

For the last sixteen years, this day has been the hardest for me to get through. I have Sydney by my side now, but I can't help but wonder what it would be like if Macie were here with us. If she were a living, breathing part of the family Sydney and I have created. There's nothing I wouldn't do to see her laughing and playing along with her siblings. Teaching them how to do the little things like tying their shoes or convincing us to let them stay up past their bedtime.

I know she would have been the best big sister, and even

though she's not physically here showing them the ropes, I can tell she's looking down on all of them.

My hands tighten on the railing as a rip of pain races through my chest.

Fuck. I miss her so much.

How come it never gets any easier? I have three amazing kids who each have a little piece of Macie in them and the most magnificent wife that this earth has ever seen, but I still miss my baby girl like it was just yesterday that she was taken from me.

It's blinding.

My nose stings with the telltale sign of tears.

A small hand tugs on my jeans. "Daddy?"

I look down to see my Sadie girl, bundled up in her puffy pink coat with a white knit hat staring up at me. "Hi, pumpkin." I bend down and scoop her up in my arms, settling her on my hip. "Is everythin' okay?"

Her chubby little cheeks shake with her nod. "Mommy said to come give you a big hug because Macie can't."

My heart squeezes and I let my eyes find my gorgeous wife softly smiling back at me. "Well, what are you waitin' for? I want my hug."

Sadie's eyes light up and she throws her arms around my neck, squeezing so hard her little body is shaking. I squeeze her back, burying my nose in her soft brown curls. "Thank you, Sadie."

She pulls back and softly places her mitten-covered hands on my cheeks. "Do you miss her, Daddy?"

I flash her a sad smile. "Yeah, peanut. Every day."

"Did the hug help?" she asks with such a serious face I can't help but chuckle.

"More than you know, sweet girl."

Sydney strolls over and pops a kiss on Sadie's cheek before leaning in and pressing a soft kiss to my lips.

Sadie giggles, her nose wrinkling in the most adorable way.

"Sadie Mae, why don't you go play with your brothers for a little bit before we head home?"

"Okay, Mommy." Sadie looks to me, studying my face for a moment. Leaning in, she whispers in my ear, "I love you for me and Macie, Daddy."

My heart swells and I can't stop the tears from welling in my eyes. "Thank you, Sadie Mae. I love you too."

A smile spreads across Sadie's face. "Mommy, do you think we could have hot cocoa when we get home? With extra marshmallows?"

Sydney chuckles and boops our little girl on the nose. "Sure, baby. Extra marshmallows sound like a great idea."

Sadie claps and wiggles her legs, silently asking to be let down.

As soon as her feet touch the ground she's off running toward her brothers. "Will! Alex! Mom said yes!" Sadie screams.

The boys both throw their hands up in the air, jumping up and down in their matching blue puffy coats and knit hats.

"We've created monsters," I say, slinging my arms over Sydney's shoulders and bringing her back to my chest.

"Yes, we have." Her hands come to her rounded belly. "Maybe we'll be able to keep this one from getting corrupted."

I laugh. "Not likely. They'll find a way no matter what."

"True," she agrees with a laugh.

"Thank you for startin' the tradition of comin' here with the kids. It means a lot to me," I say, kissing her temple.

She nods. "Macie is just as big a part of this family as any of our kids. Nothing is ever going to change that. We may not be able to see her, but she'll always have a place in our family, Chase. She'll always be in all of our hearts, not just yours."

"I don't know what I'd do without you."

"Then I guess it's a good thing you'll never have to find out, cowboy."

THE END

# ACKNOWLEDGMENTS

To think that Chase and Sydney's story is out in the world (again) is absolutely bananas to me. *A Rocky Christmas* is the result of a snowy day off of work, back in 2020. I consumed so many Hallmark Christmas movies, I decided to write one of my own—with some added spice, of course.

I will forever be grateful to everyone who gave Chase and Sydney a chance back in 2020 when they first made their debut on Episode Interactive. And I will extend that same gratitude now, to all of you who have made it this far.

Chase and Sydney, or Chaseney, as I frequently refer to them in my head, mean so much to me, and I'm truly honored to even have the opportunity to share their story with you.

To bubs, I honestly don't think I can say *I love you* or *I'm sorry* enough. The entire experience writing this book was one hell of a ride, and I couldn't do it without your support. I promise, next time around, I won't ignore your existence, or put myself on a deadline that will make me want to cry, scream, and curl into a ball. I love you forever and ever.

To my Texans, Tiff and Karli, I cannot thank you enough for listening to me yap endlessly. I appreciate the never-ending support, love, and words of encouragement more than I'll ever be able to express. I don't think I could have done this without either of you in my corner.

To my peen team, Alex and Jo, thank you for being my built-in hype women. I can't count the number of times I came to our group chat feeling like the biggest imposter, and you babes were there with pom poms and the sweetest words.

To my pseudo-mom Ruby, I don't think you know how much you've helped by sharing your knowledge of the self-publishing process and answering all of my questions. I will quite literally never be able to repay you.

To GC and DK, thank you for being my break from writing, constantly cheering me on, and checking in on my other half.

To my IRL bestie, K, you'll probably never read this, but I appreciate you and your friendship more than you know.

To Casey, you are one of my favorite people on the planet. Thank you doesn't even begin to cover how grateful I am to have you in my life.

To Ness, you have been one of my biggest supporters from the very start and I don't think I'll ever be able to express how much that means to me. Thank you for all of your chaotic Alpha notes and the endless DMs over the years telling me to do the damn thing. Well, you better get a White Claw ready, because I fucking did it!

To my amazing Alpha reader who hasn't already been mentioned, Elle. I cannot thank you enough for all your insightful comments. I appreciate the time and effort you put into every note you left and the sweet DMs you sent.

To Cindy, I'm so glad that I had someone else who came from Episode to stumble through the dark on this journey with! Thank you for being you.

To my editor, Cait, and formatter, Kay, thank you both so much for being so patient and answering all my questions. I promise to use more commas next time.

To the amazing artists and cover designers who brought *A Rocky Christmas* to life @arsiniia_, @melmul169, @mariabeatriz_j, @juniper.charm and @kjaspersendesigns. I can't thank you enough for bringing my babies to life.

To all the incredible authors and friends in the book community, I am so grateful to be here doing what I love right alongside you!

And lastly, an enormous thank you to you, my readers! I'm truly honored that you took a chance on me. I hope that Chase and Sydney will live in your hearts forever. I am so incredibly grateful for your support!

And a special thank you to Diet Coke, Reese's Caramel Cups, Sour Patch Watermelons, and David's Sunflower Seeds. I wouldn't have made it through this book without you.

# WHAT'S NEXT?

Want to know what I'm writing next? Follow me online
@storiesbyleigh

Coming Soon: Lies That Bind Duet

# ABOUT THE AUTHOR

Leigh is a caffeine addicted millennial who writes spicy, emotional romance stories. She's a pro at spelling things so wildly incorrect that even autocorrect can't figure out what she's trying to say.

When she's not fighting with her keyboard, you can find her reading, cooking, belting show tunes, or arguing about the legitimacy of central Jersey and the fact that it's Taylor Ham and NOT pork roll.

Her debut novel A Rocky Christmas was originally released on the interactive story platform Episode, where she started flexing her writing capabilities. (Technically, she also wrote Degrassi fanfics, but we're not gonna talk about that…)

Leigh lives in New Jersey with her fiance and can confidently state that it was never a phase, Mom.